THE SHARP EDGE OF FATE

THE SHARP EDGE OF FATE

The Sharp Edge Of Fate

Published by Bookwyrm Press
Copyright © TF Johnson 2023

Bookwyrm Press
www.bookwyrmpress.com.au
PO Box 9110, Harris Park NSW 2150

ISBN 978 0 6459160 0 3

First Edition

For Sam
Who always believed.
Even when I didn't myself.

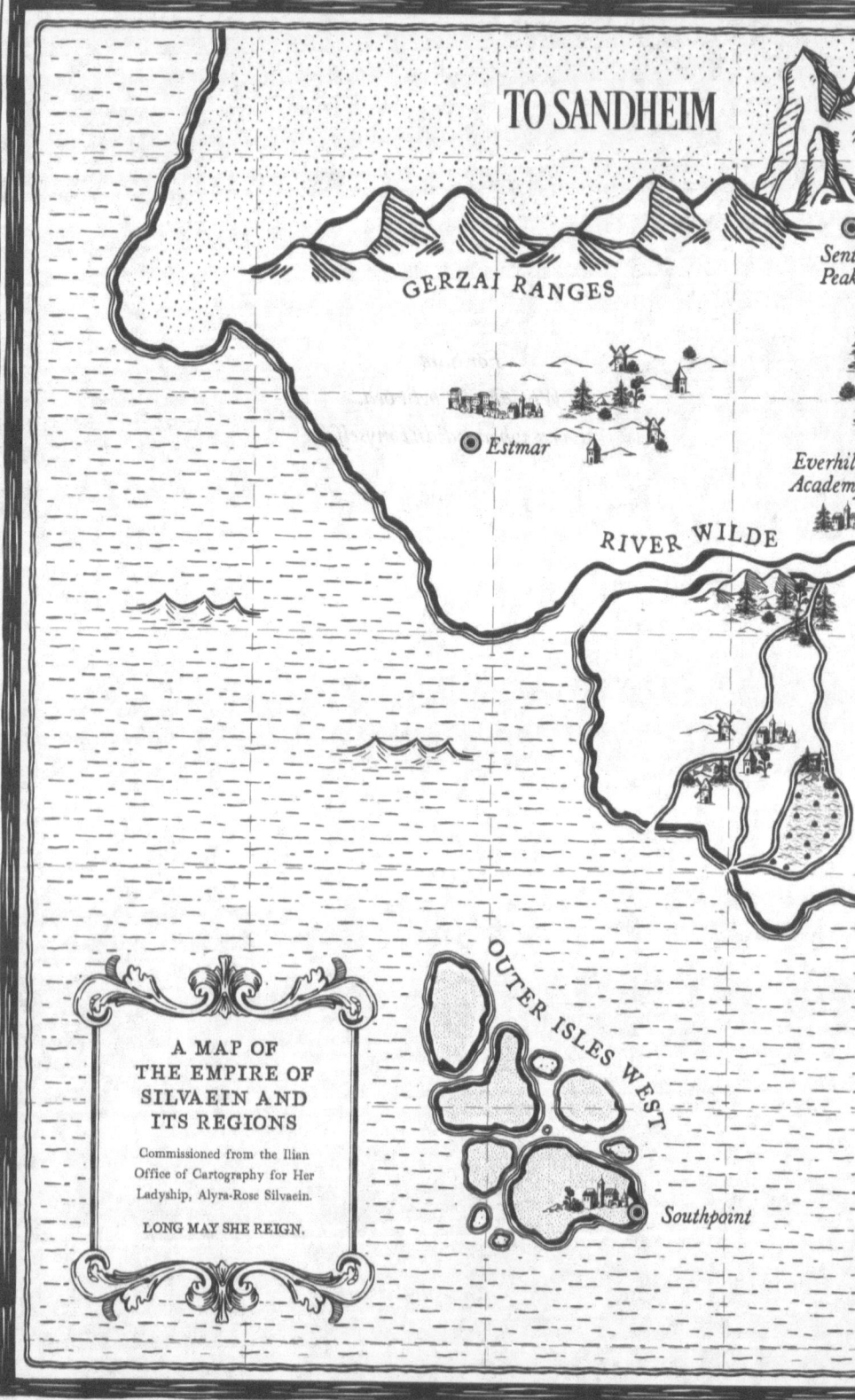

TO SANDHEIM

GERZAI RANGES

Sentin
Peak

⊙ Estmar

Everhill
Academy

RIVER WILDE

OUTER ISLES WEST

A MAP OF
THE EMPIRE OF
SILVAEIN AND
ITS REGIONS

Commissioned from the Ilian
Office of Cartography for Her
Ladyship, Alyra-Rose Silvaein.

LONG MAY SHE REIGN.

Southpoint

TO ELAROS

FOREST

...ASTER

CALLA RIVER

Port Orens

Riannivh

AMETHYST RIVER

MARRAN
MARSHLAND

Greenhaven

OUTER ISLES EAST

...SDALE

Brierwood

THE
ILIAN

SILVAEIN

ONE

Piper sat in a back corner of the pub, a half pint of beer in front of her. Condensation ran down the sides of the glass, pooling on the wooden table. It wasn't her usual drink. Or her usual pub. This one was darker than she liked; instead of bright magelights, gas lanterns illuminated a flickering path over some areas and not others. She had chosen her spot carefully; lurking in the shadows would scream she was up to no good. Instead, she sat partway between, in a space where the lamplight kept flickering, never remaining steadily dark or bright.

A book lay open beside her, clear of the trail of water currently sliding down the sloped table. Occasionally, she turned the page, though she couldn't tell you what was on it.

A cheerful hum filled the room, voices talking and laughing. The pub was almost full; Piper could only see two or three empty tables, and they were all small ones. Her gaze flickered over the room, not staying on any one person for too long. But, in her peripheral vision, she could always see him.

The man, Ten Sitram, sat at a table towards the middle of the establishment, a pack of cards spread on the timber before him. Opposite him, a short woman with yellow streaks in her dark hair – a sandstone dwarf – frowned at the hand he laid down.

A royal flush, Piper would bet. Sitram wasn't exactly subtle.

Just the other side of middle-aged, he might have had a distinguished appearance if his hair didn't creep quite so far back from his forehead. From what Piper could see, his pale hands were free of the calluses of labour. A gold chain winked around his neck, catching the lamplight.

Piper flicked a page in her book again as, across the room, the dwarf slammed her hand down on the table, her voice rising as she questioned the legitimacy of Sitram's hand. Piper wasn't close enough to hear in full, but snatches of inventive curses floated over the crowded pub towards her.

Sitram made a placating gesture. He pulled two silver stars from his winnings and passed them across the table at her.

Each cloth note threaded with silver was worth a hundred stars, so it wasn't a paltry cut. Still, from the way the dwarf glowered, Sitram had fleeced her of far more than that amount.

Piper felt sorry for the dwarf. It was hard to win against a gambler who cheated.

Sitram stood and the dwarf glanced around, perhaps looking for allies. Piper propped her chin on her hand. Her eyes flicked over the room slowly and casually, like her attention had wandered from her book for a moment.

Sitram gathered his other winnings. He slid them into a pouch, holding the notes tight as he tucked them out of sight. From the way some other patrons were following his movements, that wasn't a bad idea.

Piper sighed loudly, making the woman at the neighbouring table glance her way. She shut her book and swept it into the bag beside her on the table. The bag, made of hand-stitched leather polished buttery soft, had a large compartment at the back for her book and several pockets inside the compartment at the front, concealed by a flap. There was a place for everything she could ever want with her, including a few things she certainly wouldn't want found.

Sitram left the pub.

Piper stood and stretched out her arms, like she'd been sitting there for a while, then shouldered her bag. She flicked a few gold bits to the table and casually meandered towards the door. The coins, each worth a single star, were a pretty good tip, especially as she hadn't drunk much of her beer.

Outside, she glanced around. The tail of Sitram's coat, worn despite the warm spring air, vanished around a corner as she watched. Piper tugged her own coat closer around her throat, then, from one of many pockets, she pulled out a pair of thin black gloves. She walked as she slid them on.

The gloves did nothing to keep her fingers warm, not that warmth was an issue in the current mild weather – though in winter she had cause to wish the fabric provided greater protection from the chill. The gloves were made by a mage she'd never met: a spellbinder, who specialised in working magic into objects. These would keep her *illis*, the magical imprint that all humans had, from transferring to anything she touched.

Already, Sitram headed towards another crossroads as Piper rounded the first corner. She lengthened her stride, tucking her long braid into the back of her hood where it wouldn't snap around in the breeze.

On the street corner, Sitram halted. Piper saw why he'd stopped a moment later.

A tram headed past him, traversing the tracks covering the next street at a good pace. Piper huffed in quiet irritation. She slowed her step, keen to keep some distance between them for the moment. He didn't know she was there, and she wanted to keep it that way.

Trams were only small – a single cabin seating about fifty passengers – and it passed quickly. Sitram checked the road again, then stepped out across the tracks. Piper padded silently behind him. Her heartbeat pulsed in her throat, and she took a deep breath. No matter how many times she'd done it, this was the hardest part.

Her fingers found her stiletto blade. The hilt fit perfectly in her palm; it was her oldest blade, the first one she'd ever picked up. She felt a fondness for the weapon, not unlike the attachment one might have for their childhood teddy bear.

It was familiar, comforting. A little worn. Perfect, despite its age.

Reassured by its presence in her coat pocket, Piper released her grip.

Sitram passed under a streetlamp, the warm glow of a magelight creating a pool on the ground. It winked against the gold of his necklace and threw sharp shadows over the pavement.

Piper passed a moment later, skirting the edge of the light.

The bells of the clock tower tolled quarter to two in the morning, one soft *bong* that rolled over the city like a wave. Piper could hear voices from a few streets over; the Market District was loud even at this late hour. Sitram seemed to have no interest in joining the late-night shoppers and drinkers. Instead, he ducked left down a much narrower street, heading away from the Market District, and safety, and into the city's outskirts, the Oldtown.

Piper followed him.

The Oldtown wasn't really old. It was just poor. And, sometimes, desperate. Those who travelled to Silversdale often didn't realise just how expensive living in the capital city was. When they found themselves evicted or unable to find any lodgings in the first place, the Oldtown was where they ended up.

Every so often, the boundary of where the Oldtown started shifted back a little, as those with a little more money bought the rundown homes closest to the Market District or to Highkeep on the city's west, and painstakingly restored them. She'd done it herself a few years ago, just to get out.

She doubted Sitram would spend the money to do the same.

In a smaller street, Piper lengthened her stride, keeping her head down. Humming to himself, Sitram didn't even notice as she came up behind him, sliding her hand silently into his coat pocket. Sitram's pouch now in her hands, she ducked into an alleyway, where she emptied the contents of the pouch into her own coat, then filled it again.

She exited onto a cross street a few steps behind Sitram. Finally, Piper lifted her head.

"Excuse me!" She jogged a few steps as Sitram came to a stop, turning to her.

Piper held out the pouch. "I think you dropped this," she said, offering him a small smile.

Sitram's hand went to his coat pocket, and he blinked. "Oh." He did his owl impression again, fingers groping in the empty pocket, before he looked Piper over.

She knew what he saw. In her early twenties and barely over five feet, with curly brown hair halfway down her back in a messy braid. Pale, elfin features – though she had no elf blood in her – and silvery-grey eyes.

She saw the moment Sitram dismissed her as harmless. His shoulders relaxed, and he smiled at her.

"Thank you, young lady," he said, plucking the pouch from her fingers. "That was a very honest thing for you to do."

Piper shrugged one shoulder. "My mother taught me that good actions bring good fate," she said, which was the complete truth. And something she usually tried not to think too hard about.

Sitram laughed.

"Right she was." He glanced down at the pouch. "What's your name?"

"Bella," Piper said.

Sitram nodded. "Well, Bella, let me give you a thank you for your honesty."

"Oh." Piper's smile widened. "It's not necessary." She shifted closer, her hand finding his arm.

"I insist."

Sitram opened his pouch. For a moment, he stared at the contents; no cream-coloured notes with gold and silver threads wound through them. Those were in Piper's coat pocket. Instead, his pouch was filled with purple-black berries.

His mouth slid open, seemingly against his will. Then he looked up.

Sitram took in Piper again. This time he noticed her black coat and gloves. How her smile was just a tad too sharp to be kind.

A cold breeze filtered down the narrow street, lifting their coats.

The belladonna berries fell through Sitram's fingers. He stepped back, and as he did, Piper's fingers slid from around his wrist.

He looked down.

Barely a pinprick showed where she had slid her needle into his skin. Sitram's mouth worked. His right knee buckled, and Piper caught his arms.

"Shh," she soothed. "Shh. Don't try to speak. Speaking will make it hurt."

She lowered him carefully down to the ground, then knelt beside him.

"I'm sorry," she murmured. "But you pissed off the wrong family. Carlos was mad you cheated him."

Sitram's eyes widened, and he choked. "My– my mu–"

Piper pressed her fingers to his throat.

"No, don't talk, remember?" she murmured. "Carlos won't go after your mother now. This was the deal." She met his gaze, the whites of his eyes steadily turning red as the tiny veins in them broke down.

He sucked in a rattling breath.

Piper nodded. "Not long now," she murmured. "Time to pray, if you believe in that."

She had found that most people, no matter how much they swaggered in life, prayed when they were close to death. To Nyssa the Creator, or to fate, or even, sometimes, to the Leviathan, the Changeling, or one of the other Immortals.

Sitram's lips worked, and Piper read the name Nyssa on them. He was praying, then.

She put her hand on his shoulder. "You can let go," she murmured. "I won't leave until you're gone."

His eyes met hers again, fear wild in them. A single pink-stained tear slid down his cheek. Off-white froth specked the corner of his mouth, left there with each rattling breath.

Then … he stopped. His body twitched.

Piper's fingers found his throat. His pulse fluttered weakly for a moment. Then, it stopped.

Piper waited there for several minutes, checking the poison had worked. His tongue was swollen and blue, his fingertips a bluish purple. The whites of his eyes were red, and his muscles had seized and stiffened far more quickly than normal. She crossed his arms over his chest as they locked into place; it would take a crowbar to move them now.

Piper sat back on her heels. The pouch of belladonna berries lay on the ground beside her; three had spilled out onto the rough cobbles. Piper dropped them back in the pouch, then lay the pouch on Sitram's chest, tucking it under one hand. She wouldn't take them with her.

Piper stood. She brushed dirt from her knees, then slipped off her gloves, sliding them into an inside pocket of her coat. She found the rolled-up notes, and she pulled them out. The silver and gold threads embroidered into the fabric flickered in the light of the streetlamps, thousands of stars there, in her palms.

Piper sighed. Then, tucking the notes back inside her coat, she turned and walked back to the west, towards her apartment and her bed. Towards sleep.

If she could sleep, that was.

TWO

Lunchtime the next day found Piper in another pub. The Lily had bright, whitewashed walls displaying paintings and drawings purchased from the artisan's market, held once a month in Illusion Square, Silversdale's largest plaza. The ceiling vaulted over her head, rafters heavy with dried herbs used for cooking that leant a light fragrance to the air. Gauzy curtains at the windows swayed in the breeze. Piper had tucked the curtain in her booth behind the seat, so the sunslight pouring in from the garden fell across her table and the book she had spread there.

In the centre of the room, round tables spread with tablecloths were all currently filled by the lunch crowd. There was a fireplace against the wall behind Piper; in winter, her booth was the warmest, even next to the window.

A lovingly polished timber bar stood against one wall, an array of sparkling clean glasses stacked and hanging behind it. The Lily's proprietor – Patrik Edlam, a dark-skinned, middle-aged man – stood there. The half apron tied around his waist was spotted red in one corner by a glass of wine, knocked over as he had been pouring a drink. His customer, a woman in a mage's grey coat, sat on one of the barstools.

On the other side of the room, the man's daughter, Rose, stood on a ladder. She had a slate in one hand – dwarven Tech, rimmed in stone, with liquid light flowing between the two thin panes of glass – which she used to take stock of the bottles of wine stacked neatly on the high shelves there.

A little way across from Rose and her ladder, a staircase led upwards. Two private dining rooms and several rooms for lease took up the second floor, and on the floor above it, Patrik, his wife Lily – the pub's namesake – and Rose lived in a family suite. Rose's older brother Adam had moved out two years ago, giving them the extra room they had badly needed, especially once Lily's elderly mother Eugenie had come to live at the pub as well. Eugenie's bread was some of the best in the city, and even Patrik only complained about her a little, and mostly with a smile.

Piper flicked over a page of her book – actually reading it this time – and sipped at her latte; Rose was getting pretty good at using the coffee machine tucked in one corner of the bar.

Across the room, Eugenie opened the door to the kitchen. She slowly made her way towards the staircase and, set beside it, the door to the storeroom that had been converted to a small apartment for her when she had become too plagued by arthritis to climb the stairs.

Piper pushed her plate to one side, leaning against the padded armrest just under the window. She stretched like a cat in the sunslight, the warmth from the two suns streaming in through the window to drape over her like a velvet cloak. Out of habit, she kept a small part of her attention outwards; she noticed when the two workmen at the table near her stood and left, their lunches devoured in record time, and when the fisherwoman sat in their place and ordered "Anything except the fish and chips. *Please.*"

That made Piper smile.

The front door opened, sending the curtains swaying. A mage walked in, his coat darker than the one worn by the woman at the bar. A golden pin flashed at this throat: a spellbinder, soulmage or battlemage pin, most likely, though she couldn't see the details from this distance. He headed towards the mage at the bar.

Piper's gaze slid past him to the message board hanging just inside the door. All community places were required by law to show such boards. Amidst the usual posters – *Join the military, Silvaein needs you; Enrol in Everhill Academy, where all your magic dreams will come true; Missing; For Sale* – was a small, smudged piece of paper. Smudged, because it had been there for many years and the message board was right by the door, and small, because there wasn't a lot of information the government could put on it. It featured a crude sketch of a face that could belong to any woman, above the notice that the assassin known as the Belladonna Killer was wanted, alive, for murder. But even the ten-thousand-star reward hadn't brought forward many clues about her whereabouts.

Piper was smarter, and more careful, than that.

She supposed she could ask Patrik to take it down, but the tiny red crown in the corner of the paper meant that only a government official could remove it. Piper didn't want the Edlams in trouble for something as silly as a piece of paper. And, if she was honest, it amused her that the notice hung directly under the small bunch of dried nightshade flowers pinned to the top of the message board.

Patrik caught Piper's eye from behind the bar and held up a bottle of wine, a question in his eyes. Piper shook her head. She didn't have the body mass to drink much, and unless she was trying to blend in somewhere, she didn't drink when she was working.

Patrik offered her a small smile and stashed the bottle underneath the bar.

Now that roused her interest; Patrik only kept the best bottles down there, behind lock and key. Perhaps it was the Freyan Mahogany he ordered occasionally. If that was the case, she needn't worry. Knowing it was her favourite, Patrik wouldn't open it until she asked for a glass.

She heard a soft, sharp curse, and jerked her head around. Rose's ladder rocked, and she clung to the top rung, her face ashen in fear. She had the slate pinned between her left hand and the side of the ladder.

Patrik started around the bar, but Piper was closer. She jumped out of her booth, crossing the floor in three strides to grab both ladder and slate before either could fall.

Rose let the slate slide out of her palm and into Piper's hands. The ladder swayed again, and Piper's pulse jumped as Rose squeaked in alarm. Patrik grabbed the other side of the ladder, holding it still.

"Thanks, Piper," Rose said, putting a shaking hand back on the rung and slowly climbing down. Piper frowned as Rose took the slate from her hands.

"Are you okay?" she asked. Rose shrugged one shoulder, though her dark eyes were still slightly wider than normal.

"I'm fine," she said, her voice breathy. "It slipped out of my hands, but I managed to grab it." She clasped the slate to her chest.

"How many times have I told you to be careful up there?" Patrik said, frowning. He wrapped an arm around his daughter's shoulders and pressed his face to the top of her hair.

Rose nudged her dad with her elbow. "But I caught it!" she said proudly, twisting to smile at him, the slate in her hand.

The expensive piece of Tech would have come from Astotha or Bysage; it was impossible to be certain. The two countries had once been one but, split by civil war, they now remained at constant odds over everything, from resources to the rights to sell their Tech.

Patrik pulled back to scowl at Rose. "That thing is not worth you hurting yourself," he scolded, and Piper saw Rose's smile slip.

"He's right," Piper said. "That would have been a nasty fall."

Rose drew back from under her father's arm, a little of her spark diminished.

"You shouldn't be up that ladder by yourself," Patrik continued, his hand still on Rose's shoulder. "Next time, wait for me and I'll help you."

"Right," Rose mumbled, glancing sideways. She freed herself from her father's grip, then turned towards the kitchen.

Piper opened her mouth as the girl walked away. Then she closed it. It wasn't her business, even if she did feel for Rose. Piper suspected that, for Rose, her father's overprotectiveness was the most mortifying part of the incident. He seemed to forget that Rose was almost twenty-one.

Patrik frowned at Piper. Then he sighed. "She scared me," he admitted, running a hand through his short-cropped hair.

"Me too," Piper said softly. She rubbed her arm, and Patrik nodded, like he'd heard what Piper didn't want to say. He was overprotective. And Rose was no longer a child.

"I'll go talk to her," he said to Piper. He vanished into the kitchen after Rose.

Piper sighed and turned back to her table.

The fisherwoman at the next table tucked into her plate of roast beef, accompanied by a tall glass of something that fizzed lightly. Across the room, Patrik emerged from the kitchen, frowning again. In another booth, a tired-looking young woman – Piper assumed a nanny – sat with two small children. One had painted the booth and floor with mashed potatoes, while the other had her face and hands pressed to the window, looking at the garden outside and leaving sticky smears on the otherwise sparkling glass.

Piper bit down a smile as she stepped over an artfully lobbed blob of white – it had landed right in the middle of a whorl in the timber floor – and slid back into her booth. She shouldn't laugh. When that woman finally gave up and took her charges home, it would be Rose or Patrik who had to clean up the goopy mess. But Piper couldn't help her amusement. Especially when the giggling boy pulled back his spoon like a catapult and lobbed another lump of mashed potatoes at his nanny.

It hit her right between the eyes, and the young woman howled in frustration.

Across the room, the door slammed open. It crashed into the wall, leaving behind a dent in the message board behind it. Piper jerked upright.

A man just shy of six feet strode through the doorway, and Piper's shoulders tensed. He had roughly cut, light brown hair, swampy eyes, and a permanent sneer affixed to his face. Piper knew it was permanent, because she'd never seen him without it, even during their brief and very regretful period of dating.

Patrik shot Piper a concerned look across the room, and she shook her head minutely. While technically Patrik had the right to refuse service to anyone, getting on Saxe's nerves would only end in tragedy for the family; maybe for everyone in the pub if he was in a foul enough mood. She shut her book, clasping her hands on its cover.

Like Piper, Saxe wore weapons. Unlike her, his bastard sword was strapped across his back in plain view, defying about half a dozen laws Piper knew of. He dropped into the booth opposite Piper.

Heat flashed through Piper at his invasion of *her* space in *her* pub, but she pushed down the anger and affixed him with a cold grey stare.

"Saxe," she said tonelessly.

"Piper." The corner of Saxe's mouth curled up further, making him look feral.

"What do you want?" Piper asked.

Something dangerous flashed in Saxe's eyes, and he leaned forward. "I hear the Belladonna struck again last night," he said softly. "The upstart whore that she is, she left him in the street."

For one glorious moment, Piper imagined it. Imagined standing up as though to leave, then spinning around too fast for Saxe to catch her. Imagined sinking her dagger, the leaf-shaped one at the small of her back, into his throat and sliding it out the other side.

He'd fall forward, mouth gaping, that sneer finally wiped off his face.

Then Piper blinked, and she was sitting across from Saxe again.

"I've heard nothing about her unnamed counterpart," she replied calmly, examining her short fingernails.

Saxe reared back, fury written across his features. Piper bit back a smirk; he never had a comeback for that. He visibly ground his teeth together.

Piper leaned forward. "Why. Are you. Here?" she said, like she was speaking to a petulant toddler.

"Lore wants to see you," Saxe spat out.

Piper tensed. But she masked the action by leaning back, crossing her arms over her chest. "What does he want?" she asked.

Saxe fixed his small eyes on her, their muddy depths slight with fury like a swamp fire. "The usual," he breathed.

That was it. Why he'd come to find her on this side of the city, where the pubs and hotels and shops were light and airy, not dark and smelling of urine and spilled beer like the places he usually frequented. And why his demeanour was even nastier than usual. Saxe detested it when Lore passed over him for a job that then went to Piper.

"When?" Piper asked, and Saxe shrugged.

"Now," he replied. "Well. Hours ago. It took me so long to find you." That sneer twisted up again.

Piper clenched her fists, hidden in her crossed arms. But Saxe caught the tightening of her arm muscles anyway, and his hand strayed to his shoulder, just under the hilt of his sword. Though Piper would never start a fight with civilians around, she knew that Saxe had no such qualms. It wasn't a threat Piper could ignore.

She pushed herself up from the booth and strode across the room. Piper dropped her bag on the bar, and Patrik took it for safekeeping. He raised his eyebrows at Saxe, but Piper shook her head. He wasn't worth the effort. Now that she wasn't there to bully, he'd leave. The Lily was altogether too fancy for his tastes.

"Job?" Patrik murmured. Piper shrugged one shoulder.

"I'll find out soon, I guess," she said softly.

The door swung open again, and two policemen piled into the pub, their navy coats over their arms in the warm spring weather. One held the door for Piper, offering her a distracted smile, and she slipped out of The Lily.

Piper pushed past three women as she made her way back towards the Oldtown. She heard their soft sighs as they ogled a long white dress displayed in a shop window.

Silversdale was a large city. It took several hours to walk across it on foot, even excluding the Ilian, the other half of the city, across the river, where the factories, workshops and harbours were located. Thankfully, Piper didn't have to walk.

A tram rang its bell as Piper neared the station closest to The Lily. She broke into a jog, dodging around a man walking his dog – a small, fluffy thing with a blue bow around its neck – and turned a corner. By the time her boots hit the red-paved road one street over, the tram was moving at a slow crawl away from the station, the bell still ringing as the driver told people in no uncertain terms to get off his tracks. Piper jumped the small garden that lined the edge of the tram station. Then she reached for the wrought iron railing of the balcony.

The conductor scowled as Piper pulled herself up and over the railing. His frown vanished as Piper pressed two gold bits into his palm: the price of her fare and a small tip.

"I'm not supposed to let you on if you do that," he scolded, though Piper noticed he pocketed the coins without offering her the change.

Piper stopped herself from rolling her eyes. "But you will," she told him, pushing open the door to enter the carriage – mostly to avoid the argument she was certain the conductor would start. As he was required to stay on the balcony, all Piper got in response was a glare. She sank into an empty seat, pulling one boot up and wrapping an arm around her knee, and leaned against the window. The city blurred by as she let the conversations around her take her attention.

Trams were not as private as the people on them seemed to think. It made them good places to pick up on some gossip. To her right, a girl spoke in hushed tones to the friend sitting beside her about what Piper could gather was a romantic encounter. She rubbed her forehead to hide her grimace. That was not the kind of thing you discussed on public transport.

"Bloody murder, that's what," someone in front of Piper whispered in a voice that carried back to her.

Piper almost jumped, but she grabbed her reaction with an iron will and shoved it back down. She leaned forward, trying to catch more of the conversation just ahead of her.

"... towards the bridge in the Mage's Quarter," the voice whispered again. He glanced around, and Piper fixed her attention out the window as a cab drove past, its black horses chomping at the bit and throwing up their heads like Chaos Demons. "... swinging from the bottom of the bridge ... top of his head missing."

Piper gritted her teeth and sat back. She wasn't close enough to hear the entire conversation, but that calling card was enough. It seemed the Belladonna's unnamed counterpart *had* struck the previous night after all. No wonder the comment had annoyed Saxe so much.

The tram turned a gentle corner and came out on The Lady's Parade. The red pavement seemed to glow in the afternoon light, contrasting with the green gardens that lined the space between footpath and road. The largest road in Silvaein, The Lady's Parade ran from the northernmost point of the city, through the Oldtown and Market Districts, then on through Redwell, where the old money lived, to the palace on the cliffs overlooking the sea.

The tram rumbled through a few more stops. People got off and more got on. Piper got to her feet when an old woman stepped through the door, looking around in dismay at the lack of seats. She took Piper's seat with a warm smile, and Piper slipped outside to avoid the crowded interior cabin.

Even the balcony wasn't empty anymore; two young women leaned against the railing, chatting and watching the city pass by. The conductor glanced at them, like he was debating trying to join the conversation.

He opened the door to the carriage and leaned inside as a station approached. "Illusion Interchange!" he called.

Piper pushed herself off the railing. Before the tram pulled to a full stop at the station, she jumped off and turned back up the street towards a large archway.

Illusion Square took up a hectare of space in the Market District. A garden ran through the centre of it, large trees providing shade over grassy areas where several children currently ran, squealing in delight, watched over by parents or grandparents. Two- and three-storey buildings lined the square; mostly shops with dwellings above, though some external staircases led to shops on upper levels. Stalls packed the pavement, some purchased for weeks at a time to secure the best spots they could.

Afternoon shoppers hovered among the stalls, a hum of conversation lingering over the space. Piper tucked her braid over her shoulder, dodging around a group of young men clustered around the window of a Tech shop, where slates that ranged from the size of Piper's palm to the length of her forearm were displayed in the window. A little girl ran, screaming with delighted laughter, across the path, and Piper had to stop to avoid knocking into her. A young woman Piper assumed was her mother chased after, chocolate smeared on the sleeve of her shirt.

Piper bit back a smile. Girls that age were sassier than anyone gave them credit for; she could remember making her mother run around after her six-year-old self.

For a moment, Piper's smile wobbled. Forcing her mind away from that thought, she turned her attention back to the square.

On the other side of the square, Piper caught a different tram and rode a few more stops. She could have walked the distance, but it would have taken her hours, and Lore was already waiting.

She'd learned a long time ago that it was a bad idea to keep Lore waiting.

Piper stepped off at a station in the Oldtown and looked around. This part of the Oldtown could almost pass as the Market District, if it was a good day, and if rain had recently washed the streets.

If not … Well. Piper could smell the drains from thirty paces.

Piper left the main street and stepped straight onto dirt. One day, if these houses were ever bought by the people who'd scraped together enough money, someone might pave the street. For now, Piper's boots left little clouds of dust with each step, and dirt clung to the legs of her jeans.

The next street over was decorated with a rut as deep as Piper's ankle, made by someone dragging a wheelbarrow or very broken wagon, possibly after the last big rainstorm. Ahead, Piper noticed a patrol; policemen in a group of three here, instead of the pairs that patrolled the rest of the city. She ducked into an alley to avoid them; even with the dust, her clothes were just a little too good for the Oldtown, and she didn't want to be stopped and questioned about what she was doing here.

The smell of damp met her, and Piper wrinkled her nose. Underneath, a sickly sweet fragrance reached out to her: sewer treatment. Piper swallowed back the sick feeling that rose in her stomach and covered her nose with the sleeve of her coat.

She had not missed that smell.

She hadn't gone much further when she heard a noise behind her. Piper twisted, but not fast enough to stop a small body from running into her.

"Oof." Piper caught the boy around the shoulders and stopped them both from tumbling to the ground. As she did, she felt a hand in her pocket. Quick as a snake, Piper reached behind her and seized a bony wrist. There was a gasp, and the boy who had rammed her tried to run. She grabbed him too, then dragged them both in front of her.

Both boys paled as she looked them over. Both had the same mop of brown hair, the same freckles on the bridge of the nose. Though the older boy's eyes were brown and the younger one's hazel, they were the same shape. The younger one twisted in Piper's grip, but she'd held on to far stronger men for far longer. She didn't hurt him, but she tightened her grip enough for him to know he wasn't going anywhere she didn't want him to. The boy stopped struggling, his eyes wide and his face white.

"He don't know nothing of it." The older boy met Piper's eyes, his eyes scared but his jaw set. "I was just using him as a distraction."

The younger boy opened his mouth. After a swift kick to his shin from his accomplice, he shut it again. Piper pretended not to notice.

"Really?" Piper raised her eyebrows.

The older boy pursed his lips and looked away.

"Where are your parents?" Piper asked.

The younger boy's lip trembled. "Dead," his brother answered, his voice and eyes flat. "Dragonfever."

Piper bit back a sigh. There'd been a dragonfever outbreak in a nearby town almost six months ago, she remembered reading in the paper. If their parents had died and the boys had no one to look after them, she could guess how quickly they would have lost the roof over their heads. She could feel the bones in both boys' wrists. The older one had gaunt eyes and sunken cheeks. The younger one looked a little better; his brother, she supposed, taking care of him at his own expense. Like family should.

Piper let go of the younger boy's wrist, keeping her other hand firmly on the older child. He darted back, hiding behind his brother. The older boy reached behind him, holding his brother close, then visibly swallowed, gazing at Piper in dread. Being caught stealing earned one a magical brand from the police, made on the back of the wrist. It wouldn't hurt physically, but he'd never be able to gain employment, even when he grew up.

Assuming he managed to grow up. If the wrong person caught him stealing, the punishment would be far more lethal.

Piper pulled her wallet out of the inside pocket of her coat and flipped it open with her thumb. "No one with any sense keeps their wallet in an outside pocket," she told him.

The younger boy gasped at the glistening of metallic thread in cloth notes held in the billfold. Piper ignored him, thumbing through the stars thoughtfully. A gold star was far too much. They'd be murdered for it as soon as they tried to buy something.

She looked up at the boy and fixed him with a cool grey stare. "Don't make me chase you," she warned.

She let him go.

The boy jerked back a step. Then he froze, squaring his shoulders and meeting Piper's gaze.

She sighed. "Here." She pulled out a wad of copper stars and offered them to him.

The boy glanced between the notes and her, and slowly reached out. He took them gingerly, looking at Piper like he expected her to yank them away and laugh at him.

Piper dropped to her knees and caught his arm.

"Listen to me," she said, her silver eyes boring into his. "If you keep doing this, you'll get caught. And" – her gaze darted to the younger boy, still hiding behind his brother's back – "if you steal from the wrong person, they'll kill you."

The boy pressed his lips together. "I know," he whispered. "But I have to feed him."

Brightness glittered in his eyes, and Piper's chest tightened in pity. She sat back on her heels.

"Do you know the white building near Coral Square?" she asked, pointing towards the Market District. The boy nodded. "Take your brother and go there. Go to the white-haired man, and tell him Bella sent you. He's a friend."

"But, I–"

"Do it," Piper ordered, her voice stern. The boy wavered.

"O-okay," he stuttered.

Hoping he would do as she said, Piper let go of him. He lurched away from her, almost knocking his brother over in his haste.

Piper raised one eyebrow at him, and the boy nodded. He grabbed his brother's shoulder, then dragged him back towards an alleyway.

In the right direction, at least. If they headed for Coral Square, they'd get food and a place to stay the night. If they were lucky, maybe a foster home.

Piper lost track of them as they rounded a corner. Sighing, she forced herself to stand.

She picked her way down a few more side streets, avoiding dusty rubble and stinging nettles as tall as her thigh. The road became narrower, and she had no choice but to hold her hands up and push through a patch of the evil plants, hoping they left nothing behind on her clothes.

She climbed over a crumbling wall that had once been part of a building, that now let light and rain and fate knew what else fall on the rotten floor. Keeping to the more sound edges, Piper made her way to a door set into another wall.

This structure was in better repair than the others in the area, though still dirty and shabby. The door was washed black, the only indication of what kind of people lived on the other side of it.

Piper gritted her teeth. Then, against every desire in her body, she reached out and pushed the door open.

THREE

The door opened to a dank and shadowy hall, the walls lined with moss. Inside, it smelled like mould and old stone. Piper grimaced.

The sound of a whip cracking wetly against flesh snapped through the room, and Piper flinched before she could compose herself.

There was no whip in this room. Just a memory.

She shivered. To say she loathed this place would be an understatement.

A door was set into the wall on her right. Piper reached for the handle, the cold metal biting into her skin. Wiping her hands on her pants - touching anything in here made her feel contaminated - Piper stepped through a door low enough that she almost had to stoop. She stopped at the top of the stairs inside.

The sunken room was just as she remembered it from her last visit, down to the dirt in the corner that no one had cleaned. Dirty plaster walls stretched up to a ceiling with what looked like a burn mark in one corner. A hard bench against one wall was the only furniture. Above her head, a skylight let in the afternoon sunlight. Just enough filth covered the opening so that no one could stand on top of the building and see inside.

Piper jumped down the three stairs into the chamber, her boots making a smacking sound on the stone. Despite the warmth of the suns, cold clung to this building. It grabbed at Piper, sliding past the collar and sleeves of her coat like an invisible hand.

From here, doors led in a few directions: left to the living quarters, straight ahead to the utility rooms – including a laundry that Piper would bet hadn't been used since she moved out – and right to the training areas and single office.

Piper turned right.

The door opened straight into a training room, its walls painted white. Unlike the first room, it was clean. Bright magelights lit the space, chasing shadows from even the corners of the room. Unlike the training area Piper had in her small flat, there was no comfort in this place. No mats covered the hard stone ground, and the training dummies were weighted with lead instead of sandbags. There were no windows, preventing any curious – or stupid – city folk from peering in. Instead of the blunted weapons one might expect for training, two racks of live weapons lined one wall.

There would be no practice here. Each bout had the potential to turn deadly.

In the centre of the space, two men sparred, wickedly bladed staves in their hands. Iso, a broad-shouldered man with near-black skin, lunged overhead at the weedier Ratt. Piper, who knew Ratt didn't favour blades as weapons, watched as he bared uneven teeth and used his smaller size to duck out of the way. Not unlike she would, Piper grudgingly acknowledged. But she would do it with more finesse. She did everything with more finesse than Ratt. Stomping around to face Iso again, he had the grace of a rampaging tseoun.

A third, broader man stood watching them, his hands clasped behind his back, his suit jacket pulled tight across his shoulders. Brown hair touched his collar, and the sliver of olive skin visible at his wrists was corded with muscle. He barely twitched as Piper approached.

"Belladonna," he said, not taking his eyes off the fighters.

Piper folded her arms across her chest. "Lore." She stopped beside him, keeping a careful arm's length between them. "Ratt's going to get his fingers broken."

Lore didn't reply. Iso swung again, and Ratt brought up his staff to block. He braced the middle of the weapon with his left hand.

The angle was off. Piper could see that in the split second before the staves made contact.

There was a sharp snap and a *pop*. Ratt howled. Iso, his face blank of all emotion, lashed out. The blade kissed the pulse point in Ratt's throat, and both men froze.

Lore turned from the two of them like they were actors in a play he'd grown bored of. "By all means, you're welcome to take up their training," he said.

Red hot irritation bubbled through Piper's chest, and she sucked in air. Refusing to give him the satisfaction of knowing how much she longed to slide her dagger through his hand, she let her breath out slowly.

Lore's gaze held steady on hers, his eyes blank.

"I've told you, I'm not interested," Piper said.

Iso stalked past them without a word. He ignored Piper, and she him; that suited them both just fine. Ratt, on the other hand, glowered at Piper as he exited the room. Behind Lore's back, he spat at her. Piper pushed her clenched fists safely into her coat pockets, resisting the impulse to respond to Ratt in kind.

Lore's gaze darted down, taking in the movement. Piper forced herself to take a deep breath through her nose, squashing her emotions down to a ball in her chest. They wouldn't get to her.

They *wouldn't*.

She forced herself to meet Lore's gaze and held out her hand.

"Sitram is dead," she stated.

The corner of Lore's mouth quirked up. "And what would you like me to do about that?" he said softly. Piper's shoulders tensed, and she forced herself not to flinch. Some men yelled when they got angry. Not Lore. The lower his voice was, the more dangerous he became.

"My payment," Piper forced out through gritted teeth. She wouldn't give him the satisfaction of saying *please*.

Lore uncrossed his arms and slid his hand into a pocket. Without warning, he flung a packet directly at her face.

Only Piper's reflexes saved her. She snatched the packet out of the air before it hit, and ripped the paper off. Piper thumbed through the cloth, counting in her head.

She knew better than to trust Lore. She'd only made the mistake of not counting when she was much younger, and much more naive.

Satisfied he hadn't tried to cheat her, Piper slid the bundle into an inside pocket of her coat. Not the same pocket as her wallet, of course. She'd grown up with thieves and knew how to not be a target – and how to minimise her losses if she was.

For a moment, Lore regarded her with narrowed eyes. Then he turned. "Come," he said, beckoning over his shoulder.

Swallowing down a sigh, Piper returned her hands to her pockets and followed Lore.

The room he led her to was small. The dark-panelled walls loomed over her, pressing her down and making her feel even shorter than she already was. A desk took up half the office, a large leather chair behind it. Bookshelves dotted the walls, and an empty hearth promised the possibility of warmth that had never been delivered, at least not in Piper's experience. A hard, timber chair stood in the corner. Piper shivered at the sight of it; how the wood hadn't been stained permanently red with blood, she didn't know.

The last time she'd been in this room ... Piper pushed the thought ruthlessly away. The scar on the back of her shoulder twinged, though it had healed almost a year ago. She forced herself to take her hands out of her pockets and clasped them behind her back where he couldn't see them trembling.

Lore braced his hands on either side of the desk, his back to Piper. For a long time, he stared at the empty hearth. Her gaze darted over the exposed part of his neck, where olive skin showed behind his suit jacket, and took in the material clinging to the muscles of his back. It would be so easy to slide her stiletto through his ribs and into his heart. Or through the back of his neck, severing his spine. He'd drop like a sack of flour, if she did that, to twitch and bleed out on the floor.

Piper let herself luxuriate in the thought for a moment, drawing in a deep breath. She didn't dare close her eyes, not with Lore in the room. Maybe, after she killed him–

Piper's chest burned at the thought, destroying her daydream. She grimaced.

Lore turned. The half smirk and the glint in his eyes told Piper he knew exactly what she'd been thinking. He probably relished the thought of her trying as much as Piper did, though for different reasons.

He knew she couldn't kill him. Not without forfeiting her own life.

"I have another job for you," he said.

Piper crossed her arms. She already knew that.

"I've just done one," she said. "Get one of the others to do it."

Lore's eye twitched, and a light entered his eyes that made Piper's skin crawl.

"It's your job," he said. "You kill who I tell you, when I tell you."

His gaze flickered, for the barest second, to the thick leather book at the end of his desk. A nondescript white envelope lay on top of it, of a kind that Piper was very familiar with. The leather book held nothing worse than ledgers; though for Saxe, Ratt and Iso, there was nothing more damning than those particular ledgers.

Piper was different. Her debt was … somewhat less monetary.

"So the job pays too much for what they're worth," she said, meeting Lore's eyes coldly.

Lore leaned forward, his eyes narrowing. He said nothing. Just glared at Piper in warning.

A worm of worry sluiced through her stomach, but Piper forced herself to hold his gaze. She put her hands back in her pockets, where they could stroke the hilt of a dagger without Lore noticing.

Lore followed the movement of her arms, then refocused on her face. "The going price for this contract is two million stars."

Piper rocked back on her heels, blinking. While Lore's lips moved as he continued to speak, blood rushed in her ears and made it impossible to follow his words.

Two million stars. That was absurd. It was enough to pay someone a decent wage for about four hundred months – over thirty years.

Fate, who would hand over that much money just to have someone killed?

Lore stared at her, waiting for an answer, and Piper blinked the room back into focus.

"I'm sorry?" Her fingers wrapped so hard around one of her daggers that the sheath dug into her skin, even through the lining of her coat. Piper pried them off.

"I said," Lore repeated, his voice low and dangerous, "you will do it tonight."

Something popped in Piper's ears. She shook her head.

"No," she said. "I don't do rush jobs."

No amount of money was worth getting caught. She couldn't spend it if she were dead. And a rush job of this level … that reeked of desperation.

Desperate people were dangerous.

"You do now," Lore said.

"No," Piper said. "I don't."

He moved so fast Piper hardly saw it. In the next instant, Lore stood in front of her, his hand fisted in her collar. Piper choked as he lifted her off her feet, her coat and shirt tightening around her throat. Her hands scrabbled at his, but her short nails didn't break his skin. The toes of her boots scraped against the floor as she kicked out, looking for purchase.

Lore pulled her closer, bringing her face in line with his. His breath fanned across her face; she could smell meat and tobacco, and something else, something sickly sweet that Piper couldn't name.

"'No' isn't an option," Lore growled. "Understand?"

Piper didn't move. He twisted his grip, dragging her clothes even tighter around her neck. Her heart tripped in her mouth, cold working its way down her spine.

She had no choice. Gaping, Piper nodded.

Lore let her go.

Piper's legs buckled, and she landed on her knees. Her hands went to her throat as she sucked in a full breath.

Lore loomed over her, and Piper forced herself to look up and meet his gaze.

"You will receive two million stars if you take care of him tonight," Lore said. "If you don't, I cut your payment." His eyes glittered with something dangerous. "If he's not dead …" He left that trailing, but Piper didn't need him to finish.

Lore didn't tolerate failure well.

Piper got to her feet, proud that she did so without staggering. He watched her for any sign of weakness, a wolf looking to take down his prey. She strode to the desk, risking turning her back to him for a moment as she snatched up the envelope. Then she spun on her heel.

"You'll pay me tomorrow," she ground out, marching past him and to the door.

She tried to push aside the nagging feeling that she was going to regret this.

FOUR

Piper ducked into The Lily on her way back through town; partially to collect her bag, and partially to check that Saxe had left. Patrik raised his eyebrows as Piper slid the envelope into her bag, but he said nothing.

He knew what the envelope meant.

Rose stood by the front booths, wiping down a table sticky with someone's spilled drink. Her expression was glum. Piper nudged her on the way out and offered the younger girl a smile, which Rose returned, though it didn't reach her eyes. Rose was a cheerful girl, she just didn't like being chastised in front of people. Not that Piper could blame her for that.

Outside, Piper headed for the tram station. This time, she waited like a civilised person for the tram to pull up, then climbed aboard and paid the conductor.

She didn't go inside. Instead, she leaned on the railing, watching the city slide by her and fingering the envelope in her bag.

Two million stars … A glittering pile of money, two thousand gold-threaded notes. She could wade through it, ankle deep, in her tiny apartment. Maybe she could hire her own assassin. Someone to kill Lore, so she never had to work for him again.

Her chest burned at the notion. No, she couldn't do that.

The tram pulled into the station at Highkeep while she was still deep in thought. Piper jumped down, heading into a side street immediately. Taking a different route home every day was an ingrained habit from the years she'd lived in that awful commune with Lore and the others.

Highkeep was a solidly affluent district of the city. Though only the main road had the distinctive, and costly, red paving, the other streets were smooth and well maintained, despite the foot traffic and cabs that traversed them. While it wasn't as ubiquitous a sight as in Redwell, it wasn't all that uncommon to see an autocart trundling down the roads here. Essentially a horseless carriage, the large vehicles couldn't go as fast as a tram, but they were private. In Piper's experience, people with money valued that.

Maybe, once this job was done, she could buy one.

Piper snorted at her own folly as she arrived at her apartment building; one in a long row of stained timber buildings, the foundations made from large square blocks of stone peeking above street level.

Her ground floor neighbour looked up from her little garden as she approached. Missus Cobb put her hands on her hips and glared at Piper.

"And here I was thinking the landlady had finally evicted you," she said, her nose wrinkling.

Piper bit back a sigh and didn't bother explaining to Missus Cobb, for the tenth time, that she owned her apartment and was therefore unlikely to be evicted. "Good afternoon, Missus Cobb," Piper said instead.

Missus Cobb scowled. "Don't you take that tone with me, young lady," she said, weeds swinging from one of her gloved fists. "When I was your age, you wouldn't have caught *me* flitting around at all hours of the night doing fate knows what—"

Piper stepped past her and pulled open the door. She knew from experience that the older woman would just keep going if she stopped to listen.

"Have a good afternoon, Missus Cobb," she called, ducking inside the building to the staircase.

Missus Cobb started to say something, but Piper missed it as the front door swung shut. She sighed, rubbing her forehead. Missus Cobb had never liked her. For the three years Piper had been living in the building, she complained about everything Piper did, especially if it happened at an odd time.

If Piper had been a tenant, she was certain the older woman would have gotten her evicted long ago.

Piper shook her head and started towards the staircase.

Once an old townhouse, someone years ago had converted the three-storey structure to three apartments. A heavy timber staircase joined the three floors, and the interior walls had been rebuilt to make landings so that the apartments would be completely private.

As she crossed the second-floor landing, she heard the unmistakable sound of her neighbour's bed knocking against the wall.

The apartments were *almost* completely private.

Wincing at her unintended eavesdropping, she took the last flight of stairs two at a time, fleeing from that awkward sound. On her landing, it was more muffled.

Piper unlocked her door and stepped inside. As she shut it behind her, the sound grew quieter still, but the rhythmic thudding still made its way up through the floorboards.

She turned to her mantelpiece, where a tiny old radio sat. Piper had fished it out of a second-hand sale in Coral Square. It still worked, most of the time, and after she had cleaned it up, it didn't have any of the previous owner's greasy fingerprints on it anymore, either. It wasn't loud, but it was loud enough. The soft notes of Silvaein Radio, one of only two channels she could tune into without a spellbinder augmenting the device, filled the room. Violin and piano was far preferable to the sounds of her neighbours doing ... that.

Piper turned away from the mantelpiece and looked around.

It wasn't the largest apartment. The ceiling followed the slope of the roof, barely above Piper's head on the long sides, and reaching almost twelve feet high where it peaked in the centre. A seldom-used kitchen took up one corner and, behind it, a closed door led to the tiny bathroom. The chimney, which also serviced the rest of the building, ran right through the middle, with Piper's love seat and the huge armchair she loved to curl up in and read in front of it. A small dining table was tucked between chimney and kitchen. Piper had pushed her bed up against the back wall, on the other side of the room. The rest of the space was taken up by training mats, with one sandbagged dummy currently pushed to one side.

Piper dropped her bag on the table.

It wasn't much. The place was barely big enough for one person, there was a draft in winter, and her neighbour downstairs was ... enthusiastic in his romantic pursuits.

But it was hers.

Piper sank into one of the dining chairs – she had two, despite the fact that she never had company – and pulled the envelope from her bag. Her fingers shaking slightly, she slid the leaf-shaped blade from the small of her back and sliced the string.

The paper fell open, and Piper swallowed.

Two million stars, she reminded herself.

It was the standard affair. The first page was the writ of assassination. Not that it mentioned the word anywhere; though the documents were in cypher, it didn't hurt to be careful. Anyone who could somehow read the text but who wasn't in the know would have no clue what the paper was authorising.

Piper pulled out the next sheet of paper.

Downstairs, the sound of banging grew louder. She stopped reading to go turn her radio up, then settled back in her chair and looked over the page.

Alexander Rylan. Piper frowned as she read through his information.

Male, twenty-six. Single. University educated. Mage.

Piper's lip curled up in distaste. Trust Lore to saddle her with a mage. Mages were dangerous, especially battlemages and soulmages. Which Rylan was, the dossier did not say.

The idea of a mage made her twitch. *Two million stars*, she repeated to herself.

"Hit her again," Lore said lazily. "That will teach her to let someone escape."

Piper ground her teeth to keep from screaming as another line of fire draped across her back. The grey-coated mage stood over her, his palms full of writhing, green-yellow magic, and—

Piper shook herself. That had been a long time ago.

She turned her attention back to the paper.

Six foot four. Black hair, blue eyes. Silvaenian heritage.

Occupation: Teacher.

Piper frowned. What, by fate, had a teacher done to make someone pay this absurd amount for his death?

Current place of work: Summer Palace.

Piper shot to her feet. Even the sounds from downstairs faded from her attention as she paced from one end of her apartment to the other, twisting her fingers together.

She couldn't. There was no way.

Piper forced herself to stop pacing. Pressing her arm to the chimney, she gently bashed her forehead against it.

She couldn't go after any of the royals. Not just wouldn't, *couldn't*. It would kill her if she tried.

Piper forced herself to take a deep breath through her nose. She held it for five seconds, then let it out slowly.

He was just a teacher. He wasn't royal – at least, she didn't think he was.

Piper turned back to her table and picked up the paper again. Scanning it, she nodded, the twisting unease in her gut lessening. Nowhere did it claim he was from a royal background. Instead, it looked like he'd come from a tiny town out near Riannivh.

Piper's heart twisted at the name of the city. She missed Riannivh, the manor house on the hill overlooking smaller buildings made of purple-blue sandstone. The forest on the outskirts, trees with white trunks that grew almost transparent leaves and silver flowers in the spring and summer. The river, crystal clear, winding through the centre of the city ...

Piper pushed that thought away and took a deep breath.

He was not a royal. That was better. Still, not great – Piper rubbed her eyes, trying not to think about having to break into the Summer Palace – but better.

Piper spread the rest of the papers across her table and frowned at them. If he was just a teacher, perhaps he had a dwelling outside of the palace; even better if he had one in Redwell, where some people were too cocky to buy mage charms to alert them to intruders.

Her eyes landed on a map, and she groaned.

The map showed a rough layout of one floor of the palace. The third floor, by the label in the bottom corner. Halfway across, on the left-hand side, Piper could see a mark. A single room, coloured in blue.

Piper sighed. Not only did he work at the palace, he also lived there.

The last document was a photograph. It looked like it had been taken during a parade, because Piper could see the backs of two people's heads at the bottom of the frame.

The dark-haired man – Rylan – stood almost a head taller than the man beside him, his long hair scraped back into a horsetail. At first glance, she wasn't sure; he didn't wear the typical grey coat of a mage. But she knew it was him by the hair, the only black amid a sea of other colours. The photograph caught him twisting around, looking back along the line and frowning like someone had asked him a question.

Two redheads walked a little in front of him. The taller one, wearing a knee-length skirt and short-sleeved blouse, had her back turned to the camera.

The other ...

Piper sucked in a breath.

Piper had only seen her a few times, from a distance, but she immediately recognised the High Lady of Silvaein. It was in the way she stood, her shoulders straight and the angle of her head regal. She wore a neat blue suit that made her copper hair glow, even in a photograph.

All high ladies and their heirs had the same copper hair, and had for all recorded history.

Piper's gaze darted back to Rylan. He was *close* to them. Walking right next to a brown-haired man Piper now realised was probably the prince.

Her chest burned, and Piper rubbed at it.

Not a royal, she reminded herself. *Just an employee.*

The burning faded almost uncertainly, leaving her in peace for a moment.

Not for long, though; Piper hadn't realised the noise downstairs had stopped until it started up again, a groan making its way up through the floorboards. She glanced at her radio, but the little thing was already at full volume.

A moan joined in the symphony, and Piper shook her head. Nope.

Grabbing her papers, Piper stuffed them into a hidden, zippered compartment on the inside of her bag. Then she shouldered the bag and headed for the door.

She would be a bit early. But she couldn't stand listening to that any longer.

The city bells called out three o'clock as Piper made her way through Coral Square. Her bag, slung over one shoulder, now held a loaf of dark bread, a wheel of hard cheese and a packet of cured meats from the grocer at the entrance.

Coral Square was where the farmers market usually set up, and even in the afternoon, there was no lack of specialty foods, brought in from the farmland outside Silversdale. The space was not as large as Illusion Square and was roughly pentagonal, with flagstones that had been worn smooth by centuries of feet. Green gardens filled with flowers sat at intervals around it; some with trees for shade, and others with benches or picnic tables to rest at. People were jostling and calling out to one another around the most popular shops – the ice cream parlour on one corner was always busy. The air hummed with the sounds of people shopping and gossiping; humans, elves, dwarves and puka, all soaking up the atmosphere.

The late afternoon suns sent long shadowy spears from the tops of the buildings lining the square. Piper sidestepped a young woman, a toddler on her hip, a basket hanging off the crook of her arm. The toddler reached for Piper as she passed, and Piper wriggled her fingers in greeting. The woman glanced up at the child's bubbling laugh and took in Piper, then she moved on.

To Piper's right, a bright shop sign flapped at her passing. It displayed a cameo of a long-necked woman with an emerald green feather in her headband. Ahead of her, a sailor glanced her way. Dressed in the Silvaein naval uniform of dark blue with a griffin flying over a three-peaked wave, his gaze slid over Piper like she wasn't there. Piper brushed past him without a word, a sideways glance, or even much of a thought.

Two more naval officers stood under an archway nearby; clearly a ship had come in that day, and they had shore leave. One of them stood, his arms crossed, staring across the crowd. Like his colleague, he paid Piper no particular attention. Behind him, the other uniformed officer leaned forward, his arm braced against the stone wall. In front of him, a woman was twirling her hair through her fingers, a coy smile on her lips.

Piper rolled her eyes. Surely the man had something better to do with his one day on the shore, before he returned to sea for fate knew how long.

She ducked around a stand of fruit that was not quite in season. A man in front of her scooped up a girl who couldn't be older than three, placing her on his shoulders. A blonde woman beside him looked up at the little girl and laughed.

"Mama!" The girl waved her hands around, clipping the corner of a shop sign and causing it to swing wildly. "High!"

The woman laughed again, reaching up to take her hand. Piper tucked away a smile and pushed past them, further into the square.

A passing boy bumped her shoulder. Laughter ran through the air, and Piper dodged around two young girls chasing each other through the square. The younger one, maybe five or six years old, ran shrieking, the older girl staying just out of reach behind her. The younger girl's purple dress streamed out behind her with the movement.

Madelyn would like a dress like that, Piper thought. Perhaps she could get one made for her. It was her birthday in just a few weeks–

Someone bumped into Piper, drawing her back to the present. Murmuring an apology to the man, Piper ducked under an awning and turned to the heart of the square.

With the lengthening shadows, the fruit and vegetable stalls were quieter. Piper strode past, ignoring the calls from shop owners to come and see and sample their wares. About a quarter of the way in, Piper stopped in front of a fruit stall.

"Finally back again, hm?" the man behind said to her. "You're early today. But most of my best produce is gone."

"Most of your popular produce, you mean," Piper said without looking up. She picked up one of the pomelos, frowning at the shiny white skin, and placed it back.

"Everyone wants strawberries this time of year," the stall owner muttered, bracing his arms against his stall. He watched the periphery, where someone was more likely to try and slip a piece of fruit into their bag on the way past.

Piper picked up a small honeydew melon. Its creamy yellow skin meant it should be ripe, ready to eat right away. She grabbed a small basket from the stack next to the stall and dropped the melon in.

"Melons, is it?" the stall owner asked, and Piper nodded.

"And that pineapple," she said, pointing to the shelf behind him. "And some violaberries."

His nose wrinkled at her last request. "I'll never understand why you like those horrid things," he said. He ducked down under his bench, coming up with a large pouch. Piper took it off him and tucked it into her basket.

"Yet you always seem to have a pouch ready to go," she said, raising her eyebrows at him.

He glanced down at his till, avoiding her gaze. "That'll be thirty stars," he said.

Piper stared at him. "No way is fruit suddenly that expensive."

The stall owner pursed his lips.

Piper sighed. "Seventeen," she said.

He frowned. "You're robbing me," he accused her. "Twenty-five."

"Twenty-one, or I walk away," Piper countered.

The stall holder wavered a moment, likely trying to tell if she was bluffing, then held out his hand. "Fine," he said. "Next time, you could try asking nicely."

Sarcasm coloured his voice, but Piper ignored it as she pulled two copper stars and one gold bit from her wallet, handing them over. She didn't bother telling him that *had* been her asking nicely. Not nicely would have been at knife point.

Leaving the stall owner behind her, Piper wound her way back through the market. She ducked around another family, one boy looking around with an expression of derision that could only be worn by a pre-teen. Piper choked down a laugh.

A series of raised voices reached Piper. She paid them no mind until she rounded a corner and was stopped by a wall of navy. Piper's heart leaped into her throat for a moment, the worst-case scenario – that the police were there for her – leaping into her mind. Her hand found her dagger before she even realised what she was doing.

But the police showed her no attention. The wall of navy was only three uniforms long, now that she looked at it, with a fourth police officer, a woman, standing ahead. She held a short man with long, stringy hair, his arm twisted up behind his back.

"We know you stole the bread," she said, her voice overly patient. "Give it back and this will be a much more pleasant experience for you."

Piper pried her fingers off her dagger, drawing her hand out from under her coat.

"I don't know what you're talking about," the man said. One of the policemen upended the bag in his hands, and a sightly squashed loaf of bread fell out. "I don't know how that got there!"

Piper sidled around them, taking the closest exit out of Coral Square. Relief turned her limbs shaky – adrenaline was great on jobs, but not so much fun in the middle of a public place – and pushed aside the seed of pity she felt.

It was his fault, after all, for getting caught.

The streets immediately around the square were all well looked after, with the typical shop-and-apartment combination copied throughout the rest of the district. But Coral Square was a lot closer to the Oldtown than Illusion Square, and the streets quickly grew poorer, the pavement less even and the drains more clogged with leaves and other debris.

Piper turned down a narrow street full of small two- and three-storey apartment buildings.

One building up from the corner, a garden bloomed in a riot of greenery and colour. A wolf puka, her grey ears showing through her long brown hair, knelt beside a garden bed, a spade in one hand. Behind her, her daughter amused herself chasing her grey tail, still fluffy with baby fur.

The older puka looked up as Piper passed, and Piper nodded a greeting to her. The puka offered her a small smile, then returned to her gardening.

"Celia!" a voice boomed out, and Piper glanced back over her shoulder to see a taller puka, his ears and tail both longer than those of his mate, step out of the house. He scooped the little girl up, scolding her as he pulled a piece of bark out of her mouth.

These apartments were tiny; the largest, ground floor ones were even smaller than her loft apartment in Highkeep. Exterior staircases joined levels without so much as a balcony to step out onto. The small gardens fronted the cobbled road, gates built right up alongside. Piper trailed her hand over a worn stone fence, then over a newly painted black one. Black iron then turned to blue, and Piper stopped.

"Afternoon, Piper."

Piper glanced over to see a young woman about her age leaning on the blue fence. Why she'd chosen blue, Piper couldn't work out. Green or black or even red would have blended into the little street much better. There was a sign on the blue gate that said the occupant was a seer, but Piper had never once seen the woman with a customer.

"Hi, Beks," Piper said, stepping past the blue fence and pushing open the wooden gate next to it. Inside, Piper trod on the stepping stone to keep her feet out of the little patch of dirt that barely passed as a garden. On the other, better kept side of the fence, Beks mirrored her movements to keep pace with Piper.

"How was your day?" Beks asked.

Actually, Lore forced me into an assassination I want no part in.

"It was fine," Piper said. Then, because propriety demanded it, "Yours?"

Beks shrugged. "Average," she said. She hesitated, her dark blue gaze fixed on the apartment behind Piper.

Piper glanced back. Then she leaned on the fence. "What's up?" she asked.

Beks was weird. That much Piper could tell just from looking at her; from the dark jeans paired with brightly coloured scarves wrapped around her head like a turban, to her lack of customers. But despite that, or perhaps because of it, Piper kind of liked her.

Beks grimaced. She tugged at the collar of her shirt, staring at a point over Piper's head.

"Abby ..." She hesitated.

"What?" Piper repeated, frowning.

Beks offered a grimace, her blue eyes creasing in what Piper thought might be worry.

"She's not here," she said. "She hasn't been since this morning."

"And?" Piper pressed. It wasn't that unusual; it was a weekday, after all.

"Well ... I don't think the kids went to school today," she said.

"Fate damn it, Abby." Piper spun on her heel, heading across the garden again. For some reason, Abby really didn't seem to value her children's education. Piper did; she'd given Abby the fees for their school, so money wasn't the problem. It was a conversation they'd had many times and, it seemed, one they'd be having again very shortly.

Her fingers fumbled on her keyring, and Piper swore under her breath. Forcing herself to reign in her irritation, she fit the long key into the lock on the second try and shoved the door open. The smell of rotten eggs drifted over her like mist. Her heart skipped in her chest, and Piper gagged.

Fate. That had better not be what she thought it was.

A boy looked up from the couch. "Piper!" he cried in delight, leaping up. The book he had spread in his lap tumbled to the floor with a thud, but Caleb ignored it, shoving his mopish dark hair back from the brown skin of his face.

"Just a minute, Caleb." Piper almost threw the basket of fruit down on the rickety dining table as she flew into the kitchen. In there, the scent of rotten eggs was stronger. Piper's chest tightened, panic clawing its way up her throat.

The knobs on the stove were all off-kilter. Fate knew how long the gas had been going for. Her hands found the stove, and she turned them off. Jumping across the space, she threw open the kitchen window.

"Piper, what's wrong?"

Piper turned to see Caleb standing by the table. He looked between her and the basket of fruit, frowning.

"Caleb, where's Maddy?" Piper said instead of answering him. Fate, the little girl could be so much more susceptible to the gas than Caleb was ...

Caleb pointed over his shoulder. "Behind the couch," he said.

Piper tripped over a stray chair leg as she raced across the room. On the other side of the couch, a girl a few years younger who looked nothing like her half-brother lay in a sprawl of white-blonde ringlets, her white skin pale. She blinked big, hazel eyes as Piper leaned over her.

"Piper." Madelyn clutched her stomach. "I don't feel good."

"It'll be okay, baby," Piper murmured. "Why don't you sit up?"

Madelyn shook her head, but Piper tugged on her arm until she got her into a sitting position. The girl rubbed her forehead, then a panicked look crossed her face and she slapped both hands over her mouth.

Piper swore silently. Grabbing Madelyn around the waist, she heaved the girl up and lunged for the bathroom. They got there just in time for Piper to yank Madelyn's hair back, none-too-gently, with one hand. She used her other hand to support the girl as she vomited violently into the bath. Piper winced, the acrid smell clogging her nose and making its way down her throat.

The projectile vomit eased. Piper let go of Madelyn's waist to pull the child's hair back into a bun at the back of her head. Madelyn whimpered.

"My tummy hurts," she mumbled, leaning all her slight weight against Piper, whose back was pressed up against the wall in the small space. Piper smoothed Madelyn's hair back from her temples.

"I know, baby," she whispered. "I know."

Caleb touched Piper's shoulder, making her jump.

"What's wrong with Maddy?" he asked, concern in his brown eyes.

"Why don't you tell me what happened today?" Piper asked.

Caleb shrugged. "Mum left early," he said. "Maddy wasn't feeling good this morning, so Mum didn't want her to go to school, but she had to work, so I had to stay home too. Maddy got hungry, so I tried to make us lunch, but the stove wouldn't turn on. We found some sweets Mum had at the back of the cupboard, but ..." Caleb's stomach rumbled, and he flushed.

The panicked tension in Piper's shoulders faded. Not gas inhalation, or something more nefarious. Just two children who'd been left alone for far too long, with nothing to eat and nobody to watch them.

Madelyn chose that moment to lean forward and heave again, vomit splattering to the bottom of the bath. Caleb slapped a hand across his nose and mouth, taking a step back and bumping into the doorframe.

"Piper," Madelyn whined.

"It's okay, baby girl. It'll be okay," Piper whispered, stroking her back.

"What's wrong with Maddy?" Caleb demanded again, and Piper could hear the tears threatening in his voice.

"Come on, Caleb," another voice said, and Piper glanced over to see Beks, the back of one hand pressed to her nose, place a hand on his shoulder. "Let's give Maddy some space. Come and help me open all the windows and air out the house, okay? It's smelly in here."

Piper's shoulders drooped in relief. She nodded gratefully at Beks, and the other woman offered her a small smile.

Caleb let himself be led from the room, and Piper turned her attention back to Madelyn. The girl convulsed again, and Piper sighed. Resuming her back-rubbing duties, Piper thanked fate she wasn't a sympathetic vomiter.

FIVE

Piper carried Madelyn, now dressed in clean clothes, back into the living room. Though Madelyn clung to her shirt, Piper set her down in the old, worn armchair and disentangled her fingers.

"Piper," Madelyn whined.

Piper stroked Madelyn's clammy forehead. "Stay here, baby girl," she said.

A moment later, Piper returned to her with a bucket and a large glass of cold water.

"Sip," she said, helping Madelyn hold the glass. The girl did as she was told, though she shivered. Piper took the glass off her and tucked the throw from the couch around her legs.

"Just relax, baby," she said. "Close your eyes, don't worry about anything. I'll be right here, in this room, okay?"

Madelyn nodded.

"If you feel sick again, go in the bucket," Piper said, smoothing back Madelyn's hair again. "And sip your water slowly."

Madelyn wrapped her arms around her knees and curled into a ball.

Piper pushed herself upright, rubbing at her forehead. She could understand Madelyn staying home because she was sick; no one wanted a vomiting child at school. But to leave her *alone* ... Piper took a deep breath and glanced around.

The room was barely a quarter of the size of Piper's apartment. A love seat and armchair – old, patched and in clashing styles – were crammed in one corner. A dining table with four mismatched chairs stood in the centre of the space. The kitchen, consisting of a stove and two cupboards, made up the far wall. There wasn't even anywhere to keep perishables; Abby had to make her way to the market or grocer every day for the essentials.

Two bedrooms the size of broom cupboards and a bathroom with all its amenities jammed almost on top of each other completed the apartment.

Piper crossed the floor in three steps and dropped into a chair at the dining table, opposite Beks and Caleb, who were looking at a mathematics book together.

"It's like having groups," Beks said, pointing to a problem at the top of the page. "If you have one group of one, you have ...?"

"Two?" Caleb screwed up his face in concentration. "Isn't this just addition?"

"It's a little different," Beks said. To her credit, the woman sounded like she had buckets of patience left. When Piper tried to teach Caleb maths, her own tolerance lasted about ten minutes.

Piper cleared her throat, and Caleb looked up at her.

"Is Maddy going to be okay?" he asked.

Piper sighed and leaned across the narrow table to ruffle his hair.

"She'll be okay," she said. "But you need to be careful if you're using the stove." She gestured to the open windows, the smell of egg still clinging to the room very faintly. "That smell, it can be really bad for you." Really, he shouldn't be using the stove at all. He was far too young.

Caleb's bottom lip trembled, but Piper saw him suck in a breath. "I'm sorry I left the stove on," he mumbled. "But Maddy was hungry, and there wasn't anything else to eat except the chicken." He gestured to one of the cupboards. "I couldn't let her eat it if I didn't cook it."

Beks met Piper's gaze across the table, her expression horrified. Piper gritted her teeth together and forced herself to take a deep breath before she replied.

"Well, you shouldn't eat chicken unless it's really fresh, or it's been in an ice box, even if you cook it," she said with a lightness she didn't feel. Inside, her chest writhed and screamed at the idea that he'd been about to cook fate knew how-old chicken for them both.

Then Piper remembered what she'd been going to ask before the stove and vomiting emergencies had distracted her. She ducked her head to fix Caleb with a stare.

"Why didn't you go to school today?" she asked.

Caleb's gaze darted down to his maths book. He fiddled with the corner, avoiding eye contact. "Just didn't," he muttered.

Piper glanced at Beks, who shrugged. Well, she was just the neighbour, Piper supposed. She couldn't expect Beks to know what was going on inside Abby's household.

"Hm." Piper sat back in her chair. She crossed her arms over her chest, looking around the tiny room. There were cobwebs up in the corner. She'd have to beat them down, and hope there weren't any spiders still living in them.

Caleb fidgeted, rubbing the back of his neck.

Beks opened her mouth, but Piper shook her head to silence her, hoping the pause would prompt Caleb to offer more information. The other woman closed her mouth, then raised auburn eyebrows at her.

It crossed Piper's mind that Beks must have hair under the scarves she always wore, if she had eyebrows. Surely.

Caleb's fidgeting turned to squirming.

"Mum told us not to," he blurted out, and Piper leaned forward.

"Why'd she say that?" she asked.

Caleb shrugged. "I dunno," he said. "She just said I had to look after Maddy."

He looked up, his brown eyes wide, and Piper sighed.

"All right," she said, reaching over to ruffle his hair again. Caleb scowled at her, pushing his hair back out of his eyes. "Why don't you go get the rest of your homework, and I'll help you with it before dinner?"

Caleb huffed in complaint, but Piper could see relief in the line of his shoulders. He slid off the chair and obediently headed to his room.

Piper ran her fingers through her hair. She'd talked with Abby about this not a week ago.

Across from her, Beks cleared her throat delicately. "Why do you think Abby told them not to go to school?" she asked. Instead of meeting Piper's gaze across the table, she flicked through Caleb's mathematics book, taking note of what exercises had been completed and what hadn't.

Piper dropped her head into her hands.

"I've got no idea," she admitted. It should have been paid for; she'd given Abby enough to cover the rest of the month.

"What do you think she did with the money?" Beks asked, and Piper jerked up to stare at her. "I know you pay for both of the kids' school."

Piper realised her mouth was open, and she shut it, frowning.

"How did you know that?" she asked.

Beks shrugged, glancing away.

"I just notice things," she said. "Abby talks to me, sometimes, and she's not great at keeping secrets."

Ice washed through Piper's veins at that comment.

"What else has she told you?" Piper tried to keep her tone light and joking, but from the strange look Beks shot her, it didn't work.

Beks shrugged again.

"Not much, I guess," she said. "Just general complaints about her job – not that I really understand what she does – and ..." Beks trailed off, glancing at Piper guiltily. "And that's all, really."

Gut instinct told Piper that wasn't all. But she was also pretty sure she knew what Abby had complained to Beks about.

You should be more like Beks, Abby would tell Piper. *She's got a house with a garden, and her profession is so much better than … than* killing *people!*

Piper internally shook herself.

"Well, I'm going to find out what happened," she said. Beks nodded like she understood, then placed her hands on the table.

"Now that you're here, I'll go," Beks said, pushing herself up. "I'm late for something."

Piper rubbed the back of her neck. "Thanks." And not just for helping her air out the house.

Beks nodded. With a smile for Madelyn, who now hugged the empty bucket to her stomach, and a wave for Caleb as he came out of his room with his homework, Beks stood up and swept out the door.

By the time Piper thought to get up and see her out, Beks was already gone.

Caleb stood next to Piper and dropped his books onto the table.

"I like Beks," he said, his gaze direct. "She's nice."

A smile curled the corner of Piper's mouth.

"How do you always seem to know what I'm thinking?" she teased, poking Caleb's side. He giggled, darting away from her, but Piper caught him and pulled him into her arms to tickle him. She let him go after a moment of laughter and squirming, then pushed him into his chair.

"Have a quick look through these, and sort them into what you can do without me and what you need help with," she said, pushing herself up. "I'm going to check on Maddy, then I'll come back, okay?"

"Sure." Caleb turned to his books. The boy loved learning; his curiosity was insatiable.

Madelyn peeled her eyes open as Piper approached, blinking up at her.

"How's the tum?" Piper asked, pressing the back of her hand to Madelyn's forehead. Her face was flushed, but there was no real heat there. She didn't think the exposure to the gas had overtly harmed the two of them.

Madelyn shrugged.

"Better," she admitted. Piper nodded, smoothing back the curls that had escaped the quick bun she had put in Madelyn's hair.

"Do you want some bread?" she asked. Madelyn's face went an actual shade of green, and she shook her head. "Okay!" Piper chuckled, refastening the hair tie to more securely hold the style in place. "Okay, no food yet."

Madelyn nodded, pressing her cheek into Piper's hand.

Piper helped her drink some more water before she stood again. She then headed into the kitchen to prepare slices of bread with cheese. While she was there, she checked the cupboards and threw out the chicken Caleb had been intending to cook.

She sat down next to him, sliding the plate over. She leaned on one elbow, looking over the history book Caleb put between them.

History, at least, was something she was good at.

Piper was in the bathroom, washing her hands, when she heard the front door open.

"Mum!" Caleb cried.

Piper pressed still wet fingers to her forehead and took a deep breath.

This wouldn't be fun.

"Hi, baby," Abby said. "Quickly, help me get these things away before Piper gets here."

"But Mum, she's—"

"Not now, Caleb!" Abby's voice rose slightly at the end. "We need to figure out something for dinner."

Piper stuck her hands under the water again to wash off the last of the soap. She turned the tap off.

"Mum, Piper—"

"Maddy?" Abby called, obviously just at that moment noticing that her youngest hadn't rushed to meet her. "Where are you?"

"Here, Mummy," came Maddy's sleepy voice.

"Come on, Caleb," Abby said. Piper heard the scrape of a chair being dragged over. She wiped her hands on a towel and opened the bathroom door.

Abby stood on a chair in the kitchen, shoving things from her canvas bag into the cupboard. Her long brown hair was out and over her shoulders, tangled and messy from where she had presumably run her hands through it.

Caleb hovered around the cabinets, handing Abby things uncertainly. Abby leaned into the cupboard. "Where is that chicken? I should have thrown it out yesterday—"

"I threw it out," Piper said, leaning on the doorframe.

Abby jumped, smacking her head on the side of the cabinet.

"Piper!" she squawked, jumping off the chair and brushing imaginary dust off her worn jeans. She glanced sideways at Caleb. "Why didn't you tell me she was here?"

"He tried to," Piper said, pushing herself off the doorframe and trying very hard to keep the anger out of her voice. It simmered in her chest, restrained ... for now. "Twice."

Abby turned to her son and took in his expression. "I'm sorry, Caleb," she said, reaching out to him. Caleb resisted for a moment, then let her pull him into a hug. "I steamrolled you when I came in."

"Caleb," Piper said, stepping forward, "can you sit with Maddy for a moment? I have something to ask your mum."

Caleb glanced at Abby, then back at Piper. His dark gaze met hers, and Piper had to try very hard to keep her expression neutral.

The boy was far, far too good at reading her.

"Sure, Piper," he said finally. He crossed the room, squeezing into the armchair beside Madelyn.

Piper gestured to the door. With one more glance at her children, Abby stepped onto the porch. Piper pulled the door shut. Her hand snuck into her coat pocket, wrapping hard around her stiletto. She'd never *use* it, but the bite of metal against her fingers helped to ground her, taking the edge off her anger.

But just the edge.

"What were you thinking?" she hissed, pitching her voice low so it wouldn't carry back inside.

"I just popped out for a while," Abby insisted.

"You didn't," she said. "Caleb said you were out all day! He was going to cook that old chicken for him and Madelyn to eat!"

Abby's face went sickly white. "He didn't," she breathed.

"Thank fate he couldn't get the stove to light," Piper said. "But I came in to find the house full of gas and Madelyn vomiting and …"

"Oh no." Abby spun, reaching for the door, but Piper caught her arm.

"It's okay." She sighed, the sight of Abby's panic causing some of the anger to drain away. "They're both fine, and we aired out the place. But it could have been really bad, Abby." She crossed her arms and stared at her. "Where were you?"

Piper fixed Abby with her silver gaze, and Abby glanced away. She fidgeted, unable to get into the house with Piper blocking the door and not wanting to acknowledge Piper's question.

"I just …" Abby shrugged, wrapping her arms around herself.

Piper tapped her foot, her gaze steady. Abby fidgeted, then her shoulders slumped.

"I had to go to the healers," she whispered. "But medicine is *so* expensive. And, when I got there, he said he needed the back room cleaned, and if I could do that, he'd give me half off, and then there was a notice on the board about someone needing a babysitter, and I thought, that's something I *could* do, and the kids could have a play date at the same time and I …" She trailed off.

Piper sighed loudly. Uncrossing her arms, she rubbed the back of her neck, trying to massage away the tension she could feel building there.

"Why didn't you just send Caleb to school?" Piper said. "You could have taken Madelyn with you to the healer and everything would have been fine!"

Abby pressed her lips together, and Piper sucked in a breath. "You didn't."

"Madelyn flooded the bathroom," Abby whispered. "It got through everything and I had to rip up the carpet and replace some floorboards and there was the medicine and food and ..." She rubbed her arms. "I needed the money to fix everything."

"Why didn't you tell me?" Piper said. "I could have helped!"

"We were fine," Abby insisted.

"I just ..." Piper clenched her fists. Then she stretched out her fingers, forcing herself to relax. "We talked about this last week."

Abby flushed, looking down at the ground, misery in every line of her face.

Piper would have liked to say she was surprised. But she wasn't. There was a reason they'd had this conversation before.

"You put them in danger today," she said, and Abby flinched.

"I didn't—" she started.

"Caleb is *ten*," Piper snapped. "That is *too young* to be left alone, let alone to be looking after Madelyn, a *six-year-old*, when she's sick!" Piper hesitated, then made up her mind. "I'm going to the school tomorrow. I'll pay tuition for the rest of term to them directly."

Abby's head snapped up. "What?" she said. "You can't do that!"

"Abby, please," Piper said. "I told you, if it happened again, I would."

"But what if we need that money to—"

"You need to give Caleb and Madelyn an education!" Piper snapped. Her voice echoed around the quiet street. Across the road, Piper saw someone's curtain twitch. A man looked up from his garden bed a few houses down.

Piper grabbed onto her temper with both hands and ruthlessly stuffed it back inside her chest.

"There'll be no reason for Caleb and Madelyn to miss school again," she said. "And if you need money again, just ask me."

Abby's brown eyes filled with tears. "I just ... I ..." She sniffed, rubbing both hands over her face. "Fate, Piper. Why can't I get anything right?"

"Abby ..." But Piper wasn't really certain what to say. Or what to do about the tears.

The door creaked open before it could go any further. Caleb stuck his head out, glancing between them uncertainly.

It was too much to hope that he hadn't heard them arguing.

"Mum," he said. "I'm hungry. Can we have dinner?"

Abby scrubbed her face, turning to him. "Yes, of course, baby," she said. "Come on. I'll make something."

Both of them turned to Piper, but Piper shook her head.

"I can't stay," she said. She didn't want to sit at the table and pretend she wasn't still fuming mad at Abby for the next two hours.

Caleb's face fell. "Please?" he asked. Nothing more.

Piper tried to shake her head, but instead a sigh slipped out of her.

"All right," she said. "I can stay for a little while."

"Yes!" Caleb jumped on the spot, for once acting like a little boy, then turned around and raced inside, leaving the door to swing open and bang against the wall. "Maddy! Piper's staying for dinner!"

Piper sighed again as she stepped back inside the house, avoiding Abby's gaze.

Dinner dragged on for long, long years. Piper sat next to Caleb, trying to answer all the questions he fired her way about his schoolwork, about how the trams worked, and about Tech – his new favourite obsession.

Madelyn finished pushing her vegetables around her plate and slid off her chair. Ducking around the other side of the table, she caught Caleb's hand.

"Come on," she said. "I want to play."

Caleb hesitated, glancing at Piper. She smiled at them both.

"Go play," she told them. "I have to go, anyway."

"Aw." Madelyn's bottom lip stuck out, and Piper reached over and pulled on it. Madelyn yanked away, squealing with laughter, then ran back towards the living area.

Clearly her stomach wasn't nearly so sore now.

Caleb shot Piper a smile, then slid off his chair and went after his sister. Across the table from her, Abby huffed.

"You've got a job, don't you?" she said, quietly enough that Caleb and Madelyn wouldn't hear.

Piper gritted her teeth, then reluctantly nodded. "I do," she admitted.

Abby's jaw clenched. "You just had one," she hissed.

Piper rubbed her forehead. "I didn't have a choice in this one," she said. "He was … insistent." She touched her throat, where Lore's hand had been just hours ago.

Abby made a sound, and Piper looked up to see worry in her brown eyes. "You need to get out of there, Piper."

"I've told you, I can't," she said.

"You mean you won't." Abby's tone turned sharp, and she glared at Piper. "You know, I really wish you'd be more like–"

"More like Beks, I know." Piper pushed herself up, her chair scraping loudly over the floorboards. She grabbed her and Caleb's empty plates, then stacked Madelyn's partially eaten one on top.

"Piper." Abby caught her arm. "Please. Beks is *safe*. She's nearby and sees Caleb and Madelyn all the time. Her job is perfectly legal, but you–" she glanced towards the couches and lowered her voice. "You kill people for a living."

Though it was said in a whisper, Piper still flinched. Those words tore through her carefully cultivated armour like nothing else could.

Pulling from Abby's grip, she stalked to the kitchen and dumped all three in the sink. Behind her, Abby's chair scraped across the floor as she stood.

"Piper," Abby murmured.

"Don't," she said, her voice clipped. "I have to go."

Usually, she'd wash the plates. Or talk Caleb and Madelyn into doing it. But hurt and guilt simmered under her skin, and she had to *get out*.

"Piper, please," Abby said again, her voice low so that it wouldn't carry back to Caleb and Madelyn.

"No." Piper turned, her fists clenching at her sides. "You *don't* get to pull that crap on me. I am *not* the one that left my children alone all day today."

Abby's eyes flashed in anger. "Don't change the subject, Piper," she snapped in an undertone. "You pretend you don't care. But you know what you're doing is wrong. It's putting us all in danger."

Piper jerked back. "I pretend nothing," she breathed, her gaze darting past Abby to where Caleb and Madelyn sat on the rug, too far away to hear them. "And I am *not* your responsibility."

"Thank fate," Abby said, her mouth twisting. "You're lucky I let the Belladonna anywhere *near* my family."

Piper took a shaking breath.

"Well," she said, her voice shaking, "that's your call, isn't it?"

Abby's eyes creased, her mouth pressed in a thin line.

"Piper." Her voice softened, and she reached out. "I'm—"

"No." Piper twitched away, her pride too stung to accept the apology. She spun on her heel and marched from the apartment, careful to shut the door softly behind her.

SIX

The glow from the blue moon, Uzziel, combined with the full, red moon, Camue, to tint the night purple. It lent a faerie feeling to the landscape, no pale yellow Azah to temper the moonslight. Silversdale University cast Piper in its shadow for a moment as she passed underneath it, the darkness tugging at her coat like fingers.

Piper caught a tram for a few stops, hopping off at the edge of the Mage's Quarter.

She hesitated. Beyond this arch, a corner of the city filled almost entirely with mages awaited. The best healers, the spellbinders creating things to attach their magic to, the battlemages with their handfuls of fire and lightning, the soulmages with telekinesis and fate knew what else. And those were just the human ones. Elves, with their healing and seeing magic, and dwarves, with their runic magic also made the district their home, along with the rarer karis, puka or skinwalkers with their strange, innate magic.

Fighting down a shiver, Piper stepped under the arch.

The street on the other side was pretty. The trams ran down the middle of the cobbled stone, heated so that in winter snow would melt off the tracks. Little gardens and bushes lined the space between the sidewalk and tram tracks, with benches every so often for people to stop and rest.

Piper didn't need to rest. She turned down the first side street, then immediately left into a narrower lane.

A little two-storey building met her. Long and narrow, like many in the city, it was divided into one dwelling per level. The garden out the front was well tended, but not the riot of green and blossoms that made up the puka's garden in Abby's street. Here was mostly herbs, from what Piper could see, though she couldn't tell if they were medicinal or culinary.

Piper stepped up to the porch and opened the door. The landing here was internal; no exposed iron staircases that needed to be navigated in the cold winter air, or during a summer storm. The warm, polished timber stretched in a hallway to Piper's right, but she turned and tapped on the door to the left.

It opened almost as soon as she touched it, bringing Piper face to face with a woman.

Though Piper knew Aliana was old enough to be her grandmother, she didn't look a day over thirty. There was no grey in her brown hair, and her green eyes sparkled with good humour. Those eyes always reminded Piper of something, but she could never quite put her finger on what.

"Piper." Aliana smiled at her and extended her arm. "Come in."

Piper had no doubt that Aliana had anticipated her visit. The woman was a seer. If Beks was the entry-level, judging by her tiny apartment and nonexistent flow of customers, then Aliana was the matriarch. During the day, there was usually a line of people waiting to see her, with questions after a baby's health, whether a partner was cheating on them, or if they should make a particular investment. She had a reputation for answering all questions, no matter how trivial, with grace and a friendly smile.

Inside, watercolour paintings hung on the walls and gauze curtains let in light but kept things private. Clasping her hands in her lap, Piper leaned forward to begin the conversation. But Aliana held up a hand, frowning.

"You have a job," she said.

Piper fidgeted. It was just like looking at a disapproving grandmother when Aliana made that face.

"I do," she said at last.

Aliana's frown deepened, and she sighed. "You want to know about him," she said, and Piper nodded. Anything Aliana could tell her would give her some insight, something she could use to make this as quick and painless as possible.

Aliana leaned back in her chair, fingers stroking the arm almost absently. The air around her seemed to vibrate with sadness, a sadness that was always there. Piper didn't often feel sorry for many mages, but for some reason, Aliana felt different. Like there was real pain in her past, something more than a job she didn't like or a spurned love. Piper knew real pain. She was pretty sure Aliana did too.

Instead of interrupting her reverie, Piper rose. She let herself into the small kitchen, finding a kettle and placing it on the stove to heat. A few minutes later, armed with a mug of tea in each hand, Piper returned to the living room. She placed a mug down on the table near Aliana, then sat back in her chair, cradling her own mug between her hands until it cooled enough to sip. The mixture of green and black tea exploded over her tongue. It was one of her favourite blends – and packed full of caffeine. She'd need it, with the night ahead of her.

Finally, Aliana sighed again and shifted back in her chair. She glanced at the brew Piper had made for her, and smiled. "Thank you, sweetheart," she said. Aliana sipped her tea, looking composed despite the frown between her brows.

"You want me to tell you he's a bad man," Aliana said, and Piper fidgeted uncomfortably at the accuracy of her assessment.

"I mean ..." Piper hesitated. "That would be nice."

Aliana raised her eyebrows. "So you'd prefer me to tell you that he kicks puppies in his spare time? Maybe plots a little empire domination?" Her green eyes flickered over Piper, making Piper want to squirm like a kitten who'd just been picked up.

She resisted. Barely.

"Well …" Piper shrugged. "Empire domination might be stretching it a little. But puppy kickers don't get a second chance."

Her joke fell flat, and Aliana pursed her lips.

"So you don't want to know that he sends most of his wage home to his mother to support her?" she asked. Piper flinched. "That he's single-handedly putting his sister through school? That the High Lady regards him as reliable and steady, and a good influence on her children?"

"Well, I don't really care what the High Lady thinks," Piper said flippantly, latching onto the one thing that she could.

Aliana sighed loudly. Then she leaned forward.

"He is not a bad man," she said softly. "In fact, I would say he's a very good man."

"I don't have a choice," Piper said, her voice perhaps a little too sharp.

Aliana sat back. "Everyone has a choice, Piper," she said. Then she held out her hands. "I'm not judging you, sweetheart. I know your choices are hard. But you still have them."

Piper nodded, not bothering to disagree with her. When Aliana's mind was made up, nothing would change it. Instead, Piper stood. Somehow her mug was empty, though she couldn't remember drinking the tea.

"Thank you," she said, though she didn't think she had anything to thank the older woman for. She hadn't actually helped. But Piper slid her hand into her pocket for her wallet anyway.

Aliana waved away the payment, her eyes sad. "Any time, sweetheart," she said. "You can come and see me any time. For anything." Then she hesitated. "There's a spot in the western wall, near Highkeep. About fifty metres north of my church. You can use that to get over the palace wall."

Piper nodded, not certain what to say. She went into the kitchen, washing up her mug so Aliana wouldn't have to do it. Then she returned to the living room.

"Thanks," she said again to Aliana. "I should go now."

Aliana rose. No creaking of her joints, no hesitation. Just one smooth movement. She caught Piper's hand.

"Be careful, sweetheart," she whispered. "This thing ... It could destroy you." She frowned. "It could kill you."

A shiver worked its way down Piper's spine, but she forced her back straight.

She offered Aliana a small smile. "Not if I kill him first," she said. Then she turned and headed back into the night.

SEVEN

Piper sat on the steps of the Church of Nyssa in Highkeep, her head down and her hands clasped before her.

She wasn't praying, though that was what it looked like. Her gaze darted over the street, taking in anyone who walked past. At this time of night, there were very few passersby.

The clocks had struck two in the morning a little while ago. Piper had counted the hours while she'd been here, looking for all intents and purposes like a supplicant begging the first Immortal for some advice. Not that Nyssa would likely give any; she was just an Immortal, a being who never aged. Not all powerful, not all seeing.

Finally, after the two-bong note that signalled half past the hour, Piper stood. She turned to face the church and inclined her head – it wasn't a bad idea to be polite to the Immortal, in case she did happen to be hanging around watching – then she jumped the three stairs to the street.

Strolling as casually as she knew how, Piper made her way towards the Summer Palace. About fifty metres north, she knelt to the ground, fiddling with the laces on the front of her boot – though they were already tied – looking around through her hair.

She probably didn't need the pretence. But if some insomniac happened to look out their window, tying a shoe would look much less suspicious than loitering in the shadows.

The wall of the palace rose to her right, finely wrought iron filled in with a box hedge four feet thick. While it probably would be possible to force her way through that, it would leave Piper with scratches to her hands and face, ones the city police would be sure to look for afterwards. Piper's gaze traced up, and she grimaced.

Over it was.

Glancing around the empty street, Piper pushed herself up. She walked slowly to the wall, her stomach churning uncomfortably. She didn't know for sure, but she assumed the palace mages would have protected the ever-living stuffing out of this boundary. A faint, hazy mesh seemed to hover over the wrought iron and the hedge, shifting as she looked at it.

Piper scowled. Stupid mages.

There's a weak spot …

Barely wider than Piper's hands put together, a patch of iron glinted blackly in the moonslight. It wasn't hazy and writhing like the part next to it. Swallowing, and hoping Aliana meant what Piper thought she did, Piper gripped the iron.

Nothing happened.

Sighing softly in relief, Piper wedged her foot against one of the lower bars and pushed herself up.

The entire fence was only about twelve feet high. As Piper grabbed the spike at the top to heave herself over, it shifted. The spike screeched, turning in her hand, and Piper slipped. She came down hard on her right ankle, wedged between two of the bars, and bit back a curse. Pain stabbed up her leg.

Fate, that screech had been loud.

She unwedged her foot and hauled herself up as fast as she could. Flinging one leg over the top, Piper tumbled forward – narrowly missing another spike – and landed in an ungainly heap on the other side. She forced herself up, ignoring her smarting ankle, and dashed the short distance to a manicured garden she could see just on the other side.

A light bloomed nearby. Piper pulled her hood over her head and pressed herself behind the thickest part of the hedge, trying not even to breathe.

Two guards came into view. Piper watched them approach through the leaves, one holding a sphere of light in one hand. His coat wasn't grey, so she assumed he held a magelight rather than being a mage himself.

He held up the light, and his partner stepped forward, eyes darting over the area.

"Can't see anything," he said.

"I heard something," the guard with the light argued. The partner shrugged.

"I did too," he said. He drew a sword from his hip; police in the city didn't carry them, but guards patrolling the palace grounds did.

Piper swallowed. It wasn't like she hadn't won a sword fight before, but she desperately hoped it wouldn't get to that. She glanced behind her, but the small garden bed offered little in the way of cover. A wide expanse of lawn stretched between gardens, leaving her nothing to hide behind if she ran.

The guard with the light looked down and frowned.

"What's this?" he asked loudly, pointing.

Piper's heart leaped into her mouth. On the ground, obvious in the bright magelight, a scuff marred the green grass. Dirt churned up from underneath spearheaded towards Piper like an arrow.

The guard with the sword froze. The two exchanged a glance.

The magelight guard spoke first.

"Go wake the captain," he said, his voice soft. "We have an intruder."

"How did they get in?" Sword-guard hissed. "The fence is supposed to be spelled by the blackcoat!"

Ice doused Piper's spine, and she fought back a shiver.

Everhill, Silvaein's mage university, trained normal students as well as mages. But their magical training system was world-class, and most other countries – not just in the continent, but also beyond – had adopted the same one. Mages trained for three to five years. If they trained for three, they were gifted a plain mage's coat and the title of mage when they graduated. If they stayed for five, they picked a speciality: soulmagic, battlemagic, or spellbinding. When they graduated, they would receive a coat with their field of study's insignia on it, and the title of soulmage, battlemage, or spellbinder.

Only the spellbinders who made the coats and the mages they were gifted to touched the coats. When a mage first put one on, the pure white coat would change, fading through shades of grey to reflect the mage's power.

But sometimes, maybe once in a generation, the coat didn't stop at grey. Those mages were practically legendary.

If the High Lady had a blackcoat working for her …

Bile rose in her throat.

"No idea how he got in," the guard said after a long moment. "Go."

The sword-guard wavered a moment more, then he straightened. "Right." Turning on his heel, he jogged away.

Piper's fists clenched. There was just the one, now. If it came to a fight, she wouldn't have any trouble. But she didn't know how long it would be until the other guard got back with help.

The guard stepped forward.

"I know someone's there," he called. "Come out now, and it'll be easier for you. Just an arrest, a slap on the wrist for breaking and entering. Much better than if I find you and drag you out of there."

Everything he said seemed reasonable. Except that for Piper, as soon as they realised who she was, a slap on the wrist was not likely. More like a prison sentence, culminating in her execution in Illusion Square.

Piper edged to her left, away from the voice, careful not to make a sound. She fixed half of her attention on the guard, listening out for his footsteps;

the other half examined the ground in front of her for anything that would give her away. The last thing she needed was a twig snapping loudly underfoot.

She supposed that the benefit of sneaking through the palace garden was that the grounds were perfectly maintained. Not a fallen twig in sight.

The footsteps behind her suddenly got faster. She heard the guard grunt. Piper pushed herself to her hands and knees and scurried forward.

Saxe would laugh and laugh and laugh if he ever heard about this. Piper gritted her teeth, his malicious expression swimming in the air in front of her for a moment. She imagined stabbing it, then shoved the thought of him away.

"Come on out," the guard cajoled.

Piper crawled further forward, her eyes alert. Ahead, a gap appeared under the greenery, where the bushes changed from green and boxy to something with larger, glossier leaves. Piper squeezed herself into the gap underneath, biting back a hiss as a thorn tangled in her braid. She wasted precious seconds fumbling at it, before she forced herself to slow down. After that, it was a simple thing to unhook herself.

The footsteps approached again, and Piper pressed herself further into the bush. Something velvety brushed her face.

Piper froze, but it was a flower, not a spider. Purple-black blooms as large as Piper's hand opened to the night, a dusting of gold and silver pollen on the petals. A sweet and spicy scent surrounded her.

Nightflower. It was not a popular variety of bush, for many reasons, including that the flowers only bloomed at night.

Through the foliage, Piper watched as the guard approached. He rubbed at his eyes, blinking. Then he sneezed. His grip tightened on his sword, and he stepped back. He blinked again, squinting towards the nightflower bush.

"I know you're here," he growled. "And I'm really getting sick of this game. Come out now!"

The gravity of his words was lost when he sneezed three times, explosively. Piper sat in the shadow under the bushes, staring at him. He must be allergic to the nightflower.

"Come out!" he snapped, stepping forward again.

Piper clenched her fingers in the dirt. Her hand brushed against something smooth, and she glanced down. A small pebble. Piper turned it over in her fingers, then she looked up.

The guard sneezed again, wiping at his streaming eyes.

Piper twisted and threw the pebble as hard as she could. It pinged off the marble base of a topiary, and the guard's entire body jerked in that direction like a marionette.

Piper launched out from under the bush. The guard started to turn back to her, but he was too slow, his vision impaired. To make matters worse for him, he sneezed again.

Piper dodged around the sword – he kept it raised despite not being able to see; clearly the man was trained well – and jumped for his back. He was far taller, but she'd had plenty of practice. Her left arm, her stronger arm, wrapped around his throat, her right bracing it and pulling it back. Both of her feet landed on the ground again, bending him backwards to increase the pressure on his throat and put him off balance to fight back.

And he *did* fight. But, quickly, his body went limp.

Piper grunted as his entire weight fell on her. She maintained the hold for another few seconds, then released it to lower the guard to the ground.

As soon as she let go, he let out a weak groan. Piper glanced at the outline of the palace in the distance, then at the nightflower bush. She wasn't certain how allergic this guy was.

Grabbing him by his coat, she dragged him a few metres away. The muscles in his face twitched, his eyelids fluttering.

Piper pushed herself up. There was no time to spend on the guard. She took off, running across the grounds. She had to be far away from here, and in cover, before the first guard got back with others.

The palace hulked above her.

In all fairness, Piper didn't think it would hulk during the day. From what she had seen from outside the grounds, it was actually quite pretty, made of pale stone, with big windows and pitched roofs in blue and purple tiles. Vines wound up the western side, where they could soak in the morning sun, and several smaller buildings in the same style dotted the grounds to the east.

But in the dark, after two in the morning, with no lights on inside and lit by the purple moonslight, it definitely hulked.

In the distance, Piper could see the sweep of magelights over the grounds, attached to the figures of guards. Piper couldn't make out their details from this distance, but they moved systematically, sweeping the grounds for any sign of her.

Piper shook her head and glanced back up the wall. She assumed there was someone inside, waking the High Lady and her family. They'd be moved somewhere safe, somewhere the intruder would struggle to get to. Somewhere with guards to protect them. Maybe that would work in her favour, she tried to convince herself. Maybe the guards would be so preoccupied with the royal family, they'd never even consider that someone else might be a target.

She really hadn't planned on being noticed so early in her mission.

Piper turned away from the grounds, stalking down the palace walls. First, she needed some kind of entry point. Above her, a balcony curved, almost an entire wall of glass behind it. If there were doors, Piper was certain they would be locked tight against the night.

She needed something less conspicuous. Something a tired employee might have overlooked.

Piper made her way around the palace, keeping close to the walls so she couldn't cast a shadow over the grass. Behind her, she could hear the low voices of the guards calling to each other. Her heart lodged in her throat, and Piper swallowed it back down.

She turned a corner, and the pungent smell of horse hit her like a wave. Piper screwed up her nose, hay and manure and fate knew what else clogging her nostrils. She could make out a two-storey building in the distance, one that must house the animals. A curved fence ran beside it, and beyond that was a larger paddock. The moonslight stained the grass a faint purple, washing all other colour from the scene.

Closer to the palace, a low, walled garden sprawled. This was not a manicured garden, like the ones behind her. This one was a well-ordered jumble, filled with leafy greens and herbs.

A kitchen garden. And where there was a kitchen garden ...

Piper turned, scanning the side of the palace for the kitchen door. It wouldn't be far. When something's cooking, no one wants to walk a long way to get some extra herbs.

A large timber door sat in the pale stone, whitewashed to help it blend in. Piper glanced over her shoulder, taking in the distance to the waving lights of the search party. Then she darted forward.

Piper tried the handle, but she wasn't surprised to find it locked. She knelt down, the stone path hard under her knees. Slipping three slim picks out of the top of her boot, Piper stuck one in her mouth. The other two she slid into the first lock. She felt around blindly, searching for the pins to push back, to unlock the door. She found one, then slid the pick in further to search for another.

A sound behind her made Piper jump, her hand slipping. She heard the click of the lock slipping back into place and swore around the pick in her mouth. She had her knee on the edge of one of the pavers; the hard line dug into her. Piper shifted, wincing as blood rushed back to the area, and manoeuvred her picks again.

She knew, roughly, where the first pin was, so it was faster this time. The next pins gave her far more pain. Piper's heart thumped, bile burning in her throat.

Voices reached her ears; they were close. She couldn't make out the words yet, but they grew louder and louder. Piper's hand slipped again, two pins sliding back into place.

A litany of curses flew through her mind, but Piper didn't allow herself to say them out loud. Her hands shook as she tried to force her picks to cooperate.

Stupid Lore. This was his fault. This was why she didn't do rush jobs.

A glow of light appeared near the corner of the building. It was just far enough away that it didn't reach the door to give her a bit of light to work with.

Stupid mage, pissing people off.

She could hear conversation now. Variations of *I want him found* rattled through the air. Piper had a moment of being faintly insulted that they assumed she would be a man.

Stupid her, for being bullied into this.

Footsteps sounded around the corner.

If she'd had time, if she'd pushed back harder, she could have researched, could have–

The lock clicked.

Piper leaped to her feet. Grabbing the handle with both hands, she twisted it quickly. Then she set her shoulder against the door.

It swung silently open, and Piper almost cried in relief. She threw herself inside just as the light rounded the corner. So, so quietly, she eased the door shut. There was a key in the other side of the lock. Piper turned it, the faint click as loud as a gunshot in the small space.

Then she held still, held her breath. Held everything.

"I don't know," the voice on the other side of the wall said, muffled through timber and stone. "Like I said. We just found the scuff mark after hearing a noise in the garden."

The other person was silent for a moment. The door rattled, and Piper slapped her hands over her mouth to stop herself from yelping in surprise.

But, seemingly satisfied by the locked door, the rattling stopped.

"Whoever he is, he left Merle alive." This voice was feminine. "Battered. Very groggy. But he's not badly hurt."

"I haven't seen any other sign of them." At least this one didn't assume Piper was a man.

The voices were moving away, likely to check any other entry points. Piper let out a shaking breath, thanking fate, Nyssa, or anyone else who would listen that someone had left the key in this particular door.

She turned.

She was in a small mudroom. A long bench with a huge sink sat to her right. To her left, pairs of gumboots lined the wall, some still muddy. The smells of earth and hay and garden filled the space.

Piper carefully knocked her boots on the mat and crossed the room. It opened into a slim hallway, darkness pressing on all sides. Piper hesitated, waiting for her eyes to adjust after the purple gloom of the moons outside.

She was in the east wing, Piper knew. A few metres to her left and right, the hallway turned at an angle, vanishing into darkness. If she went left, she'd reach the entrance hall, and the grand staircase. They said the staircase was made entirely of glass, though Piper thought that was probably only partially true.

She didn't have time to waste on curiosity. Piper slipped to the right, away from the main body of the palace.

Glancing inside the room immediately to her right showed Piper a larder, its shelves stacked high with sacks of flour and other nonperishables. The next door along Piper didn't open, but she could feel the chill radiating from it. A cold room, for perishable storage.

The next door had a zigzagging line engraved in its wood. Piper pressed her ear to the door, then, gingerly, turned the handle. It creaked a little under her palm, loud in the silent hall.

Piper sighed in relief as she saw a set of narrow stairs leading upwards. Though she was loathe to, Piper shut the door behind her. Her best chance of getting out of the palace was for no one to realise the path she'd taken, and though open doors made for quicker exits, it wouldn't be quick if every guard in the palace was waiting for her.

Piper jogged up the stairs as silently as she could. At the top of the third flight, Piper stopped to drag in a breath. She was fit, but running up that many stairs so quickly would challenge anyone. They were long flights too, each storey of the palace being taller than the ones in her apartment building. The place had very lofty ceilings.

Piper pressed her palms to the door marked 3. The map had said the third floor. She was fairly certain that all the staff rooms were on this side of the palace.

When her breathing had evened out, she slowly eased the door open. This one was quieter, only offering a muffled groan as it swung towards her. Piper stepped out, glancing around.

She was in a plush hall. A single lamp glowed over the staircase, its light turned low. If these were the staff apartments, like she thought, that made sense. Some of the kitchen staff would need to rise early and get bread baking before the High Lady wanted her morning toast. Piper imagined it wouldn't be a nice result for anyone who kept the High Lady waiting for her breakfast.

Edging to the side, where she felt a bit more hidden even if there wasn't anything to shield her, Piper slid the map out of her pocket.

She tilted the paper to the lamplight. With her free hand, Piper traced along the sides until she found the stairwell. It wasn't marked, but it was the same shape and on the same stretch of corridor shown on the left-hand side of the map.

Piper touched the coloured mark of the mage's room and gritted her teeth. She was on the wrong side of the wing. There was a bank of rooms running down the middle, then another against the wall on the front side of the palace. From where she stood, against the back, she'd have to go all the way to the front of the wing, towards the centre of the palace. The mage's room was near the doors, so at least she wouldn't have to double back too far.

79

Piper cursed under her breath and folded her map back into her pocket. She turned left and eased down the hallway, sticking against the wall like a burr. There was no real place for her to hide, and at any moment everything could go horribly wrong, especially now with the guards on alert and she—

Piper forced herself away from that line of thought. Panicking would not achieve anything. It would just make her sloppy, which meant mistakes. And mistakes got you killed.

She'd seen an assassin panic on a job, three years ago. He hadn't made it. She'd had to jump off a roof to escape, slicing her calf open on a rusty bit of metal. She still had the scar. From then on, Piper had refused to work with anyone else.

At the end, the hall turned. Piper pressed herself against the wall, glancing around the corner. A set of double doors sat in the wall in front of her, leading, she presumed, back into the palace proper. An alcove sat at the front of the room, large windows overlooking the front courtyard of the palace. Through them, Piper could make out the manicured front gardens and driveways, all tinged purple. A cluster of armchairs sat in front of them, a coffee table between them; it would be a nice place to sit on a sunny day.

Piper pushed herself off the wall. The middle of the hall was exposed no matter where she walked, so Piper picked up her pace, striding across the space as fast as her short legs would allow without actually running. Being fast would do her no good if someone heard her.

She was halfway across when the handle of the big doors moved. For a split second, Piper froze, her body cold and stiff as ice. Then reality smacked into her, and Piper launched herself across the room.

There was nowhere to hide. The armchairs weren't big enough, and there were no curtains on the windows. Piper threw herself into the space behind the door as it pushed open.

The door swung in front of her, and Piper held her breath. If she didn't, she was certain it would saw in and out of her chest.

Light edged around the door.

"I don't know," a man said in response to a question Piper hadn't heard. "The captain just said there was an intruder, and we were to wake him. He'll stay with the family while we search."

Two backs passed the edge of the door, leaving it open with Piper behind it. They were dressed in the dark blue-and-grey uniform of the palace guard, crimson stripes around their biceps. Both had swords at their hips, and one had the white griffin that meant he was a healer stitched on his shoulder.

The healer's companion grunted. "Better him than me," she muttered, running her fingers through her hair and messing up her neat bun. "The High Lady gets cranky when she doesn't sleep."

Piper swallowed, edging out from behind the door a little more to watch them. They passed the first door in the hall, then stopped at one on the left. The healer reached up and knocked on the door. Without waiting for a response, he opened it. It shut behind him with a snick.

Piper chewed her lip, hesitating. If her memory served her ...

She pulled the map out of her pocket, trying not to let the paper rustle, and bit back a groan.

The two guards had just entered the mage's room.

Piper rubbed her forehead. Her target was surely now awake and moving around, and about to be moved out of her reach. Her heart set up a steady thrum, no longer beating in time. Her stomach twisted sickly.

Fate, everything she touched just went so *wrong*.

She had to get over there before he left. But, as Piper made to step out from behind the door, the one down the hall opened again. The guards stepped out, the woman straightening her hair and the man grimacing. They glanced at each other, then at the door.

"... give him a few," Piper heard, and the woman nodded in agreement. They strode back towards her, and Piper eased behind the door again; no sudden movements. In the dark, sharp motion was more likely to attract the eye than something slow and smooth.

She held her breath again as they passed. Piper waited excruciating seconds for their footsteps to fade. Then she ducked out from behind the door and strode as fast as she dared down the hall.

She checked her map one last time, before laying her hand on the doorknob.

It turned soundlessly, effortlessly, under her fingers. Piper pushed the door open.

Inside, a single lamp lit the room. Piper blinked, getting her eyes to adjust to the sudden brightness.

A king bed pressed up against one wall, rumpled from where the inhabitant had thrown the covers off and not pulled them up. Two chairs and a table sat in front of one of the two large windows, and fully stuffed bookshelves stood against another wall.

In front of a chest of drawers stood a man. Piper recognised him instantly. Alexander Rylan was even taller in person, towering well over a foot above her. He looked up as the door clicked closed behind Piper, fixing her with a bright blue gaze.

"Who are you?" he asked, frowning as he stuffed his arm into a sleeve. He yanked the shirt closed, covering the edge of a tattoo.

She offered him a small smile. "Bella," she told him.

Rylan huffed through his teeth.

"Look, Bella," he said. "Tell them I'll be there as soon as I can. I *literally* woke up about a minute ago." He shoved his hair back out of his face, grabbing a leather band to tie it back off the chest of drawers.

"I'm not here for that," Piper said.

"Then whatever it is, tell me while I walk." Rylan's long legs ate up the distance to the door.

When Piper didn't move, he caught her arms, moving her bodily out of the way. Piper wrapped her fingers around his wrist, bared by his rolled-up sleeves.

"I'm sorry about this," she said, not even really lying.

His head jerked around to hers. Then his gaze snapped down. His mouth opened as Piper withdrew the fine needle from his skin, and he sucked in a breath.

His knees buckled.

"Shh." Piper caught him, and almost swore out loud. Fate, he was heavy. "Don't speak. That makes it worse."

She couldn't hold him. Her muscles screamed at her as she lowered him to the ground, trying hard not to drop him. The collar of his shirt pulled across from her grip, and she saw the curving tattoo again.

Piper patted his shoulder, relief flooding her body like a drug. She'd done it.

"If it's any consolation, I'm not after the royal family," she told him. His blue gaze fixed on her, eyes wide. His mouth gaped open, and he tried to say something, but Piper shushed him. "No, don't. That will make it worse."

She pulled a small pouch of berries from her bag, tucking them inside his top pocket. His hand came up, wrapping around her wrist, and Piper hissed at the burning, tingling sensation his hand left behind. Magic. Trying to fight back. But there was a small dose of Mage's Dust in her poison, stopping him from reaching his power properly.

His grip faltered, and Piper yanked her arm free.

Behind her, the door opened. Piper leaped to her feet.

For a split second, the two guards she'd seen before just stared at her. Piper's chest constricted. Like the dying man behind her, she couldn't draw a breath.

Piper bolted.

The woman snapped out of her shock first. "Grab her!" she yelled as Piper lunged around the other guard. His hand wrapped around her arm before she could get past him, yanking Piper around.

The woman knelt beside Rylan, and the male guard hauled Piper closer.

Piper pivoted on one foot, bringing her knee up in the surest way to make any man let go of her. He went white. His grip slid off her, and he keened as he dropped to the ground.

Piper spun on the ball of her foot and ran. The door slammed shut behind her, loud as a gunshot in the night. Piper hurtled down the hall, hearing a shout of surprise come from somewhere behind her. Her heart spasmed in her chest with each panting breath.

Around the corner, Piper tripped over a spindly little table. The vase on it went flying, crashing behind her as she recovered. She slammed, palms first, into the stairway; the door banged against the wall as she shoved it open.

Piper half tripped, half ran down the stairs. She jumped the last six steps on the ground floor and landed hard. Her ankle, still weak and sore from scaling the fence, buckled underneath her, and she landed on all fours, skidding across the stone. She gasped, her breath rasping in her chest like a file. Her ankle throbbed painfully.

Above her, a door slammed open.

Piper shoved herself to her feet, biting back a whimper at putting her ankle underneath her. She shoved the door with her shoulder, stopping on the other side long enough to close it, hoping desperately they wouldn't know what level she'd got out at.

Her boots slapped against the hallway floor as Piper forced herself into a run again. In front of her, the door to the pantry opened, and a sleepy-looking man, his hair mussed, stepped out. He had a bag of flour in his arms and an apron belted around his waist.

"What?" he asked.

Piper shoved past him, and he swore, staggering back through the door. She barrelled into the mudroom as she heard the clatter of someone else exiting the staircase.

"She went that way!" she heard the cook yell. In her mind, Piper imagined him pointing frantically towards her.

Piper fumbled with the key in the door, losing precious seconds. Then she had the door open. Seizing the key, Piper yanked the door closed and then locked it from the outside.

Something – or, more likely, someone – slammed into the door, making Piper jump. She spun on her heel, tossing the key into the garden. The person on the other side of the door roared.

The grass sped past underneath her as Piper hurtled towards the nearest fence, sprinting like creatures from the Winterland were on her heels. Maybe they were. She could almost feel the hot breath of a Chaos Demon on the back of her neck, making the loose curls stick to her skin. Her breath rasped in her chest, like someone had taken sandpaper to her lungs.

Behind her, she heard a shout. Whether it was someone from the house or someone from the garden, Piper didn't know, but a moment later, light washed over her.

"Halt! Stop!"

She didn't.

The wrought iron fence came closer. Black spots appeared in Piper's vision, washing the purple moonslight out. She sucked in a breath that felt like fire.

She could hear footsteps behind her now, gaining on her. Then, the thunder of hoofbeats.

The fence was in front of her. Piper leaped, grasping the top railing in between two of the spikes.

Her hands sizzled, like she'd grabbed a coal straight from the fire, and Piper screamed. But the hoofbeats grew closer, and she could hear the snorting of the horse now. A huge beast, she was certain, its eyes rolling and hooves the size of dinner plates, ready to smash her skull in like warhorses in history books did and–

And even if the horse didn't kill her, the guards would.

Piper hauled. Never in her life had she been more grateful for the pull ups Lore had made her do every day for eleven years; the ones she had been doing on her own for the past three, unable to break the habit. She pulled her body weight up, finally lodging her good foot on an angle between two of the bars.

It gave her the leverage she needed. Piper pushed herself up and over, the tail of her coat catching on one of the spikes as she leaped from the fence. She landed hard.

There was a crash, then an inhuman scream. Piper turned, yanking her hood down so her face was in shadow, to see the horse rearing away from the iron that Piper assumed burned it as much as it had her. Its rider kicked out, hitting the fence with a heavy boot and making it clang. He shouted a curse into the night, then hauled his horse around.

Pointing for the gate.

Piper shook herself. She forced herself to her feet, her ankle protesting with every bit of weight on it.

Hobbling, Piper ran from the palace.

EIGHT

Piper caught a tram a few streets over, the relief of taking her weight off her ankle making tears spring to her eyes. She got off in the Market District and pushed her way into an all-night bicycle hire shop. An extra star across the counter had convinced the sleepy-eyed clerk to forget to take her name.

She rode to Highkeep and returned the bicycle at the station closest to the Oldtown. Then Piper jumped on another tram, her hood tucked around her like she was hiding from the brisk wind. The conductor barely glanced at her, instead leaning against the railing and yawning over an enormous metal flask that smelled of coffee. She got off three blocks from her flat, then dragged herself down a side street and into a small alley, the kind that no one liked to be in during the dark hours. She approached her building from behind as the suns poked at the western horizon, turning the sky a washed-out gold.

She tiptoed through the front door, easing it closed as softly as she could. No movement from Missus Cobb's apartment, thank fate. Piper didn't have the energy to deal with her.

Her ankle protested with every step up the staircase. Her neighbour on the second floor was quiet for once, clearly worn out from his afternoon activities.

Piper breathed a sigh of relief as she unlocked her front door, then locked it again behind her. For good measure, Piper dragged a dining chair over the floor and propped it under the handle to stop it turning.

She wasn't being paranoid. Paranoia would be doing this without reason. And given that she had just broken into the palace and assassinated one of the staff …

Piper dragged her feet as she approached her bed. Even moving was difficult. Her arms and legs felt heavy; the adrenaline from the encounter with the mage and the chase was seeping from her. Her wrist burned, though there was no visible mark there.

Piper dropped down on her bed, face first, not even bothering to remove her boots.

Exhaustion claimed her in seconds.

A pounding on her front door woke Piper from a very deep sleep.

She groaned, dragging her pillow over her head. That muffled the sound enough that she could almost ignore it.

It halted, and Piper let out a sigh of relief. They must have decided she wasn't home. That was good. It meant she could go back to sleep.

The pounding started again, louder.

"What?" Piper snapped, throwing the pillow. She swung her legs out of bed and stood, then staggered as her ankle protested the sudden weight on it. She gasped, catching herself against the chimney – it really wasn't a very big apartment – and gritted her teeth.

The pounding stopped.

"Delivery for Piperlyn!" someone called.

Piper groaned, pressing her forehead to the stone. They always pronounced it wrong. Very few people in Silversdale knew her by that name. That the courier had it ...

Piper hobbled towards the door. She shoved the dining chair away and yanked the door open to scowl up at the courier. He looked far too happy, a small smile crinkling his lips and the corners of his eyes. There was a small cardboard box in his arms.

Piper glared. "You're pronouncing it wrong," she said.

The courier blinked at her. "I'm sorry?" he said.

Piper gritted her teeth. "You're pronouncing it wrong," she said. "It's Piper-*lyn*. Not Piper-*leen*. Like Madelyn." Her eyes narrowed. "And do you know what time it is?" she demanded.

"It's almost noon," the courier said smoothly, and Piper blinked. She'd slept through all the morning bells? The courier's smile widened, and he held out the box. "I assume you're Piperlyn?"

"Yes," Piper said, sighing. There was nothing for it.

She signed the clipboard propped on top – not with her real signature, she hadn't used that in years, nor the one she used for Lore and his contracts – and took the box. The courier took back his papers, then offered her another bright smile.

"Have a fate-blessed day, miss!" he called as he turned towards the stairs. Piper kicked the door closed behind him and rested her forehead against it, groaning again.

Even if it was nearly noon, it was far too early for this.

Piper locked her door and dropped the box on the table. She couldn't ignore it for long, but her hair was snarled and patches of dirt and not a few grass stains marred her palms and the knees of her jeans. Thank fate her duvet cover was navy blue and wouldn't stain, but she'd still have to take it to the cleaners.

Piper stripped, leaving her clothes in a pile in the middle of the floor – there were advantages to living alone – and made her way into the bathroom.

Her shower was barely larger than she was, but it ran in continuous hot water no matter how long she stood underneath it. Piper washed her hair, watching tiny twigs and bits of leaf spiral down the drain along with water the colour of mud, then scrubbed at the green stains on her hands. Leaving them there would be a dead giveaway; the police would be looking for someone of her description.

Piper groaned. She pressed her forehead to the tiled wall, slick from the shower spray.

Fate. She needed an alibi.

There was only one person she could ask to risk that for her. Good thing he was probably the one who'd sent the box on her dining table.

She stretched out her shower as long as she could, until her fingers and toes resembled flesh-coloured prunes. But eventually, she had to leave her haven of hot water behind. She put on a pair of old, soft jeans and a long-sleeved shirt, and went to stand at the kitchen table. The hot water had helped her ankle, but it still hurt to put weight on it. Her hair was wet, dripping into the towel Piper used to blot it dry – vigorous rubbing would only tangle her curls into an unmanageable snarl. Dropping her towel over the back of her chair, Piper slid the small blade out of the back of her belt and sliced open the tape. She lowered herself into a dining chair to read the note she pulled from inside.

> *I would ask if it was you, but I have a funny*
> *feeling I won't like that answer.*
> *The Lily, 2pm. See you there.*
>
> *P.S. Use the ointment on your ankle. Your limping*
> *will be a dead giveaway, and they're already*
> *looking for you.*

Piper sighed. He was right; he wouldn't like that answer.

She groped around in the tissue paper, and her fingers found a small glass jar. She pulled it out, frowning. It didn't look like much. But, when it came to healing, that was more often the case than not. Piper cracked open the lid and sniffed. She screwed up her face at the scent of chamomile, garlic and ginger. Dutifully, Piper scooped a gob of the gelatinous ointment onto her fingers, then rubbed it into her ankle.

The zap of magic working made her jump, then Piper moaned in relief. Cold to the touch, whatever magic was in the ointment, helped by the herbs, sank into her skin immediately, working its way through muscle and tendon.

Piper stretched out her leg, experimentally twisting her ankle from side to side, flexing and pointing like a dancer. It still twinged, especially on a twist, and Piper rubbed some more ointment into it. That was all that was in the jar, those two palmfuls. It took the entire thing to put her ankle to rights.

Piper shuddered, hating the thought of how much that tiny jar of ointment would have cost. But he was right; limping through the city was a bad idea, and not only because the police might notice. If Saxe found her injured, arrest would be the least of her worries.

Her stomach chose that moment to growl loudly, and Piper sighed. The clock on her mantelpiece, beside the radio, said it was only half past twelve, far too early for her meeting. But The Lily would have lunch.

Grabbing her book from the side table and her bag from where she'd dropped it the night before, Piper headed for her door.

Piper sat in her usual booth at The Lily, though not in her usual seat. Instead, Piper faced the wall, the second booth at her back.

It was not a comfortable way to sit. Piper's fingers itched to draw her dagger, just to have it closer, even though she knew logically that it only took a split second to draw from inside her coat. She stared at the book in front of her, only able to focus half of her attention on it.

It was a relief when someone sat down behind her.

Piper gestured across the room to Rose. The younger girl's face morphed into an instant grin; she knew Piper well enough to know the request would be a coffee, which meant she got to play with the machine.

Piper twisted sideways, her long hair sliding over one shoulder and partially screening her. It didn't take Rose long to arrive with her coffee. When she did, Piper took a long, appreciative sip.

There was a chuckle from behind her.

"Dare I guess how much coffee you've had today?" the man asked from the adjacent booth. Piper clamped down on the desire to turn and face him; that would defeat the point of them sitting behind each other. It was all about plausible deniability.

"This is only my second," she said primly. She didn't bother telling him she'd only been awake for two hours.

He let out a grunt. "What were you thinking?" he asked, his voice much quieter.

Piper forced out a sigh through her teeth. "I had no choice," she replied just as softly.

Rose took his order: a double shot of espresso. Piper could have told Rose that, not that she would ever contemplate letting slip how well she knew him. Rose left to make the coffee.

"You say that a lot," the man said.

Piper sighed again. "I really didn't," she insisted. She turned a page in her book, lifting her latte to her lips. Rose arrived a moment later, espresso in hand, and the man thanked her softly.

Piper sat silently – though she couldn't see him, she knew he'd be taking a sip of his coffee. She heard the soft chink of the cup being placed back down in the saucer.

The man sighed. "You promised me," he said, and Piper grimaced as fire flared through her chest.

"I wasn't after any of them," she said. "Just someone who works for them." The burning faded with her words, and Piper rubbed her breastbone.

It was an uncomfortable sensation, the effect of a fate oath.

He sighed loudly, rubbing the back of his neck; Piper saw the flash of a brown sleeve in her peripheral vision, then a flick of pale hair.

"If anyone asks, you were with me last night," he said after a moment. "We were playing poker."

Piper chuckled. "I lost, I assume," she said. She was rubbish at poker, and he was far too good. Whenever they played in truth, he cleaned her out.

He just laughed in response.

"How are the boys?" Piper asked.

"I know a woman who lost her daughter to dragonfever," he said. "She was happy to look after them both."

Piper nodded, satisfied. It was why she'd sent the two street urchins to him, after all.

She heard him sigh.

"Stay out of trouble," he said. "There's been a few unexplained bodies in the last few weeks. Not from your lot, or mine."

Piper gritted her teeth. "It's scum like that ..." she growled, clenching her fists.

"I know," the man agreed.

Piper heard a crack behind her. She winced – he must have been stretching his spine to produce that noise.

"You know that's not good for you," she chastised.

"Yes, Mother," he said with a chuckle, and Piper rolled her eyes. If she'd been sitting next to him, if there hadn't been two benches between them, she'd have elbowed him.

"Don't blame me when you're thirty and you can't move your head." She finished her latte, staring mournfully into the depths of her cup.

She could almost feel his tension behind her when he spoke again. "How ... How are they?"

Piper rubbed her face. Part of her wanted to tell him the hard truth. But that didn't feel fair on any of them. "They're good," she said, smiling softly. "They're all good." She would have given all the money in her wallet to be able to see his face at that moment. In her peripheral vision, she saw him nod.

"Good." He cleared his throat. "I'm glad."

Movement behind her told Piper that he stood. Their conversation was over.

Piper hesitated.

"Thanks," she said softly. "For the ointment."

She glanced up to catch him as he flashed her the fastest smile possible.

"Hey, I owe you for the last time, I'm sure," he said. Then, without saying anything else, he turned from his table and walked towards the bar to pay his bill.

Piper didn't look at him, keeping up her facade of reading her book. Her mind skipped through their past encounters. They'd stopped counting who owed whom years ago, but if Piper were honest with herself, the tally probably had her in the red. They were both in a dangerous line of work, and having someone to occasionally stitch you up after a fight was a good thing, especially when it came with no strings attached.

The door swung shut, and Piper felt the tension in her shoulders ease. She wasn't scared of him, but it would never be relaxing for two people like them to meet in a public place.

Rose approached her table, glancing at the empty spot behind her. "Did you know him?" she asked.

Piper blinked at her. "No, why do you ask?"

Rose's eyes flicked over Piper. She was far more perceptive than anyone gave her credit for. She shrugged one shoulder. "You laughed," she said. "I assumed he said something funny."

Piper smiled at her. "I was laughing at my book," she lied.

Rose rolled her eyes. "You're reading history," she said dryly, leaning on the table beside her.

"History can be funny!" Piper protested.

Rose didn't even try to hide her snort. "Sure," she said, disbelieving. "Another coffee?"

Piper hesitated. She should go check in with Lore; she didn't usually, but this was not a usual job. But … it was still early, and her book was interesting.

"Why not?" she said, smiling. Rose beamed at her, then turned to scurry back to the coffee machine.

Piper smiled. Then, standing, she switched back to the correct side of her booth. With the hearth to her back, she could relax enough to crack open her book and actually absorb the words.

Rose dropped off her coffee, a cappuccino this time. Piper shot her a distracted smile. She opened the window to let in the spring breeze, drifting across the fragrant lavender Lily planted in the garden outside, and tucked the curtain behind her seat again. Finally, Piper curled up in the corner of the booth to soak in the rocky history between the elven country, Freya, and the military powerhouse of Krauthuum.

NINE

Lore wasn't there. Piper had knocked, and there had been no answer. She'd picked the lock, but was greeted by nothing but an empty desk.

The ledger was gone. When Lore wasn't there, it was tucked into a safe Piper couldn't crack. Locks were one thing, but a safe was entirely out of her league.

Piper cursed stoutly, kicking the leg of the desk for good measure. That made her toe throb, even through her boots, and Piper hissed. She spun and yanked open one of the desk drawers. Pens and paper greeted her, and Piper ripped one of each out.

She left the note on his desk, stalking back towards the door. She didn't bother to catch it before it slammed shut behind her. Then, her toe throbbing from kicking the desk, her arm throbbing from where the mage had grabbed her and her head throbbing from lack of sleep, Piper left the building.

The next evening, Piper stumbled off the tram. It had been a good day, a quiet day. She'd slept in until midday and then stretched, exercised and read her book. She'd finally got to the part that discussed the first war between Freya and Krauthuum, and that had been enlightening.

The elven nation was no match for Krauthuum's military might. But they were cunning. That was, perhaps, even more thrilling.

All day she'd been trying not to think about the argument she'd had with Abby on her last visit. Part of her didn't want to apologise. That part still stung every time she thought of Abby's expression when she'd said *you kill people for a living*.

The male wolf puka, whose name Piper didn't know, nodded to her as she passed his yard. He was sitting on his front porch, a pipe in his hand. Piper waved, suppressing a wince when her wrist throbbed with the movement, and trudged down the road.

Beks' apartment was dark, locked up tight against the evening air. Either she was a very early sleeper, or she was out.

The city clock tolled six as Piper touched Abby's gate. It swung open under her grip, without her having to unlatch it, and Piper blinked. It was unlike Abby not to latch the gate after her. Piper couldn't remember a time when she'd got here and found it unlocked. Abby might not like growing things in her garden, but that didn't mean she wanted small animals to find their way in easily. Piper's gaze traced up past the stepping stone and to the porch.

Where the front door stood ajar.

Piper's heart jumped into her throat. Cold sweat prickled into life over her shoulders, and it was only force of will that stopped her from shivering. She leaped forward, then stopped herself, cursing silently.

Piper crept the rest of the way to the porch on silent feet, her hand wrapped around her stiletto. The smaller, leaf-shaped blade pressed against the small of her back, a comforting pressure.

She skipped the creaky step and peered through the door.

Her heart slammed in her throat, and Piper strangled her panic down. She wrapped her fingers tighter around her blade to stop them from shaking.

Inside, the sky-blue pot Abby used for her utensils had been smashed on the floor, pottery shards and metal spoons everywhere. Beyond that glimpse of the kitchen, Piper couldn't make out anything inside.

Swallowing her heart back down, Piper eased through the door.

The front room of the cottage was deserted. Piper straightened, her grip shifting on her stiletto as she looked around. The door to the bathroom hung open, sagging off one hinge where it had been pulled from the doorframe. Piper gritted her teeth, edging across the space and trying to take in every corner at the same time. Her heart fluttered unevenly.

A damp towel sat on the bathroom floor. One of the tiles was scuffed with something red; closer inspection told Piper it was blood.

She swallowed, bile rising in her throat. She had to swap her dagger between her hands to wipe both palms on her jeans. Before she rose, Piper drew her long dagger from her boot. It wasn't one she liked to have out that often; it was better as a surprise. But the idea that someone had been in the house with Maddy and Caleb and Abby, that there was blood in the bathroom that might belong to one of them ...

Piper tightened her grip, easing out into the main room. Though every instinct screamed at her to sprint out and find them, to find the three of them and get them out, Piper shoved them ruthlessly down.

She reversed her long blade so it lay along the underside of her left arm; she'd need more finesse with that blade, to lunge and slice. Her stiletto was better for bashing and stabbing.

Desperately hoping the open front door and gate were because Abby, Caleb and Madelyn had run out that way, Piper edged towards the two bedrooms. The kids' bedroom door hung open, showing rumpled beds and Caleb's book on the floor.

Caleb didn't have many books, and he was fastidious with them. There was no way he'd just drop it on the floor, given a choice.

Piper spun on her heel, swallowing hard to work moisture into her paper-dry mouth. She crossed to Abby's room and turned the handle slowly, to stop it squeaking.

This was the smaller of the two bedrooms. A double bed was squeezed in the tight space, touching both walls. The bed was made, pulled pin straight as soon as Abby had got out of it, no doubt. The bed and a wardrobe were the only things in the room; there was room for nothing else.

Glancing behind her, Piper slowly crept inside. The kids' beds were low, but this one was much higher, on a simple iron frame.

Piper eased the door shut. Her boots would be showing to anyone under the bed. She paused for long enough to swipe her palms on her pants again, then Piper steeled herself to move.

She dropped to the floor as fast as she could without hurting herself.

"Piper!"

Piper yanked her arm out of the way as Madelyn wriggled out from under the bed like a worm from the abyss. She threw herself at Piper, narrowly avoiding the stiletto blade.

Piper dropped it to the floor with a clatter and wrapped one arm around the girl. Madelyn burrowed into her as Piper pushed herself to a sitting position.

Caleb worked his way out from under the bed with more difficulty, the rabbit toy Piper had given Madelyn for the previous Yule in one hand. His face was the palest Piper had ever seen it. She worked an arm out from around Madelyn and held it open.

For the first time in a year, Caleb threw himself into her arms without any hesitation.

"It's okay," Piper soothed, feeling Madelyn's tears soak into her shirt. Caleb sniffed, his arms wrapped in a stranglehold around Piper's neck. "It's going to be all right."

Her stomach churned. She'd got mad at Abby just days ago for leaving them alone; surely she hadn't done it again. And then there was the blood. And the broken door. Piper swore silently, pressing her cheek to Madelyn's hair and sucking in a breath.

Fate, this was not good.

Caleb wriggled, and Piper loosened her arm for him to pull back. He ducked his head, scrubbing at his cheeks with the back of his hand.

"What happened?" Piper asked him.

Caleb sniffed loudly, then looked down at the bunny in his arms.

"There was a man," he whispered, his voice shaking. "He knocked on the door, then he shoved in before Mum could stop it." He looked up and met Piper's gaze. "He took Mum!"

"M-ma-ma-mama!" Madelyn sobbed into Piper's shirt, and Piper cuddled her, Madelyn's head tucked under her chin.

"It's gonna be okay," she promised. "I'll find her. I'll find your mama."

"How?" Caleb said, his voice breaking.

Piper pulled him closer.

"I don't know yet." She couldn't lie to him. "But I'll figure it out."

TEN

Piper closed the door to her apartment behind her, biting back a sigh.

Madelyn was crying again, big, silent tears streaking down her cheeks. Caleb sat curled in one of the armchairs, his face pale under his brown skin.

Piper had comforted. She'd cajoled. She'd even tried distracting.

Nothing calmed them enough to sleep.

Piper rubbed her forehead. It wasn't really fair of her to expect it, but she didn't know what else to do. She'd planned to wait until they were asleep, but ...

She'd told Abby two days ago she couldn't leave them alone all day. How much worse was she if she left them alone all night?

Even if it was to find their mother.

Piper pushed off her apartment door and took the stairs down two at a time. She hesitated on the second floor. Maybe she could ... She shook herself. That was a stupid, stupid idea. She couldn't hear anything from inside, so he probably wasn't home anyway.

Piper took the last flight of stairs and halted outside Missus Cobb's home. Taking a deep breath, Piper reached out and knocked at the door. She stood there for several minutes, staring at the timber door, her palms sweating. Piper swallowed and was lifting her hand to knock again when the door opened.

Missus Cobb filled the frame. Crossing her arms over her ample bosom, she fixed Piper with a glare. "What do you want?" she demanded.

Piper tucked her hands into her pocket to hide her nerves. She offered Missus Cobb a small smile.

"Missus Cobb," she started, but the older woman just rolled her eyes.

"I don't see why you need to come down here and bother me," she complained, and Piper snicked her mouth shut. "It's bad enough that I have to listen to Royan and his dalliances at all times of the day and night. Then I've got you tromping in here at five o'clock in the morning, making a fate-awful racket …"

She continued on, Piper blinking at her.

She'd tiptoed in like a mouse the other morning. The stairs hadn't even creaked under her weight. She'd closed her door as softly as possible, and then fallen straight asleep.

Yes, Royan was loud. And occasionally Piper was too. But if Missus Cobb didn't like that, maybe she should move out of the city.

Piper sighed loudly, cutting off whatever tirade Missus Cobb was working herself up to.

"Okay," she said, offering the other woman a smile that felt wooden on her face. "Never mind, then." Piper turned on her heel and marched out the front door.

"You get back here young la–" Missus Cobb's words cut off as Piper closed the heavy front door behind her, hearing it lock.

It would only be a moment before Missus Cobb realised that she could continue to berate Piper from the garden. She may be cranky, but she wasn't stupid.

Fate. Piper rubbed her face with both hands. She wasn't certain why it had seemed like a good idea to ask Missus Cobb to keep an ear out for Caleb and Madelyn for the ten minutes she'd likely be gone. Maybe it was just that she couldn't think of anything else.

Piper turned as she heard the garden door open. She speed-walked towards the police station on the corner, ignoring Missus Cobb calling after her.

"And she's been gone for how long?" the bored-looking police officer asked Piper over the desk.

The inside of the police station was bright and airy, even in the darkening night. Magelights hung in brackets on the walls, lending the waiting room a cosy glow. Two doors opened behind the officer's desk; Piper didn't want to know where either of them went.

She bit back a sigh. "Like I said," she repeated, with all the patience she could muster, "I don't know. I went to her house today and found it broken into, blood in the bathroom and her two children alone."

"And are you a family member?" He noted down precisely nothing.

"No," Piper said, hiding her clenched fists behind the table. "I'm just a friend."

"And her two children?" The officer's eyebrows rose, and he fixed Piper with a cool stare. "Are they with a relative?"

It took Piper all of three seconds to realise her mistake. She couldn't admit Caleb and Madelyn were with her. She wasn't related to them in any way. If she hadn't already said she was just a friend, she might have been able to get away with a lie that she was their older sister, or maybe even that she and Abby were in a relationship. But one look at the police officer's face told her that would not pass. They'd be taken off her and placed in the foster system until Abby could be found.

She couldn't let that happen.

"Yes," Piper forced out, trying to keep her voice even. "They're with an … aunt. Roberta is her name."

Roberta was the first queen of the desert kingdom Eswye. The oldest of thirteen, her father had no sons to inherit. Roberta had changed the ascension from the eldest boy to the eldest child, regardless of gender.

"An aunt?" the police officer asked, and Piper nodded. "Do you know where Roberta lives?"

"In the Market District," Piper said, the lies coming one after another now. "Though I don't know her exact address off the top of my head."

The police officer seemed to accept that. He nodded, scrawling something in his notebook. "I can't lodge this until she's been missing for forty-eight hours," he told Piper. "If you come back with the aunt's address, I'll send someone out to do a welfare check."

Piper nodded, though she had no intention of doing that.

The police officer glanced at her. "And your contact details?" he pressed.

Piper gave him her real address. It seemed silly not to, when he could look out the station door and see her step into her apartment building. If he thought she was lying about that, maybe he'd realise she was lying about the kids and their imaginary aunt. Even worse, he might decide she was lying about Abby being missing at all.

She was back out on the street again in less than ten minutes. She rubbed the back of her neck, trying to ease the tension headache she could feel building. It felt like a Chaos Demon was pounding the inside of her skull with a hammer.

Piper shook her shoulders out and started down the street.

She bought two hot chocolates from the late-night cafe across the road from her apartment, served by a girl who looked barely fifteen but handled the milk steamer like she'd been born to it. With the two hot chocolates and a bitter *frede* – an elven pastry made from folding coffee grounds into the raw dough until it was brown and smooth – on a cardboard tray, Piper turned back to her apartment building.

Missus Cobb had gone inside. Piper jogged up her stairs, passing the second floor, and came out at the attic level a moment later.

Then she pushed the door open.

"Piper!" Madelyn thumped into her, and Piper grunted, narrowly avoiding spilling the hot chocolates. The little girl sniffed, and Piper shuffled her across the space until she could deposit her burdens on the dining table.

Piper sat in a chair and pulled Madelyn into her lap. "What's wrong, baby girl?" she murmured, stroking Madelyn's blonde hair back from her face.

"I thought you weren't coming back," she whispered. "I thought you were gone like Mummy."

"Of course I came back, baby," Piper whispered. She looked up, casting around for Caleb, only to find him hovering uncertainly in the bathroom doorway.

She held out her hand to him and smiled. "I bought you both a hot chocolate," she said. "Would you like to drink them before bed?"

Madelyn stared at the mugs, her eyes wide. Caleb crept closer.

"Mum doesn't let us have hot chocolate before bed," he said softly.

Piper fought back a wince. "Well you can't have them every day," she said. "But just this once, because we've all had a bad day, it's okay."

Madelyn didn't need any more encouragement. She took the mug in both hands, and Piper had to grab it as well to stop her from spilling at all over them both. Caleb edged up to the table too, sliding onto the second chair and reaching for his own drink. The two of them drank, Piper silently stroking Madelyn's hair. Madelyn asked to try the *frede*, and Piper let her, correctly predicting the girl would screw up her face at the bitter taste.

Caleb stared towards the empty fireplace, a frown between his brows.

It didn't take long for Madelyn to doze off, curled against Piper's chest. The half-finished hot chocolate slid out from her fingers and Piper caught it, a little liquid tipping onto her jeans. She swept Madelyn up, carrying her over to the bed. It was only a double; the perfect size for Piper, who never had company. But it wouldn't fit all three of them.

Piper tucked Madelyn into the far side, against the wall, and straightened. When she got back to the kitchen table, Caleb looked at her.

"I can sleep on the couch," he offered.

Piper smiled, wrapping an arm around his shoulders and ruffling his hair. "No, sweetie," she told him. "You take the bed. I'm not tired yet anyway."

Caleb blinked at her, sleepy and owlish. Then he nodded, not quite smiling his thanks at her.

Caleb finished his hot chocolate in silence while Piper picked at the *frede*, trying not to frown.

ELEVEN

Piper woke up the next morning with a crick in her neck, her back twisted at an awkward angle. She groaned, rubbing both hands over her face. Her little love seat was not big enough for a fully grown adult to sleep on, not even one as short as Piper.

A sore back was only the first of her issues that morning.

Caleb didn't want breakfast. He wanted to leave, to go through the city and start looking for his mum, no matter how many times Piper told him that Abby wouldn't just be standing around in Illusion Square. Madelyn did want breakfast, but she wanted Frosted Fruits – a sugary cereal meant to taste like fruit, though it didn't taste like any fruit Piper had ever eaten – which Piper did not have. Piper tried to talk them both into toast, to no avail.

Then Madelyn complained about sharing a bed with Caleb.

Caleb shot her a glare. "At least I didn't put my feet in your back all night!" he snapped.

"Enough!" Piper yelled.

Both Caleb and Madelyn jumped. Madelyn stared at Piper, her mouth hanging open, and Caleb took a step back from the table.

Piper dragged in a breath through her teeth and very slowly placed both hands down on the tabletop.

"You will both eat your breakfast," she told them. "Without fighting. Am I clear?"

Madelyn's mouth closed, then opened again. Then she closed it and nodded.

"Caleb?" Piper asked, looking at the boy.

He stared at Piper like he'd never seen her before. Piper tapped her fingers on the table, and his gaze darted down to her hands.

"O-okay," he said, stumbling over the word. Piper gestured to them both to sit and turned into her little kitchen.

A few minutes later, two pieces of toast were in front of each child. Piper perched on the arm of her love seat, her coffee in one hand, keeping an eye on them both as they slowly chewed. She drummed her fingers on the table, her thoughts far away.

Fate, where was Abby? Piper rubbed her mouth. She could think of far too many possibilities, none of them happy.

Ultimately, Piper needed to find her. Though she had no clue where to start. And in the meantime, her place was too far from Caleb and Madelyn's school, and – her back twinged, and Piper winced – too cramped to fit them all.

"Piper?" Caleb asked, jolting her out of her reverie. "Aren't you going to have breakfast?"

Piper blinked at him for a moment. Then she realised she couldn't very well tell them she didn't want breakfast, not when she'd made both of them eat.

"I had mine before you got up," Piper lied.

Caleb frowned at her. "We got up when you did," he said.

Piper sighed, rubbing the back of her neck. "I didn't sleep very well," she admitted.

Madelyn looked up from her plate, toast crumbs smeared on the side of her face. "Why not?" she asked, her mouth full. "Were you worried about Mummy too?"

"Finish your bite before you start talking," Piper scolded gently. "Yes, I was worried about your mum." Among other things.

"What are we doing today?" Caleb asked, pushing his empty plate away. "Are we looking for Mum?"

Piper pinched the bridge of her nose and let out a long breath. "*I* am going to look for her," she said, emphasising that they wouldn't be accompanying her.

Caleb's face fell. "But–"

"Please, Caleb." Piper held up her hand. "I don't want to have this argument with you right now. If you're finished, could you please go and wash your face, and then pack your bags?"

Caleb's eyes widened. Madelyn's filled with tears.

"Are you sending us away?" she asked. "Is it because I was bad?"

"What?" Piper bolted upright as Madelyn buried her face in her hands. "No, baby girl." She jumped up, rounding the table to wrap her arms around Madelyn.

"I'm sorry!" Madelyn wailed. "I'll be good!"

"Oh, sweetie." Piper picked her up, shuffling Madelyn around so that she could sit on her chair, pulling the girl into her lap. "That's not it at all. I'm sorry."

Piper stroked Madelyn's long hair.

"Shh, baby girl, shh," Piper breathed. "I'm not sending you away. I promise."

Madelyn burrowed her face into Piper's shoulder, sniffling, and Piper resigned herself to tears and likely snot on her shirt. She pressed her cheek to the top of Madelyn's head, brushing her hair back.

"I promise I'm not sending you away," Piper said. She met Caleb's eyes over his sister's head. He fought them back, but she could see the tears gathering there. "I'm not sending either of you away."

THE SHARP EDGE OF FATE

Caleb blinked, making a single tear slide down his cheek. But he nodded. "Okay," he whispered.

Piper extracted one arm from around Madelyn and offered it to him. Caleb hesitated, then stepped forward for Piper to wrap him in a one-armed hug.

He pulled away quickly. "I'll go pack," he said, his voice despondent.

"Caleb," Piper called, but he ducked around the chimney and out of her sight, and with Madelyn still crying in her lap, Piper couldn't get up to go after him.

She sighed, pressing her forehead to Madelyn's hair.

"It's going to be okay," she promised. "I'm going to find Mummy. And until then, you can stay with me. I promise."

Madelyn sniffed, then nodded.

"Okay," she whispered.

Piper sighed. Then she pulled back.

"Why don't you go and wash your face?" she suggested, wiping at the tears on Madelyn's cheeks. "Then we can get ready to go."

Madelyn nodded again, her eyes downcast. She slid off Piper's lap and walked towards the bathroom.

Piper rubbed the back of her neck, feeling the tension there mounting.

"Fate," she breathed, quietly enough that she didn't think Caleb would hear. Then she pushed herself up. She needed a fresh shirt, and then to help Caleb and Madelyn get ready to leave.

They loved the trams.

Piper would have walked more if she were by herself, but with the two children and their bag in tow, it was much easier to take the trams all the way to the Market District, even if it meant changing at The Lady's Parade. When Piper finally stepped into The Lily, she had a child hanging off each arm.

The only two patrons in the pub so early in the morning glanced up as they passed, then looked back down. One, a wood elf judging by the deep umber of his skin and the pointed ears that sliced up through his black hair, had some sort of game open in front of him, with a wooden board and tiny pegs made of ivory. The other, a human, flicked open her newspaper and sipped at her coffee.

Patrik's eyes bulged when he saw her.

"Uhm, Piper ...?" he trailed off, his eyebrows forking towards his hairline.

Piper offered him a smile. "Morning, Patrik," she said, as cheerfully as she could before eleven o'clock.

He blinked at her, apparently speechless.

"Oh!" The voice came from behind Piper. She spun to see Rose coming out of the storage room. She crossed to Piper at a pace just short of running, smiling hugely at Madelyn and Caleb. "Hello to you both!"

Caleb took a step back. Madelyn pulled her hand out of Piper's to clasp behind her back, looking up at Rose through her hair.

"You're really pretty," Madelyn said softly.

Rose crouched down before her. "So are you," she said. Madelyn giggled.

Smiling, Piper turned back to Patrik, who looked no less confused.

"I need a favour," Piper said without preamble.

Patrik nodded. "Of course," he said without question. "Anything."

"Maybe favour is the wrong word," she said, grimacing. His eagerness to help made her uncomfortable. "I need a two-room suite. We can't stay at my apartment, it's too small. Do you have a room we could use?"

Patrik hesitated. "Lily wouldn't let me hear the end of it if I charged you," he said uncertainly.

"And I wouldn't forgive myself for not paying," she said with a reassuring smile.

He nodded. "The family suite," he said. "Come on up. Rose'll show you."

Piper turned to see Rose, who was holding one of Madelyn's hands and smiling at Caleb. The boy looked a bit uncertain, and Piper ran her hand over his hair, mussing it. He glared at her, swiping it out of his eyes, and Madelyn giggled.

"Come on you two," she said. "Let's go see the room we'll be staying in."

Madelyn gasped. "We're staying in a hotel?" she squealed in delight.

Caleb scowled. "It's a pub, not a hotel," he muttered, but Madelyn didn't seem to hear him. Rose beckoned to them, then turned and led Madelyn towards the stairs.

On the first floor, Rose waved them to the end of the building. A door with red trimming was set into the timber walls, its colour setting it apart from the other entranceways. Rose unlocked the door and pushed it open.

"Wow!" Madelyn gasped.

Piper had to admit, the suite was nice. The door opened to a cosy living room, a pot-bellied stove against one wall in lieu of a proper fireplace. There were two large couches and an armchair, and a dining table set underneath the window. The kitchenette was just a bench with a kettle for brewing tea and powdered coffee, but that was about the extent of Piper's cooking skills so would suit her fine.

Madelyn let go of Rose's hand and ran to one of the three closed doors. Throwing it open, she gasped again. "The bath is big enough to swim in!" she cried in delight.

Piper followed her. The bath wasn't quite that big, at least not for an adult to swim in. Compared to the tiny tub at Abby's place, though, Piper wasn't surprised that Madelyn was impressed.

The little girl raced from the bathroom, quickly discovering a bedroom with two twin beds, one pushed up against each wall, and the master bedroom, with a queen bed in the centre of the space.

Piper squeezed Caleb's shoulder, and he looked up at her.

"Don't you want to have a look around?" she asked him.

"I want to go home," he said.

Piper bit back a sigh. "We can't do that, baby," she told him.

"Don't call me baby!" he snapped. Piper blinked as he pushed her hand off his shoulder, then marched into the room with two beds. The door slammed in its frame after him.

"Oh dear," Rose said softly.

Piper rubbed her forehead. "Fate," she muttered.

"Piper?"

Piper opened her eyes to see Madelyn standing in front of her, hands clasped behind her back again.

"What's up, baby girl?" Piper asked, forcing a smile.

"Why is Caleb mad?" Madelyn asked, her forehead creased in a frown.

Piper sighed and knelt down so their eyes were at the same level.

"Caleb is upset that you're not at home, and he's worried about Mummy," she said.

Madelyn's bottom lip stuck out. "But you said you'll find Mummy," Madelyn said. "You will, won't you?"

"Of course, baby girl," Piper said softly, smoothing back her hair.

Madelyn shot Piper a smile, though this one wobbled.

"I'm going to go tell Caleb you're going to find Mummy," she said. Then she turned on her heel and ran to the door. She burst through it without knocking, and it slammed shut behind her.

"They're cute kids," Rose said, casting Piper a sideways look.

Piper rubbed her forehead. "They're my friend's."

"Okay …" Rose quirked her eyebrow, and Piper offered what she was sure was an unconvincing smile.

There was a soft knock on the door, then Patrik pushed it open.

"Everything okay?" he asked Piper, and she knew he didn't just mean the room.

"Their mother is missing," she said, with a glance towards the closed bedroom door. Rose gasped softly. "I don't know where she is, but she vanished some time yesterday. The police won't open a case looking into her until she's been gone for forty-eight hours, so until then it's just me looking for her."

113

"What are you going to do?" Patrik asked, and Piper shrugged.

"What else can I do?" she asked. "I have to find their mother."

"Will you take them with you?" Rose asked.

Piper shook her head. "They have school from tomorrow," she said. Then she glanced at Rose, hesitant. "How much does babysitting usually go for?"

"When I'm babysitting for Adam, he usually pays me about thirty stars an hour," she said.

"If I have to go out today, if I pay you the same, can you keep an eye on them?" she asked. "I'll set them up so they don't need someone to watch them the whole time, but if you could check on them ..."

Rose glanced at Patrik, who nodded. "You can take the afternoon," he offered. "It's been quiet, anyway. And I'll come and get you if I need you."

Rose smiled. "Thanks, Dad." Then she turned back to Piper. "Sure, I can look after them."

Piper sighed, feeling some of the tension in her neck and shoulders ease.

"Thanks, Rose," she said. Then she turned to Patrik. "How much do I owe you?"

Patrik wrung his hands in his apron. "Going rate is two-fifty-six a night, but–"

"No buts." Piper held up her hand, cutting him off. "That's the going rate and you can't be out of pocket because you're doing me a favour."

"But–"

"No," Piper insisted. "No. I'll pay." She ran her hands through her hair. "I'll pay this afternoon for the first few days, at least."

That was all she had on her. She had some money in the bank, but it was tied up so that Lore couldn't get to it ...

Lore. Piper sucked in a breath. Lore. Of course.

A small smile curved the corner of her mouth, and Patrik frowned. "I don't like that look," he said.

Piper chuckled. "Don't worry," she said. "It won't be any trouble for you."

Rose giggled.

"The implication of that is that it will be trouble for someone else," Patrik grumbled.

Piper's smile widened. "Don't worry about it," she said. "I've got this under control."

And she did. Or she soon would.

TWELVE

Early afternoon sunlight trickled between buildings, casting fingers of shadow and light across the pavement. Piper glanced across Illusion Square, lengthening her stride. She'd stayed at The Lily longer than she intended.

The square slowly got busier as those who started early – who worked in trades or cafes – finished their workday. Piper ducked past a fruit seller, who tried to give her a strawberry to sample, then dodged a mother with a young son hanging off her hand. She left the square and hopped onto another tram.

It felt like hours later that she finally arrived at her destination. The squat building hunched in the Oldtown like an ugly, vicious dog. Piper shoved down a looming shudder as she entered, marching through the main room and training area. She didn't bother knocking before she forced her way into Lore's office. He sat behind his desk, his boots up on the polished timber. Across from him, Saxe sat in a hard wooden chair.

Saxe shot her a dirty look, but Lore just stared.

"I want a word," Piper said through gritted teeth.

"Go on." Lore steepled his fingers, and Piper clenched her fists.

"Alone."

Lore glanced from her to Saxe and back again.

"Ah. A lover's spat."

Piper ground her teeth, imagining for a moment that she could slowly peel the skin off Lore's face. And then feed it to Saxe.

She let out a breath.

"Alone," she repeated.

"Whatever you have to say to me, you can say it in front of your partner," he said.

Saxe glared at Piper. She could practically feel his feral joy at her misery.

"Fine," she spat, turning back to Lore. "Do you know who took Abigail Brown from her apartment yesterday?"

Lore looked at her. "Who?"

"Abby," Piper ground out. "You should remember her; she cleaned this dump for you for a year."

"Ah. Her." He shook his head. "I have no idea what you're talking about."

Piper's heart performed a painful leap. She stared at Lore for a long moment, but he held her gaze. Damn it. If she'd been alone, Piper would have kicked the heavy desk.

She forced herself to take a calming breath. There was something else he could do for her, then. "I want my payment for the mage," she said. She wanted to ask who wanted him dead, and why, but bit her tongue at the last minute. That didn't matter to her, or to Abby.

Lore's gaze turned cold. "I won't be paying you for that," he said.

"Excuse me?" she growled. Piper crossed the room in three steps, smacking both hands onto the desk. Saxe was beside her in an instant, gripping her wrist.

Piper turned to Saxe. She may not be able to beat Lore, but Saxe did not have the same protection. Shaping all her frustration into a blow, Piper jabbed his armpit. Saxe swore as his right arm flopped to his side uselessly.

He reached out with his left and caught her by the braid, dragging her head back. Piper bit back a yelp of pain and grabbed his little finger, forcing it backwards. Saxe grunted, but restrained any sound of real distress.

"Enough!" Lore roared.

Breathing hard, Piper stumbled back a step from Saxe. The other assassin eyed her warily as he put the chair between them.

Lore pointed at Saxe. "Out," he ordered in a clipped voice.

Saxe never ignored Lore. He spun on his heel and marched out, slamming the door behind him. Piper turned back to Lore, but he was faster. Grabbing her wrist, he yanked her over his desk.

Piper grunted as her back hit the timber. Twisted, she had no leverage to fight back. Piper gritted her teeth, forcing down the panic, and reached her free hand for a dagger.

Lore caught that wrist too.

"You," Lore spat in her face, leaning over her, "failed."

Ice, as cold as the half-frozen harbour in winter, crawled over Piper's skin at his words.

"I did not!" she gasped, struggling to take a full breath. "I killed him!"

"And did you watch him die?" Lore breathed. Something Piper had never seen before, something more than fury or bloodlust, flickered in his eyes.

Piper stiffened.

"No, I thought not," Lore said.

Piper twisted, but Lore held her in place. He gripped her hand and smashed it against the corner of his desk. Piper convulsed, biting her tongue to stop from crying out in pain.

"You know how I feel about failure," Lore said softly. He leaned his weight on her hand, and Piper tasted blood. It took her a moment to realise she'd bitten through her lip. "I told you what would happen. I'm halving your money, and if you don't follow through with this by the end of the week, it will be your execution."

He offered her what some people might consider a smile. If she'd had a hand free, Piper would have rammed a blade straight through his mouth.

"You absolute and utter–"

"Tsk." Lore cut her off before she could call him a name she might come to regret. "That's no way to speak to your betters, girl."

Finally, he let go of her wrist. Piper was on her feet in a flash, the wall to her back. She cradled her hand to her chest.

"I hate you," Piper said. It was petulant, and immature, but she couldn't stop herself.

Lore snorted out a laugh.

"You're running out of time," he said.

"If you–"

"If I what?" Lore interrupted, not waiting to hear her threat. "What'll you do, hm? Kill me? Go ahead and try, Belladonna; it'll be the last thing you do."

He wasn't wrong.

Piper spun on her heel and marched out the office door, right hand cradled carefully in her left. Saxe stood outside, leering as though he'd been eavesdropping; he probably had. Piper paused, then spat at his feet, narrowly missing his shoe. He stepped towards her, murder in his eyes.

"Saxe," Lore said through the open door. Saxe fixed Piper with one last glare, before vanishing back inside.

Piper's eyes stung as she sped back through the main room and out the door into the Oldtown. She'd gone down three streets and into an alleyway before she stopped and put her back to a wall. She pressed her uninjured fingers against her eyes. Lore was a bully; unfortunately, he was also true to his word. If she didn't bring him proof of death, and soon … She shook her head. That couldn't happen.

She needed a doctor. Nursing her right hand, Piper raced from the Oldtown.

Healthcare was subsidised by the government in Silvaein, but Piper needed to keep her treatments off the books, and that wasn't free. Her hand hadn't been broken, thank fate. There was no instant fix for broken bones; a healer couldn't set bones, not without the risk their magic would fuse them together wrong. Now, a white bandage strapped around her hand, Piper hurried back through the Market District. Her wallet, ominously light, pressed against her from the inside of her coat.

Most of her money was wrapped up in a trust that she couldn't touch for another year. Piper had learned the hard way when Lore muscled his way into her finances; she never kept much readily available. But that meant she had less than the price of two weeks of accommodation, even if she bought nothing else. Their room fee included two meals a day, and school would provide lunch for Caleb and Madelyn. She still had herself to think of for one meal on schooldays, and one meal for all three of them on weekends.

Lore hadn't paid her. Piper snorted, catching the attention of a police officer standing outside a cafe, likely waiting for his partner. His gaze darted over her, frowning when he saw the bandage on her hand.

Piper breezed past him before he could stop her, her heart hammering in her throat.

The mage couldn't be alive. She'd left him only a moment before she usually would; there was no way he could have got help fast enough. Not with the poison she used. Not when the only nearby healer was incapacitated from a knee to the groin.

Piper blinked as someone behind her cleared their throat. She stood in the doorway to The Lily, blocking the entrance. She glanced back to see a man – a mechanic by the oil stains on his fingers – frown at her.

"If you'd move, lass," he said, gesturing to the door.

"Sorry," Piper muttered, stepping to the side. The breeze blowing between the buildings tugged at her hair, bringing snatches of conversation and the scent of the sea to her. Straightening her shoulders, she slid inside the pub.

The early dinner crowd was starting to trickle in. Half of the tables were occupied, and from the bar, Patrik offered Piper a distracted wave as he poured a beer. Rose looked up from the table she was taking orders from and smiled.

"Hey," she said, stepping to the side as Piper passed. Then, "You look awful."

Piper laughed humourlessly. "I don't feel great," she admitted. "How were they while I was gone?"

Rose shrugged one shoulder. "Not happy," she admitted. "But they were fine. I've mostly been up there, but as it started to get busy I've been going up after every table."

"Thanks, Rose," Piper said, rubbing the back of her neck. "I'll head up now so that you can get back to work." She checked the clock above the bar and almost winced. "I owe you four and a half hours."

Rose waved her hand.

"Don't worry about it," she said, but Piper shook her head.

"It's only fair," she said.

Rose bit her lip. "All right," she said, frowning. "If you're sure."

"I'm sure." Piper squeezed her shoulder, then looked over at Patrik. She offered him a small wave. "I'll bring the kids down for dinner in a bit."

"Okay." Rose smiled. A man on the other side of the room waved to catch her attention. "Talk to you later!"

Piper smiled distractedly at her, then headed for the stairs. She took them two at a time, stopping in the hallway to stretch out her shoulders and sigh. Her hand twinged.

You failed.

But she hadn't. She'd felt the needle slide into his flesh. Felt him shuddering in her arms, trying to breathe. There was no way he'd found a healer in time. Not at three in the morning, in a dark palace, with incapacitated guards with him.

He was dead.

"So this is where you're hiding."

Piper spun, then froze.

She was seeing things. Her imagination had conjured him up, because she'd been thinking of him. She was hallucinating. She'd gone mad.

It was definitely one of those things, because the alternative wasn't possible.

Alexander Rylan leaned against the far wall, his blue eyes cold and hard as flint. Piper took a step backwards, her heel bumping against the door behind her.

"What the fu–" Then she remembered Caleb and Madelyn were on the other side, and could likely hear her. "Fudge … stickles," Piper finished lamely.

The mage raised one eyebrow at her. "What?"

"What the fudge-stickles?" Piper stuck out her chin, edging back until her palm pressed against the door. "How the fudge-stickles are you here?" With each use of fudge-stickles, the mage's face grew more bemused.

"Did you really think I was dead?" he asked her, his gaze travelling over her. Then he shook his head. "Maybe it was the poison. I remember you … taller."

"Well you know what they say about good things," Piper snapped.

"I severely doubt you're a good thing," he said.

Piper's breath caught in her throat.

He wasn't dead. She was in so much trouble.

Piper's hand tightened on her coat pocket, but it was empty. She only carried poisons when she had a job to do, and she only prepared enough for each job. The rest of the time, her distilling set and her poisons lay locked up under layers and layers of protection at her little apartment.

Rylan's gaze flicked away from her and around the hallway.

"I'm surprised," he told her. "This pub is nice. Not the kind of place I'd expect to harbour a fugitive." He fixed his eyes on her again. "You know this means I'm going to have to have them arrested."

"They don't know," Piper lied. She pressed her shaking hands against the timber wainscotting behind her. The texture of paint, the tiny lines from a brush, was like sandpaper against her fingers. Rylan hadn't moved from his casual position against the wall.

"They don't know," he repeated.

Piper shook her head. "They've got no idea." At least, Rose, Lily and Eugenie didn't. The three of them made up a "they," so it wasn't really a lie.

Fate knew why she was rationalising lying to a man she'd tried to kill.

In the room behind her, something thumped. Rylan's eyes narrowed.

"What are you hiding in there?" he asked suspiciously.

"Nothing," she said. Then, mentally, she smacked herself.

Well done, idiot, you may as well have just said something!

She needed to get him away from the door. Preferably, out of The Lily. Maybe, if he thought he was alerting the authorities, she'd be able to get him in a quiet street and sink a dagger into him. It wasn't the same as a poison, and she didn't have any berries on her to leave, but dead was still dead.

Dead would still get her paid.

"Look." Piper stepped forward, though her heart hammered in her chest. "All right. You've got me. We should leave before someone sees us."

The mage pushed himself off the wall with his shoulder, striding the three steps across the hall to tower over her. "Why would it matter if anyone sees us?" he asked, his eyebrow lifting again. Piper took a shaking breath, imagining sinking her dagger through it and slicing it clean off.

"Um." She didn't have a good answer for that. "Collateral damage?"

Rylan smirked. "You assume you'd be a threat to me," he said.

"I am a threat to you," she snapped, scowling.

Rylan chuckled, his blue eyes never leaving Piper's. "No," he said. "I want to see where the Belladonna was running to."

"Don't call me that," Piper growled. She stepped into the doorway and braced her arms on either side. "There's nothing in there."

"Right." He took a step forward. "Open the door."

"No," Piper said.

"For fate's sake." He closed the distance between them, grabbing Piper by her shoulders and trying to bodily move her out of the way. But Piper locked her elbows; the only way he'd get her away was if he broke her arms.

"Leave it alone, mage," Piper spat.

He shot her a glare, his blue eyes burning with raw power, and Piper almost squeaked in alarm. She expected him to reach out, to force some kind of magic on her to make her move, but Rylan just brought up one leg, slamming his foot into the door with his considerable height and strength. It crumpled inwards.

There was a squeal, and Piper yanked herself from his grip. She stumbled backwards into the room, stooping to pull the long dagger out of her boot as she moved.

"Get behind me!" she said. Caleb dived off the couch, seizing Madelyn and pulling his sister into relative safety behind Piper's back.

Piper planted her feet, sliding the leaf-shaped dagger from the back of her belt and holding its blade between forefinger and thumb. She didn't know if he would attack them with magic; if he worked for the palace, he was likely a battlemage, able to throw handfuls of fire or lightning at her. A dagger in his eye would stop him regardless.

But Rylan didn't move. He didn't even seem to breathe, watching them in bewilderment.

Madelyn pressed against Piper's back, her arms wrapping around one of Piper's legs.

"Who is he?" she whispered. "Why is he standing there like that?"

Rylan blinked at her voice, his eyes darting over both Caleb and Madelyn.

"I'm not sure why he isn't moving, baby girl," Piper said. She felt Madelyn's grip around her leg tighten, and she dropped her hand to run her fingers comfortingly through her hair, making sure only the hilt of her dagger was anywhere near the girl. Rylan followed the movement, taking in Madelyn's comfort, even with a dagger hilt rubbing the top of her head.

"What does he want?" Caleb asked.

"I don't know that either," Piper said.

Rylan looked at her. "You thought I would hurt them?" he demanded.

"I know next to nothing about you," she retorted. "It's not a chance I would take." She pointed to the door with her dagger. "Get out."

His eyes followed the line of her arm, to the little dagger still held between her forefinger and thumb. Her other hand, the bandaged one, twinged when she tightened her grip on the long dagger.

Rylan's gaze flicked back to her face. "Is your aim any good?" he asked.

In response, Piper flicked her hand. He didn't have time to do any more than suck in a breath before the dagger stuck in the wall behind his shoulder, quivering from the force of her throw. Several strands of blue-black hair floated down to land on Rylan's shoulder, stark against his white shirt. One more dagger, and she could collect on that contract.

Piper's gaze darted down to Caleb and Madelyn. If they weren't here, she'd have done it.

Rylan twisted, looking at the dagger in the wall behind him.

"I'm being nice," Piper told him. "I won't tell you again. Get. Out."

Rylan crossed his arms. "No," he said, and Piper blinked at him. "I have questions for you, Bella. You're going to answer them."

Madelyn tugged on Piper's coat. "Why is he calling you that?" she asked.

"No reason, baby," Piper answered. She slid her hand inside her coat, pulling out one of the twin narrow daggers inside. These were better for throwing.

Rylan's eyebrows both rose this time. "How many knives do you have?" he asked, sounding impressed despite himself.

Piper fixed him with a glare. "Come closer and find out," she said.

Caleb wrapped his arm around Piper's.

"Piper, you can't kill him," he whispered, loud enough that his voice carried through the room.

"I can if he's going to hurt you or your sister," Piper said, shaking Caleb off.

Rylan met her eyes across the room.

"I swear by fate," he said, and Piper's breath stuck in her throat, "I will not harm either of them."

She'd only ever seen one fate oath broken. To break a fate oath, whether by action or by lying, was to die painfully. And not quickly. It had taken the poor man almost five minutes to die, screaming in agony the entire time, clutching his chest.

The mage stayed standing.

Not in pain. Not dying.

Piper lowered her long dagger, stooping to slide it back into her boot sheath. The other, smaller dagger she kept between her fingers for the time being.

He hadn't sworn he wouldn't hurt *her*, after all.

Madelyn peered out from behind Piper. "Is he going to hurt us?" she asked.

Piper ran her fingers through the girl's hair again, no dagger in between them this time.

"No, Maddy," she said. "He won't hurt you."

Madelyn stared up at him. Piper couldn't see from her angle, but she thought the girl's mouth might be hanging open.

"He's so big!" she whispered.

Rylan glanced at Piper, then back down at Madelyn. Then, slowly, he dropped to his knees. It was a long way down. But finally, he knelt near the door and smiled at Madelyn.

"Maddy, is it?" he asked, smiling at her. "Is that short for something?"

Madelyn let go of Piper. She crept across the floor, stopping just out of arm's reach.

Madelyn looked up – even kneeling, Rylan was taller than her. She clasped her hands behind her back and swung back and forward slightly, her hair falling across her eyes.

126

"Madelyn," she said shyly.

Rylan's smile widened. "It's a pleasure to meet you, Madelyn. I'm Alec." Rylan glanced at Piper. "I need to talk to your mum."

Madelyn's face crumpled. "But Mum's not here," she said.

Rylan stared at her, blinking. Caleb stepped forward, putting himself between Piper and the mage even as Piper tried to drag him back.

"Our mum's missing," he said, and Piper could hear the suspicion in his tone. "How do we know it wasn't you who took her? You're threatening Piper."

Rylan's mouth worked open and closed, like a fish, and before she could stop herself, Piper snorted. He fixed her with an icy-blue glare, rising to his feet in a surprisingly agile move.

"Well, either way I need to speak with your ... Piper," he said.

Piper narrowed her eyes at him.

"No, that's not what's going to happen," she said. "You're going to leave, and you'll never see us again."

Something burned in those blue eyes, something Piper couldn't put her finger on.

"Not likely," he said, in a voice that shook, not with nerves, but with something Piper didn't want to identify. Something like power.

Piper opened her mouth to snap something back at him – what, she wasn't too sure – when Madelyn turned to her.

"Piper." She tugged on Piper's sleeve again. "Can Alec stay for dinner? I'm hungry."

"Of course you are, baby girl," Piper said, picking her up to brace the girl on her hip. "Ry– Alec was just leaving, so he can't stay."

They'd have to work out a new place to live. They couldn't stay here, not with Rylan knowing where she was. But she had to feed them both first. And then convince them that they had to move.

Piper felt her left eye twitch, frustration and stress broiling under her skin, but she forced herself not to show it.

Rylan shrugged in a way that would have been nonchalant, if he hadn't kept his gaze on Piper the entire time. "I think I'm hungry too," he announced.

Piper glared at him, but he didn't seem to notice. Maybe she could push him down the stairs and he'd break his neck. Maybe she could convince him to go down first, then sneak Caleb and Madelyn out through the window.

Maybe—

"Piper?" Madelyn tugged on Piper's braid to get her attention.

She hissed in surprise. "You can't pull on people's hair, baby girl," Piper scolded her.

Madelyn pouted. "But I'm hungry," she said again.

Piper bit back a sigh.

"All right." She lifted Madelyn to the ground and took her hand. "Come on, both of you. Let's get some dinner."

THIRTEEN

Piper felt eyes on her throughout the meal, which they ate in the pub's common room. There was Rose, frowning at the tense set of Piper's shoulders; Lily, sticking her head out of the kitchen to see Piper's almost untouched plate; Patrik, glancing at her between serving the customers that came up to talk to him at the bar instead of waiting for Rose to take their orders at the tables.

And there was Rylan. The fate-damned mage walked to the bar, talked to Patrik for a moment, then settled himself at a small table across the room – one where he had a clear view of the booth Piper sat in.

Fate knew how the mage had survived. How he'd found her. Piper's skin prickled uneasily, and she stopped herself short of shivering. Her heartbeat tripped a nervous beat in her throat, refusing to stay in its place. No matter how many times she swallowed, she couldn't work moisture into her paper-dry mouth.

Grinding her teeth so hard she was surprised they didn't crack, Piper turned back to Caleb and Madelyn. Both had mostly empty plates, and Madelyn yawned, slumping sideways on the bench.

"I'm sleepy," she murmured. Piper stroked her hair back.

"All right," Piper said. "Let's go up to bed." Or maybe to the room to pack. She could carry Madelyn, even if she was asleep. Piper glanced at Caleb. "Are you finished?"

He nodded, his brows creasing into a frown. "What about Mum?" he asked. "Are we going to look for her?"

"Caleb, that's what I've been doing today," she said. "I'm not stopping. I promise. But I can't leave the two of you alone all the time."

Caleb's frown deepened. "Surely there's something you can do tonight," he said, his voice just shy of a whine.

"I …" Piper trailed off. She suddenly smacked the tabletop with her hand. "Shoot, I can't believe I forgot that."

"What?" Caleb asked, fixing her with a look. Piper pushed herself out of the booth.

"Stay here," she told him. "Neither of you move, understand? I'll be one minute."

She didn't wait for either to agree before she ducked across the room to the bar.

Patrik looked her over. "What's got you so flustered?" he asked.

Piper pushed her hair back out of her eyes and sighed.

The mage was watching her. She could feel it.

"That list is too long to recite," Piper admitted. "Have you got some paper?"

"Of course." Shooting her a curious look, Patrik retrieved a pad of paper and a pencil out from under the counter. It was the kind Rose took orders on all day long. Piper huffed a laugh, imagining her recipient's surprise, but scrawled a quick note across a few pages.

When she was finished, she handed them to Patrik. "Can you leave these for me?" she asked.

130

Patrik's eyebrows rose. "In the usual spot?" he asked, and Piper nodded. "Sure."

"Thanks." Piper glanced back at the booth to see Madelyn with her head on the table, her long hair trailing in the leftovers of Piper's salad. She almost sobbed out loud.

Patrik sighed, clearly seeing the same thing Piper did. "No luck finding their mother?" he asked, his voice soft, and Piper shook her head.

"Fate, I'm not even sure what to do next," she admitted. Then she glanced at him. "I have to keep looking. But I don't think it will be until tomorrow, while they're at school."

"Good idea," he said. "At least at school they'll both be supervised and out of your hair."

Piper smiled sadly. "Yeah." She sighed again. "Night, Patrik."

"See you tomorrow," he called as she stepped away. Piper didn't bother to say he might not. She offered him a wave over her shoulder, winding through the tables full of patrons and dodging Rose with a tray full of plates. She stopped beside the booth.

"Come on, both of you," she said, gathering Madelyn's hair out of her plate. "It's shower time, then we need to talk about some things. And you've got school tomorrow."

Caleb scowled. "I don't want to go to school," he said. "I want to help you find Mum."

"We'll talk about it in the morning," Piper said, with no intention of changing her mind. "Come on."

Madelyn whined until Piper picked her up, then laid her head on Piper's shoulder. Piper hitched Madelyn into a better spot, resigning herself to salad dressing on her shirt. She extended a hand to Caleb. To her surprise, he took it.

Across the room. Rylan rose from his table.

Piper stiffened. Madelyn felt it and lifted her head from Piper's shoulder.

"What's wrong?" she asked.

"Nothing, baby girl," Piper soothed. Madelyn blinked big hazel eyes, before laying her head down again. Piper tugged gently on Caleb's hand. "Come on. Let's go."

She led them towards the stairs. Rylan followed.

Piper's heartbeat spiked in her chest. She could get Madelyn and Caleb inside. He'd said he wouldn't hurt them. She could lock the door and make a run for it out the window. Maybe he'd chase her.

But ... Surely he'd know she'd come back for them. So all he'd have to do was wait.

Inside the suite, she let go of Caleb's hand and placed Madelyn down. Madelyn yawned, and Piper caught her shoulders.

"It's shower time," she said firmly.

"But I'm tired," she said. "I don't want to."

"Too bad," Piper said. "You have to, and you have to wash your hair."

From Madelyn's gasp, that was the worst punishment in Rhealgo. But, eventually, Piper half cajoled, half bullied her into the bathroom. Extracting a promise to call her if she needed help washing her hair, Piper closed the door. She pressed her back against it and sighed.

A shoe scuffed the floor, and Piper turned her gaze to Caleb.

"Am I going to have to fight with you too?" she asked him.

Caleb stuck out his bottom lip, but then he shook his head. "No," he said finally. "When Maddy's done, I'll have a shower too."

"Good boy," Piper said, reaching out to run a hand through his hair, but Caleb twitched away from her grip, scowling.

"I'm not a boy anymore," he snapped.

Piper knelt down before him. "You'll always be a little boy to me," she said, smiling gently. "I remember when you were just this tall." She held out her hand, and Caleb scrunched up his face.

"I was never that small," he argued.

Piper smiled. "Everyone was that small once," she told him. "Why don't you go and get your clothes ready for your shower? I'm sure Maddy won't be too long."

Caleb nodded. Turning, he headed towards the bedroom, pulling the door closed behind him.

Piper huffed, running her hands through her hair where it had escaped her braid. She'd pack. That's what she'd do. And, when they were both showered, they'd steal out the window and head back to her place, and—

"I didn't expect to find the Belladonna playing house with two children."

Piper shot to her feet. Rylan leaned against her doorframe, his arms crossed over his broad chest.

"Do not call me that," Piper hissed, stalking across the sitting room towards him. "And go away!"

Rylan shook his head. "Nope," he said, popping the *p*. "You're going to get the two of them into bed. And then we're going to talk."

"I am not talking with you," she said.

Rylan raised one black eyebrow. "The alternative is I have you arrested and we talk in Silversdale Prison," he said.

Piper froze. "You can't do that." If he threw her into prison, Madelyn and Caleb would have no one. They'd have to go into foster care. No one would be looking for Abby anymore. Fate knew what would happen to any of them.

That fate-damned eyebrow inched higher. "Try me," he said.

Piper clenched her fists.

The bathroom door cracked open. "Piper," Madelyn called. "My hair is tangled."

"I'll be there in a second, baby," Piper called over her shoulder. Behind her, she heard the bathroom door close again.

Piper pressed a finger into Rylan's chest, and something ticklish zipped up her arm.

"Get out of my doorway," she breathed. "And fate help me, if I come out to find you've irritated Caleb in any way ..." She left the threat hanging.

One corner of Rylan's mouth quirked up in a sarcastic smile. "Try it," he said, "I dare you."

Piper backed up a step. She wasn't running, she told herself. She forced herself to hold Rylan's gaze until her other hand touched the door. She pulled it open and vanished inside.

Madelyn stood in front of the mirror, an oversized blue towel wrapped around her. Her hair was a snarled mess, some shampoo suds still visible where they hadn't been rinsed out properly.

"Okay, baby girl," she said, pulling Madelyn back towards the shower. "Let me help you fix this."

Piper closed the door to the second bedroom softly behind her.

Caleb had taken less than five minutes in the shower, but he'd sworn up and down that he'd scrubbed every inch of him. It wasn't late, but Piper had found him a couple of books to read in bed, and settled him and Madelyn in the twin room.

The mage still occupied her doorway, looking out the window towards the darkened city.

Piper stalked across the room. "Well?" she demanded, crossing her arms. "What do you want?"

Rylan snapped his gaze to her. His attention *should* be on her. The fact that he didn't even consider her to be enough of a threat to keep his eyes on her when they were in the same room was infuriating. Piper ground her teeth. Again.

"Come on," he said. He jerked his head backwards. "I don't want to talk here where they can hear us."

"I'm not going anywhere with you," Piper snapped. "I have two children ten and under in that room. I am not leaving them alone so that you can berate me."

"I'm not berating you," he said. "I'm actually trying to have a civil conversation with you. Considering that you tried to kill me a few days ago, I think I'm being more than reasonable."

Piper bit the inside of her cheek. She didn't have a response for that. "Well ... You're still lurking in my doorway," she snapped. "Which you broke, by the way."

Rylan rolled his eyes. "Come on," he said, stepping back into the hall. "Let's talk."

He gestured to a door opposite her, and Piper narrowed her eyes.

"You do know that these rooms aren't just here for your pleasure, right?" she asked waspishly, bracing her hands on the doorframe. "They're there to rent out."

"Oh I know," Rylan tossed back at her. "I've rented this one. That way I can keep an eye on you, and make sure you don't disappear." He fixed her with his blue gaze. "Don't try to disappear."

Piper clenched her fists. She glanced back, towards Caleb and Madelyn's door. There was no lock on it, no security. Piper looked at the splintered wood of the main entrance. There was a dent in it from Rylan's kick.

"Fix the door," she said.

Rylan blinked at her. "Excuse me?"

"You think I'll just leave them to go talk with you?" she asked, gesturing behind her. "They are children. I'm not leaving them alone unless I can lock this door. So fix it."

Rylan frowned. For the first time, Piper didn't think it was directed at her.

"My magic doesn't bend that way," he said after a moment.

It was Piper's turn to blink at him. "I'm sorry?"

"My magic doesn't bend that way," Rylan repeated, like he was speaking to a slow child. "I can't fix the door."

"Then I'm not leaving them." A thrill of triumph ran through her.

"Oh for the love of sweet fate," the mage said. He dug a hand into the pocket of his jeans and pulled out a small mechanical ... scorpion?

"What's that?" Piper asked warily.

She'd never seen a real scorpion before. They were more typical in hot, arid climates like Sandheim and Eswye. But the little mechanical

135

creature was exactly like she had imagined, down to the tiny bulb and stinger on the end of its tail. The gears and pulleys were miniscule, like someone the size of a faerie had worked on it. But faeries weren't real, not outside of story books, so he had to have bought it from somewhere.

A tiny, blue-black spark flared to life in its eye pits. The scorpion twitched, its tail flickering forward over its head. Piper jerked back with a yelp. It scuttled off Rylan's hand to the doorframe, where it sat at head height – his head height, not Piper's.

Rylan turned to her. "Happy?" he deadpanned.

Piper shook her head. "I have no idea what there is to be happy about."

Rylan sighed, like she was the greatest nuisance he'd ever come across. The feeling was mutual. Piper narrowed her eyes at him, crossing her arms over her chest.

"Use your words, mage," she said.

His eye twitched, and Piper heard him drag in a breath.

"This will stop anyone other than you or me entering this room," he said in a long-suffering tone. "Will this satisfy?"

Piper narrowed her eyes at him. "No," she said flatly.

He crossed his arms. "Too bad." He jerked his head behind him. "Shall we?" It wasn't really a question.

"Fine." She didn't think she had a choice, not with the look Rylan pinned her with.

The mage nodded. He stepped out of the doorway and into the hall. Silently, he opened the door on the other side.

With his back to her, Piper fingered the hilt of her dagger. Her stiletto would do the trick nicely. The blade was made for stabbing. If she sank it at the right angle past his spine ...

Rylan turned around before Piper could act. Her thoughts must have shown on her face, because he glared at her.

"Don't even think about it," he said, gesturing inside.

Piper hesitated a moment longer. Then she stepped past him.

His suite was much like hers across the hall, except he only had two doors off the sitting room instead of three. In the middle of the small space, between the couch and armchair, Piper turned on her heel, crossing her arms over her chest.

"What's with the scorpion?" she asked, before he could open his mouth.

Rylan raised one eyebrow at her. "You've never seen a construct before?"

Piper frowned. "Why does a battlemage have a construct?" she asked, not willing to admit that no, she hadn't. "You can just blast your enemies with fire, or electricity, or whatever."

"Human magic doesn't work that way," he said. "We work with energy. We can't just create an element." He crossed his arms, mimicking her pose. "And I'm not a battlemage. I'm a spellbinder."

"Oh." That made things much better, actually. Piper's rigid stance relaxed a bit, and her gaze darted over him. Maybe she'd be faster than he was. If she timed it right, maybe she could slip her dagger through his ribs.

Rylan snorted.

"You've just made three erroneous assumptions," he told her. "First, you assume that because I'm a mage, I can't fight. Second, you assume that because I'm a spellbinder, I'm weak. Third"–he narrowed his eyes–"you assume I won't do whatever it takes to defend myself."

Piper gritted her teeth. She couldn't in all fairness say that any of that was false. But she wasn't interested in being fair.

"You're wrong," she said loftily. "Right now I'm thinking that you're interrupting my evening, and that you need a haircut."

Rylan's arm jerked, like he was going to lift it up to touch his hair but stopped himself.

Point. Piper smirked, refusing to think about the one-ups he'd scored on her.

Rylan uncrossed his arms to gesture to the couch. "Sit," he said, his voice clipped.

"I am not a dog," she snapped.

"Then stand," he told her, dropping into the armchair. "I really don't care." He leaned forward, bracing his elbows on his knees, and fixed her with that bright blue stare. "Why did you try and kill me?"

Piper looked away. There was a dent in the pipe of his pot-bellied stove. She'd have to see if Patrik could get it fixed; it might leak smoke into the room and suffocate a customer. Though, if it suffocated this customer ...

"Because someone paid us to," she said after a moment, deciding on the truth.

His eyebrow rose. "'Us'?"

Piper shot him a look. "I'm not the only ... person like me in the city," she said. Then, because standing while he was sitting was starting to feel stupid, she dropped huffily onto the couch.

"So I should expect someone else to come looking for me?" Rylan asked.

Piper shook her head. "No," she admitted. "You're mine. No one else will come for you."

Yet, she added. But she kept that to herself.

Rylan nodded, rubbing his chin in thought. "Who hired you?" he asked.

Piper shrugged. "No idea. I'm not privy to that information."

To her immense surprise, Rylan leaned back, the intensity fading from him. Rubbing his hands over his face, he let out a sigh. "Well, I suppose that was a bit of a stretch," he admitted, almost to himself.

Piper stared at him for a good moment. He was just sitting there, not looking at her, basically defenceless ... Her fingers caressed the hilt of her stiletto through her coat.

She could do it. But ...

"What do you want with me?" she asked instead. Curiosity nagged at her now. Besides, as much as he threatened it, he didn't seem like he was about to turn her in.

Rylan dropped his hands and fixed her with that blue stare again. "Their mother," he said, with a jerk of his head back towards the other room. "Your ... partner?" He danced around the word delicately, sounding for the first time like he was trying not to offend.

Piper shook her head. "My friend," she corrected. "What about her?"

"When did she go missing?" he asked.

"Yesterday some time before three," Piper said.

"And do you know of anyone who'd want to hurt her?"

"No," Piper said. "Why? Why do you even care?"

"Because," Rylan said slowly, "I'm starting to wonder if her disappearance is linked to another disappearance. One I'm investigating." He frowned, staring in the direction of the stove.

Piper shifted forward on her seat, curious despite herself.

"Why would you think they're linked?" she asked.

"No real reason," Rylan admitted with a shrug. "Just a feeling, I guess. But, when you're a mage in Silvaein, you learn to listen to your feelings. Sometimes there's more to them." He scrubbed his face with both hands again. "It could be nothing," he continued after a moment. "It could just be one big coincidence – my person goes missing, you try to kill me, your person goes missing. But I don't like coincidences."

That, at least, was something they could agree on. Piper chewed her lip. Then she asked the million-star question.

"Who else has disappeared?"

Rylan braced his elbow on his knee, leaning towards her. His blue eyes pinned her to the couch.

"Prince Jairus of Silvaein."

Piper felt her heart beat three times before she could force out a response. "What?" she demanded, her voice strangled.

Rylan's gaze flicked over her. From the curls escaping her braid to brush at her cheeks, to her boots, and back again, his eyes took her all in. Then he leaned back, nodding as though satisfied about something.

"You didn't have anything to do with his disappearance, did you?" he mused.

"Of course I didn't!" Piper snapped, smacking her hands on her thighs. "No royals! Never, ever! That's suicide, and the worst thing for the economy!"

Rylan blinked at her. "Good. You're sensible."

Piper fingered the hilt of one of the twin blades on the inside of her coat, considering using him for target practice again. Her leg jittered, and Piper pressed one hand down on it to try and keep it still.

"You're mad," she said, shaking her head. Then she narrowed her eyes at him. "Is that why you tracked me down? You thought I had something to do with it?"

"It's not a complete stretch of the imagination," Rylan said, reaching into his pocket. "You certainly like to make a statement." He produced a small pouch. The same one Piper had slipped into his shirt pocket the night she'd tried to kill him.

She shook her head. "That's exactly why it's a stretch," she argued. "I don't make people disappear. I leave messages. Did you find my kind of message wherever it is he vanished?"

Rylan's eyes narrowed. "No," he said. "I did not."

Piper nodded, rubbing her fingers along her blade through her coat. Who'd be mad enough to kidnap a prince? Another country, maybe?

"What about the crime families?" Rylan asked, leaning forward again. Piper's heart jumped into her throat, and she swallowed. "I know there are several in Silversdale."

"Like in any big city," Piper said, waving a hand dismissively. "It's possible but unlikely. The reason they're in the position they're in is because they like their money, and going after the royal family stops that money flow."

"You know them," Rylan accused.

"We run in some of the same circles," she admitted reluctantly. She knew most of them mainly by reputation. She only knew one personally.

"Which one is your boss?" Rylan asked, crossing his arms.

Piper snorted. "None of them," she said. "Lore is an ass of epic proportions; he's also an idiot. He can barely keep the assassins in line. He's not smart enough to run an entire sect of the city."

"Lore, hm," Rylan mused.

Piper bit the inside of her cheek. She shouldn't have let that name slip. Then again, she really, really didn't care if this mage grabbed Lore and dropped him in the Lord General's lap.

Rylan steepled his fingers, staring over them past her. He tapped his fingers together, his attention far away. Piper's leg started jittering again, and she pressed down on it with both hands this time.

Rylan's gaze flicked to her. "I want to see where your friend went missing from," he said.

It took a good second for Piper to process what he'd said. When she did, she scowled.

"Why?" she demanded.

One of his eyebrows rose. Again.

"I really don't think you're in much of a position to be arguing with me," he said.

Piper shot to her feet. She crossed the three steps between them, glaring at Rylan, her fists clenched. Seated, he was finally shorter than her.

"Let me get one thing straight," she hissed. "This," she gestured between them, "is no partnership. I am not working with you."

He leaned back, crossing his arms, and cocked his head to the side.

"Even if it helps you get your friend back?" he asked. "Get those kids their mother?"

Piper froze. "Damn you to the Winterland," she whispered.

Instead of being offended, Rylan chuckled. "That's not the first time someone has told me that." He sounded almost cheerful. Then his expression darkened. "Let me be straight with you," he said. "Right now, you are more valuable assisting me than resisting me. That is why you're standing here, free." He braced his arms and fixed her with his gaze. "Don't make the mistake of crossing me, Bella."

Piper dug her nails into her palms. "You have no idea about me, Rylan," she spat. "Let's keep it that way."

Rylan's eyes narrowed. "How many people have you killed, Belladonna?" he said flatly. "How many families hate you?"

Cold raced down Piper's spine. She fought back the shiver, barely, and fixed Rylan with a stare that could have flayed his flesh from his bones.

Then she turned on her heel and strode from the room.

Rylan didn't try to stop her. Piper slammed his door shut, letting him hear the full force of her displeasure. Inside her own suite, she leaned back against the wall and buried her face in her hands.

How many families hate you?

Too many. She shivered, sightless, accusing eyes dancing behind her closed lids. Far too many.

Piper shook herself.

She didn't need much light to see her way around the room; Azah was in the sky tonight, and the pale gold light of the crescent moon slid in through the window. It gilded the couch, sparkling off the mirror over the mantelpiece. Piper glanced at her bedroom door, then at the still open door to the hall. Rylan's scorpion sat in the doorframe, its little brass parts shining like gold.

Piper ignored it and cracked open the door to the room Caleb and Madelyn shared. Their twin beds were each almost as big as the bed in her apartment. Piper gently closed the door and sat on the edge of Madelyn's bed, brushing her blonde curls back from her face. Across the room, Caleb lay on his side, his hand on the cover of his book.

Piper couldn't bring herself to move them again, even if the desire to get away from the mage nagged at the back of her mind. Sighing softly, Piper lay back on Madelyn's bed. In her sleep, Madelyn curled into Piper's side.

She couldn't trust Rylan. He wanted to find the prince; he didn't care about Abby.

If he found the prince, he'd leave her alone.

If she were smart, she'd knock him out and deliver him to Lore as promised.

Piper rested her cheek on Madelyn's hair.

Maybe she'd get lucky. Maybe something would kill him in his search for the prince, and she could claim it was her. Or maybe he'd get bored hassling her and scurry back to the palace on the next available tram.

So long as he forgot to turn her in before he went, that might be the best available outcome.

FOURTEEN

"Come on!" Piper cried, grabbing Madelyn's hand.

"Piper, stop pulling!" Madelyn complained, tugging back.

Piper ignored the girl's plea. Instead, she picked her up and raced down the stairs two at a time, almost tripping over the bottom one and sending them both to the floor.

Caleb stood by the bar, talking to Rose as she filled coffee orders. The pub was quiet at breakfast time; usually just the few people who stayed overnight would be there. Rose did a good job, but Piper knew of two or three absolutely amazing coffee places in the city that were much more sought-after breakfast locations.

Piper skidded to a stop next to Caleb and caught his shoulder. "Come on, Caleb, time to go," she said, with a distracted nod to Rose.

"But–" Caleb started.

Piper grabbed his hand and dragged him out the door. "Come on, quickly!" Piper put Madelyn down and pulled them both into a jog.

"Piper," Caleb said. Piper ignored him.

They were almost past The Lily when a hand wrapped around Piper's arm, pulling her to a stop. She reacted on instinct. Dropping both Madelyn and Caleb's hands, she spun, stepping forward so they were both behind her, the heel of her hand striking upwards.

It hit Rylan's nose with a grating crunch.

He staggered back a step, letting go of her to cover his face with both hands. A stream of words that Piper were certain were curses left him, though they were muffled by the blood dripping down his face and hands.

"Oh," Piper said.

"Fuh," Rylan said. At least, that was what it sounded like. Piper was pretty certain it wasn't what he actually meant. "Whad'ya do tha for?"

He winced as the words pulled at his face.

"You grabbed me," Piper said, pressing a hand to her chest, where she could feel her heart pounding like a rampaging tseuon. "What did you expect when you grab an – a person like me!"

Madelyn stared between Piper and Rylan, her mouth open. Caleb had one hand pressed to his mouth – in shock or to contain laughter, Piper couldn't be certain.

The city bells tolled, and Piper swore under her breath. "Come on." She grabbed Caleb and Madelyn again. "You're going to be late."

"Lade?" Rylan demanded, pulling one bloody hand away from his face to fish around in his pocket and produce a handkerchief. "For whad?"

"For school!" Piper snapped.

"I don't want to go to school!" Caleb said. "I want to help find Mum!"

Piper drew in a long, calming breath. "You have to go to school, Caleb," she said in a gentler tone. "You have to learn. I will keep looking for your mum while you're there, okay?"

Caleb stamped his foot at her, and Piper stared at him. She couldn't remember a time in the last six years that he'd had a tantrum.

"I want to come!" he repeated.

"Piper's righ'," Rylan said, making Piper's head snap around to him like she was on a string. "You've godda go do school. Bud I'm gonna help her look for your mum an' my friend while you're dere. Is thad okay?"

Caleb blinked at him for a long moment. Not a yes, but also not an argument – that was better than most of the responses Piper had got.

"Come on," she said, tugging on both of their hands again. Caleb and Madelyn followed her a few steps.

Piper hesitated. Sighing, she looked back over her shoulder.

"There's a healer near the school," she said.

Rylan blinked at her in surprise, the handkerchief steadily turning redder and redder.

Piper narrowed her eyes. It was the most of an invitation he was going to get, and if he didn't like it …

Rylan followed her.

Piper hurried Madelyn and Caleb across the square and to the nearest tram station. The two-minute wait for the next service was torture; add to that the looks they got over Rylan's clearly broken and still bleeding nose, and Piper would almost have been happier to walk.

But just almost. If they did, Caleb and Madelyn would be so late for school they might not be let in for the day.

Piper picked Madelyn up again to get off the tram; it was easier than trying to get her to jump the narrow gap between tram and platform with her little legs. Caleb jumped off after them, with Rylan bringing up the rear. They hurried around a corner and onto a quaint little street. Trees lined the road, which was just wide enough for two cabs to pass. The cobbles were swept clear of horse manure, though they wouldn't stay that way. No autocarts would come down here; those with enough money to own one would be sending their children to the fancier schools in Redwell or Highkeep.

The school gates towered well over Piper's head, their wrought iron wrapped in ivy. They stood open, though they would close soon, keeping anyone not a student outside. Parents milled around the opening, hugging and kissing goodbye, pressing books and homework and bags into their children's hands.

Piper dropped to her knees to one side of the gate and pulled Madelyn into a tight hug.

"Be a good girl today," she said. "Don't forget to bring your homework home, and I'll help you with it before dinner."

Madelyn nodded against Piper's neck, then pulled back. She glanced at Caleb, then both fixed their eyes on Piper. They looked so different; Caleb with dark skin and hair, Madelyn with fair colouring, a smattering of freckles across her nose already, and white-blonde hair.

Caleb caught his sister's hand, squeezing it. "Will you come and get us early if you find Mum?" he asked.

Piper smiled at him and ruffled his hair. He pulled back with a frown. "I can't promise that," she said. "Learning is important. But I do promise I'll do everything I can."

Caleb's frown turned into a scowl. But, slowly, he nodded. "All right," he said.

Piper squeezed his arm. For a moment, Caleb let her.

Then he stepped back, breaking the contact. He looked over Piper's shoulder, and Piper looked up in time to see Rylan nod to them both.

"Have a good day," Rylan said.

Madelyn smiled up at him. Then she grabbed Caleb's hand and dragged him towards the school entrance. Piper rose, watching as they vanished behind the ivy-covered gates. Then she turned. Rylan stood behind her, bloody handkerchief in one hand. His nose was purpling, and blood streaked his top lip where he'd clearly tried to wipe it off.

She sighed. "Come on," she said. "Healer's this way."

Piper stood outside the cafe opposite the healer's office, a coffee in one hand. She leaned against the corner of the building, debating.

She could try leaving. He'd never notice until he'd finished with the healer. Noses were one of the few broken bones healers would set, possibly because the cartilage was so easy to manipulate. When he came out, he'd be good as new.

Not that he was any good new. Or any way, really.

But, if she stayed with him, she could find a way to drop him in Lore's lap. Something had gone wrong with the poison, but a knife to the heart or throat would drop him for certain.

Piper rubbed her forehead, feeling a headache building there.

"You didn't get me one."

She snapped her head up to find Rylan standing in front of her, arms crossed. His nose was straight again, and its usual colour, no traces of blood on his face. Piper narrowed her eyes at him.

"I don't know you," she said. "I don't like you. Why would I get you a coffee?"

"Peace offering?" Rylan said, one of his eyebrows lifting. "Bribery so I don't get you arrested?"

Piper snorted. "You assume I can be arrested. Are you calling the army?" Bravado never went astray. She'd learned that early on with Lore and Saxe.

Rylan just shook his head. "Don't go anywhere." He vanished into the cafe.

Piper seethed, glaring at his back as he stood at the counter. Then, just to spite him, she moved to lean against the building opposite. When Rylan left the cafe, he looked at the spot she'd been standing and glared. A flash of dark blue appeared around his hand for a split second. Then he looked up and met Piper's gaze across the street. Coffee cup in hand, Rylan stalked over the cobbles towards her.

"You try my patience, Bella," he said.

"Do not call me that," Piper snapped.

"I'll stop calling you that if you tell me who hired you," he retorted.

"I already told you, I don't know," Piper snapped, her free hand flying to her hip.

Rylan stared at her for a moment. Then he gestured to the street. "Well? Where does your friend live?"

Piper took half a step back, her boot bumping into the stone wall. She couldn't tell if he believed her or not. "Why do you want to know that?" she asked suspiciously.

Rylan rubbed his eyes with his thumb and forefinger. "I told you last night," he said slowly, like he thought she wasn't all there. "I want to look around where she went missing from."

Piper gritted her teeth. "You assume I'll just let you into her house."

"Why are you fighting me so hard?" he asked instead of replying.

Piper blinked at him for a moment, certain she'd misheard. "I don't know you," she repeated.

Rylan shook his head. "Haven't you ever worked with someone before?" he asked. "It generally works better if you are at least civil to them."

"I don't work well with others," Piper said, fingers finding her stiletto through the fabric of her coat. Rylan caught the move and clearly guessed what she was doing. He narrowed his eyes.

"Well that's too bad, because you're stuck with me," he said, taking a sip of his coffee. "I won't let you take those two children and run again." He met her eyes. "That's what I thought you were doing this morning."

She couldn't deny that she'd thought of it. "You still shouldn't have grabbed me."

"Noted." The corner of Rylan's mouth twisted up in a smirk, and Piper scowled at him. "Now, where does your friend live?"

Piper wavered for a moment longer. Finally, she huffed.

"This way."

Rylan trailed her through the city, not commenting as they took a tram and then wound through the narrow streets on the poor side of the Market District. They turned onto Abby's street, greeted by the riot of colour that was the puka's garden. The female puka stood on the porch, a tray of seedlings in front of her. She looked up at the sound of Piper and Rylan's footsteps.

Her gaze slid over the mage, but she offered Piper a smile and a nod. Piper waved back before they passed on.

The mage said nothing as Piper led him through the bare garden and up the stairs into Abby's little apartment. Piper paused inside the door. It looked much the same as when she'd left two days ago, Caleb and Madelyn in tow. The spider web in the corner had grown a little, but the pot was still in pieces across the floor, utensils still scattered, and the bathroom door was still off its hinges.

Behind Piper, Rylan hummed.

"What?" she asked, stepping to the side.

"Not sure yet," he murmured, slowly peering around the apartment. It took two long steps before he stood in the centre of the small room.

Piper shivered, rubbing at her arms, and turned away from him. She would ignore the main room. There wasn't much there, and that was where the mage was doing ... something. Piper was certain she didn't want to know what that something was.

Instead, she stepped into the bathroom. The smear of blood on the floor had darkened to brown, stark against the pale, chipped tiles. Her foot nudged something, and Piper looked down. A hairbrush lay half in the shadows behind the open door, its handle sticking out. Piper knelt, looking it over.

It was Abby's, she was pretty certain. That round barrel would be useless brushing something like Piper's curls or Madelyn's ringlets, but would be perfect for Abby's straight brown hair. Abby wasn't terribly vain, but she did like to look her best if she was heading out. She'd use the barrel to try and get some volume into it, so it didn't look so thin and limp.

She'd been getting ready to go somewhere, then. Piper's gaze flicked over to the counter, where a compact of foundation lay open, a sponge next to it spreading orange-tinged powder over the counter.

"Find anything?"

The voice made Piper jump and let out a very girlish yelp. Her head smacked into the door handle, hard.

"Owowowowow *fate*." Cradling the top of her head in both hands, Piper plopped down and glared up at Rylan, standing over her. His mouth hung open, and he blinked down at her in shock. "If you like yourself not stabbed, don't ever sneak up on me! I'd have thought you learned that this morning!"

"Looks to me like you're hurting yourself right now, more than me," he said.

Piper glared at him – she couldn't refute that, not when her crown set up a steady throbbing that reminded her of the kind of bass music played at the nightclubs in the Market District at two in the morning.

Rylan sighed. "Do you need a healer?" he asked.

"No!" Piper said so sharply he started. "No healers." Piper forced her feet underneath her and stood, even though the movement made the top of her head throb.

For a moment, Rylan stared at her. Then he held up both hands in a placating gesture. "All right," he said. "No healers." He jerked his chin behind her. "What did you find?"

Piper massaged the top of her head gingerly and turned back to the room.

"Abby was getting ready to go out when someone attacked her," she said, gesturing to the brush on the floor and the makeup on the counter. "Where she would have been going, I don't know. It wasn't a school day, so she would have had to leave Madelyn and Caleb alone."

Piper winced, guilt spiking through her. Rylan noticed.

"What?" he demanded, closing the distance between them. "What is it? Do you know where she is? Where they might have–"

"No!" Piper snapped, just to shut him up. "No, I just ... It's nothing, okay?"

Rylan crossed his arms and set his legs, staring down at her. "It's not okay." She felt ... something roll off him, and had to force herself not to shiver again.

Piper stepped out of the bathroom, looking around the main room as an excuse to put some space between them. Rylan stalked out of the room after her. The back of her neck prickled as Rylan crossed the room, towering over her with his arms crossed. "I need you to tell me what you're thinking," he said.

"I don't need to tell you anything," Piper snapped. "This whole intimidation thing won't work with me, Rylan. I've faced off against scarier men than you before breakfast."

Rylan uncrossed his arms. He took a breath, rubbing both hands over his face, being careful of his newly healed and probably still tender nose. "I'm not trying to intimidate you," he said, his voice muffled. Then he dropped his hands and met her gaze. "Bella–"

"Stop calling me that!" Piper yelled.

"I'm not–" Then he took another deep breath and held out his hands. "I'm not trying to intimidate you," he repeated. "I'm trying to figure out what happened here. I need to find him. I can't make you understand how important this is."

"You actually care, don't you?" Piper asked, curious despite herself. He seemed personally invested in this search, more than if it were just his job. "Why?"

Rylan grimaced. "I ..." He shook his head. "I just do, okay?"

Piper crossed her arms, glaring at him.

Rylan sighed. "I ... The High Lady hired me as Jai's tutor straight out of uni, no experience beyond teaching classes to first years in Everhill. He's only seventeen." He held out his hands. "I've seen you with those two children. You understand wanting to protect someone."

Piper rubbed her arms. "Seventeen isn't so young," she said.

To her surprise, Rylan shot her a half smile. "I suppose it might not seem like it to you," he said. "I don't think I want to know what you were doing at that age. But he's not you. He's a young seventeen."

At seventeen, she'd ... Yeah. She didn't really want to remember what she was doing at that age, either.

Piper huffed. "All right," she said. "I get it. You're looking out for people too."

She shivered, the chill in the air going down her spine. Glancing around the room again, she noticed a slight fog had formed on the glass of the windows.

"Will you please tell me what you were thinking before?" Rylan asked. Piper could hear, in his voice, the effort it cost him to be polite to her.

"I just ... The last time I was here, I had a big fight with Abby over her leaving the kids here alone." She rubbed the top of her head distractedly and checked the palm of her hand – no blood. "That's all. Nothing that would help you with finding your... friend." She couldn't make herself say the word prince out loud. It felt too absurd, like this was some kind of sick joke.

"Well, it's ..." Rylan started, then trailed off.

Piper glanced at him, to find him frowning at the same windows Piper had just noted. "What?" she asked, hugging her elbows.

"Do you feel that?"

Piper shook her head. "Feel what?" she asked.

He looked at her, taking in how she had her arms huddled around herself, hands rubbing at the thick feeling against her arms. "That," he said, pointing to her hand.

Piper glanced down, but there was nothing there. "I don't–"

Rylan's face went white. "Get out," he said.

Piper took a step back from him. "What?"

"Out!"

153

He didn't wait for her to respond. Rylan grabbed Piper by the arm and leaped across the room, physically dragging her out of the apartment behind him.

"Ow!" Piper yelped, tripping down the stairs and into the street. "What—"

Behind her, she felt a great, rushing cold. Piper spun, yanking her arm out of Rylan's painful grip.

Hoarfrost coated the inside of all the windows. Frost radiated out of the doorway in a spiderweb pattern, circling around the doorway on the porch. The old, ratty curtains stood stiff in the windows.

Piper took a step forward, but a hand wrapped around her arm.

"The last time you did that, you got your nose broken," she forced out. Her voice sounded strangled, and Piper cleared her throat.

"Yeah, I have a feeling you won't be breaking it this time," Rylan said weakly. He let go of her and crept forward. "Stay behind me," he said.

"Trust me, Rylan, I have no plans of approaching this much magic," she said. Her voice was stronger this time, though Piper couldn't stop herself from wrapping her arms around her chest again, hugging her elbows.

In response Rylan just said, "Hm."

Piper stopped at the edge of the porch, not quite game to climb the stairs. Rylan took them all in one step. He tapped the frost with his foot, then hissed in pain.

"Fate that's cold," he said, thumping the side of his boot against the porch. Ice dripped into the garden.

"Why isn't it melting?" Piper asked.

"Magic," Rylan said. "It was a mage trap, set here to catch whoever came in. Most likely me, maybe you."

"But I was here before," she argued. "With Madelyn and Caleb."

Rylan shrugged, leaning through the doorway to peer around inside. "Maybe there was some kind of time lapse on it," he said, sounding distracted.

He turned to face her. Piper's arms were tightly wrapped around herself. He frowned.

"What?" Piper snapped, shoving down a feeling of self-consciousness under his scrutiny.

"Do you feel it again?" he asked, his voice deathly quiet.

"Feel what?" Piper asked.

Rylan jumped off the porch. He beckoned, and Piper gladly followed him out of the garden and into the street. There, Rylan examined her, his blue gaze taking her in from the top of her head to the bottom of her boots.

"What you felt inside," he said. "I should have noticed it earlier. You were rubbing your arms almost as soon as we walked in."

Piper forced herself to let go of her elbows. "So?" she asked uncomfortably. Her fingers twitched, wanting to wrap back around her, but Piper held them down by force of will.

Rylan's eyes narrowed, like he knew what was happening.

"How long have you been able to feel magic?" he asked her.

Piper blinked at him. "I'm sorry?" she said.

Rylan gestured back towards the apartment. Despite the warm spring day, the ice showed no sign of melting.

"I've only met one person who would feel magic like that before." He rubbed his chin. "She was a particularly talented warlock." He cocked his head to the side, his eyes fixing on Piper's. "Your eyes–"

"I am not a warlock!" Piper snapped. "I am not a mage!"

"Your eyes are just the right colour of silver that if you had a warlock starburst, and it was silver instead of gold, no one would be able to tell," he said. "Of course you're a mage. Your *illis* is so strong I could track you across the city with it."

Piper's mouth popped open. "Rylan," she said a moment later. "I don't know how else to tell you this. I am not a mage. I have no magic."

"Unless you were tested when you were thirteen and seventeen, you may not know," Rylan insisted. "Many mages don't know they have magic until something truly traumatic happens–"

"Trust me," Piper interrupted, proud her voice didn't break. "If my magic hasn't flared by now, it never will. All humans have an *illis*. That doesn't make me a mage." Rylan opened his mouth, presumably to argue again, but Piper looked away. "Can we just …" She gestured back to the apartment and took a step towards it.

Rylan caught her arm. "No," he said. "We can't go back in there. No one can, actually." He let go of her to rub his hand over his face again – a habit, it seemed, when he was thinking. "I need to go get the constabulary on this. If anyone goes in, and that mage trap goes off again, it will kill them."

"But it was just a little ice," she said.

Rylan shook his head. "Make no mistake," he murmured, "if we had been inside, it would have frozen us solid. That was some powerful magic. I almost didn't feel it until it was too late."

He sighed.

"Come on," he said. "I need to think about this. Let's go and find the police, and then get a coffee and something to eat."

He turned from her, heading back down the lane. His stride was a bit shorter than it had been before.

Piper glanced over her shoulder at the apartment. Frost covered the doorframe and the inside of the windows. Through the open door, Piper could see the couch; it looked like it had been left out in a blizzard.

She shivered, then jogged to catch up with Rylan.

FIFTEEN

Piper hung back as Rylan spoke with two police officers. One, a tall wood elf with dark skin, had a purple streak through the front of his black hair. The other, Piper assumed his watch partner, had furry white ears sticking up through his pale hair; he must be some kind of puka, though she couldn't see his tail from this angle.

They both nodded at Rylan, and the wood elf clasped Rylan's forearm. Then they turned and strode away.

"Well?" Piper asked when the mage rejoined her.

He yanked at his hair, pulling it out of its horsetail just to gather it and tie it off again. "They're looking into it," he said. "Liam – Inspector Riveralli, the wood elf – he's a mage too. He'll make sure no one enters the place until I or someone else has had a look at it and made sure it's not dangerous."

"You ..." But there were too many things in that statement to question. Piper shook her head. "I thought elves couldn't be mages?"

"Hm?" Rylan glanced at her. "Oh. He's half human. His human side gives him his magic, his elven side his appearance."

"Oh," Piper said.

"Come on," he said, changing the subject and taking off down the street. "I'm hungry. Chasing after you this morning meant I skipped breakfast."

"How can you be hungry?" Piper had no choice but to follow him, if she didn't want him trailing her through the city again, apparently following her *illis*. Stupid mages. "We're looking for missing people. Doesn't that just kill your appetite?"

"Nothing kills my appetite," Rylan said. "Do you like burgers?"

Piper blinked at him, pausing on the spot. "Burgers?"

"Yes, burgers," Rylan answered distractedly. Before she could say anything else, the mage had already moved away down the street, his attention fixed on something in the distance.

Sighing, Piper started after him.

She caught up to Rylan as he paused outside a restaurant. Piper looked through the doors to see inside.

Booths littered the space, not unlike the booths in The Lily. These were all brightly coloured, the vinyl seats torn and patched with different colours. Paintings hung over almost every inch of the walls, masking the white paint behind more colours and shapes. She spotted a caricature of the Lord Trader, a universally disliked man called Gervas who controlled trade and commerce for the nation.

Rylan pushed the glass door open.

"Alec!" a waitress, blonde hair in a thick braid down her back, bundled up to them, beaming. "We haven't seen you for a while!"

He smiled at her. "Hi, Janie," he said. "I've been busy."

The waitress grabbed a menu from the stand near the door and gestured to him. "Come on, then," she said. "Your booth's free."

"Thanks," Rylan said. Janie turned her back, and Rylan gestured to Piper over his shoulder as he followed her.

Piper blinked, rubbing the top of her still sore head again, and crossed the room. The tiles under her feet were cool, a black-and-white check pattern that had been mopped perfectly clean. Rylan slid into one side of the booth, the red vinyl creaking under his weight. Piper dropped into the opposite side, her seat royal blue.

Janie placed the menu in front of Piper and smiled at Rylan. "Your usual?" she said, and he nodded.

"Yes, thanks, Janie," he said.

Janie smiled. Then she turned her attention to Piper. "And you?" she asked.

Piper scanned the menu. She wasn't entirely certain what half of the items were.

Janie and Rylan waited on her answer.

"Um ..." Piper's gaze flicked over the paper, searching for something even recognisable. "The grilled chicken." At least she knew what that meant. She'd never even heard of an Elswye-spiced pork pattie before.

"One healer burger and two fighter burgers coming up!" Janie said cheerfully. She grabbed Piper's menu, then turned away from them.

"You come to a burger place and you order the grilled chicken?" Rylan asked her.

Piper ignored him. She glanced around the diner, then leaned forward, her elbows on the table. "Did the inspectors say anything else?"

Rylan rubbed both hands over his face, then leaned back. "Not a lot," he admitted. "Just that they would keep people away from the area, and not let anyone inside."

The idea of Beks coming home to ice on the doorstep and going inside to check on Abby and the kids was ... unpleasant. Especially if that ice was as powerful as the mage said it was. Knowing the site would be guarded eased a tension in her chest that she hadn't realised was there.

"How do mage traps work?" Piper found herself asking.

Under the table, Rylan crossed one ankle over his opposite knee.

"Mage traps are a djinn invention," he said after a moment. "They used to be called kali traps, after their most powerful sub-species. Essentially, they trap a mage and draw them inside a bubble of magic, with the intention of killing them. Some mage traps are mental, and some are physical," he added. "Either way, the point is they ensnare you unless you can break free."

"How do you break free?" Piper asked.

"By being stronger than the person who cast the trap," Rylan replied. He reached out, fiddling with the salt shaker in the middle of the table. Piper watched as he spun the cylinder of wood around and around and around and ...

"How do you know if you're stronger than them?" Piper asked after a long moment.

Rylan gave a humourless laugh. "You get caught in the trap and break it," he told her.

"So, we ..."

"Were lucky." Rylan shrugged one shoulder. "The trap was just preparing. If we'd been there for even a moment longer ... Well. We'd have found out if I'm more powerful than whoever cast it, I suppose."

Piper stared at him, wide-eyed.

"It's never a good idea to mess around with mage traps," he said.

Piper said nothing. Instead, she sat back in her chair, rubbing her right wrist, the wrist Rylan had grabbed the night she'd tried to kill him.

"How did you survive it?" The question popped out before Piper could stop it.

Rylan blinked at her. He opened his mouth to reply–

"Here you are," Janie appeared at their table again, sliding two large glasses of water and two bowls of hot chips towards them. "Your burgers will only be a minute."

"Thanks, Janie," Rylan said.

Piper glanced around the room as the waitress left. It was quiet enough that no one was close to overhear them – but a quiet room meant their voices would carry. Piper took her glass between her hands, rolling it between her palms. Perhaps this wasn't the best place for this conversation.

Rylan took a chip from the bowl closest to him. A crease appeared between his brows.

"I don't really remember much," he said after a moment. "One of the guards was a healer. The other guard dragged us together. The next thing I knew, the High Lady was there." He met Piper's gaze. "She's a very powerful healer. She forced the poison out of me." His eyes narrowed. "What was in it?"

Piper pursed her lips. She looked at the wall, taking sudden interest in a screen print of purple unicorns standing over an orange lake in a field of blue grass.

"I was sick for days," Rylan said.

"You shouldn't have survived," Piper murmured before she could stop herself. Rylan shot her a look, and she crossed her arms. "No one has before."

"I won't apologise for spoiling your perfect record," he said dryly.

Janie appeared at that moment, a plate in each hand. She slid one down in front of Piper – grilled chicken and salad on a toasted, seeded bun – and the other, she handed to Rylan.

Piper stared.

He had two burgers. Each was huge, with two meat patties, several slices of cheese and a stack of other fillings. He lifted one to his mouth, then quirked his eyebrow at Piper.

"What?" he asked.

Piper just shook her head. Turning her attention to her own food, she cut her burger delicately into quarters. When she looked up again, half of his first burger was already gone.

"How do you eat like that?" Piper asked, half awed, half disgusted.

Rylan swallowed his bite before answering. "I like food," he said, shrugging. Then, when Piper glared at him, he added, "My *illis* burns a lot of calories. I need to eat a lot."

Piper dabbed her fingers on a napkin, reached for one of her chips – they were perfect, thick cut and crispy on the outside, fluffy and light on the inside – and pointed at him with it.

"I've never heard or read anywhere that an *illis* would burn that many calories," she said.

Rylan started to reply. Then his gaze fixed on her wrist.

His blue eyes widened.

"What?" Piper turned her hand over.

She gasped.

Around her wrist, where Rylan had grabbed her in what she thought were his death throes, a shadow moved under her skin.

She dropped her chip with a yelp. She scratched at the skin, but that did nothing to stop dark lines from forming, coiling around her wrist like a snake. Scales defined themselves. Legs. And then wings.

Piper sucked in a breath as the shadows solidified into the shape of a dragon, wrapped around and around and around her wrist.

"So that's why he told me to grab you," Rylan breathed.

Piper turned to him. "What did you do to me?" she demanded.

Rylan held up both hands. "I didn't do anything," he protested.

"You sure as fate did!" Piper snapped, shaking her wrist at him.

Rylan caught her hand and pushed it down to the table, glancing around.

"Stop that," he murmured. "You're causing a scene."

"I will cause a scene if I fate-damned want!" Piper jabbed his chest. "What. Did you. Do. To me?" She punctuated the words with pokes until Rylan caught her hand, forcing her to stop.

"Firstly, like I said, I didn't do anything," he said.

"Bull!" Piper snapped. "It's exactly where you grabbed me when I ..."

She trailed off, realising how loud she was talking. Across the room, Janie busied herself with the napkin holders. A couple near the window cast disgruntled looks at her and Rylan.

Piper stood. "I'm leaving," she hissed.

"For fate's sake!" Rylan stood as well. Even across the booth, he towered over her. He grabbed her arms and pushed her back down. "Sit and listen. Just listen for a moment."

Piper looked down at her wrist. The thick lines there shone like oil on water, not quite black but a kind of beetling colour, with red and green and blue all thrown in at the same time. The reflections changed when she twisted her wrist, the marks catching the light.

The bottom of her stomach yawned. She'd read about marks like these. Ones that looked like a mirage on the skin, where the colour never quite settled.

"You've got a fate mark on your arm," Rylan said.

SIXTEEN

Piper shook her head, hard. It didn't make any sense. There was no way.

Why by fate would someone choose me for a fate mark?

Her gaze snapped up. To the open collar of Rylan's button-up shirt. To the mark there, curling up the column of his throat. The one that glistened, not quite black, like oil on water.

Piper pointed, words sticking in her throat. Rylan glanced down, then lay a hand over his neck, grimacing.

"Well, yeah," he said, answering her unspoken question. "Like I said. This is clearly why he told me to grab you."

Piper stared at him. *He?*

"You gave your tattoo a gender?"

"It's a fate mark, not a tattoo," he said. "It's literally a connection to an Immortal. Yes, he has a gender. Yours does too."

Piper looked down again. Under her pale shirt, she could just make out faint lines curling further up her arm, to her shoulder. It looked like it was still growing.

"I don't understand," she whispered.

Rylan sighed and sat back. He touched the mark on his throat. "I suppose, if she's marked too, that means I can't have her arrested if she annoys me, hm?" Piper blinked at him. It didn't seem like he was talking to her.

A moment later, he chuckled. "I'll keep that in mind."

"You talk to your …?"

Rylan shrugged one shoulder. "I talk to my Immortal," he said. "You probably could too, if you tried."

"Nope." Piper shook her head. "Not going to happen." She held out her arm to him. "Get it off."

Rylan stared at her for a moment, shock written across his face. Then he laughed.

"You're kidding, right?" he said.

"You're a mage," Piper argued. "Get it off."

Rylan shook his head. "I'm good," he said, "but I can't make an Immortal do what it doesn't want to do."

"It doesn't want me!" Piper snapped. "It's made a mistake."

A rumbling started on her wrist. It travelled up her arm, reverberating through her body. Piper swallowed as she realised what it was.

A growl.

As quickly as it had started, it stopped. Piper stared down at her hand, at the whip-like tail wrapping around her wrist.

Rylan leaned forward. "What did he say?" he asked.

Piper crossed her arms tightly. "Nothing," she said. "No one said anything."

Rylan sighed. "Whatever you want to tell yourself," he said, turning his attention back to his meal.

Piper picked at her burger, her attention fixed on the mark around her arm. It wasn't until Rylan stared at her expectantly that she realised he'd asked her a question. "I'm sorry?" she said.

"I said, what do you know about Shiv'ek?"

"They're ... Chaos Demons, right?" she hedged.

Rylan nodded. "They're not just *any* Chaos Demon, though." Both burgers and all of his chips were just ... gone from his plate, Piper noticed. "They're the most powerful Chaos Demons."

"What makes them more powerful?" Piper asked, curious.

Rylan shot her a look that, for the first time, she thought might be close to approving. But that was a stupid thought. She didn't care if he approved of her or not.

Piper pinched her leg, hard, under the table.

"They're like Immortals," he admitted. "Undying unless killed, very strong, and extremely magical. They also have some powers the Immortals don't, or won't, use. I'm not sure which, and Laithos hasn't expanded on that."

Piper let that sink in. There were several things she didn't understand, but one main one stood out. "Laithos?" she asked.

"Mm hmm." Rylan reached across the table and stole a chip from her bowl. Then he tapped the tattoo on his throat. "Laithos."

"Oh." She didn't know what else she could say to that one, except that it was madness to give a tattoo, even a fate mark, a name.

The growling sound echoed through her again, and Piper flinched.

Rylan narrowed his eyes at her. Piper blurted out the first thing she could think of to avoid the question she was certain was coming. "And why do you feel the sudden need to educate me about Shiv'ek?"

"Ah." Rylan sat back, grimacing. He rubbed his forehead with the back of his hand, then met her gaze again. "Well ..."

"Spit it out, Rylan," Piper snapped when he trailed off again.

"You know that magic you felt at the apartment?" he asked.

Piper shook her head. "I don't know what I felt," she insisted, though part of her screamed that was a lie. She'd definitely noticed a slimy, heavy feeling pressing at her bare arms, pushing against her like thick, oily water. She shivered, wrapping her arms around herself, her appetite well and truly gone. Rylan, on the other hand, reached across the table again, stealing another chip.

"Well," he said, "the magic there. I'm ninety-nine per cent certain it was Shivian magic."

For several long seconds, Piper stared at him.

"You're saying that the person who took Abby was—"

"A Shiv'ek, yes," Rylan said, nodding.

Piper's stomach churned. She pressed a hand to her chest, forcing herself to suck in a long breath through her nose.

"Let me check I understand this," she said after a moment. "The person who took Abby is more powerful than an Immortal?"

"At least as powerful," Rylan admitted, "and likely less moral."

Piper's hand, pressed to her shirt, was shaking. "Fate," she whispered, not able to make a sound more coherent than that.

Rylan crossed his arms, regarding her. Piper glanced at him and forced her hand to drop into her lap.

"There's more, isn't there?" She wasn't sure how she knew it. But one look at Rylan's expression, the set of his mouth and tension at the corners of his eyes, told her she was right.

Rylan sighed.

"Shivian or not," he said softly, "it matches the feeling left behind where Jai was taken too."

"Oh." There was nothing else she could think of to say.

Rylan nodded grimly, reaching for another of Piper's chips. She pushed the bowl across to him. Rylan's eyebrows forked up, and he opened his mouth.

"Save it," Piper said before he could get a word in. "I'm done, anyway."

"You sure?" he asked.

Piper nodded. The mage helped himself to Piper's chips, while Piper brought one foot up on the bench seat and wrapped her arms around her knee. Her gaze slid over the unicorn painting and landed on the one next to it, of orange griffins whirling over blue buildings on yellow ground.

"How do you know it's Shivian magic?" she murmured after a moment.

Rylan glanced at her. "I don't for certain. But ... I read a lot. And, having felt both places, the magic is definitely the same." He propped his chin in his hand and looked at her. "It'd be interesting to see if you could feel the magic in the palace library, but it was a month ago now. It's faded."

"Hang on." Piper held up a hand. She hissed out the question, in case Janie was eavesdropping as she walked past. "He vanished from the palace?"

Rylan nodded. "Yup." He looked like he'd sucked on a lemon, his lips pursed together so hard they almost vanished. "Right underneath our noses."

"Huh." Piper sat back in her seat, watching him.

He stared towards the far wall, a frown between his brows. His blue gaze was dark and heavy, and the fingers on his right hand tapped repetitively on the tabletop, the remainder of Piper's chips forgotten in front of him. He blinked, then his gaze slid to Piper again.

"What?" he said.

Piper shook her head. "Nothing."

A rumbling started at her wrist again. Piper tensed, but ... the tone was different this time. It was less growling, and more ... purring?

Did dragons purr?

"If you're done," Rylan said, "we should head out. We've only got a few hours before Caleb and Madelyn are finished with school for the day."

"Right." Piper rubbed both hands over her face. "Fate."

SEVENTEEN

They tried some of the places Piper knew Abby had worked waiting tables at recently. Then some of the shops she and the prince might both have visited; there were not many of those. The kinds of shops Abby could afford didn't generally cater to royalty.

Hours later, they stood in the middle of Illusion Square, waiting for the line in front of them to move so they could replenish their caffeine.

Piper rubbed her eyes. "Fate," she muttered.

Beside her, Rylan nodded. "That about sums it up," he agreed.

"This is what you've been doing?" Piper asked. "For a month?"

"Yup." Rylan rubbed his forehead and sighed. "A fate-damned month, and nothing to show for it."

The lady in front of them made an affronted noise. Casting a dirty look back over her shoulder, she tugged her child – maybe three or four years old, Piper thought – away from Rylan and his swearing. Piper chuckled under her breath.

"What?" Rylan asked as they closed the gap.

"Just thinking, if she's affronted by you saying 'fate,' she's in for a nasty surprise in the rest of the city, is all." She shrugged, and Rylan laughed as well.

"I forget to censor myself," he admitted.

"Yes, I'd noticed." She recalled his muffled, oddly pronounced words when she'd broken his nose that morning.

They stepped up to the coffee stall – one of the best in the city – and Piper ordered her latte. She paid, then stepped aside.

"A double shot long black, please," Rylan ordered. "Three sugars."

Piper blinked at him. "You're kidding me, right?" she asked.

"Hm?" Rylan glanced at her, handing over a copper note.

"Three sugars?" Piper shook her head.

Rylan pushed at her arm, and Piper stepped to the side so the next person could order.

"What?" he asked. "There's nothing wrong with sugar in coffee."

"Yes, there is." There was something wrong with sugar in anything, as far as Piper was concerned.

Piper looked away from the coffee stall, her gaze sliding over the square. In the distance, she could see a few girls in long dresses gathered around the paned windows of a millinery. Hats. Piper shook her head. She'd never understood them. But, looking at those young ladies, they might be coming back into fashion.

One of the girls turned, tossing long brown hair. Even from this distance, Piper thought she caught a flash of green eyes.

She sucked in a breath.

"What?" Rylan asked.

Piper tapped her fingers against her leg. "I can't believe I didn't think of that," she breathed.

"Think of what?"

"Latte and long black, three sugars!" The girl called out their coffee orders. Taking them with a distracted smile, Piper shoved the sugary concoction into Rylan's hand.

"Come on," she said. "I have an idea."

Piper led Rylan at a brisk clip through the city. At least, it was a brisk clip for her; Rylan just lengthened his stride, his long legs allowing him to easily keep up with Piper. She hurried towards the archway that led into the Mage's Quarter, and Glimmer Street. Here, Rylan paused. He caught Piper's arm, drawing her to a stop on the footpath beside him.

"You know," he said, "I'd really rather not involve any mages we don't have to."

Piper brushed him off. "I don't like mages, either," she said. "But Aliana might know where they are."

"What?" She heard Rylan's question behind her as she moved, but Piper didn't bother to stop and answer him. She turned a corner, then went into the narrow alleyway.

Rylan didn't answer as Piper pushed open the entry door.

She rapped on the timber briskly. "Aliana?" she called.

There was no answer.

Frowning, Piper reached out. The handle turned smoothly under her fingers.

"What …?" Piper murmured, as the door opened and she stepped inside.

It looked like no one had ever lived here. All the furniture was still there. But it all looked new, like it had just been bought. There was not a speck of dust or a cobweb anywhere.

Footsteps thudded on timber behind her, and Piper turned. A smaller man jumped the last two stairs on the staircase, then looked up.

"Good afternoon!" he called, his face breaking into a smile. "Are you here to look at the apartment for lease?"

"For lease?" Piper glanced around. "I was looking for the lady who lived here not two days ago."

"Ah, her." He offered Piper a small smile. "She said she had an emergency, and had to go home. Shame to lose a great tenant, but what can you do?" He stepped inside the apartment, looking Piper over. "You know, this would make a great apartment. If your friend came back to the city, she might come looking to rent this back. If you lived here, she'd find you right away." His gaze flickered over to Rylan, and back to Piper. "It's got three bedrooms and a yard. A great place to start a family."

Piper barely bit back a snort. Behind her, Rylan coughed.

"Thanks," Piper forced out. "I'll think about it. Do you know where she went?"

The landlord shook his head. "No, I'm sorry," he said. "She didn't leave any contact details. Settled all the bills before she left."

"Right," Piper said. "Thanks anyway."

Much to the man's disappointment, Piper led Rylan back out of the apartment building. On the street, she rubbed the back of her neck, stretching out her back and groaning.

"That would have been too easy, wouldn't it?" she asked, speaking mostly to no one. "To have a seer point us in the right direction?"

Rylan grunted. "She might not have known, anyway," he said.

"She always seemed to know everything." Piper glanced back over her shoulder to find him frowning down at her. "She knew how to get to you."

His frown deepened. "How *did* you do that?" he asked.

"There's a weak spot in the fence near the Church of Nyssa," she said, waving her hand dismissively. "I climbed it there."

Rylan narrowed his eyes at her suspiciously. "You're just telling me this? What do you want in exchange for this information?"

Piper gestured to the path in front of them and stepped forward.

"Nothing," she said truthfully, her boots tapping on the cobbled street. "It's not like I need to sneak back in there to get to you. You've very conveniently put yourself in the room across the hall from me. As for the future ... I told you, no royals."

The *bong, bong, bong-bong-bong* of quarter to three rang through the city, and Piper swore.

"Fate, I'm going to be late!"

They arrived at the school at ten minutes past three, Piper's breath sawing in and out of her lungs. She straightened her shoulders, propping her hands on her hips to open up her chest and help her recover after the mad dash. Beside her, Rylan wasn't any better. Despite his long legs, Piper was fast, and he'd had to work to keep up with her.

But he had kept up, she had to admit grudgingly. And he hadn't complained once while he did.

"Well," Rylan said after a moment. "That was fun."

Piper chewed on her bottom lip, watching the mage out of the corner of her eye while most of her attention stayed on the students starting to trickle out of the school gate. She'd barely even thought, that entire day, about how to kill him and dump him into Lore's lap. She sighed, gingerly running a hand over the top of her head. If Abby's disappearance really was linked to the prince, maybe it would be good to have him around. Maybe he'd help her find Abby.

Pain throbbed through her temple, and through the bump on the top of her head.

"What are you scowling at?"

Piper smoothed her expression. "Nothing."

"Uh huh." Rylan rolled his eyes. "If you keep doing that, you'll end up with wrinkles."

Piper snorted. "I'm twenty-three," she said. "I don't think I have to worry about wrinkles just yet." Rylan glanced at her, but Piper ignored him as another flash of pale hair made it through the gate.

"Piper!"

Piper stepped forward, dropping to her knees as Madelyn flew at her. Piper wrapped the little girl in a tight hug, burying her face against blonde hair.

Caleb approached them more slowly. When Piper looked up, she caught him staring up at Rylan. Then his attention slid back to Piper.

"Did you find Mum?" he asked by way of greeting.

A lump lodged in Piper's throat, and she swallowed.

"Not yet," she admitted. "But I promise we won't stop until we find her."

Piper, at least, would never stop looking.

Caleb's face fell. Piper reached for him, but he stepped back.

Rylan clasped him on the shoulder. "Come on," he said, forcing a cheerful smile – for Caleb's benefit, Piper assumed. "Let's head back. I'm sure you're hungry, right?"

"Yep!" Madelyn threw out her arms, smacking into a woman's leg as she passed. Piper sighed and caught Madelyn's hands.

"Come on," she said.

EIGHTEEN

The next two days passed much the same. Piper, mage in tow, would drop Caleb and Madelyn off at school in the morning. Then, the two of them would spend the day in the city, searching in strange corners, talking to people and doing everything else the two of them could think of.

So far, they had no leads; not on the prince, nor on Abby.

That afternoon, Rylan shot Piper and the kids a distracted nod, then vanished up the stairs towards the rooms. Piper stayed downstairs long enough to check with Patrik – no, there was still no message for her – and to organise two hot chocolates and a coffee, a homework treat. Rose promised to bring the drinks up to their room.

Piper took Madelyn's hand and took both children upstairs, through the door Patrik had repaired the day after Rylan broke it down. Madelyn dumped her backpack inside the door and ran into her bedroom. Caleb followed her, his own bag bouncing on his back. Piper stooped and picked up the bag, then rubbed the muscles at the back of her neck, trying desperately to convince the tension lingering there to fade, just enough that she could get the kids through homework and dinner.

A knock sounded on the door. Piper blinked, shaking off her despondency. Dropping Madelyn's bag at the dining table, she turned and pulled the door open.

She'd been expecting Rose with their drinks. Maybe Rylan, a frown fixed on his face.

She hadn't expected two grey-uniformed police, the orange bands of Highkeep around their upper arms, to be standing there.

"Miss, erm …" The first officer scanned a piece of paper in his hands, clearly looking for a surname. When he found none, he looked up at her. "Piper?"

"Yes?" Piper said carefully. Her grip around the door handle tightened at the look the two officers exchanged. She eased her weight back on one foot, readying herself to move.

"May we come in?" the second guard asked.

"I'd really rather you didn't," Piper said, bracing one foot behind the door.

There was movement at the top of the stairs. Piper's gaze flicked that way. Another police officer, an older one with ranking stripes wrapped around his bicep, crossed his arms and frowned at her.

Piper swallowed, her attention darting back to the two in front of her. She could feel her hands shaking. Her palms were sticky, her fingers sliding on the metal door handle.

"Miss Piper," one of the officers in front of her said, forcing a smile. "I'm afraid that isn't an option. We have a search warrant for your address in Highkeep and for the suite you're renting here."

Ice drenched down Piper's spine. They knew. She didn't know how. Maybe Saxe. Maybe Lore. Maybe–

"Our colleagues went to your apartment, and you weren't there," the officer continued. "They haven't gone in yet. They won't, if you cooperate now." He leaned forward. "You don't want your door broken open for all the beggars and thieves, now do you?"

What would it matter? If she was in prison, the beggars and thieves could have her apartment. It wasn't like she'd need it. She'd be treated to the crown's hospitality – for a while, at least.

"I ..." She couldn't force more than that word out. Her voice sounded strangled.

She'd end up in The Pit. The deepest, darkest part of Silversdale Prison. Where the murderers and rapists and true psychopaths went, ones who'd never find their way out. But she would find her way out, if only for her execution at the High Lord's hands, in Illusion Square, as it had been done for hundreds of years.

She couldn't feel her hands. Or her feet. Somehow, her legs hadn't buckled. They couldn't buckle. Not if she needed to run.

But if she ran, she'd be leaving Caleb and Madelyn.

"Piper?" Like her thoughts had summoned her, Madelyn pushed the door to their bedroom open with a bang. "Who's that? Is it Alec?"

Something flashed in the older policeman's eyes.

"They're here!" the one who had spoken first said.

The second one, the stockier one, dropped his shoulder and slammed it into the door.

Piper stumbled back, tripping over the edge of the rug and landing half over the coffee table. The pointed corner dug into her hip, and she gasped in pain.

"Piper!" Madelyn squealed as one of the policemen made a grab for her.

"Maddy!" Piper took her by the arm, yanking her behind her back. The policeman went for Piper instead, but Piper brought up her elbow, jamming it into his throat.

He dropped, gagging and gasping as he tried to draw in a breath.

"Piper!" Caleb shouted. Piper spun to see the first police officer, one hand hard on Caleb's arm. Piper reached for him.

A fourth officer, a woman Piper hadn't even noticed in the hall, stepped between them and snapped her hand out in a punch that Piper only just got her arm up in time to block. The block was sloppy, and the force of the punch sent Piper's own elbow towards her temple.

"Stand down, young lady!" the oldest officer snapped. "You will regret it if we have to use force!"

Piper was pretty certain they were already using force. "Let go of Caleb!" she snapped. The other police officer pulled Caleb closer, his free hand going past the revolver on his belt to the baton there.

The female police officer didn't have the same qualms. She yanked her slim metal pistol from its holster, pointing the barrel towards Piper's forehead.

Piper's field of vision narrowed to that cylinder. Nothing beyond it existed. She lashed out, stepping forward. Her fingers wrapped around the woman's wrist, forcing her hand to the ceiling, where a bullet would lodge into the plaster and not into anyone in the room. She twisted, and there was a sharp crack of bones snapping. The woman cried out, the gun falling from limp fingers.

It hit the ground with a loud clatter, and Madelyn squealed. She hadn't heard a bang, but Piper's heart leaped into her throat all the same.

The woman staggered back a step, and the older police officer's beet-red face appeared in Piper's vision.

"What the f–"

"Is there a problem here?"

Piper spun, gathering Madelyn in her arms.

Rylan stood in the doorway, both arms braced on the frame above his head. His lips were pressed into a thin line, his blue eyes flinty.

Fate. She was going to prison. And Caleb and Madelyn would be alone.

Madelyn squeaked as Piper hugged her too tight, but she didn't try to wriggle out of her grip.

"B-Blackcoat Rylan," one of the police officers stammered.

Blackcoat Rylan.

Blackcoat.

Blackcoat.

Spots danced in front of her vision, and Piper remembered to drag in a breath.

Rylan's eyebrows drew together in a scowl. "Well?" he demanded when no one said anything else. "What's happening here?"

The female police officer had slumped into a puddle on the floor, her good hand wrapped around her broken wrist. One of the men pulled Caleb behind his back, like he thought Piper would lunge for him while they were all distracted.

She might have.

The first police officer stepped forward. "Sir, you're interfering with an official investigation, and I insist you step aside. We're looking into the case of two kidnapped children who—"

"Do they look kidnapped to you?" Rylan thundered.

The police officer flinched.

Piper blinked uncertainly. *Kidnapped?* They didn't know about her?

The police officer opened his mouth to argue, but the senior man stepped forward. "You don't know who you're talking to, boy," he said to the police officer. It was his voice, Piper realised. He was the one who'd addressed Rylan as ...

The senior officer turned to the man holding Caleb. "Let the boy go," he said. The officer hesitated for a split second, then let go of Caleb's arm.

"Piper!" Caleb dived across the room. Piper flung an arm out to him, staggering back with the force he hit her with. She fell, dragging both children to the coffee table. Caleb and Madelyn pressed as close as they could to her.

"It's okay," Piper breathed. She kissed Caleb's temple, then Madelyn's hair. "It's okay. I'm here."

Caleb sniffed. Madelyn shook. Piper looked over their heads and glared with everything she had in her.

The police officer who'd held Caleb back had the grace to flinch and look away. The other one, who'd faced off against Rylan, didn't.

"She broke Tia's wrist!" he cried. "She was resisting official police business!"

"She was pointing a gun in a room with children in it!" Piper cried, her voice breaking. "Be glad that's all I did!"

"You did what?" Rylan glowered at the woman on the floor. Tears were streaking down her face.

"That's enough," the older man said, stepping forward. He pointed to the mouthy officer. "Boy, pull your head in. You're a rookie. And you don't know—"

"I don't care who he is!" the officer snapped. "He's—"

"Conducting my own investigation on behalf of the High Lady," Rylan interrupted. The rookie officer's mouth dropped open.

The older man sighed. "Perhaps we could discuss this like gentlemen, Blackcoat Rylan."

Rylan's lips pressed together.

"I'd be delighted, superintendent," he said. "Downstairs. With your officers out of this room."

Piper thought the police superintendent would argue. But he just sighed again, nodded, and gestured. "Arren, get Tia back to the station," he said. "She needs that wrist looking to."

The police officer who'd held Caleb nodded. Crossing the room, he hesitated as he passed Piper. "Sorry," he murmured, so quietly she almost missed it. Then he helped the woman up, and the two of them left.

The superintendent turned to the last man. "Wait for me outside," he said, in a tone that left no space for argument. The man flushed, then turned on his heel and marched from the room.

The superintendent turned to Piper.

"Sorry, ma'am," he said, touching the brim of his hat. "But if you wouldn't mind coming with—"

"No!" Madelyn threw her arms around Piper. "Don't go!"

"I'm not going anywhere without you," Piper promised softly. Caleb tightened his arms around her.

"I guess it's just you and me, superintendent," Rylan said, jerking his head towards the door. "We can send up for Piper if we need to."

The superintendent huffed, but allowed Rylan to gesture him from the room. The mage made to follow him. As he gripped the door handle, he glanced back, his blue gaze meeting Piper's.

He nodded, once.

Then he vanished through the door.

It took almost an hour for Piper to calm Caleb and Madelyn down. The hot chocolate Rose brought up shortly after, accompanied by a plate of snacks, helped. So did talking Caleb into a quick shower, and then arranging for Rose to bring up their dinner, so that they didn't have to go down to the dining room. The superintendent could still have been there.

She'd come so close to losing them ... Piper shivered as ice prickled down her spine.

Now, Caleb leaned on his hand at the dining table, his maths homework in front of him. He scowled down at the page, his pencil making a dent in the paper of his notebook.

"I don't understand," he insisted.

Piper rubbed her forehead. "It's groups," she tried. Again. It was the same conversation they'd had every night that week, working on multiplication.

"Piper," Madelyn interrupted from where she sat opposite. "I can't read this word."

"Just one sec, baby," Piper said. She was certain her hair must be standing on end from all the times she'd run her fingers through it. It was definitely falling out of her braid. One long curl brushed the back of her hand, and Piper impatiently pulled the tie from the end and shook out the tangled mane. "Let's ..." Piper trailed off, uncertain what needed to come next in that sentence.

Behind them, the door opened. Piper turned, sighing in relief. That must be Rose, and the appearance of their dinner. They'd have a break and she could figure out how to—

The person who stepped through the door was not Rose. Alec met Piper's gaze and raised his eyebrows.

"What?" he asked.

Piper frowned. So apparently she thought of him as Alec now.

"Nothing," she said, turning back around. "I thought you were food."

"Ah." He accepted that like it was perfectly reasonable. "What are you doing?" he asked.

"Maths homework," Caleb said, in the same tone as Piper would say *having lunch with Saxe*. "But I don't understand it and Piper keeps getting frustrated."

"Piper, I can't read this word," Madelyn said again.

"I'll be just a minute, baby," she repeated, holding up one finger. "Just let me help Caleb first, then I'll help you."

She turned back to Alec.

"Did you need something?" she said. She needed him to go away before Caleb and Madelyn completely forgot they were supposed to be doing schoolwork and instead peppered him with questions.

Alec shrugged instead of answering her question. "I can help, if you'd like." He gestured to the table and the children.

He's mad, she thought. If she had any choice, homework was not how she would be spending her evening.

"Why?" she asked.

"I minored in mathematics," he said, another shrug rolling across his shoulders. He crossed to her in two strides, then leaned over to peer down at Caleb's book. "Ah, multiplication." He glanced at Piper again. "Do you want help?"

"Yes please!" Caleb said, before Piper could reply. "Piper gets frustrated when I don't understand." He looked at Piper. "Doesn't minor mean less?" he asked her.

182

Piper touched his cheek. "In this case, it means he learned it at university, but he didn't study it as much as something else. It was his second-best subject."

"Oh." Caleb nodded. "That makes sense."

Only to a ten-year-old. Piper smiled at Caleb. Then she glanced back at Alec, hesitating.

The mage smirked at her. "It might be my second-best subject, but I'm still pretty good," he said. "Show me what you're working on."

Piper pushed away from the table as Alec dropped into the chair on Caleb's other side.

"Piper," Madelyn said.

"Yes, baby girl," Piper said, sliding into the chair next to her. "I'll help you now. I'm sorry it took so long."

"It's okay." Madelyn curled into her side, opening the book she'd been reading.

"Let's start this page again," Piper said. "Then we can try that tricky word."

She felt Madelyn nod, her hair brushing Piper's shoulder. Across the table, Alec leaned over Caleb's workbook, pointing to things.

"Here it is," Madelyn said, pointing, and Piper dragged her attention back down. "Be-ah-oo ..." She trailed off, her face scrunching up.

"That is a hard word," Piper admitted. She pointed to the letters on the page. "You're trying to sound it out, which is good. But sometimes, when these three letters are together they make a *yoo* sound instead."

"Oh." Madelyn scrunched up her face. "Why do they do that?"

"I'm not sure," Piper admitted. "Sometimes, Rhealgan has funny rules with words like that. You'll learn all about them as you start reading more." She nudged Madelyn. "Why don't you try sounding it out now with the *yoo* sound?"

"Okay." Madelyn snuggled closer into Piper's side. "Be-yoo-ti-ful. Beautiful!"

"That's exactly it, baby." Piper kissed the top of her head, and Madelyn twisted to look up at her.

"What does it mean?" she asked.

Piper's smile slipped for a second. Any six-year-old girl should know what that meant. She should be told it every day.

"It means really pretty," Piper said.

Madelyn beamed up at her.

"You're beautiful, Piper," she announced, and Piper laughed.

"So are you, Maddy." She tapped Madelyn's nose, and the little girl giggled.

"You're making this too hard in your head," Alec said from across the table. "It's groups."

"Everyone says that, but it doesn't make sense!" Caleb snapped.

He threw his pencil down, and it clattered across the table towards Piper and Madelyn. Piper stopped it with one hand. She opened her mouth to berate Caleb for his tantrum, but Alec didn't look bothered by the outburst. Instead, he pulled Caleb's blank notebook towards him and reached out with his own pen.

"It's like this," he said. "If I have one group of three apples, how many apples do I have?"

Caleb frowned. "Three?" he said sulkily.

Alec nodded. "Exactly," he said. "Now."

He reached out, and Piper craned her neck to see him draw a second group of three circles a little way along from the first.

"Now I have two groups of three apples. How many do I have?"

"Six," Caleb muttered, scowling.

"Yes, that's right," Alec said. He moved his pen along the page some more. "What about three groups of three?"

Caleb hesitated for a moment.

"... Nine?" he asked uncertainly.

Alec grinned. "That's exactly it," he said, his voice bright with praise.

Caleb's answering grin was just as bright.

Madelyn tugged at Piper's arm, drawing her attention back.

"Piper, I'm bored," she said. "Can I stop doing homework now?"

Piper glanced at the clock on the wall. "Five more minutes," she said. "Then dinner should be ready. Okay?"

Madelyn pouted, but she turned her attention back to her book. Piper flicked distractedly through the rest of Madelyn's work; basic maths and something with coloured fish on it.

Madelyn kept reading out loud about a horse that was looking for its beautiful mane – what this was supposed to teach, Piper had no clue – while across from them, Alec talked Caleb through the rest of his three times tables. A small, determined smile stayed on Caleb's face as he worked his way to the end of the sheet.

A tap came at the door before it swung open. Rose stood in the doorway, a tray propped up on one hip. It carried four plates, filled with food. She brought it in, her movements brisk.

"Oh good," Rose said when she saw Alec. "Your dinner's here too, do you mind grabbing it?" She deposited the tray on the table and, before anyone could say anything, she waved to the kids and vanished back downstairs; clearly, they were busy.

Alec ruffled Caleb's hair. "You're doing great. Keep it up, and you'll have all your times tables sorted soon." He waved to Madelyn, who smiled shyly at him, then scooped up one of the plates – the one with the double helping.

Caleb glanced at Piper, prompting her with a pointed look.

"Wait." The word slipped out of Piper before she could stop it. From the corner of her eye, she saw Alec turn. She was pretty sure his eyebrows lifted.

The corner of Caleb's mouth turned up a little.

Piper's leg jittered, and Madelyn pressed down on it with both hands, the motion clearly bothering her.

Piper took a deep breath. She forced herself to make eye contact.

"You could stay." She jerked her head towards the dining table. "For dinner, I mean."

"Sure," Alec said, dropping back into his chair next to Caleb. He was smiling. "Thanks, guys."

Piper busied herself with getting Caleb and Madelyn to wash their hands. Anything to avoid thinking about the line she'd just crossed.

NINETEEN

When Piper stepped out of Caleb and Madelyn's shared bedroom later that night, it was to find her living room empty. The dinner plates had been cleared off the table. After their meal, Piper had helped Caleb with his history homework, while Alec sat on the floor, teaching Madelyn some game with long, thin sticks. She couldn't see the sticks either, now.

Piper shook herself. An empty apartment was good. It was what she was used to. There wasn't homework spread across the dining table, or toys on the floor to trip over and break her neck. There was space to exercise, to do a proper routine, one with knives out and everything. She could wash her hair without interruption. She could read a book.

Piper hesitated. She headed for the door, then stepped into the hall. She heard a satisfying click behind her.

She hesitated again.

Piper tapped on the door opposite with one knuckle.

This was stupid. She should be spending this time preparing for tomorrow. Maybe she should go downstairs and see if Patrik had heard anything about–

The door opened. There was a towel in front of her, laid over a soft white shirt. She dragged her gaze up.

Alec's hair was damp, sticking up from where he must have been rubbing it with the towel.

Realising her hand was still in the air, Piper lowered it.

"Um …" She wasn't even sure why she was there. "Sorry. You're busy."

"It's fine." Alec's blue gaze traced over her. "Want to come in?" He pushed the door open.

Piper stared at the scene he had revealed. Paper littered every available surface, from the dining to the coffee table. A huge map of Silvaein was stuck up on the wall, with an almost-as-large map of Silversdale next to it. Coloured putty and pins had been stuck into both.

"What is this?" she said, stepping inside. Behind her, Alec sighed. Piper turned back to see him yank the towel from around his shoulders. Walking to the bathroom, he chucked it inside and closed the door.

He gestured around the room. "I can't stop," he said. "I need to find him."

Piper turned back, running her gaze over the maps.

"Fate," she breathed. "When do you sleep?"

Alec chuckled. "Honestly? From about two to six in the morning."

Piper turned to see him run both hands over his face. Now she was looking, she saw the obvious shadows under his eyes. She frowned.

"Why didn't you say something?" she asked.

"You're parenting," he said with a shrug. "It's not like you're spending your nights cavorting or anything like that. You're busier than I am."

He rolled his shoulders; Piper could hear them crack from across the room. He glared down at the coffee table, running his hands through his hair and making a frustrated sound. "I just …"

"I know," she said. Her legs suddenly felt like they had lead weights attached to them, and she sank onto the couch. "Me too."

Alec sighed and dropped heavily into an armchair. "There's too much to look at," he admitted. Then he looked at her. "Maybe there's something you can see. Something I've missed."

It was almost a plea. She rubbed her temple.

"I don't know how much use I'll be," she admitted. "This is way out of my depth." She looked up, meeting his gaze. "Most of my cases are handed to me. This kind of legwork ... it's not what I'm good at."

Despite her words, she gathered some of the papers off the table. Tucking her feet up under her, she curled into the corner of the couch, spreading the pages across the arm. She frowned as she read. They were witness statements, mostly from people who had seen the prince in the Market District, or ...

"The Mage's Quarter?" Piper asked.

Alec nodded. "Jai's going to Everhill next year," he said. "He's pretty powerful; at least, I think he will be, after he's trained. It's always hard to tell at first."

Piper rubbed her forehead. "I don't even ..." she trailed off, not bothering to finish that sentence. Her gaze trailed back down to the papers.

Most of the statements felt coincidental. None of the ones she'd read seemed to mention the prince disappearing. Did they even know he was gone? Surely they had to. Alec couldn't hide the fact that the prince was not where he should be. But then again, no one they'd spoken to in the city seemed to know he was gone. No one in The Lily had heard anything about it; if it had come up, Patrik would have told her. If there was even a rumour, it would have got back to Piper through ...

She sighed. He still hadn't answered her message. That could mean a few things; either he couldn't answer for some reason, and she was pretty sure she would have heard about a power play if there was one, or he was gathering information.

Fate, she hoped he was gathering information.

She looked up to find Alec watching her.

"What?" she asked.

"How'd you get her to drop the gun?" he asked. "The police officer, I mean."

Piper blinked at him. "This is what you're asking me right now?"

Alec shrugged. "It's a useful skill," he said. "Especially doing what we're doing."

Piper placed the papers down. "You think the Shiv'ek will shoot us?" she asked.

Alec huffed, leaning back to run his hands through his hair.

"No," he said. "This Shiv'ek will be mine to deal with. But pistols are getting cheaper, and more and more common."

Piper thought for a moment. Did he really want to know?

"I broke her wrist to disarm her," she said finally. "But what I did today was a bit sloppy. I panicked. It's not the right way to disarm someone."

He leaned forward, pressing his elbows to his knees. "How would you usually do it?"

Piper opened her mouth to answer. But then Alec pulled something from the armchair beside him. Piper leaped to her feet, swearing.

The pistol glinted in the lamplight, and Alec glanced down at it.

"It's not loaded," he said, standing. "I do know how to empty a pistol."

"How about we check that?" Piper said, her hands feeling far too light for her body.

The withering look the mage shot her was almost laughable. But he clicked the barrel to the side, tipping it up. When no bullets fell out of the revolver, Piper let out a small sigh of relief.

Alec held the gun in his right hand, raising it to point at her. At her chest, Piper noted, not her head. More likely to hit, but, if she was fast, less likely to hit something vital. If the gun were loaded, and he shot at her. He waited for her move.

Piper lunged. Alec's mouth popped open, and he tried to bring the pistol up.

She was faster. She pushed his arm back across his body with her left hand, locking her elbow so Alec couldn't bring it back across. She wrapped her arm around his, pinning the arm with the gun against her chest. Then she grabbed the pistol in her right hand and twisted.

Alec swore. Then Piper stepped back, the pistol in both hands.

He blinked at her as she held the pistol steady, aiming for his forehead.

"Huh," he said after a moment.

Piper shrugged, relaxing her stance. "If you knew what you were doing, maybe it'd be a little harder for me to get it," she said.

"Are you any good a shot?" Alec asked.

"Remember the throwing knives, the day you broke down my door?" she asked.

Alec winced. "About that—"

"Save it." Piper waved one hand. "Well, I wouldn't try that with a gun. I'm not certain I wouldn't hit you."

"Good to know the aim is *not* to hit me, then," he said dryly. Piper snorted.

She handed him back the pistol.

"I suppose I should return this," he said.

She gave the gun a closer look. "Wait, is that the same gun from earlier?"

"I found it under the couch when I was playing with Madelyn," he said. Cold drenched Piper's spine. "Didn't think it was a good idea to leave it there with the kids."

"Yeah," Piper whispered, shivering. She wrapped her arms around herself. Then she swallowed. "Thanks."

Alec just nodded. They stood there for a moment.

"So," she said eventually, pointing. "Something you want to tell me, Blackcoat Rylan?"

Alec followed her finger to the coat rack, and his coat hanging on it. He winced.

"Well …" He hesitated. "What is there to say, really?"

"Why didn't you say anything?" Piper demanded, dropping back to the couch.

Alec didn't answer right away. He crossed back to his armchair and sat. Then he leaned forward, his arms braced on his knees, staring at his hands.

"I ... When people find out," he said slowly, "they tend to react one of two ways. And honestly, your derision was kind of refreshing."

"I am not derisive," Piper argued.

Alec laughed. He leaned back, shooting her a smile across the room.

"See what I mean?" he said. "You're not afraid of me. Nor are you sucking up to me. Instead, you're arguing with me." He held out his hands. "I mean ... it's not that bad, is it?"

Piper frowned. Her gaze traced over his face, taking in his open expression. It felt like she was seeing him unguarded for the first time.

"I don't know many mages who would think that being powerful is a bad thing," she said softly.

"It's inconvenient," he said after a moment. "My magic. It's big. But what I'm trained to do, what I love, is using small bits of magic for maximum effect." He got up, crossed the room in three long strides and pulled the coat from the rack. Then he went back to Piper. He held the coat out, the insignia on the breast catching the lamplight.

"I didn't pick this by chance," he said, pointing to the interlocking spellbinder crest. "I picked it because this matters to me." He sank back into his chair, dropping the coat over the arm. "Maybe it would be better if I was a battlemage," he muttered, almost to himself. "Maybe it'd be easier to find him. Maybe they never would have dared take him." He buried his face in his hands.

Piper didn't know how to answer that. Instead, she pushed to her feet, crossing the floorboards with a soft thud of bare feet against the floor.

"What kind of information have you been gathering?" she asked.

Alec pulled himself up. Then he crossed to the wall beside her.

"Let me take you through it all," he said.

"Piper," Patrik called as they were leaving The Lily the next morning. Piper turned to him, a half-eaten piece of Madelyn's toast in one hand,

Madelyn's bag in the other and coffee in a waxed paper cup clutched precariously between her forearm and her chest.

He took one look at her and chuckled. "Now you know how hard it is to raise kids," he told her. Then he held up an envelope. "This came for you."

Piper's gaze darted over it, then she sucked in a breath. The leaf-green seal shone back at her, the early morning light through the windows turning it fluorescent.

"Finally," she breathed. Dropping Madelyn's bag to the floor, Piper reached for it.

"What does this mean?" Patrik asked her, frowning.

"I don't know," Piper admitted. "I haven't even read it yet."

"Does he have something he wants you to do?" he pressed.

"I don't think so," she said. "He didn't when I talked to him last."

Patrik pursed his lips. He leaned forward so his voice wouldn't carry.

"Rose asked who he was, last time he was here," he murmured. "Was convinced the two of you were talking, even though you were in different booths."

"Fate," Piper said softly, rubbing her forehead with the hand that held the envelope. "I'm going to have to move our meetings."

Patrik sighed. "As much as I trust you both to be here," he said, "that might be the safest option."

Piper laughed without humour. "I'll add it to my list of things to do," she promised.

"What's on your list of things to do?" Alec asked from behind her.

Piper started. She hadn't heard him cross the room; for someone so big, he could move pretty quietly.

"What's *not* on my list?" she asked, deflecting. There were some things that it was better to keep him in the dark about, and this was one of them.

He frowned, like he could hear her thoughts. But that was absurd. Telepathy was rare and, as far as Piper knew, a mage could never read the thoughts of a non-mage.

Piper shook herself mentally, forcing her expression neutral. That only seemed to make Alec more suspicious, if the hard set of his mouth was anything to go by.

"Piper!" Madelyn sped towards Piper, her arms outstretched. Piper, hands full, looked frantically for somewhere to put her coffee down safely. Before disaster struck, long arms, clad in black sleeves rolled up to the elbow, plucked Madelyn from the air mid-jump.

"Maddy," Alec scolded, settling the girl on his hip. "You've gotta look before you jump, okay? Piper didn't have any hands to catch you. You could have got hurt."

Madelyn's face fell. "I'm sorry," she whispered.

"It's okay, I'm not mad at you," Piper said. "But Alec's right. You've gotta be careful, baby."

Madelyn nodded. Her arms tightened around Alec's neck, and she buried her face in his shoulder. For a moment, Alec blinked. Then he sighed. He cupped the back of Madelyn's head with one hand, offering her a hug. Then he put her down.

"Come on," he said. "If we don't go now, you're going to be late."

"Right." Piper shook herself again, brushing off the fog that had descended over her like ... well, like fog.

Piper stuffed the letter inside her coat and grabbed Madelyn's bag.

"Come on, Caleb," she called to where he sat at the bar, talking to Rose. He scrambled off, waving to the older girl over his shoulder, before racing over to join Piper and the others.

"Piper?"

"Hm?" Piper said, watching Caleb and Madelyn walk towards the school gates. Caleb held Madelyn's hand – right up until another boy his age called his name. Then he dropped it like a hot potato. Madelyn frowned at her brother and said something Piper couldn't hear.

"Piper," Alec said again, nudging her shoulder with his arm.

Piper snapped her attention back to him. "Sorry!" she said. "I was ..."

"I know," Alec said. "But they're just walking through the school gates. Nowhere could be safer; I should know. One of the first things the High Lady asked me to do when I started working for them was check the enchantments on schools."

Piper stared at him. "You did what?"

"I checked–"

"No, I got that!" Piper interrupted. "I just ... I guess I didn't even realise there were enchantments on the schools."

Alec shrugged one shoulder. "There didn't used to be, before the coup. But there are now. The ones on this school keep weapons out and children in, except at designated times or in emergencies."

"Huh." Piper shook her head. "That's ..."

"You're about to come out with some spiel about magic and how we use too much of it and how you don't like mages," Alec predicted, his mouth twisting in a sarcastic smile.

Piper shrugged one shoulder and looked away.

"Actually ..." She couldn't believe she was about to admit this. "I was about to say, that's good to know. Here, at least."

Silence. Piper looked up to find Alec staring at her, his mouth slightly open.

"I do think we use too much magic, though!" she snapped. "And I still don't like mages!"

Alec closed his mouth. "Oh I know," he said. His blue eyes glinted in amusement, and he gave her a real smile. "Trust me. I know."

Piper glared at him. Alec laughed.

"Come on," he said. "Let's get started."

Piper held up one finger, remembering the envelope in her coat pocket. She pulled it out, broke the seal and started skimming the letter.

"What's that?" he asked. He shifted to see over her shoulder, but was written in a cypher she and the sender had made up. Alec wouldn't be able to read it.

> *Piper,*
>
> *I'm sorry it took me so long to reply.*
>
> *Have you heard anything more about Abby? How are the kids? You should keep them with you, if you can. That's the safest place for them. I heard there's a mage hanging around the city, looking for someone. Do you know anything about that?*
>
> *Abby isn't the only one who's vanished. I've included a list of people, children mostly, whose parents have contacted me in the last year. None of them were seen again.*
>
> *I don't know if it's connected, but I've heard a disturbing rumour. We should talk about it in person.*
>
> *There's another issue we need to discuss. Meet me at the W on Asdiel night. We can talk then.*
>
> *–A*

Piper pulled out the second page and sucked in a breath. "We need to go back to The Lily," she said.

TWENTY

Piper hurtled up the staircase, startling Lily as she descended with her arms full of linen.

"Sorry!" Piper called back over her shoulder, taking the stairs two at a time. She heard Alec's much more polite "Sorry, ma'am" behind her. She skidded to a stop before Alec's room, trying the handle, and turned to him when it was locked.

"Well?" she demanded, gesturing.

Alec eyed her cautiously even as he reached into his pocket. "Well what?" he demanded. "What are you doing?"

Piper waved the piece of paper at him again. "This!"

"I have no idea what 'this' is!" he retorted.

Piper pushed the unlocked door open and almost tumbled inside in her haste. She jogged across the room, stopping before the enormous map of Silversdale. Grabbing a pin, she tacked the piece of paper next to it.

"Help me with this," she said, gesturing.

Alec's footsteps sounded behind her, heavy on the timber. He frowned at the piece of paper, his finger trailing down the list of names.

"What's all this?" he asked. "Are these locations? I don't know where any of them are."

Piper forced herself to slow down. To stop, even though that almost physically hurt. She took a deep breath.

"It's ... something," she said. "I'm sure of it."

Alec traced his finger over the list of names. "How did you get this?" he asked.

"A little birdie told me." She waved a hand dismissively. "It's not important. What's important is the information."

She grabbed some more pins and coloured putty.

"Read the locations to me, and the dates," she ordered.

To her surprise, Alec gave her little more than a sideways look before he complied. He read the list aloud and Piper pinned frantically, colour coding the putty based on dates of disappearance. Ten minutes later, she stepped back to look at the map.

Little coloured dots littered the sepia landscape. Piper frowned at them, turning her head to the side. If she did that, and squinted, she could kind of–

Hands wrapped around her shoulders, pulling her back. Piper lashed out with an elbow, but Alec wrapped a hand around her arm.

"Look," he said.

Piper sucked in a breath.

She'd been too close to see it before. But the pins ...

They marched in a perfect semi-circle on the opposite side of the river. Piper shook Alec off, stepping closer once more. Now that she'd seen it, she couldn't unsee it.

"That's ..." Alec trailed off. In her peripheral vision, Piper saw him cross his arms.

"He's operating from somewhere," Piper murmured. She traced a circle on the map. "Somewhere here."

Beside her, Alec nodded. Piper stepped back to get a better look.

"Why the Lower Ilian?" she asked. "That floods at this time of year." The snow melts from the mountain flowed down the Amethyst River, then broke free, filling the floodplain before draining into the ocean.

"Maybe because it's cut off?" he suggested. "I've never been down there. How hard is it to get around?"

"Depends on the year," Piper admitted. "Most of the time, it's not too bad. Ankle deep, maybe. But sometimes, like this year, the river bursts and floods *everything*." She traced the main street that ran between the Ilian and the Lower Ilian. "These streets are all basically canals. The first few blocks are okay, but anything after this"– she tapped a spot on the map – "and you're swimming." She thought for a moment, then added, "Most people have evacuated, so patrols wouldn't be necessary. There'd be no one there, now."

Alec looked at the list again and rubbed his jaw. "Why children?" he wondered aloud. He shook his head. "I don't know. But I know someone who might."

"I'll come with you."

Alec glanced at her. Then he nodded. "Sure," he said. "Fate. Maybe we'll find them." He let out a shaking breath.

"Maybe." A small, hopeful smile curled the corner of Piper's mouth.

Alec saw it. His answering smile was full of relief.

If you don't follow through with this, it will be your execution.

Reality washed over Piper like ice water. It didn't matter how much the mage helped her with finding Abby. It didn't matter if the prince stayed missing, or if they found these other children. Alexander Rylan was still a target; her target.

He was already dead. He just didn't know it yet.

Alec's expression faltered. "What?" he asked.

Piper wrapped her arms around herself and forced a smile she didn't really feel.

"Nothing," she lied. "Let's go talk to your little birdie. I'll send mine a message too. He'll expect a reply."

Alec glanced over at her, a frown appearing between his brows. Finally, he nodded. "All right," he said. "Let's go."

Piper felt her smile wobble. But she followed him from the room and downstairs.

They walked in silence through the city. When they got on the tram, Alec paid the conductor without asking, then leaned on the railing.

"What is it?" he asked softly.

Piper glanced at him, then away. "Nothing," she lied again.

Alec kept his eyes on her, but Piper turned her attention to the distance, letting the city slide past her.

It was for the best. She'd got too close; she'd let her guard down. Fate, if she kept going like this, she'd start to like him.

They'd find Abby. And if they had to leave the prince behind …

Piper grimaced, rubbing at her breastbone as it burned.

… maybe they'd have to find the prince. Then they may as well find the missing children. Their families should get to know what had happened to them.

After that, she had to kill the mage. He'd understand, maybe. Hopefully he wouldn't hold it against her.

Piper shook herself. It didn't matter if he held it against her. He would be dead. Even if the Creator took him to the Summerland, with its rolling fields and lush forests and endless magic, she'd never see him again.

Piper was under no illusions. It wouldn't be the Summerland for her. She'd be in the Winterland, at the Glacial Cliffs, probably near the top where the wind howled endlessly. Where the Chaos Demons came from, before someone was crazy enough to allow them passage into Rhealgo.

Piper shivered.

"Hey." Alec nudged Piper's arm. "We're here."

While she'd been distracted, they'd moved through half the city. The tram trundled to a stop on Glimmer Street. The purple flags of the Mage's Quarter hung from the streetlamps, and Piper stiffened.

Alec jumped off the tram before it came to a complete stop; it was good to know she wasn't the only one who did that. Piper followed him off, glancing around the street.

"Where are we going?" she asked. She pictured the area on the map, surrounded by pins, and touched her fingers to her dagger. "We know where to go."

"But we don't know why," Alec said. He ran his fingers through his hair, then retied his horsetail. "I don't like not knowing why."

Piper rubbed her forehead, then grabbed Alec's hand to check the watch on his wrist. Not even noon yet. They had plenty of time.

Time for what? a snide voice in her head asked. *Time to do your job?*

Piper shook it away. *I don't have a choice.*

They walked a little way up the street before Alec stopped. Piper traced her gaze up the building next to them, her breath catching in her throat.

The storefront ran longer than any of the fronts in the Market District. The frame was painted dark green, interspersed with huge glass panes.

Behind that glass were books.

Thick and thin, leather-bound and cloth. Tall books. Books so small they could fit in the palm of her hand. One sat on a lectern, propped open to a fantastical two-page illustration. A copy of *The Combined Histories of Rhealgo*, bound in crimson leather, stood in a stand near the doorway.

The bell above the door tinkled as Alec went in, pulling Piper from her wide-eyed rapture. He waved at her impatiently, and she ducked inside after him.

A flagstone floor met her boots, stepping up slightly to warm floorboards a few metres away. To her right, Piper could smell coffee; a tiny cafe had been installed there.

A small woman bustled out from behind the bookshelves. She was tiny, even shorter than Piper. Brown hair tumbled over her shoulders, liberally streaked with a delicate shade of pink. Where the sunslight hit the strands, they turned luminous. When the dwarf saw Alec, her face changed from a professional smile to a genuinely pleased grin.

"Alec!" She crossed to him, holding out her arms. Alec stooped, bending almost in two to return her hug.

He pulled back. "It's good to see you, Hazel," he said. Then he turned to Piper. "This is Piper. She's … working with me."

Hazel offered Piper a kind smile, then turned back to Alec.

"Liam said he ran into you a few days ago," she said, worry in her voice. "Something about a mage trap?"

"Unfortunately," he confirmed with a nod. "Thank fate Liam and his partner were nearby, so they could make sure no one else got caught up in it." He ran a hand through his hair. "That's why I'm here, actually. Is Liam around?"

Hazel nodded. "It's his day off," she said, "so he slept in. Let me go see if he's awake."

She turned, hurrying towards the back corner and an ornate spiral staircase. The stairs made little noise under her slippers, despite her being a dwarf – dwarves were built shorter but far heavier than humans, typically.

Piper turned to Alec. "So," she said, "old girlfriend?"

Alec snorted. "No," he said. "She's with Liam, and has been for years. I knew her in university, vaguely. We reconnected when I got to the city to teach Jai."

"Hm." Piper stepped up onto the floorboard, trailing her fingers over the bookshelf.

Notebooks of all shapes and sizes packed this one. She trailed her fingers over the spines, feeling leather and cloth and hand-stitching. In her peripheral vision, she watched as Alec trailed down the opposite shelf. His eyes fixed on her. Piper could feel them, like fire against her neck, following her movements.

Piper clenched her fists.

The clattering of feet on the staircase interrupted them, and Piper jumped. She stepped back, peering around the bookshelf. The wood elf Alec had talked to just a few days ago jumped the last two stairs to land with a thud on the floorboards. Hazel followed him more delicately. She smacked his arm.

"What have I said about that," she said.

He grinned. "Sorry, baby." He wrapped an arm around her shoulders.

Alec stepped out from behind the bookshelf, holding out his hand.

"Liam," he said, smiling. The inspector withdrew his arm from around Hazel's shoulders and reached out to clasp Alec's arm.

"What brings you out here?" Liam asked. Then he frowned. "It's not that mage trap again, is it?"

"No, not this time," Alec said. "We've found ... something strange."

"Hang on." Hazel held up her hands. She glanced around the shop, then turned to the door. She turned the sign around, flicking the lock with a click. Then she turned back. "If this is anything to do with the case you've been telling me about, I don't want my customers walking in on it." She gestured to the cafe. "Clara is out, but I can make you something."

"You don't have to—" Alec started, but Hazel nudged him hard enough that he stumbled a step to the side, laughing. Piper blinked. Fate, dwarves *were* heavy.

"It's no problem," Hazel said, smiling.

"Thanks, baby," Liam said, planting a kiss on the top of Hazel's head. He was almost as tall as Alec, so he had to bend a long way down. Hazel pushed him away, smiling up at him, then headed to the cafe.

"C'mon," Alec said, beckoning Piper over. Piper stepped away from the bookshelf.

"She's the woman who was with you the other day," Liam said, looking surprised to see her. Suspicion laced his voice.

"Piper's helping me," Alec said as she joined them. "Needless to say, Liam, this cannot leave this shop."

"What do you take me for?" Liam demanded. Pulling a chair out from a table, he sat. Alec followed suit, and then both glanced at Piper.

Piper looked at Hazel, feeling bad sitting while Hazel waited on them.

"Don't worry about it," the dwarven woman called, like she could read Piper's mind. "Sit!"

Piper did, albeit reluctantly. Unease prickled the back of her neck, for no good reason as far as she could tell. Perhaps it had something to do with the way Liam watched her. It felt like fire ants were crawling all over her skin.

Piper rubbed at her arms as the sound of the coffee grinder started.

"What is it?" Liam asked Alec. The coffee machine started to hiss, and his eyes flicked momentarily to Hazel. He frowned. "Whatever happened with this mage trap … you don't think it's going to bring danger back here, do you?"

Liam seemed very protective of his … girlfriend? Partner? Wife? Could elves and dwarves even get married, legally? Piper frowned. She'd never thought about it. She supposed they could, here in Silvaein, but what did their families back in Freya and Drummonia think of it? Perhaps Liam was from Freydell. She'd heard the elves there were progressive. And the ones in the Ayran Cluster were all half-elf at most.

Alec shook his head. "I don't think so," he said. "I just wanted to run some things by you, to see if you had any insight. Maybe you've heard something I haven't."

Liam glanced at Piper again, curiously. He nodded. "Of course."

Alec leaned forward, bracing his elbows on the little table. "Piper's friend has gone missing," he said. "As has … someone I'm looking for."

Liam nodded. "The prince."

Alec started. "You knew about that?"

Liam shrugged. "Wasn't that hard to put together, actually. I haven't seen you outside the palace this much in years."

Alec grimaced at his words. "I clearly need a life." But the joking fell flat, even Piper could tell that. She wound her fingers together under the table, forcing her hands away from her blades. She didn't need them in here. It was a bookshop, for fate's sake.

"Today," Alec said, "Piper's ... informant sent her some information." He rubbed his chin. "What do you know about children going missing?"

"All children under the age of eighteen, except for my friend," Piper said.

The grinder stopped. Liam rubbed his jaw with one hand, the scratch of stubble against skin loud in the sudden quiet.

"Children go missing all the time in cities, unfortunately," he said, his expression pensive. "There's often not much for us to go on in terms of finding them."

Alec pulled a tourist's map of Silvaein out of his pocket and spread it across the table. "They all vanished from places equidistant from this area, here," he said, circling the spot in the Lower Ilian.

"Something in here could be a kind of haunt, or base maybe," Piper added. "Somewhere to take them back to."

"Huh," Liam muttered. He leaned back in his chair, his gaze fixed on a point past them, a frown between his dark brows. The purple streak in his hair glinted in the light. "Let me think," Liam said. "Just let me ..." He rubbed his forehead. "What is this city coming to? Children disappearing, mage traps ..." He looked up at Alec. "Rumour at the station is *she* came after you. Belladonna berries and everything."

Piper stiffened. She clenched her hands in her lap, her fingers almost creaking with the pressure.

Alec cut her a brief glance, opening his mouth.

Liam frowned. "Does she have anything to do with this?" he asked. "The Belladonna, kidnapping children?"

"No," Alec said. "At least ... No, she doesn't."

Piper's heart spasmed in her chest.

Liam sighed. Then he looked at Piper. "And what do you ..." He stopped. "Informant," he whispered, his gaze darting over Piper. His eyes fixed on her hip, where Piper belatedly realised her coat was pulled awkwardly over her stiletto blade.

"Tell me she's not," he growled, looking at Alec.

Piper froze. She couldn't breathe.

"I …" Alec stumbled, his eyes wide.

Liam lunged across the table.

Piper saw him. Knew, in her mind, what to do to stop him. She hesitated a moment too long. His hand clasped around her arm, and Piper gasped. Liam stood, dragging Piper with him as he did. The chair screeched underneath her.

"Get off me!" Piper slapped at his hand.

"Liam!" Hazel cried, starting around the counter.

"Stay back!" Liam spat. His fingers dug harder into Piper's arm, and she bit her tongue to hold back a cry.

Her fingers twitched near the hilt of her blade, but she stopped herself. There was no bounty out on him. And she couldn't. Not in front of Hazel.

Liam shook her arm, making Piper's teeth sink further into her tongue, and she seriously rethought her nonviolent approach.

"Let go of her, Liam," Alec thundered.

"You," he spun to Alec, dragging Piper with him and almost tripping her over. "You brought the Belladonna into my *house*, with *my wife*."

Alec opened his mouth – to say what, Piper wasn't certain. But Liam's attention on the mage gave her the opening she needed.

She spun, digging her free elbow into the hollow under Liam's exposed ribs, then jabbed her fingertips into his armpit for good measure. Liam hissed in pain. His grip slackened. Piper wrenched her arm from his grip and sprinted for the door.

"Get back here!" Liam roared.

It took Piper precious seconds to throw the lock. Then the door was open, and she flung herself out. She didn't stop running until she'd put four streets between them. Piper sank back against a townhouse wall, her breath sawing in and out of her chest.

Liam hadn't followed her. At least, she didn't think he had. She hadn't heard any footsteps, nor a policeman's whistle.

Fate. A policeman. Four-letter curse words flitted across Piper's mind, but she was too breathless to force them out. A *policeman* knew who she was. Knew her name and what she looked like.

Piper sank down the wall a little way before she forced her legs to catch her. Her hands shook, and she pressed them to the bricks.

He hadn't come after her, but it was only a matter of time. Maybe he'd called his partner – the puka with the pale ears. The rest of his station, maybe. Alec might have given him her address at The Lily.

Alec. Piper seethed. If that damned mage hadn't needed to know *more . . .*

Piper looked up. The suns still made their way towards the east. A pounding throbbed behind her eyes.

She didn't *run.*

And she had to know what he was planning.

Piper turned on her heel and made her way, much more slowly, back towards Glimmer Street.

Piper snuck her way over the back fence of the bookshop, into the yard. It was a riot of colour, flowers blooming in the spring sunsshine and trees spreading sweet-smelling pollen into the air. A table and four chairs sat on the patio, and there was a fire-pit in the middle of the plush lawn. Hazel and Liam must spend a lot of time out here.

Piper pushed her way towards the back window of the building. Pressing herself against the wall to one side, she could just see a sliver of the bookshop interior past the curtains. Liam sat, his arms crossed. Alec stood beside him, both arms braced on the timber tabletop, a scowl on his face. Neither man looked pleased.

Piper glanced at the window. It was the kind that opened with a simple latch, not much to secure it. Sliding her hand to the small of her back, she drew her leaf-shaped blade from the back of her belt. It was slender and razor sharp.

A peel of paint chipped off the window-frame as the blade slid between the bits of timber. She had to wriggle it for a moment, but eventually Piper got it in place to flick open the latch. She eased the glass up, leaning closer.

"I *told* you—" Alec was saying, but Liam threw up a hand and cut him off.

"That's not good enough, Alec!" he snapped. "You brought her in here knowing full well who she was, putting Hazel in danger!"

Piper twisted, trying to see more of the shop, but a shelf blocked her view.

"What are you doing?" asked a soft voice from behind her.

Piper spun. Hazel stood there, a small book in one hand and a pen in the other.

Piper blinked at her. "I'm …" Her voice stuck in her throat, and she swallowed. "How did you know I was here?"

Hazel gestured to the window. "I felt my runes break," she said, holding up the book. "I'm a dwarfsmith."

That explained it. A dwarfsmith was trained in their runic magic. They had to draw the runes to use them, Piper was pretty sure. If she could just separate Hazel from her book …

Hazel took a step backwards, accurately reading Piper's expression.

"I don't want to hurt you," Piper said. "Your husband seems to think I'll kill you all."

"Will you?" Hazel demanded. She sounded calm, but her grip tightened on her book, on her pen.

Piper reached for her coat, her fingers brushing her stiletto through the fabric.

She saw Hazel swallow. "I don't think you'll hurt me," she said, like that would make it true.

Piper didn't answer. Her fingers itched to draw her stiletto. It would be so easy. Hazel wouldn't be able to draw a rune as fast as Piper could draw a dagger.

She palmed the hilt. Hazel flinched.

On the other side of the window, footsteps sounded.

"You had better keep your side of this, Alec," Liam said, his voice a growl. "When you're done with her, she comes in." Then he raised his voice. "Hazel?"

"I'm out here!" Hazel called breathlessly.

The footsteps grew closer.

Piper turned on her heel. Racing for the closest fence, Piper vaulted it, dropping into the garden beyond seconds before the back door creaked open.

TWENTY ONE

Piper stood near the entrance to the school, watching the other parents mill around the street. They paired off in small groups, chatting with other parents who probably had children the same age.

That must be nice, Piper thought bitterly. To have other parents the same age as you. People you could ask for advice when you were flying by on a hope and a prayer, or laugh with over something silly your child did. Friends.

Footsteps sounded behind her, and Piper clenched her fists.

"There you are," Alec said. He stopped beside her, glancing down from his much taller height. "I couldn't find you after the Mage's Quarter."

"You couldn't find me because I left," Piper said shortly, keeping her gaze fixed down the street. She should move closer, but the bell hadn't rung yet, and she wasn't certain she *did* want any of the other parents talking to her. She wasn't certain what she'd say if they started on standard adult topics.

So, what do you do for a living?

Alec frowned. "I get you're mad, but–"

"Mad?" she repeated, her voice deadly quiet. "Mad does not *begin* to cover it, mage. If you hadn't dragged me along to see your friend–"

"Dragged?" Alec interrupted. "I did not *drag* you along. You *offered* to come with me!"

"And if I'd known you were going to see a police officer, I wouldn't have!" Piper snapped. "Now he knows something that I have kept quiet for fourteen years."

Alec stared at her, his mouth open. "Fourteen years?" he breathed, his eyes wide. Piper clenched her fists.

"That is not something we are discussing!" Her voice rose until it almost broke on the last word, and Piper forced herself to take a deep breath.

"When this is over, mage," she spat, "when this is over ..."

She wasn't certain what she was going to threaten.

You had better keep your side of this, Alec.

Piper crossed her arms. "When we find them," she said softly, "we're through. Understand?"

Alec frowned. "I can't let you disappear," he said.

"They know who I am," she hissed through clenched teeth.

Alec went very still. His blue gaze flickered over her face.

"I won't let you hurt them," he said, his voice quiet.

Piper reeled back, feeling like she'd been slapped across the face. His eyes stayed fixed on hers, power glinting in the blue depths. She clenched her fists.

"I need to go get Caleb and Madelyn," she spat. Without waiting for him to reply, Piper spun on her heel and marched down the street, past the other parents.

Caleb and Madelyn found her right away. Madelyn offered a squeal of excitement, throwing her arms around Piper's waist and hugging tight. Piper smoothed back her tangled hair – it hadn't stayed in the ponytail she'd put it in that morning – and smiled at Caleb.

"Hey you," she said.

Caleb offered her a smile that didn't quite reach his eyes. "Hi." His gaze slid past her, landing on something over her shoulder. "Hi, Alec," he said, and the peace Piper felt at seeing them died a painful and gory death. She managed to keep the smile on her face, but only just.

"What do you say we get a treat on the way home?" she said, holding out a hand to Caleb. "What do you feel like?"

"Ice cream!" Madelyn cried.

"Doughnuts!" Caleb protested.

"Cookies!" she chimed in.

"Brownies!"

"Cinnamon–"

"Okay!" Piper nudged them both. "Okay. The bakery it is. C'mon. Let's go."

"Yes!" For the first time in a week, Caleb shot Piper a completely unreserved smile. She beamed back, her chest tight.

Then Caleb turned. "Are you coming too, Alec?" he asked.

Piper's mood plummeted to the cobblestones.

"Alec has something he has to do," Piper said before the mage could reply. "So it's just going to be the three of us."

She waited for him to argue. To protest that he wouldn't let her out of his sight, especially with Caleb and Madelyn in tow. She heard him sigh.

"Piper's right," he said. "There's something I need to do right now. I'll meet you back at The Lily."

Piper didn't look at him. But Caleb smiled at the mage, and Madelyn waved at him around Piper's legs.

"Bye, Alec!" she called. "We'll bring you back a treat!"

Piper took both of their hands, tugging them away before Madelyn could promise any more.

TWENTY TWO

Piper knew she should make the two children do their homework. Instead, she hunted down Patrik, and asked for the back door key. Holding Madelyn's hand, she cajoled them both towards the tiny door. She fit the key in the lock and pushed the door open.

It wasn't often that a building in the Market District had a personal yard, but The Lily was one of those few. It wasn't large; a small vegetable patch, two trees and a grassy area. But Madelyn clapped her hands together in delight.

"It's just like the playground at school!" she said. Pulling her hand from Piper's, she spun to Caleb and jabbed his shoulder.

"Tag! You're it!" Before he could react, Madelyn threw up her hands and raced to the other side of the yard, shrieking with laughter.

"Hey!" Caleb pelted off after her. Piper shifted her weight to one foot, smiling as they chased each other. Madelyn grabbed a tree in a bear hug and declared it "bar." Caleb ducked around the tree, and Madelyn shrieked in laughter.

Behind Piper, the door creaked open. She stiffened, inexplicably knowing who it would be.

Footsteps scuffed the grass. Then *that mage* appeared in her peripheral vision. He had his arms crossed over his chest.

"I half expected you to not come back," he said.

"I need to find Abby." And that was the only reason she was still here.

"Look, Piper–"

"Don't." Piper held up her hand. "I'm not interested in hearing it."

She had until they found the prince. That boy mattered to him more than anything else. Once they'd found him, Piper wouldn't be useful to him any longer. So she had until then to find Abby. "What did the inspector tell you?"

She needed to get an idea of how much time she had before she had to kill him. And then she had to leave. The inspector would know it was her. He knew her name now, and what she looked like. Piper clenched her fists.

Would Lore let her go? Would the others?

Alec ran his hand through his hair. "That area of the Lower Ilian is the first to flood," he said. "On a bad year, it's the first evacuated, the longest left deserted. The people left over two months ago."

Piper nodded.

Alec looked at her. "Piper," he said again, but Piper shook her head.

"I don't want to talk about it," she said coolly. Alec's mouth snicked shut. "Let's just focus on the Lower Ilian." She looked at him fully for the first time in hours. "Does water affect your magic?"

He wavered, like he didn't want to tell her. "Yes," he admitted finally. "Water, pardon the pun, dampens my magic."

Piper didn't laugh. She just nodded, her mind reeling.

The Lower Ilian, then. That was the place to do it, where he couldn't fight back as effectively. He may be a spellbinder, but he was also a blackcoat. That meant he could be dangerous. But without his magic …

Another thought occurred to her.

"Can you fight?" she asked him. "Without magic, I mean."

214

"Are you asking because you plan on killing me?" Alec asked.

Piper shoved down her astonishment, trying to keep guilt off her face. She frowned at him.

"I'm asking because we're about to go into one of the most dangerous places of the city, where there are quite possibly several kidnapped victims and a Shiv'ek, and by your own admission your magic won't be at its best," she said waspishly.

Alec looked at her for a long moment. Piper stuck her chin up in defiance, willing her thoughts deep below the surface.

His eyes narrowed. "I can fight with magic, even if it's dampened," he said in a warning tone. "I may have majored in spellbinding, but I took battlemagic classes." He glanced sideways at her. "But I wouldn't need magic to beat you."

Piper turned to him, her eyebrows rising. "I beg your pardon?" she demanded.

Alec shrugged. "Look at you," he said, gesturing with his shoulder. "You're what? Five foot? And there's no muscle on you. I'd take you out easily."

"I'm five *one*," Piper argued. "And believe me, if I wanted you dead, you'd be dead."

"You tried that," he said, amusement in his voice. "And aside from breaking my nose, you've never actually overpowered me physically, or anyone else that I've seen."

"I've been training as a fighter for fourteen years," Piper said, her voice carefully sweet. "How long have you trained for?"

"Long enough," Alec said dismissively.

"Right now, mage," Piper snapped before really thinking it through. "You and me." She pointed to the grassy area.

"You really think you can beat me?" he asked. "You. Are. Tiny."

Alec's gaze flicked over her, and Piper saw the corner of his mouth tilt in a smirk. She took a deep breath, forcing her fists to unclench at her sides. The frustration faded to a simmer in her gut, rather than racing through her chest. Piper took another deep breath in through her nose, letting it out slowly, and the simmer died down to a glow.

"No magic," Piper said, a floating feeling in her chest. She felt an emptiness that hadn't been there just a few minutes ago.

"I won't need it," he boasted.

She needed this. Needed to know what he could do. Needed to know how he would come at her, when he realised what she was going to do. He'd realise. She wasn't conceited enough to think she could outsmart him, and take him by surprise. The man was a blackcoat, and a teacher to a prince. You didn't get there by being dumb.

Alec's gaze flicked over her coat, lingering where it pulled over a knife hilt near her hip.

Piper rolled her shoulders. Then, gripping her cuffs, she peeled the coat off.

She dropped it to the side, moving a few steps away so she wouldn't get tangled up in it when he attacked.

She still had the leaf-shaped blade at the small of her back, and the long dagger in her boot. She could feel both as she moved. But her stiletto, and the throwing knives she kept near her chest, were both out of reach.

"How do we know who wins?" Alec asked. He scuffed his foot at the grass, but the area was smooth and flat.

"Trust me, mage," she said, "you'll know." She moved her weight to her toes.

Alec shifted his weight. Then he threw a punch at her chest. It was much faster than Piper had expected, and with much more force behind it. She twisted out of the way, and the blow that would have winded her instead slid past.

She sucked in a breath. "You can punch," she admitted grudgingly.

"I played Teravalon at Everhill," he said with a smirk, bracing both hands in a block and deflect position. It was good, but Piper could already see two ways around it: under and to the left, and over near his nose.

"What position?" she asked. Teravalon had seven people on the field at any time, and they had to be incredibly fit, because the ball was enchanted to never stop moving.

"Midfield," Alec said. "They tried me on goals for a while, but midfield was a better match for me."

Piper hesitated. "Midfielders can't use magic," she said. Strikers could; that was their job, to throw magic at the other players to try and control the ball. The goalkeeper, too, could use shields to help block the enormous goal.

"That's why I preferred it," he said. "Everything else at Everhill revolved around how strong my magic was. I liked that the game didn't."

He lunged at her, attempting some kind of grapple. Piper pushed his hand across his chest, twisting him awkwardly around himself. Then, in a moment of immaturity, she reached up and yanked the tie out of his hair. Black strands fell across his face.

Alec grunted. "That wasn't fair."

"Fair?" Piper jumped back, balancing on the balls of her feet. She waggled the band between her fingers, causing Alec to scowl. "A Shiv'ek isn't going to be worried about what's fair. You had a chance to grab me; you messed it up. If I was trying to kill you, would you have let me get so close? I could knife you in the gut before you could do anything about it."

Alec narrowed his eyes. But she wasn't going to kill him like this. Not at The Lily, where it would make business harder for Patrik and Lily, who had only ever been kind to her. Not in front of Caleb and Madelyn, who seemed to actually like the mage.

In the Ilian. Where the water would make it easier.

Alec lunged. Piper turned with him and ducked under the punch. He'd overextended himself. As he recovered, Piper landed a hard punch in his ribs.

"You're slow," she taunted.

His eyes narrowed. He stepped towards her, snapping his left hand out in a way that would probably knock down a Teravalon player. Piper ducked again, taking advantage of their closeness to throw a punch at his exposed stomach.

It was like punching a wall. Alec grunted, and pain travelled up Piper's arm, even though she'd thrown the punch well. Punching Saxe in training was nothing like that.

That moment of distraction, of pain, cost her. Piper didn't see his right-handed cross until it connected solidly with her jaw. She stumbled backwards, hands coming up defensively.

"Hey!" Caleb shouted.

Piper looked up. Caleb stalked across the ground towards them while Madelyn watched on, her mouth open in horror.

"You hit her!" Caleb shouted. He jabbed a threatening finger at the mage, who was almost double his height.

Alec didn't even seem to notice the boy yelling at him. He stood rooted to the spot. His mouth hung open, his eyes wide.

"Fate," he whispered, horror in his voice. "I expected you to dodge!"

Piper rolled her jaw gingerly. "Caleb," she said. "It's okay."

"He hit you!" Caleb whirled around, his fists clenched by his sides.

Piper crouched down to his eye level. "We're practicing," she told him. "Practicing is important. Sometimes, when you practice fighting, people hurt each other. But I'm okay."

Caleb frowned. He reached out, and Piper let him turn her face to look at the side where Alec had hit her.

"Why do you need to practice?" he asked. Piper took his hands.

"Because the bad people who took your mum might want to fight us," Piper said. His dark eyes fixed on hers. Piper wrapped both her hands around his. "Okay?"

Caleb bit his lip. "Okay," he said. Piper smiled and squeezed his hands.

"Keep playing with Maddy," she whispered. "I need to show this mage he can't beat me just because he's bigger than me."

Caleb chuckled. "You can beat anyone," he said. Then his expression sobered. "You'll get Mum back."

He pulled free, and Piper let him go.

When she got Abby back, would she ever see them again? If she had to leave the city, and Abby didn't want to ...

Piper pushed that thought away and got to her feet. Alec's gaze traced over her jaw as Piper faced him.

"I thought you'd dodge," he repeated.

"When I didn't, you should have pressed your advantage," she told him, frowning. "That's what Lore would have done, and she'd have more than the one bruise."

Alec rubbed his stomach where Piper had punched him.

"I'm not going to hit a woman while she's helpless," he said.

Piper's mouth fell open.

"Helpless?" she spluttered. "I haven't been helpless since I was nine years old!"

"Still—"

"Is that what they taught you at Everhill?" Piper interrupted. "Don't press an advantage, wait for your opponent to recover? Because in the real world, that gets you killed!"

"I can't just hit you like the people I played Teravalon with!" Alec snapped. "I'll hurt you!"

Piper closed the space between them. Alec jerked back, but Piper hooked one foot around his ankle.

Alec overbalanced, slamming into the ground hard.

"Don't. Underestimate. Me."

Piper spun, pacing back a few steps. Her chest heaved, and she could feel her heart thundering under her shirt. She hadn't been treated like a delicate wallflower for fourteen years.

Piper turned back to face him.

"Are you actually going to try?" she demanded. "Or do you give up?"

Alec glowered at her, pushing to his feet. "I don't give up," he spat.

Piper held out her arms. "Well, then?"

She struck. Alec wasn't prepared for her; she caught him off guard. He brought up his arms in a block that intercepted Piper's left wrist, but her right snuck underneath to find the hollow beneath his ribs. Her right hand. Which Lore had crushed not a week ago.

Pain radiated from the backs of her fingers, and Piper sucked in a breath. She should have known better than to punch with that hand.

Alec lunged. Piper dodged. She punched his arm, hitting a bunch of muscle in a way that would make it partially numb. Alec grunted.

"You were holding back before," he accused, then he threw another punch.

Piper pushed it to the side, narrowly avoiding him. "So were you."

He was pretty good, actually. The Teravalon training showed; he deflected well, pushed her aside and almost danced out of the way of some of her blows. He went for grapples more than punches, though he didn't succeed in actually grabbing her.

But, as physical as Teravalon could get, it still had rules.

And Piper didn't have to play by them.

He lashed out, and Piper spun under his arm. Behind him, she twisted and landed a solid kick to the small of Alec's back. He stumbled.

"You need to be faster," Piper said. "And you're predictable."

She grimaced when she realised what she was doing. She shouldn't be teaching him to fight her more effectively. She should be working out the easiest way to kill him.

Alec made a sound rather like a growl and darted towards Piper. Catching her around the waist, he tackled her to the ground, not bothering to break her fall. The air left Piper's lungs as she found herself on her back, looking up at the sky.

Now *that* was not predictable.

Before she could catch her breath, Alec knelt beside her, grabbing one of her wrists.

Instinct took over. She lashed out with her legs, catching Alec in the side. He let go of her arm with a stout curse. Piper twisted, this time catching him in the shoulder and head, her stomach muscles screaming at her from the movement.

He fell sideways, and Piper used the momentum to roll to her knees and launch herself at him. He might have been bigger, but Piper's knee found the middle of Alec's chest, pinning him down. She caught his right hand, his dominant hand, with her left, and pinned it over his head. With her other hand, she covered Alec's face, pressing her fingertips against his eyelids in warning.

Under her, Alec stilled. His breath came raggedly. Piper could feel it against her wrist.

Piper tapped her fingers on Alec's closed eyelids. "You're blind," she said. She squeezed the wrist pinned above his head. "You're disarmed." She took her hand off his face, and Alec's eyes flicked open as Piper flicked his throat with one finger. "And you're dead."

They sat like that for a heartbeat. Alec's eyes were fixed on hers, power burning with blue-black fire in their depths.

Piper bit the inside of her lip. Maybe that had been a mistake.

Small feet, attached to small legs in a worn blue skirt, appeared in her vision. "Piper?" Madelyn asked softly.

Piper pushed herself off Alec. She used the movement to mask her face as she schooled her expression. When she met Madelyn's hazel eyes, she could smile again.

"What's up, baby?" she asked, holding out her arms. Madelyn took her hands carefully.

It had been a bad idea. She'd scared the children, and now Alec knew what she was capable of. She'd have been better off with him underestimating her.

Piper took a shaking breath and picked Madelyn up. She could feel the little girl shake, and one of her hands wrapped around Piper's braid, tugging it just enough to make Piper wince.

"Come on, Caleb," Piper said, holding out her hand. "Let's go do homework."

Caleb stared at her from where he stood a few metres away, his eyes wide. His gaze darted between Piper and Alec, still sprawled on the ground behind her. For a moment, Piper didn't think Caleb would move. Then, slowly, his eyes still too wide, he edged towards her.

Piper paid Alec no more mind as she gathered her children and headed back inside.

Later that evening, Piper sat in her living room. Alone.

It was a strange feeling. The last few days, she'd barely been alone for longer than the time it took her to shower. Even then, if she took more than three minutes, she'd have at least Madelyn, maybe both of them, knocking on the door. She'd learned a few days ago to use the lock; Madelyn thought nothing of throwing it wide open and stepping inside.

Piper sighed, rubbing her forehead.

Alec was smart. There was no way he hadn't realised what she had. He'd probably known it the entire time.

They weren't both getting out of this.

Like her thoughts had conjured him, Piper's door opened. She looked up, fixing the mage with a scowl. "What?" she demanded. "Don't you knock anymore?"

"I would if the door wasn't open," he said, brows raised. "If you don't want me here, just lock it."

Piper dragged a breath in through her nose, choosing to ignore that comment. "So, we're going to the Lower Ilian tomorrow?"

Alec dropped himself into the armchair. "Yep," he said. "Seems like the best place to look. It's the best … Well. It's the only real lead we have."

"Fine." Piper got to her feet.

"Where do you think you're going?"

A hand latched around her arm, and Piper spun. Her leaf-shaped blade was in her hand before she thought about it, resting against Alec's pulse point. His eyes widened.

"Give me a reason," she breathed. "I dare you."

"Are you going to Hazel and Liam's?" he demanded, gaze turning hard. "I warn you. No matter how good you think you are, you're not likely to get past a mage, a dwarfsmith and the two puka that live with them.

"What do you think?" she asked instead of answering.

His grip tightened on her arm, and Piper bit back her gasp of pain.

"I told you before, I won't let you hurt them," Alec said. "I screwed up. Not them. Don't do it."

For perhaps the first time in eleven years, Piper's hand wavered on her dagger. Of course he'd assume the worst. She was a killer, after all.

Piper ripped her arm from Alec's grip. "I'm going downstairs to see if Rose can pick the kids up from school tomorrow if I'm late," she said. "Don't flatter yourself, *mage*. You don't impact my life that much." She spun on her heel and marched for the door.

"What happened?" he said.

Despite herself, Piper paused, her hand on the doorframe.

"What happened when?" she asked, not turning.

She heard a scuff, then footsteps.

"We're good together, Piper," he said. "You're smart. You know the city. We've made more progress on finding both Jai and Abby in the last few days than I made in a month by myself. So what happened?"

Piper clenched her fingers, and she realised she still had her dagger in her hand. She slid it into its sheath.

"You know what happened," she said softly.

She couldn't be certain. But she thought Alec flinched.

Piper pushed the door back open and took the stairs to the main room two at a time.

TWENTY THREE

"I don't understand," Madelyn said. "Where will you be?"

Piper dropped to her knees and took one of Madelyn's hands.

"I might be here," she reminded the girl. "But I might not be. Either way, it will be me or Rose who picks you up this afternoon. Don't go with anyone else. Understand?"

"Does this mean you know where Mum is?" Caleb asked.

Piper reached up and cupped his cheek. For once, Caleb didn't pull away.

"Maybe," she said, the only honest answer she could give him. "I don't know yet. But maybe."

Caleb frowned. "You won't disappear too, will you?" he asked softly.

Piper patted his cheek. "No," she promised. "No. I won't leave you alone."

She hoped it was a promise she could keep.

Madelyn wrapped Piper in a tight hug. "Please find Mummy," she whispered.

Piper kissed the top of her head. "I'll try my best," she breathed, quietly enough that the girl wouldn't hear. She pulled back, and Caleb surprised her by squeezing her hand of his own volition.

"Don't disappear," he said.

Piper smiled at him and nodded. "Go on." She gave them both a gentle push. "Have a good day."

Madelyn offered Piper a watery smile, her eyes large in her face. Caleb reached down and took his sister's hand.

"Bye," Madelyn called, waving. Caleb tugged her inside the school.

Piper ran her hand over her side, feeling the bumps in her coat pockets. That morning, Rose, likely sensing Piper's foul mood when they'd spoken the night before, had added a bowl of violaberries to their breakfast tray. They were probably intended to cheer her up. But Piper, not wanting to be cheered up, had just refilled her pouch and slid it into her coat, where the weight pressed against her ribs.

She ducked her head, taking a deep breath. The tightness in her chest eased, just enough for her to breathe normally again. The stinging in her eyes receded when she blinked hard a few times.

Find Abby. Ditch the mage. Leave the city.

Piper's chest burned, and she grimaced.

Save the prince, she added reluctantly. *Then ditch the mage.*

Permanently.

"Time to go," that same mage said from somewhere above her.

Piper pushed to her feet, and the motion forced him to back up a step. "Fine," she said.

Piper's boots tapped on the stone bridge spanning the Amethyst River. The tram tracks lined the middle of the space, bracketed by a wide lane on either side for carts and autocarts. A raised footpath kept pedestrians out of the rain in spring and summer, and the snow in winter. Tidy garden beds, not even a foot wide, separated the footpath from the road. Far below them, the river chugged lazily past. The purple algae that gave the river its name bloomed around the support pylons and turned the foam mauve and lilac. They stung with tiny paralytics, just like a jellyfish, when touched by bare skin.

Once, when she'd tried to run away, Lore had plunged her arm in a barrel full of those algae.

Piper rubbed her arm and looked away from the water.

Alec walked at her side without saying a word. She wasn't paying that much attention to him, instead training her gaze straight ahead.

It'll be your execution.

She had to do it. Even if they didn't find the prince, she had to. She had no choice.

Without looking, she jumped down the step from the bridge to Factory Road. She ignored the pedestrian crossing, instead darting diagonally across the tram tracks. Behind her, she heard Alec swear. An autocart honked, then she heard the slapping of footsteps behind her.

"You need to be quick here," Piper said without looking back. "You're not in Redwell anymore, Rylan."

She felt him bristle behind her. "You're assuming that I–"

Another autocart screeched, almost clipping them. Piper grabbed Alec's sleeve and tugged him to the other side of the road before he could get them both killed.

"Save it," she said. "You're in rush hour around the factories. And you won't win against an autocart."

They might be more expensive than horses, but autocarts didn't need the same kind of care that animals did, making them popular with factory owners who worked long hours.

Behind her, Alec scoffed. "Nothing wrong with a horse," he muttered.

Piper opened her mouth to reply, but stopped herself. She'd thought, as a spellbinder, he'd be interested in the carts; she was surprised that he seemed to actively dislike them. But she was determined not to be curious.

It didn't matter what he was interested in, or what he liked and disliked. Not to her.

A huge building made of corrugated metal stretched over Piper's head; one of the many factories that called the Ilian home. They lined Factory Lane and marched towards the river, petering out in the narrower streets off the main road. There were few shops on this side of the river, beyond corner stores and grungy eateries, and while the roads were well maintained out of necessity – they were needed for transporting goods up and down – only the main street and the bridges had tram tracks across them.

The street started to slope downwards under Piper's feet. She heard a rustle behind her and glanced back to see Alec pulling out a map.

"If what Liam said is right," he mused, almost to himself, "we should hit the flooded area soon."

"In a few streets," Piper agreed, turning her gaze forward again.

They wound away from the main road, heading downhill towards the floodplain. Piper ducked sideways into an alleyway, feeling dampness radiating off the stone retaining wall by her side. Alec loomed behind her, silent and stoic. She slid her hands inside her sleeves; it was a tight fit, with the way the material clung around her wrists, but there was enough give there that she could do it, giving herself somewhere to put her hands where they couldn't fiddle with her daggers. Or stab Alec.

Her fingers met an unexpected texture, and Piper yelped. She shoved up her right sleeve, her eyes wide.

"What?" Alec demanded, spinning to her.

The dragon tattoo was still wrapped around her wrist, the tip of the tail vanishing under the bandage on her hand. It glistened green and purple and black in the light from the suns, oil on water. It didn't look any different from the hundred or so other times she'd looked at it in the past few days.

"What is it?" Alec repeated. He reached for Piper, but she pushed his hand away.

She ran her fingers over the back of her wrist. Clearly defined scales met her fingertips. Piper could feel each ridge, feel the hard points of the edge of the spines that ran down the dragon's back. She pulled her hand away, clenching it when she realised her fingers were shaking.

"Why is it textured?" she asked carefully.

Alec grimaced. "Ah," he said. "That."

Piper looked up at him, narrowing her eyes. "You knew this would happen?" she snapped.

"I didn't know it would happen so quickly!" he protested, holding up his hands. "It took two weeks for Laithos to get a texture on my skin." He touched his throat, running his fingers along a tentacle.

Piper traced it with her eyes. "What is it, anyway?" she asked, curious despite herself.

"An Immortal?" he offered snidely, raising his brows. Piper's fingers brushed the hilt of her dagger, but she tamped down the impulse to draw it and stab him in the neck.

"I mean," she growled, "what animal is it?"

"They'll get upset at you if you call them animals," Alec commented idly. Then, when Piper's glare grew heated, he sighed. "He's a kraken."

"Why are a kraken and a dragon Immortals?" she wondered out loud. All the stories she'd read said that Nyssa created such creatures from the primals, the race that had walked the planet before the cataclysm, and before magic.

Alec shrugged. "I'm not sure," he said. "Laithos is cagey about it. Maybe your Immortal will tell you."

"It won't tell me anything," Piper muttered under her breath. She spun on her heel, continuing down the alleyway. As she walked, her fingers found their way to the textured skin on her wrist. That almost rumbling started up again in her mind, and Piper pushed it away.

She kept half her attention on Alec as they walked. They hadn't found the water yet; that meant his powers were still at full capacity, whatever that might be. She hadn't seen the scorpion construct since the first night and had no idea if he kept it with him. She didn't know if the construct's poison could incapacitate her, or if it wouldn't be strong enough to get through her defences.

Piper chewed her lip, her gaze tripping over the buildings on all sides. Her boot came down with a slapping sound, and Piper glanced at her feet. Water seeped up through the cobblestones from the oversaturated ground. She scuffed at a loose paver, and it shifted in place, sending tiny waves racing for her boot.

She hummed in thought.

"And so it starts," Alec murmured beside her.

"And it only gets deeper from here," she said. Her boots were waterproof, to an extent. But they wouldn't stand up against something like this for long.

Piper stepped forward, grimacing. The water splashed under her feet, making her wince. There'd be no sneaking through here. After a long pause, she heard Alec approaching behind her. His footfalls were heavier, the water splashing more under his boots than her own.

Damp stone walls – timber would rot quickly here – stretched above her head, topped by corrugated metal roofs. Tiles were expensive, and thatch would let in the damp. And rot. So much rot.

"How do you suppose they keep out the mould?" Alec murmured.

Piper shrugged one shoulder. "I don't think they do," she said. She gestured to the corner of a building. Water stains stretched up its side, most down lower, but some all the way to the roof. Someone had patched that corner at some point, timber beams holding down a sheet of metal. The timber was greying. It looked like something had some along and gnawed out the inside, leaving just the barest outline behind.

"This is not a kind area," he said.

Piper laughed without humour. "Most of this city is not kind," she told him. "At least, not when you have no money." She saw Alec open his mouth, likely to argue, but Piper forged ahead.

The water slowly rose up the sides of her boots. Around one corner, and her shoes started to make a noticeable splashing sound with each step. Another street, and water shushed as she moved. A twist in the road, and the tops of her boots were covered. She stopped when it got to her ankle.

Any higher and it would seep in around her laces. As much as she didn't want wet feet, that wasn't what made her pause.

Piper grabbed Alec's arm as he stepped past her. His muscles tensed under her hand. She pointed. Ahead of them, a patch of violet algae floated, caught against the side of the building.

"Not a good idea," Piper said.

Alec followed her gaze and muttered something under his breath. "I have no desire to be stung by that stuff again," he said aloud.

Piper glanced at him. "Not fun, is it?"

Alec looked at her, both eyebrows rising. "No, it's not fun," Alec said after a moment, turning his attention back towards the water, and the algae.

Piper had never lived in this area, even when she was at her poorest. Only the really stubborn and the really desperate stayed in the Lower Ilian. But, if she did live here, she didn't think she'd just wait for the water to rise. She doubted those who did were that passive, either. Piper glanced around.

There. Around the side of the building, not even as wide as her boot, a narrow ledge of timber protruded, supported by iron stakes. It would take her weight easily. Piper grabbed the handhold bolted into the side of the building and pulled herself up. The timber creaked under her, but held fast. Piper nodded, then glanced up to find Alec watching her, one eyebrow raised.

"I don't think that's going to hold me," he said.

Piper edged forward. "Feels pretty sturdy," she said. "Your choice is this or walk through the water."

Alec screwed up his face. "That is not much of a choice," he said. Piper snorted. He stared at her, and Piper realised what she'd done. She turned from him, shoving the momentary amusement she'd felt down into a ball in her stomach.

Dead, she reminded herself. He was already dead. He was just walking around for a few hours more.

He wouldn't leave the Lower Ilian.

There was a creak behind her, and Piper turned. Alec pulled himself onto the narrow walkway, teetering a little.

"Right," he muttered, glaring apprehensively at the timber under his feet. "Let's get on with it."

TWENTY FOUR

The timber slid under Piper's boots as she made her way across the street. She gritted her teeth, her left hand clutching the gutter above her head in an iron grip. The board shook with every step she took, and almost dislodged with every step Alec took behind her.

Piper glanced down to her right. The water rose steadily up the side of the buildings; they were still descending into the floodplain. More and more violet algae dotted the street, and Piper shivered.

Perhaps rebuilding with stilts would help, but rebuilding anything in the city was expensive. Materials had to come from somewhere, and even when they were made in the city, the bigger businesses and more wealthy residences would always be served first. Even if they did have stilts, they'd have to figure out some walkways. The algae interacted poorly with mortar, and so much water would rot wood in a heartbeat, as was evidenced on every house with timber repairs.

Piper edged around a corner, then stopped. A muffled curse sounded from behind her.

"What are you doing?" Alec asked. Piper looked over her shoulder. He hung precariously, halfway around the corner. One hand was clenched in the gutter, his knuckles white. His other hand gripped a windowsill near Piper's elbow, his muscular forearm corded with the strength of his grip.

Piper glanced down to the plank underneath her. "There's no more path," she said. She twisted, grabbing a shutter with one hand to help her balance as she turned around on the narrow plank.

"Whoever put it here didn't just jump into the water and swim," Alec said shortly. "It must continue somewhere."

"Yeah, I'm looking," Piper snapped half-heartedly. Her boot slipped on the gummy timber, and Piper's grip on the gutter tightened, her heart leaping into her throat and pounding a staccato beat.

She really, really didn't want to fall into that water.

There was nothing to her left. The building across from them was too far to jump to, even if she could see a foothold to aim for. And in this damp, there was no guarantee anything would hold her if she landed on it.

Piper glanced right, but her vision filled with black hair shining blue in the light of the two suns. Huffing, Piper turned again.

Further to her left, the street narrowed into something more like an alleyway. The buildings would be close enough to move between there. But there was nothing pegged into the side of the building that she could use to get down the wall.

Look up.

Piper jumped at the voice, nearly losing her footing. She looked at Alec. "What did you say?" she asked.

Alec blinked at her. "No one said anything," he replied, his voice tight. His voice was far more strained than the one she had heard.

A rumbling, comforting purr started up her arm.

"Oh no," she said vehemently. "We are not doing this!"

"What–" Alec started.

"I am not talking to you," Piper snapped.

Alec's blue gaze flicked over her, then down her right arm. He smirked.

"Ah," he said. His smugness was somewhat ruined by the way he clutched the corner of the building.

Piper glared at him. "Not a word, mage," she said.

She did what the voice suggested and looked up. Not far from her hand, a black scuff marked the gutter; the kind left behind by black-soled shoes. She couldn't see much of the roof itself from this angle; couldn't tell if it was flat or steep, rotten or sound. She let go of the window and grasped the gutter with both hands.

"What are you doing?" Alec asked.

Piper ignored him. Getting one foot on the windowsill, she pushed herself up. Even with her foot on the window, she could only just get her chin to the gutter. She jumped.

Beside her, Alec swore. She heard him slip, then a clatter that she assumed was him grabbing the shutter she'd just let go of. She could feel his arm beside her leg.

Piper raised her body over the edge, her arm muscles trembling at what felt like the worst pushup of her life. They screamed at her to let go and drop back down. Her arms straightened, the roof stretching before her at far more of an angle than she had hoped. Piper slipped, pitching forward. She couldn't contain a yelp, and Alec swore again. But she rolled, yanking one foot up and catching her heel in the gutter.

It shuddered. Then it held.

"Oh thank fate," she breathed.

"I'll assume you're not dead, then," came Alec's voice from below her. Piper shook her head, then realised he couldn't see her.

"Still alive," she confirmed. "Roof's kinda steeper than I expected, though."

"Great." She heard the creaking of the timber plank, then two hands appeared on the gutter. "Move out of the way."

Piper scooted to the side, using her hands on the corrugated metal and heels in the gutter to crab-crawl sideways. The gutter creaked, and Piper yanked her feet out of it so fast she slid down the roof. She braced both hands, hissing as the friction burned one and the other scraped against a bolt.

"What was that?" Alec asked.

"Nothing," Piper ground out. She slipped another inch or so down the iron, the bandage on her right hand making for poor purchase against the metal. "Just hurry up so I can brace my feet again. I'm slipping."

Alec let out a soft curse, and the gutter shook. Piper hooked one heel over the edge, pulling her leg back to try and brace it. Her thigh and stomach muscles screamed from her cramped-over position. Her left hand dug further into the bolt; Piper didn't dare move it. A wet trickle slid down her palm.

Alec's hands flexed, the muscles standing out. Agonisingly slowly, Alec's blue-black hair appeared over the top of the gutter. Then his shoulders.

He grunted, one arm over the edge. "Move."

"I really can't," Piper said, strain in her voice.

Alec pushed himself up a little further, groaning with the effort. He hooked one leg over the edge of the gutter. Piper felt it buckle under her heel and pressed harder, back into the roof.

Then Alec rolled. He let out another curse as his back slammed into the roof's pitch. His left arm flung out, and he gripped the peak to pull himself up.

"That was harder than I thought," he muttered.

"Yep." Piper unclenched from her half-foetal position, sighing as her stomach muscles relaxed. She slid another inch down the roof, and wedged her heel into the gutter.

It gave way under her with a screech.

"Fu–"

She shot towards the edge, the bolt tearing into her palm. Something hard fisted in the back of her coat, pulling it tight. It jerked tight across her shoulders and underarms, pulling her arms up into the air. Her legs hung off the edge, swinging over the water below. It wouldn't be deep enough to break her fall.

Behind her, Alec grunted. Then he heaved. Piper scrabbled for purchase with her feet as he hauled her back up the roof to sprawl beside him. He pinned her to the roof with one hand, loosening his grip enough that Piper could move her arms again. She reached out with one hand and grabbed the gable.

She winced as she held up her other hand, examining the blood seeping from the slice on her palm. "That was not as fun as I imagined."

Alec pushed himself up. His forehead creased as he took in Piper's palm, then he looked at her. "Can you swim?"

"What?" Piper blinked at him, and Alec gestured to the street below them.

"I'm trying to work out if I'll have to dive in after you if you fall," he said. "Can you swim?"

Piper pushed herself upright, bracing herself against the pitch of the roof, careful of bolts this time.

"I can swim," she said. Alec raised an eyebrow at her, and Piper scowled. "Okay, I can't swim well. But well enough not to drown. Besides," she added, glancing down into the street, "at least on this side of town, the bigger issue is hitting your head when you fall."

Alec grunted in agreement, rubbing the back of his head.

Piper craned her neck, looking towards the corner of the roofs. "Come on," she said, nudging Alec with her foot so she didn't have to let go of the peak. "It looks a bit flatter over there."

Alec glanced over, then groaned. "I have to get across the not-flat part to get there, though," he complained. But he pushed to his feet, gripping the roof with one hand and holding out the other for balance on the steep roof.

The roof further along was flatter. At the edge, Piper glanced down at the water below her, swallowed, then jumped, crossing her fingers desperately. She landed hard on the other side, the metal clanging underneath her.

Piper glanced back over her shoulder, then scurried out of the way for Alec. With his much longer legs, he barely needed to jump, which made Piper glare at him resentfully.

The next roof across was completely flat. And on the one after that ...

"Oh thank fate," Alec said when he saw the walkway spread out across the corrugated metal of the roof. As Piper watched from relative safety, he gingerly picked his way across the rooftop towards her, having to check each spot before he put his full weight on it. With one hand out to grab onto the corrugated metal if he did fall through, and his legs spread wide, he looked like some odd kind of crab or spider.

"You are making this way harder than it needs to be," Piper said.

Alec fixed her with a black look. "Just because you're so tiny you weigh nothing," he muttered under his breath. He reached Piper and sighed in relief as he stepped onto the thick wooden boards of the walkway. "This feels much better," he admitted, testing the feel of the wood under his boots.

Piper glanced down. Where the metal had flexed even under just her feet, the boards held steady despite Alec's greater weight. He raked his hair out of his eyes with one hand, and looked over the rooftops.

"I'm glad this place has these, at least," he said, scuffing his boot against the timber beneath them.

Piper had to agree with him. She shaded her eyes against the glare of the suns on the rooftops, the light bouncing off the metal to stab at her eyes. Roofs of all heights and pitches patched together as far as she could see. Their newfound timber path wound around one much steeper roof, vanishing from sight.

"It still doesn't help with the flooding," she said, glancing over the side of the building.

"No, but at least people bigger than you can move around," Alec said, casting a glance Piper's way. Then he pulled the map from his pocket. "Where do you suppose we are?"

Piper crossed the boards to stand beside him as Alec unfolded his map of Silversdale. He folded it back over itself so only the Lower Ilian was visible.

She hesitated, glancing back the way they'd come. "If this is Factory Lane here, and we took this street before we climbed up the roof ..."

"I think we crossed over to this street on the roofs," Alec said, pointing. "So that'd put us here?"

"Maybe?" Piper shrugged.

Alec rolled his eyes. "How do you ever find your way to any of your jobs?"

"Landmarks," she said, her voice clipped. Then she spun on her heel. "Come on." Her back ramrod straight, Piper marched off in the direction she thought was right. Fate help Alec if he tried to correct her – she'd likely stab him.

She'd have to stab him anyway; she didn't have any of her poisons.

Piper looked at the water below. She couldn't tell how deep it was. Was it deep enough to drown a man as tall as Alec? Even a foot of water could be deadly if he hit his head on the way down. With the windows and shutters and fate knew what else hanging into the street, a head injury was almost a given.

A single beam crossed a larger gap between two buildings. The one on the other side had a second storey; smaller than the first, the stone walls stretched upwards, creating two-tiered terraces, one with a little table and chairs on it. Though Piper couldn't fathom who would want to sit and look out at this part of the city.

Piper started to edge out, but Alec caught her arm.

"Let me go first," he said. "If it breaks, and I go down, I'm a stronger swimmer than you."

"I don't think the water's that deep," she argued, but when she peered down, a dark, murky colour filled her vision. She couldn't see the bottom, nor the shapes of anything that might have been left on the ground when the floods started.

"Do you want to test that?" Alec didn't wait for a response to his question. Instead, he took Piper's shoulders and moved her out of the way. Piper didn't protest. He eased out on the timber board, testing it before he gave it his full weight. Then, in three quick, somewhat reckless strides, he was across.

Alec turned to grin smugly back at her. "Piece of cake," he said, gesturing.

Piper rolled her eyes. "Whatever." Not wanting to be shown up by him, Piper nudged the heavy board with the toe of her boot. It barely moved. Swallowing, and hoping to fate that it continued to stay put, Piper stepped onto it. It wobbled with her weight, sending Piper pitching forward. Alec reached for her, but Piper stumbled straight across the board and into the opposite wall.

She stood there for a second, trying to force her breath to stop heaving in her lungs.

"See?" he said from beside her. "That wasn't so bad."

Piper turned to him and jabbed him in the stomach as hard as she could. Alec doubled forward. His foot slipped. Already off balance, he swayed, his face a mask of panic. Piper's heart leaped into her throat.

One of his flailing arms hit her in the face, and Piper grabbed him. The material of his shirt bunched under her fingers. She hauled him back, and Alec slammed into the wall beside her. They stood for a long moment, staring over the wall. The murky water gurgled against the stone below them, violet algae sprinkled through it.

Realising she still had a hand pressed against his chest, Piper forced her fingers to unclench from Alec's shirt.

"Right," she said. "No more falling. From either of us."

Alec nodded. "Deal," he said.

Piper cursed herself as they made their way across the rooftops again. She should have let him fall. If being near water dampened his magic, fate knew what being drenched in the stuff would do. Cut it off completely, maybe.

There was also the algae. If he fell in a patch of that, it would partially paralyse him. At the very least, it would make it difficult to move. She could slide a dagger into his throat and cut the artery there without any resistance. He'd bleed out in seconds. It would be virtually painless, if she was smart about it.

And it didn't matter if it was painless, Piper told herself crossly, stomping across another timber board. What mattered was that she get the job done. And quickly, before Lore decided she'd deserted.

The fate of a deserter was not at all pleasant.

Piper took another step forward, and a hand like steel wrapped around her forearm. Alec jerked her back, and Piper stumbled into him. She turned, scowling.

"What was that for?" she snapped. Alec inclined his head. The board she'd been about to step on rested precariously between two others. Any weight on it, even as slight as hers, would likely cause it to slide into the street below.

"Oh," Piper said.

"Want to tell me what's got you so preoccupied?" he asked her.

Piper scowled, wrapped her arms around herself, and tilted up her chin. "No," she said, turning away.

"Right," he said sarcastically. But he let Piper draw into the lead, both of them careful to avoid the loose board.

She should keep an eye out for those. If he tripped on one, he'd be off balance. Startled. He probably wouldn't even notice her dagger sliding into his neck. It'd have to be his neck, she'd decided. Anywhere else was too easy to miss. He'd still die from a heart-wound, but if she got it wrong, it would take longer. He'd be in pain.

Her fingers brushed her stiletto through her coat. But that wouldn't do. The stiletto was best for stabbing, for bashing. She'd need something with a razor edge.

The knife in her boot, or even better, her leaf-shaped blade. That was easier to get to. Her gaze flickered to the side, taking in his height. She'd have to be fast. If he blocked her, grabbed her, she wouldn't break free. He was far stronger than her.

Beside her, Alec made a half-amused sound. She met his gaze and sucked in a breath, her feet sticking to the board underneath her.

His eyes burned with blue-black fire, lingering somewhere beneath the irises. They swept over Piper, scalding her skin even through her clothes.

"Are you going to do it?" he asked, his voice rolling like soft thunder.

Despite herself, Piper took a step back. "Do what?" she tried.

Alec blinked, and the glow in his eyes faded. "We both know what you're thinking," he said.

Piper clenched her fists. She tilted her chin up, forcing herself to meet those burning eyes, no matter the power in them.

"I haven't decided yet," she lied. She had decided. She had to.

Alec let out a sound that was half chuckle, half huff. He blinked again, and his eyes were their normal sky blue.

"All right, Bella," he said, and Piper stiffened. "I'll play your game for now." He gestured to the rooftop. "After you."

Piper gritted her teeth and stepped forward.

The water rose, or the buildings sank, until the flooding reached just beneath roof level. Algae floated past in patches, bright purple against the murky water. Piper swallowed. Anything could be in that water. Snakes or crocodiles, though the latter were rare in the city. Even the occasional kappa was known to appear and drag someone down into the depths.

Alec nudged her in the back. "Look," he said.

The buildings ahead of her changed. No more metal roofs padded with boards; these were made of stone. "We're at the old abbey," she whispered. She twisted, glancing up at Alec. "From when Silvaein was first founded."

Alec frowned. "It's still standing?" he said. He leaned towards it, cocking his head and studying the architecture.

241

"It's a religious site, so no one wanted to dismantle it I guess," she said with a shrug. She tilted her head back. "How do we get across?"

The abbey didn't have a wall – at least, not one that Piper could see above the water. The closest building had a gap of at least five metres between it and where they stood.

"I can't jump that," she said, pointing.

"I'd struggle to jump that too," he said dryly. "There has to be another way across."

Piper tilted her head, taking in the scene. Sunlight glittered off the water as far as the eye could see, turning the grey-brown liquid sparkling. The abbey itself took up a large, circular footprint at the edge of the Lower Ilian, almost exactly like–

"This is it!" Piper reached up and yanked the map from Alec's top pocket.

"What?" Alec said. "What is it?"

She didn't have the skill of folding the paper back on itself to create a perfect square. Instead, she knelt and spread the map out on a dry part of the roof. "Look," she said, pointing. "It's just like the map my informant sent me. See here?" She drew a curved line on the map with her finger. "This is where the children went missing most recently. Mostly from the Oldtown, a few from the Market District. Then here" – she drew another line inside the first – "these are the ones who went missing before that. A few in the Oldtown, but mostly in the Lower Ilian." She looked up at Alec. "The poorest districts. Where people are less likely to be missed."

Alec sat back on his heels, frowning. "Parents and neighbours would notice they were missing," he said.

Piper shook her head. "Parents, maybe," she said. "But they'd have a hard time getting the police to really look for them." She hesitated. "Most of the time, when a parent from the Oldtown or the Lower Ilian reports a child missing to the police, it's a farce. They're already long gone on a black ship."

Alec flinched. "Surely not."

"It's sad, but true." Piper shrugged. "Unfortunately, some people are so poor they have nothing to sell but their children."

Children that went away on the black ships never came back. No one knew where they went, but it was safe to assume it was somewhere other than Rhealgo. Somewhere there was a market for child slavery.

Alec was silent for a moment. When Piper looked up, it was to find him studying her.

"There's something you're not telling me about those ships," he said, his tone close to accusatory.

Piper laughed without humour. "I almost ended up on one myself."

Alec's blue eyes went wide. "Your parents—"

"My parents weren't in much of a position to do anything, at that point," Piper said. She held up one hand before he could try to get more out of her. "We're not talking about that right now." She gestured back to the map. "I didn't notice it on your map. It didn't have the abbey marked. But the abbey is right in the centre of the blank space, between where all the children went missing."

Alec hummed in thought. When Piper looked up, it was to find him rubbing his jaw, his gaze fixed on the buildings in front of them. "That is very interesting," he murmured. "One of the few places with liveable space above the water line, separated by tonnes of water and abandoned buildings."

Piper rocked back and forward on her heels. "Do you think they could be in there?" she said quietly.

Alec shrugged. "It's possible," he said. "And to be honest, possible is better than I've had in a month."

Piper chewed her lip, bracing her arms on her knees. "I think we can get into the upper bailey this way," she said, touching a part of the map where it looked like the buildings were close together. "We'd have to circle around, though."

Alec looked out over the abbey. "I don't think we have a choice in that," he said. "I can't see me making that jump, unless there were Chaos Demons on our heels."

Piper snorted. "And even then, I'm ending up wet," she muttered.

Alec swept up his map and stood. "Come on," he said, peering out over the water. "Let's try and get into the bailey as soon as we can. I don't want to be there at nightfall."

Piper shuddered. Attempting to pick their way across rooftops with just the moons to guide their way was not something she wanted to contemplate. Pushing herself up, she followed the mage across the stone roofs.

TWENTY FIVE

Piper's boots tapped on stone. After such a long time hearing only tinny creaks and the soft thud of leather on timber, it was a foreign sound.

They'd been silent for a while. Alec, in the lead, kept his gaze trained on the abbey as they slowly circled it, back-switching across roofs to avoid the larger gaps. Piper knew a lot of that was for her benefit; some gaps he'd be able to jump with his much longer legs, if he were alone.

Piper peered over a roof, frowning at what she saw. "Does the water look like it's going down to you?" she called.

"Street's rising below us," he said. "That's why all these roofs are getting higher."

Piper glanced back. Now that he said it, she could see the roofs behind them step down until they plateaued almost a hundred metres behind them. The roofs stretched out, water glittering between them, until the buildings rose again, then turned into the three- and four-storey-tall factories of the Ilian, close to the river.

Sunlight glittered off something on the roofs behind them. Piper squinted, shading her eyes with one hand. The glint vanished behind a chimney stack, and Piper's heart leaped into her mouth.

She spun around so fast she almost tripped and fell into the water below. Ahead of her, Alec glanced at his watch.

"I'm hungry," he complained. "Maybe we should stop soon and—"

Piper latched onto his elbow, tugging him forward.

"Hey!" Alec snapped, yanking his arm from her grip. "What do you think you're doing?"

Piper grabbed at him again. "Someone's following us," she hissed.

Alec stiffened. He started to turn, but Piper yanked him back around.

"Don't turn around, you idiot!"

"Are you sure?" Alec asked.

"I mean, it could be a coincidence that someone is taking the same path as us across a part of the city that is currently deserted." She dragged him forward, around the second storey of a building, where they wouldn't be as exposed.

"A yes would suffice," he said.

"Yes, I'm sure!" Sorely tempted to kick him, Piper jumped the gap between two buildings.

Alec followed. "Did you see who it was?" he asked.

"Just a flash," she said. "No idea what caused it. Could be a weapon. Could be the crown jewels for all I know. I just know they're following us."

"When you spend your life following people," a voice drawled ahead of them, "it's only natural to know when you've become the prey."

Ice crawled up Piper's spine. A familiar figure, with muddy blonde hair and swamp-green eyes, stepped out from behind a porch. A bastard sword lay strapped across Saxe's back.

"What are you doing here?" Piper spat. Alec glanced between the two of them, sweeping one foot back and readying himself. He didn't know what he was getting himself into. What Saxe lacked in subtlety, professionalism and stealth, he made up for in cunning and brute strength. He was a deadly fighter, even for her. If Saxe attacked, the mage was dead. He didn't stand a chance.

A smirk lifted the corner of Saxe's mouth. The skin around her wrist itched, and Piper clenched her fist, avoiding the urge to look down at it.

"Oh, it's not just me," he purred. Soft footfalls sounded behind her. Piper spun on her heel, putting her back to Alec's. Iso stopped several metres back, crossing his arms over his chest. His long daggers, almost half the length of Saxe's sword, glinted at his belt, reflecting the sunlight off the water. That was what she'd seen flash, Piper realised.

The soft screech of metal on metal met her ears, and Piper's gaze jerked up. Ratt crouched on the roof above their heads, his lips twisted in a manic smile that showed all his yellow teeth. His brass knuckles scraped a bit of tin on the roof in a repetitive, stroking motion.

Piper's fingers wrapped around her leaf-shaped blade. She couldn't even recall drawing it.

"This is a cull," she breathed. Iso's face stayed impassive, but Ratt's smile widened, displaying mottled pink and white gums.

Behind her, Saxe tsked. "What did you expect?" he asked. "It's what we do to traitors."

"Lore's deadline isn't up yet," she called. She wanted to face him. Having her back to Saxe felt like having her back to a rampaging lesser tseoun. Like she'd get teeth and claws in her throat before she could breathe, before she could blink. But she didn't dare take her eyes off Iso and Ratt, either.

"Lore's impatient," Saxe said dismissively.

Ratt didn't scare her. He was too straightforward, too blunt. The other two, however …

Piper shifted enough that she could make out Saxe and Iso both in her peripheral vision. They'd deliberately placed themselves so that she couldn't quite focus on both of them at once.

Iso shifted, and Piper's attention snapped to him. "Lore said you have a choice," he said in his heavily accented Rhealgan. She'd never asked where he came from. Had never cared. It felt important now. What if his culture forbade unprovoked attacks?

Saxe let out a sound like a growl.

"What's Lore's choice?" Piper asked, feeling the weight of her blade in her left hand. If she could get to her twin throwing knives before they realised what she was doing, maybe she could drop two of them before they reached her.

One on one was far better odds than three on one.

"You already know that," Iso said. "Kill the mage."

Behind her, she felt Alec tense.

"He has something I need," she said, heart thudding in her throat. "I'll kill him when I'm done."

It was the truth. It had to be the truth.

Iso shook his head. "Lore won't wait," he said.

"He shouldn't have to wait," Saxe snarled, and Piper spun to him. "If you won't kill him, I will," Saxe continued.

Alec stood between them.

Piper shook her head. "I said I'll kill him," she snapped. "He's my mark. Not yours."

Iso's hand rested on one of his blades. Ratt licked his lips, his gaze alight with greed.

Saxe straightened, pretending to wipe mirth from his eyes.

Piper's hand tightened on the hilt of her dagger.

Saxe crossed his arms, a smug sneer curling his lip. "Do it, Belladonna," he said, his voice taunting. "Or don't. If you don't, I'll relish killing you myself."

"Lore would never let you," Piper said, narrowing her eyes at him.

Saxe laughed again. "He never said I couldn't."

"He wants you alive, Piper." Iso's expression was unreadable. "You won't like the punishment he's devised. It's … intense."

Piper swallowed the sick feeling in her mouth. She knew just how *intense* Lore's punishments could get. The bandage on her hand was child's play, barely the equivalent of a slap on the wrist. Lore was a master of pain.

If she killed Alec now, in front of these three, Lore would have no choice but to pardon her. And give her the money. He couldn't bully all four of them.

Alec's eyes fixed on her, something like fury burning in their depths. She felt her breathing stutter in her chest. Something ticklish dragged its way across her skin, plucking at her, moving her coat and her hair in a nonexistent breeze that flowed towards the mage.

Saxe uncrossed his arms. One hand crept up to his sword, ready to unsheathe it. There was a soft rasp; one of Iso's daggers coming free. Brass glinted on Ratt's knuckles.

It had to be now. With the water to dampen his power. With Saxe, Iso and Ratt watching. Iso might kill him quickly. Saxe would not. He'd draw it out as long as he could; he tended to scalp his victims while they were still alive. She didn't know what Ratt would do. He always lost to Iso in the bouts she'd witnessed, but she'd never fought him herself. With those brass knuckles, it would be death by blunt force trauma, and that was never a nice way to go.

Piper took a step back, her weight settling onto her right leg. She bought her left arm up in a fluid, lightning-fast movement. The tip of her blade rested between her forefinger and thumb.

Alec's eyes widened. Magic gathered around his hand. But, like she had told him in The Lily's backyard, he was too slow.

But Alec wasn't her target. Saxe was. And Saxe wasn't too slow. The dagger that should have sunk into his heart instead lodged in his shoulder.

Saxe bellowed, clapping his hand over the wound. Crimson streaked down his chest and arm. "You bitch!" he roared. He yanked her dagger from his shoulder, dropping it over the side of the building.

Piper's world narrowed. The dagger flipped over, drops of scarlet dribbling into the air. She shoved Alec aside. He staggered, swearing. Piper dived.

She wrapped her hand around the dagger as it plunged over the edge of the roof, the bandage on her hand a barrier between her flesh and the blade. For a second, her heart slammed in her chest, a sick feeling crawling through her like fire ants at the thought of losing the dagger.

Something crashed behind her, and Piper threw herself around. Saxe was nowhere to be seen. A trail of red spotted the ground, leading away. Both Iso and Ratt had stayed.

Alec threw up his arms. A flicker of blue-black magic lit the air.

Iso threw his dagger; it lodged in the magical shield. He snarled, pivoting on his back foot. Behind Alec, Ratt circled, trying for an opening. Alec threw out a hand, and something blue-black flashed out too quickly for Piper to see. Iso danced around it, pulling his dagger free as he did.

Piper leaped to her feet, her boots flying over the stone roof. Iso turned a moment too late and Piper crashed into him, her shoulder landing in his gut. He grunted, his reflexes unable to save him from five foot one of pissed-off assassin. Piper landed on top of him. She rearranged her grip, bringing her dagger down towards Iso's throat.

Iso's arm snapped up, blocking her. The hilt of his dagger slammed into Piper's unprotected side, and she saw white. Piper fell sideways. She flung out an arm, landing hard on her elbow but saving her head from the cold stone.

Iso loomed over her, one long dagger glinting in the sun.

Piper brought up one boot, snapping it against the inside of his thigh. Iso swore, going down hard, and Piper flipped herself up. She spared a glance over her shoulder.

Alec's fiery black shield held. As she watched, the mage lashed out with a handful of blue-black magic. Ratt dodged.

Iso lunged. Piper dragged her attention back to him, ducking under his lunge and drawing her long dagger from her boot in the same movement. When she spun back around, Iso faced her, one of his daggers held in both hands. Hers looked like a toothpick next to it.

Iso met her gaze. "No hard feelings," he said.

Piper shrugged. "Maybe a few."

She lunged. Iso deflected her longer dagger, but Piper brought up her smaller blade, still slick with blood, before he could block. His head jerked forward. Piper gasped in pain as his forehead connected with hers, and both daggers slid through partially numb fingers as stars flashed across her sight.

There was a splash behind her. Piper hoped to fate it was Ratt who'd fallen, because if it was Alec …

Iso swiped. Operating entirely on instinct, Piper grabbed his wrist with both of her hands. His fist landed in her gut, and Piper choked. She twisted his wrist, a sharp crack echoing across the water. Iso cried out. His dagger fell from limp fingers, and Piper caught it. He stumbled back, drawing his second dagger with his good hand. Piper reversed his, holding it in her left hand, and extended her other arm.

Iso's dark gaze darted over her, uncertainty in his eyes for the first time. He was usually so calm and collected. His fingers tightened around the dagger. His left hand. His weaker hand.

Piper lunged. Iso brought his dagger up a fraction too early. Piper bashed his hand aside with her forearm, his dagger going wide.

Her left hand plunged towards him. Sharp metal pierced his leather vest like it was made of butter. The dagger sank into Iso's chest, to the hilt, and his mouth dropped open. His dagger slid from his fingers, hitting the rooftop with a clatter. Piper's free hand gripped his upper arm, holding him tight against her so he couldn't get away.

He didn't try. Instead, his other hand grasped her shoulder.

She felt cool metal against her arm, and looked down.

Not a knife, like she had expected. A wedding ring. Not a black widower's band, either. A ring of warm gold, lovingly polished and free of grime or blood, that glowed against his deep brown skin.

Her eyes met his. She understood. "I'll make sure it gets to her," she breathed.

Iso let out a long breath. He nodded, once, his face creased in pain.

"Fate guide you," Piper breathed, "and Nyssa welcome you with open arms."

His eyes flickered open, landing on hers for a moment in surprise. Then he groaned. His eyes slid shut, and his knees collapsed. He went limp, his hand falling from her shoulder.

Piper gently lowered his body to the ground, clasping his hands over his chest.

TWENTY SIX

Leaving Iso in his final resting place, Piper grabbed her dropped daggers and raced towards where Alec and Ratt still fought.

Alec stumbled back as Ratt launched another barrage against his blue-black shield. It flickered in the sunslight. Water soaked Alec's leg up to his thigh.

Piper didn't know if the shield was weaker now because of Alec's proximity to water, or because of Ratt's unrelenting attack. Either way, she hadn't just committed treason to see the mage killed by someone as disgusting as Ratt.

While she had been fighting Iso, somehow a street had gotten between her and Alec. Piper didn't remember crossing it; even in the middle of a fight, a four-foot jump was something she would have noticed. Alec must have retreated over it to try and get some distance. Too bad Ratt had followed him.

Piper took a flying leap, her arms windmilling wildly as she prayed to fate that she hadn't misjudged the jump. She collapsed rather than landed on the other side, her right leg buckling underneath her and her palms skidding across the stone.

She looked up. Ratt had backed Alec towards a wall, where he'd have nowhere to manoeuvre. Nowhere to run, even if he could turn his back on the assassin.

"Oi!" Piper bellowed. Both turned to her. Alec's shield flickered.

Ratt grinned, his yellow teeth glinting in the sunlight. His tongue swiped out over his lips like a giant amphibian. "Too late," he said. He flung out his arm. Something black glittered in the air between him and Alec.

"Shield!" she screamed.

Alec threw up his hands without question. The blue-black fire flared into life again, covering him like a dome.

The glittering powder slid through it. It settled on the mage's shoulders, his chest.

Alec's eyes went wide. He thudded to the stone floor in a heap. Ratt leaned over him, his knuckles raised.

Piper leaped between them. Brass knuckles scraped against the metal of her dagger, a screeching sound rending the air. Ratt gnashed his teeth at her, and Piper brought up one boot to kick him, hard, in the gut. He stumbled back, putting space between him and Alec. Piper followed, stalking after him, flipping the long dagger between her fingers so it lay pressed against the inside of her forearm.

"You're a coward, Belladonna," Ratt said. "You should have used it on him the second you knew he was a mage."

"I am not a sadist, like the rest of you," Piper hissed. But Ratt just laughed, like that was a badge of honour.

"No, you're not," he said, his gaze sliding over her. Piper kept hers fixed on his eyes; that's where he would give away his next move.

Ratt licked his lips again, trying to sidestep towards Alec. Piper closed the distance between them, forcing him backwards to stay out of reach of her long dagger.

"You do understand that two million stars is enough to settle all of our debts to him, don't you?" Ratt hissed. "How high are yours, that you'd pass it up? And for a mage?" His lip curled on the word, and briefly Piper wondered what had happened to cause so much hatred in him. She pushed the thought away, stepping to the side to block Ratt again.

"It's none of your business." She pressed him again, and he fell back further.

His face twisted in fury at being denied his prize. "Or do you like being under Lore's thumb?" he spat. "I never took you for a masochist."

"I'm impressed you know a word so big." She knew better than to get angry at his taunts, but fury simmered under her skin like fire just the same. Heat travelled up her right arm from the fate mark, but not a burning heat. It felt like sitting too close to a fire and roasting one part of your body.

The warmth settled around her chest and a long, rumbling growl sounded in her mind.

Ratt lunged. Piper ducked under a swing from the brass knuckles and lashed out, but Ratt avoided her dagger. He lunged again, and Piper had to leap back to avoid him.

The other assassin turned to the offensive, striking with a speed and aggression that Piper was hard pressed to keep up with, never mind attack against.

Fate, she swore. Either she'd vastly underestimated him, or he'd been playing them all since the moment Lore recruited him.

Piper lashed out, scoring the side of Ratt's face with her long dagger. His cheek hung, flapping sickly with his movements.

He hissed and surged forwards, forcing her back a step. Her boot met the edge of the roof, but Piper didn't dare look back. Further behind and to her left, Alec lay slumped in a heap; she could just make him out at the corner of her eye. Ratt grinned.

Piper ducked down and used all her strength to bury her shoulder in Ratt's stomach. The air left his lungs in a surprised *oof*, and he stumbled back. One heel caught on a loose piece of stone, and he sprawled, off balance. Piper knelt on his chest in the next instant, catching his dominant wrist.

"Was it worth it?" he croaked, a grin still wide across his face. "Was it worth choosing that mage over your own people?"

Piper pressed her dagger down to his throat. "You are not my people," she breathed.

Ratt laughed. "You're dead," he said. "He'll kill you. Wait and see."

Piper drew her dagger across his throat, and he choked on his own blood.

She left him dying on the stone. Quickly, she stumbled her way over and dropped to the roof beside the mage.

"Come on, mage." Piper patted his cheek roughly, and he groaned. "I know you can hear me." Piper's palms stung with the effect of the poison. Mage's Dust was like that; it was unpredictable, but saved its real effect for mages.

He was so still. Piper's fingers found Alec's throat, letting out a shaking breath when she found the pulse pounding there.

"Okay." Piper withdrew her hands, sticking them into her outside pockets. "It's okay. I'll figure this out." She would find nothing in her pockets to help. There was no cure for Mage's Dust, and it made it impossible for mages to access their magic. That was why she used it in her tinctures.

"Come on, come on, come on." She slid her hands up and down her chest, stopping when she found a lump in her inside pocket. "Oh fate," she breathed.

Rose's violaberries, the ones she'd been too cranky to eat. Fate, the woman must be part seer. Piper yanked the pouch out of her pocket and poured them out on Alec's chest. They spread out, a purple-black wave. There had to be enough.

Alec's eyelids flickered. When he forced them open, his eyes were dark with pain. They fell on the berries between Piper's fingers and went wide with fear. He tried to pull back, barely managing a twitch.

"Fate damn it, hold still!" Piper hissed, grabbing his jaw. He clenched it shut. Her fingers dug into him in frustration. Then she realised.

"They're not nightshade!" she exclaimed. "They're violaberries!" Then, when Alec's jaw didn't relax. "Look!"

She threw one into her mouth and chewed furiously, swallowing before she even tasted it. She was loathe to waste them. But if it got him to eat them without fighting her …

Alec's eyes hardened, his jaw tightening. Piper touched his cheek.

"Please, Alexander," she whispered.

With a muffled groan, his eyes slid shut, his head lolling back against the stone.

Piper swore. She pried at Alec's jaw, but with one hand, all she could manage was a tiny gap between his teeth. "Please don't bite me," she said. She pushed a violaberry past his lips.

Dark purple juice, too much for the berry to logically contain, erupted from the fruit, turning Piper's fingers and Alec's teeth purple. She touched his throat, leaving behind a purple thumbprint.

"Swallow," she coaxed. After an age, Piper felt his throat muscles contract, then relax. "That's it." Piper grabbed another berry off his chest. Violaberries were a natural antitoxin; she just had to hope they would suffice as a cure for the Mage's Dust.

Please, please fate, let them work.

Maybe it was her imagination, but she thought he relaxed. Just a little.

Finally, the pile on his chest was gone. Piper tipped her pouch upside down again, shaking it vigorously. Nothing came out. Swearing under her breath, Piper stuffed it back into her inside pocket, then grabbed Alec by the shoulders. "Alexander." She shook him, hard, with no regard for the fact he'd just been poisoned. "Alexander. Wake up."

He didn't move. Piper shook him again, feeling a hysterical edge stab into her chest.

He groaned. He tried to raise his hand, but it flopped uselessly back down to his side.

"Oh thank fate." Piper pressed a shaking hand to her chest, heedless of the purple mark it would leave against the grey linen of her shirt.

Alec tried to lift his hand again. This time, he got his hand over his face. "Fate that hurts."

Piper reached for him. "Just … breathe, I guess," she murmured, her fingers finding his pulse. It beat erratically under her fingers. "Do you feel nauseous?"

"Nauseated," he said, and Piper blinked at him.

"What?"

"It's nauseated, not nauseous," Alec mumbled. "And yes, I feel like I might throw up. Whatever those berries were, they were disgusting. And they smell awful."

"Those berries saved your life." Piper couldn't quite give the words the acidity she intended.

She pressed her fingers into her forehead, sitting back on her heels. Taking a deep breath, she tried to calm her still-galloping heart.

Then she frowned. A tinge of something nasty came with the faint breeze. Piper took another breath through her nose, and gagged. It was stronger now. A foetid stench, like raw meat left in the sun to rot.

A wailing, undulating cry sounded behind her, and Piper spun, almost falling on top of Alec as she did.

Something crouched on the roof facing them. Its body was humanoid. Under corpse-white skin, Piper could see every plane of its skeleton. Dark, shaggy hair hung in ropes around its head, tufting from its protruding spine. Branching antlers framed its face, sharp enough to slice. Its long legs were covered from ankle to knee in something dark that could be mud, or something else entirely. Too-thin arms, also dark, bent backwards. It walked on its knuckles like a tseoun as it descended the roof. Its claws clicked against the stone.

Long limbs took the gap between the buildings in stride. It stopped beside Ratt's body, and lowered its head.

"Sweet fate," Alec breathed behind her. Piper couldn't tear her gaze away from the creature to look at him. Instead, she reached back, feeling until she grabbed his arm.

"Get up," she whimpered. There was a sucking, squelching sound, and the creature made a noise that could only be satisfaction. It set every hair on Piper's body on end.

"What is it?" Alec whispered.

Piper squeezed his arm, hard. "Get up!"

The thing jerked its head up. Blood streamed down its mouth, dripping off its chin like scarlet rain. Something fleshy hung between its pointed teeth. It slurped the fleshy object up with slow relish, then licked its lips with a tongue white as its skin. Piper clamped a hand over her mouth and nose.

Eyes blacker than a moonless night bored into Piper, sucking in the sunlight.

It turned its attention back to Ratt. With those razor-like claws, it ripped open his shirt. Then it lowered its head again.

"Alexander, get up!" Piper tore her gaze away, spinning on her knees. Alec had one arm underneath him. He gaped at the creature, his face almost as white as its skin. "Get up!"

"I don't think I can," he breathed.

Piper stared at him. Then she spun around, in time to see the creature raise its gore-covered face again. Watching them.

"Get up." Piper grabbed Alec by the arms, heaving him. She grunted with the effort, and Alec scrabbled both feet against the ground, trying desperately for purchase.

"Everything is numb," Alec gasped, "like I've got pins and needles all over my body."

"I said get up!" Piper snarled. Behind them, a bone cracked. She bit back a whimper.

Alec grasped the wall beside him. Piper yanked his arm, jamming her shoulder under his armpit. She heaved. She was by no means weak, but he was the heaviest thing she'd ever lifted.

Alec stumbled like he had vertigo, but got one leg underneath him. She wrapped her arm around his waist. Most of his weight draped over her shoulders, and it was all she could do to stand. His face pressed into her hair, and Piper could feel his harsh breathing against her neck.

Piper urged him forward, her eyes fixed on the creature. "Step," Piper breathed. Alec stumbled, but they were moving. Somehow, the two of them got across the gap she'd jumped just moments before, Alec gripping Piper in an effort to stay upright.

She couldn't see Iso's body; just a smear of blood on the stones. Maybe the sound of their fight had attracted it.

Something cracked behind them. Piper spun, almost pulling Alec off balance. Her heart leaped into her mouth.

"Get ready to run," she breathed.

The creature stepped over Ratt, clutching one forearm. Two long claws speared through the palm of Ratt's hand. Piper watched with sick detachment as the corpse stayed put, the arm pulling away as the creature moved.

She stumbled back a step, pushing Alec with her. "Run," she said.

"I don't think I can–"

The creature lunged.

"RUN!" Piper shrieked.

Piper heaved Alec away, keeping him upright almost entirely through willpower as they raced across the rooftop.

Behind them, Piper could hear the clacking of claws on stone. She glanced back and bit down a scream.

The creature snapped at their heels. Piper dropped her weight onto one foot, snapping the other back with all the force she could and smacking it across the face with her boot. The creature recoiled, wailing. Piper yanked Alec forward, not daring to stop.

Alec's breathing heaved in and out of his chest. He sounded like a freight train on its way through Silversdale. He had his arm around her, his other hand pressed to his side. Every muscle in his body trembled with pain and exertion.

He shouldn't be running. He shouldn't even be moving.

Another snarl came from behind them. Piper drove Alec onwards.

"I can't. Keep. Running," Alec forced out between harsh breaths. His entire body shook in Piper's arms.

"Don't stop," she begged. "Please don't stop."

Somehow, the mage found a burst of speed. They staggered around a chimney, Piper half propping him up, half dragging him along. He made an inarticulate sound. Piper's eyes widened.

"Dead end!" he cried. They were back at the abbey wall. The gap between the buildings stretched before them, metres of water sparkling in the sun.

Piper's heart dropped into her stomach.

"Jump," she whispered.

"What?"

Piper shoved Alec's arm from around her shoulders.

"Jump!" she yelled, pushing him towards the gap.

Alec glanced at her, then behind her. Magic flickered to life around his hand, then his face contorted, the magic dying.

"Go! I'm right behind you!" Piper spun, not waiting to see if he listened to her.

The creature jumped the gap in the buildings behind them. Piper cast around, her heart in her throat.

The creature stepped towards her.

A clothesline leaned against the corner of the chimney, half folded down. Piper grabbed the metal end, throwing it. The creature reared back in surprise, one of its long antlers caught in the fine line. It bellowed, yanking back.

"Piper!" Alec yelled.

Piper spun. He stood on the other side of the gap. Dry, so he hadn't fallen in.

Behind her, Piper heard the line snap. She leaped forward, fear lending her feet wings. Alec's face creased, his gaze trained behind her. The creature screeched, and Piper heard another line snap.

Piper launched herself from the edge of the roof. Water sailed by under her feet. Her arms flailed. She wasn't going to make it. Her legs were too short. She hadn't taken enough of a run up. She'd land in the water. If she hit something on the way down, she was dead. She'd drown.

If it fished her out, the creature would eat her.

She plummeted, too far from the stone to reach out and grab it. Alec leaned forward.

His hand closed around Piper's arm, and he yanked.

Piper gasped in pain as she jerked through the air like a ragdoll, straight into Alec. He grunted, stumbling and falling. Piper landed across his chest on the other side.

A screech like fingernails on a blackboard rent the air, and Piper shoved herself up with a gasp. The creature paced on the other side of the water, clothing line tangled around its antlers.

Underneath her, Alec groaned.

"Sorry!" Piper pushed herself up and off him, but Alec waved a hand.

"'S not you," he mumbled. "You're not that heavy." He ran both hands over his face.

Piper looked up again. The creature made no move to cross the water. It snarled, baring long fangs at them and shaking its antlered head threateningly. When its right hand touched the water, it jumped back, spitting like a cat.

Piper took a shaking breath. "Come on." She grabbed Alec under the arms and helped haul him to his feet, despite his weak protests. After one last glance back at the creature, Piper propped Alec's arm over her shoulder and they made their way across the rooftop.

TWENTY SEVEN

"Stop," Alec groaned.

Piper glanced back. They'd made a little progress, and she couldn't see the creature anymore. But she could hear it. Its undulating cries sent a cold feeling down her spine, making her shiver. She'd rather not stop, but Alec was not doing well and she was struggling under his weight.

She turned, spotting a low wall where they could rest. It might have once been part of a second-storey terrace, with raised dirt beds and a broken stone bench. Piper put Alec's back to the wall and helped him down.

He scrubbed his hands over his face, shuddering as he did. Piper dropped her bag and rummaged through it for her water.

"Stop, stop." She caught Alec's hands as he tried to rub his face again. "You're going to make it worse. Here."

Unscrewing the cap with her teeth, Piper poured her water bottle over Alec's hands. Then she caught his chin, tilting his head back. "Hold your breath," she murmured.

Alec stiffened. Piper trickled water over his hairline, letting it trace over his eyebrows and cheekbones, hopefully washing off the worse of the poison.

A hand closed over hers. "Thanks," Alec said very softly. Piper nodded, awkwardly, sitting back on her heels while he washed glittering black dust off his arms.

Piper's hands stung, and she glanced down. Her fingers were black with the stuff. Mage's Dust might not cause the same excruciating pain in non-mages, but prolonged exposure …

Alec cleared his throat. "You could have left me," he said.

Piper started, turning to him. "What?"

Alec capped her water bottle, holding it out to her. "You could have left me," he repeated. "Why didn't you?"

Piper looked away, feeling her face heat. She fiddled with her coat sleeve; in the sunlight, she could see the faint shimmer of Mage's Dust on the black fabric.

"Honestly?" she said, after too long a pause. "The thought didn't actually occur to me." Piper glanced back at Alec through her hair. His blue eyes were fixed on her face, his expression thoughtful.

"What was it?" he asked.

"Mage's Dust," she murmured. "A poison that only affects mages. The more powerful you are, the worse it is."

Alec held out his hands. He frowned, and fire appeared in his palm. Then he hissed, and the fire winked out.

"It's making it painful to access my magic," he said.

"It also does that," she said. "You shouldn't even be able to use your magic. No one has been before."

"You've used it before?" he asked, his voice cold.

Piper flinched. "I …" Her voice stuck in her throat. Piper swallowed, but the lump stayed lodged there, like a protest.

"You?" Alec pressed.

"I … made it," she admitted slowly. "With some help. Lore had a mage, and he …"

Piper forced herself not to shiver.

"I took the dust with me the next time Lore had us spar – his magic against me, without any weapons." She still had a burn mark across her back from that day. Her shirt had melted onto her skin; since then, she never wore clothes of man-made cloth. "Well. I kept it in my pocket, and when I had an opening, I ..."

"Used it," Alec filled in, after a moment of silence.

"He died screaming in pain." It had been one of the most awful deaths she'd witnessed. Piper met Alec's gaze with defiant eyes.

"Did you give the recipe to them?" Alec asked.

Piper shook her head. "No," she said. "It was my discovery. They couldn't make me hand it over."

They'd tried. With fists and weapons and more magic. But she hadn't given in to them.

Alec pursed his lips, silent for a long moment. He pulled his water bottle, larger than Piper's, out of his own bag, and splashed his face and the back of his neck with water. "Those three?" he said finally, jerking his head.

Piper shrugged as much as she could without letting go of her elbows. "Assassins," she said. "Iso, the dark-skinned one, and Ratt, the one who poisoned you, they were partners of a sort. Saxe, the stupid one ..." Her lip curled. "He is – was – my partner."

Alec's eyebrow rose. "What does having a partner mean?" He kept the water flowing, now rinsing his hands again. "There's one of them looking after you?"

"I can't stand Saxe," she said, fixing Alec with a glare. "And he would gladly see me dead. So, no."

Alec rubbed his chin. "That's cold," he said.

Piper laughed without humour. Alec looked up at her, completely calm, his blue gaze intent.

"That's cold?" she asked. She twisted so her left side faced Alec and shoved her sleeve up as high as it could go. Above her elbow, a star-shaped scar showed starkly against her tanned skin. "You see this? When I was sixteen, Saxe and I sparred. He got me on the ground, and he shoved his entire knife through my arm." Alec went white. "Then he twisted it and pulled it out. Then he did it again. And again, until I stabbed him." Piper stopped and took a shaky breath. "He severed nerves, tendons. If it weren't for A– someone who helped me, I would have either bled out or lost all use in my dominant arm. I would have been useless, then, and they would have killed me, or worse." Piper yanked her sleeve down and turned away from the mage.

For a moment, Alec didn't say anything. "Why didn't you report him?" he asked eventually. "Child abuse ... That's illegal. And you were a minor."

Piper sank onto the wall. "Do you really think anyone would care?" She shook her head, not waiting for his answer. "It doesn't matter, anyway."

Alec slowly got to his feet. "Fine. It doesn't matter right now." He glanced around. "So what next?"

Piper pressed her lips together, angling her head so that her hair fell across her face. "I don't know."

Alec's boots scuffed against the stone as he walked around her, taking in her hunched shoulders. His gaze flicked down to her hand, and Piper realised she held the hilt of her stiletto. "You're scared," he said softly.

"Of course I'm scared!" Piper gripped her elbows so tight her arms ached. "You saw them!"

"You killed two of them. With no major injuries to yourself."

"Saxe escaped," she breathed, shaking her head. "He knows what I did. Lore will brand me a traitor."

And Lore was a thousand times worse than Ratt, Iso and Saxe put together. She shivered, despite the warmth of both suns beating down at her.

"What will they do if they catch you?" Alec asked, his voice almost gentle.

Piper shrugged one shoulder. "Fate knows," she said. "Lore is creative." She glanced down at her bandaged hand.

"Did he do that?" Alec asked.

Piper nodded. "When I tried to refuse your job."

Alec raised his brows. "You tried to refuse me?"

"I don't like rush jobs," she admitted. "There's too much risk."

"Well," Alec said after a pregnant pause, "we'll just have to make sure he doesn't get you, then."

Piper rolled her eyes. Shoving herself up, she pushed past Alec to look back the way they'd come. The city sprawled ahead of them. Logically, Piper knew it wasn't that much higher than where they stood. But it looked like it had climbed a small mountain.

"Don't get ahead of yourself," Piper said. "You still have your deal with the inspector to fulfil, after all."

"What?" Alec asked. Piper turned to find him blinking at her in puzzlement.

"Doesn't matter." Piper stooped and grabbed her bag from the ground. "Let's go before whatever that thing was decides it can swim."

"Piper." Alec caught her arm. But Piper shrugged him off, stalking off along the terrace.

Piper shivered as they trod the terrace. It wound around a central structure, the tallest building in the area, reaching up another storey into the air. The garden beds were long dead. Maybe once, they had been full of flowers, a place for supplicants to come and pay homage to Nyssa or to fate. Maybe to both. Maybe they prayed to the Leviathan. Or the Changeling, though Piper had never heard of anyone praying to the third of the three most powerful Immortals. Maybe people prayed to all of the Immortals, together. The Lady of Light was a popular figure in some countries.

Something throbbed behind Piper's eyes, and she fought down another shiver. Swallowing felt strange: sticky, and heavy. Alec had drained her water bottle washing the Mage's Dust off himself, so although a drink would be blessed at that moment, it would have to wait.

The stone of the walls fitted together almost seamlessly, the surface so smooth Piper wasn't certain she could scale it.

Piper forced another swallow in her parched throat and straightened. Her shoulders tried to hunch forward, but Piper forced them back and straight. Her gaze darted over the wall as she followed Alec around a corner.

The terrace opened in front of them, and Piper sucked in a breath. Stonework scrolled over the face of the building, clearly the work of master carvers. Intricate sigils etched the wall, and the terrace stretched out towards an expanse of open water.

Piper hardly noticed as Alec wandered towards the building. Instead, her feet took her, almost of their own accord, to the garden.

She could see it. See a priest, a nun, maybe Nyssa herself, standing here. It had to be a courtyard below. She could just imagine it filled with people. Rich people in jewel colours. Poor people in worn work clothes. Children with dirty faces; children with plump, happy faces. Widowers, and old crones. All with their faces turned up towards this spot, to where a person they trusted stood. Preaching, maybe. Or offering words of comfort.

"Piper!" Alec called. "What is it?"

"Nothing," she said. Piper jumped off the step – she hadn't even realised she'd climbed it to look down into the water below – and hurried towards him. "What are you doing?"

"I'm not sure," Alec murmured, running his hands over the glyphs on the stone. "There's something here. I can feel it. But I'm just not sure what."

Piper frowned. "How do we even know this is the right place?" she asked.

Alec looked her up and down. "We know," he said.

Piper froze. Now that she'd stopped rubbing them, a sticky feeling crawled up her arms. She tried to suck in a breath, and the air stuck in her throat.

Alec's hand landed on her shoulder.

"Breathe," he told her, rummaging in his bag. "It's just the magic you're feeling. I feel it too, but" – he shook his head – "not as strongly as you do."

He handed her his water bottle. With a grateful glance, Piper unscrewed the top and swigged.

Alec turned from her, back to the wall. The glyphs formed an archway most of the way up towards the windows on the next level, though there was nothing between them but blank stone.

Piper slid Alec's bottle into the top of his bag. "What … What is it?" she asked.

Alec didn't turn to face her; Piper saw one shoulder rise and fall in a shrug, his other hand trailing over the wall as he walked down it.

"I'm not sure," he called to her. "Your *illis* seems to be particularly susceptible to this type of magic."

"That's not helpful," Piper muttered, swiping at the sticky feeling on her arms. "Fate, stop it."

The magic did not stop sticking to her. It writhed over her arms like an eel, or something else particularly unpleasant. A squid or octopus or … or a kraken?

Piper shook her head as a disapproving rumble flowed through her from the fate mark on her wrist. Piper wasn't certain how she knew it was disapproving. But she did.

She sighed, rubbing her forehead. Then turned her attention to the wall. The pale stone glowed in the sunlight. The smaller sun's darker light seemed to ripple across the ground, like it did every afternoon. The inside of her stomach gnawed with hunger at that realisation. Fate, with the morning they'd had, she hadn't even realised what time it was.

Piper's hand brushed the stone, one of the carvings rough under her fingers.

It lit up.

Piper gasped. "Alexander?" she said. From further down the wall, the mage grunted.

The stone in the archway turned a soft, shimmery gold. Piper's fingers twitched, and she found herself reaching towards it. Something on her wrist tugged, like it was trying to drag her back.

THE SHARP EDGE OF FATE

"Piper, don't!" Alec roared from beside her. Piper turned to look over at him, but her fingers brushed the gold. Something yanked her forward, then she stumbled through the wall.

270

TWENTY EIGHT

Piper blinked at the sudden darkness.

"What ..." She tried to bring up her hand to rub her eyes, but it was attached to something. Something with long fingers that dug into her through her coat.

Piper yelped, recognising Alec's hand. Spinning, she placed one hand against the stone wall, trying to push away. As soon as her fingers touched the stone, it turned gold again.

Alec stumbled the rest of the way through, knocking into Piper and yanking quickly away. He filled the space with a selection of four-letter words, holding his hand to his chest. Piper watched, open mouthed, the scene lit by the faint golden light the archway gave off when she touched it. After what felt like an age, Alec turned to her. He scowled at her hand on the stone.

"Stop touching that!" he snapped. Piper yanked her hand off the stone like she'd been burned, plunging them both into darkness. For a moment, all she could hear was Alec's harsh breathing. Her heart beating somewhere near her throat, Piper swallowed.

"Alexander?" she said, when she was certain her voice wouldn't shake. "I can't see anything."

"Just don't move for a sec," he muttered, then cursed under his breath. "Ah!" Alec held up his hand, and a soft blue-white light blossomed in his palm. Piper blinked, forcing her eyes to adjust to the sudden brightness.

Alec rounded on her. "What did you think you were doing?" he demanded.

Piper crossed her arms. "I don't know what you're talking about."

"Just ..." Alec rubbed his free hand over his face. "Don't touch stuff. Especially stuff with Old Rhealgan runes on it."

"These are Old Rhealgan?" She reached out, not to touch, but just to—

Alec's hand closed around hers. "I said," he ground out, "don't touch."

"Yes, Your Highness," Piper sniped.

Alec flinched. "Seriously, Piper." He let go of her and ran his hand through his hair, messing up his horsetail. Then he sighed. "Here." The speck of light flew through the air towards her.

Instinctively, she snatched it out of the air. A pale blue, semi-translucent stone the size of a golf ball, but flatter, sat in her cupped palms. Runes that looked like they were drawn in soot wrapped around it in a thin band, and Piper had to push away the childish urge to see if she could smudge them.

"What is it?" she asked.

"Runestone," Alec said, gathering his hair again. "Dwarven version of a mageligt."

Piper glanced at him, her eyebrows creeping up. "And you have one because ..."

He huffed. "Like I said before" – hair tied, he reached over and plucked the stone from her hands – "I have trouble with small magics, like creating light. This is the easier, because I'm not creating anything. I just have to feed a little of my *illis* into it, and it lights up." He held out his hand, and the light brightened to the point that Piper had to shield her eyes.

Then it dimmed.

"More *illis* means brighter," he said, as Piper blinked stars from her vision.

"Huh," she said.

Alec didn't seem to notice. He turned from her, frowning at the wall. "Now this ..." he murmured, "... this, I have no idea."

He reached out. Piper flinched, waiting for the arch to fill with golden light again, but it stayed stubbornly dull. Alec's frown deepened, and he traced his hands over it. Piper edged closer, curious despite herself.

Her elbow brushed the wall and gold filled the space.

Piper jerked back with a yelp. So did Alec, narrowly avoiding having his hand stuck halfway again. He turned to Piper. She'd expected anger, but instead a deep curiosity filled his blue eyes. He cocked his head to the side.

"Interesting," he murmured. "Something specifically about you, about your *illis*, is reacting with this wall."

Piper wrapped her arms around herself. "I don't have any magic to react," she said, but Alec shook his head.

"I think we both know that's not true." His gaze slid over her, and Piper swallowed nervously. Then he sighed. "We should see where this goes," he said.

Piper nodded, rubbing at her arms. Then she stopped.

"Alexander?" she said, and the mage turned to her. "I think the magic is stronger in here."

Alec frowned. Turning, he held out his hand, the light bouncing off the inside of the space. Piper looked up. Stone arched above her head. Two balconies jutted out from the upper storey into the void. One had a mosaic of a brown-haired woman behind it; the other, a swirling purple and blue nebula. Nyssa, and fate.

She turned back, her gaze flicking over the archway again. "I don't think this arch was always bricked up," she said.

273

"Hm?" The light swept over her, Alec holding it high to light the wall. Footsteps sounded until he stood beside Piper. "I think you're right," he murmured. A far paler, newer stone blocked out the inside of the runic arch.

"I didn't see it from the outside," she said. "Everything is too dirty, with the floods and the soot from the Ilian."

"I wonder ..." He trailed off, stepping forward.

It took a moment for Piper to realise he wasn't waiting for her. She jogged after him, slotting into place at his side. "Wonder what?" Something sticky pressed against the back of her neck, but Piper forced her arms down by her side.

"Many things," Alec admitted. "Right now, what this place is."

"You don't think it's just an abbey?"

"No," Alec said, unnecessarily.

Piper didn't think it was either. Not with the sticky feeling that clung to her arms with every step, like she'd stepped in chewing gum, but all over her body.

There were no stairs in the entryway. A mezzanine ran around the walls well above their heads, and at the back was a passageway, a shadowy smudge in the light of Alec's magelight. Piper's steps slowed when they got there.

Alec glanced back when he realised he'd left her behind. "I think this one is just a normal passageway," he told her.

"Gee, thanks," she muttered under her breath. But she did lengthen her stride to reach the arch at the same time as him. They stopped. Alec ran his gaze over the arch, then stepped up to touch the sides. Piper glanced over her shoulder, the skin on the back of her neck crawling. She shivered.

"I feel like something's in here with us," she said.

Beside her, Alec admitted, "I do too." He squatted down, his attention on one of the runes at the bottom of the doorway. Piper peered over his shoulder. It looked like a jagged trident. Alec traced a finger over it and, even though she couldn't see his face, Piper could almost feel his scowl.

"What does that mean?" she asked.

Alec was silent for a long moment. "Nothing," he said.

Piper frowned at him. She lined up her shot and kicked.

"Ouch!" Alec twisted, falling to one side and grabbing his ankle. "Did you just kick me?"

"Did you just dismiss me?" Piper retorted.

Alec stared at her for a moment. "You know," he said, after a long pause, "I think I liked you better when you were giving me the cold shoulder."

Piper narrowed her eyes, and he held up a hand.

"All right!" He shuffled to the side, likely so he didn't get kicked again. "It really is nothing. I just saw this rune used a lot in university as a base by someone."

"A base?" Piper knelt down beside him, tilting her head to get a better look at the rune.

"People who aren't … good at spellbinding, they need a base to anchor their spells to," he said. "That's really all."

Piper glanced from the rune to Alec, and back again. Alec pushed himself up, then glanced at Piper.

"Come on," he said. "Let's see what we're working with here."

Piper jumped to her feet after him, glancing around the corridor. Rather than being round or square, the ceiling came to an arched point above their heads. Alec kept his gaze forward, a frown fixed between his brows, but Piper's glaze flitted off the stones. They fit together with the same workmanship as the exterior walls. Piper could barely see the cracks between them, and no mortar held them together.

They walked together in silence for a long moment before Alec nudged Piper with his elbow. "So," he said. "Alexander?"

Piper stared ahead. "Yup."

"Why? I mean, Alec works well enough for most people."

"Deal with it." Piper looked up at the dancing shadows over their heads. "Or we're going back to Rylan."

Alec chuckled. "Yes ma'am."

Piper responded with a half-hearted glare before turning her attention back to their surroundings.

She let out a breath. Fate, she'd never seen First Era architecture like it. That they could make something like this without magic, without Tech …

Something in her peripheral vision caught Piper's attention, and she turned.

She jumped back with a yelp, knocking into Alec and sending them both staggering. Alec swept her behind him with one arm, the other stretching out, blue-black fire racing up its length.

"What?" he said.

Piper pressed a shaking hand to her chest. "Nothing," she admitted. She pointed to the wall, where there was a drawing. Piper stepped around Alec, a frown forming on her brows.

It was almost lifelike, carved into the wall with so much detail the creature had depth. The black eyes bored into her, even from the stone backing, and the antlers twisted rather than branched. When Piper's gaze darted over the rest of the drawing, she saw that it was definitely more … feminine.

Piper stared at a female version of the creature from the rooftops. Who would have taken the time to draw it in such painstaking detail, she had no clue, but it was exquisite. Piper shivered and glanced away.

Then she realised something. "What was that?" she asked, gesturing to Alec's arm, still outstretched from where he'd pulled her behind him.

"Ah." Piper's mouth dropped open as the light from his magelight flared. He was … embarrassed? "I was hoping you wouldn't notice that." Alec squirmed, then sighed. Rubbing his face with his free hand, he shrugged. "It was habit, okay?" he said. "I'm used to doing it with Jai and the princess."

"And you're lumping me in the same category as royalty because …?" Piper couldn't resist needling.

Alec threw her a dirty look, the magelight fading again. "What I'd really like right now," he said, avoiding the subject entirely, "is a camera." He crossed the hall, peering at the drawing.

"It's so lifelike," Piper said, and Alec nodded.

"I get why it scared you," he said, reaching out. He stopped himself just before he made contact, his fingers hovering over the creature.

Piper rubbed her arms, fighting back another shiver at the magic sticking to her skin. She edged closer to Alec. "Do you know what it is?"

Alec shook his head. "No idea," he said. "I've never seen anything like it before. It's almost..." He shook his head. "But that's not possible." He glanced up. "Let's keep going."

"Wait." But the mage stepped away from the carving without her. Piper jogged across the hall to keep up with him.

Not far from the drawing, a smaller archway appeared from the gloom. But this one appeared to be bricked up by normal means; Piper couldn't make out a rune anywhere around it.

Alec ran his hand through his hair, looking it over. "Someone didn't want people in here," he said after a moment.

"That makes it sound particularly ominous." But she couldn't exactly argue with him. Alec hummed in thought, tension around his eyes. Piper stooped, sliding her longest dagger from her boot. Alec glanced over at the movement, then raised his eyebrow at her.

"And when you were being sucked through a magical doorway, you didn't feel the need to draw your knife?" he asked.

Piper glared at him. "Keep the sarcasm to a minimum, mage, or I'll stab you." Alec just snorted.

Piper's boots scuffed the stone floor as she turned, peering around. If she squinted, she could make out bricked-up windows in a wall curving away from them to the right. "What is this place?" she breathed. She was certain the abbey hadn't looked like this when it had been built. There would have been light, for one thing.

"Something ... strange," Alec said.

Piper turned, facing down the hall. "I suppose we go this way, then," she said.

He didn't respond, but fell into step beside her as she made her way through the dark. The air pressed down on them, thick with the smell of dust despite the water outside. Their footsteps sounded softly, muffled somehow by the space. A chill crept up through the stone, one Piper could feel even through her boots. Darkness spread on all sides. Piper's gaze flicked over the left wall as they walked, counting the windows. Three. Five. Eight. They came in pairs and threes, marching out of the darkness like good little sentinels. She imagined people on the other side. Standing, watching, through the blind openings.

Piper shook herself. That was just fanciful.

"I think we're spiralling," she said, coming to a stop. The wall was blank stone, with no more windows.

Alec's footsteps stopped. "Of course," he breathed. He stretched his arms out, so long they almost brushed both walls. Piper had to step back or risk an arm across the face. Alec hung his head back and drew in a deep breath. "Oh, yes," he said. His voice *rumbled*. Piper swallowed, taking an involuntary step back from him.

Power she couldn't see but could sense wrapped around Alec's arms. It travelled over his body, a heat and pressure pushing against Piper from several steps away. She backed up again, and it spread out, forcing her further away. Piper gasped as her back met the wall.

The sound seeming to remind him of her presence, Alec turned. Black fire swirled in his eyes, more than she had ever seen before. It overflowed, spreading down his cheeks like flaming tears. Blue-black fire wrapped around his wrists, rubbing against his arms like a cat.

He stepped closer.

Piper's feet stuck to the stone as she tried to sidle away. The broiling power pressed her against the wall, slowly squashing the air from her lungs. Each breath was harder to draw in.

He stopped before her, his fire-eyes burning into hers.

"You thought you had the upper hand in the Ilian, didn't you?" Alec murmured. His voice was soft, but it made the stone shake all the same.

Piper pressed her shaking hands to the stone behind her back, her voice stuck in her throat.

Alec chuckled. "Maybe out there." He reached out to run his fingers through one of Piper's curls. "But in here, in this spiral ..." He wrapped the curl around his finger. Again. And again. And again. Spiralling, incessantly spiralling, forever spiralling ...

He leaned closer. "You were going to kill me," he whispered.

Piper did the only thing she could think of. She brought up her hand and, with all her strength, she slapped him across his face.

Alec stumbled back. The pressure vanished so fast she fell to her knees, gasping as she hit the stone with nothing to cushion them. Her head snapped up, her gaze on Alec. The mage rubbed his hands over his face, then looked up. His eyes, when they fixed on her, were their normal sky blue, and Piper let out a shaking breath.

"Thanks," he said, his voice rough. "I needed that."

Piper pushed herself up slowly. "What happened?" she asked.

Alec winced, pushing himself up using the opposite wall. He took a step towards her, and Piper took one back. He held up his hands.

"It's the spiral," he said. "They're ... dangerous for mages. They make magic more chaotic, uncontrollable." He glanced at her, apology in his blue eyes. "If you're not expecting them, they can make you lose yourself."

Piper's grip tightened on her dagger. "You were going to kill me," she accused.

Alec shook his head. "No, not kill you." He rolled his shoulders, twisting at his neck until a soft popping sound reached Piper's ears.

Piper still eased back another step. "Will it happen again?"

Alec's mouth opened. If she hadn't been watching him, she might have missed it. He closed it again and took a deep breath. "No," he said. His voice reverberated with power again, but it was more ... controlled, this time.

This time, Piper didn't fear him. She felt her shoulders and arms relax from the instinctive defensive stance she'd taken. Alec noticed, the corner of his mouth quirking up in a smile. He tucked his hands into his pockets.

Piper sighed. She reversed her grip on her dagger, laying it flat along the underside of her arm.

Alec's tiny smile widened into a smirk, and Piper glared at him, daring him to comment.

He didn't. But Piper still knew what he was thinking.

She could have stabbed him, when he'd had her against the wall. But ... she didn't.

Tucking that irritating thought towards the back of her mind, Piper turned and started down the spiral again, keeping one eye on Alec beside her. Just in case.

TWENTY NINE

Several doors branched off the spiral. They passed what might have once been a meeting room, with a dilapidated table and broken chairs; a tiny study, books in the bookshelves turned to dust bound by empty leather covers; a room with a lock that Piper had picked, only to find a distillery inside.

Alec shivered as they walked. When Piper glanced at him questioningly, he just held out a hand. "I'm fine," he said. "I can just feel the spiral tightening. It's trying to pull me in, but now that I'm more aware of it, I can resist it."

"You'd better." Piper's grip on her dagger tightened, and she shot him a warning look that, to her ire, just made the mage chuckle.

"I don't think you're going to stab me," he said. "Not after all that."

All that. With Saxe, Ratt and Iso. With the creature.

She shrugged and looked away, not certain how she wanted to answer.

The smell of old stone pressed in on her from every angle, the darkness lit only by Alec's magelight. The light never faded, never wavered, making everything feel ... timeless. Still. Like a pool of water, the surface as smooth as glass.

They trod around another curve, and the hall ended at a door. A dark one, though Piper couldn't really make out the colour in the light of the magelight. Something was smeared across the front of it. The sight shattered the still, calm pool in Piper's mind, and kicked her heart up into her throat, for no reason other than it was different. Piper swallowed, forcing herself not to rub at her arms again.

"Alexander ..." She trailed off, then took a shaking breath as Alec glanced at her. "The magic. I feel it here. It's strong, stronger than I've ever felt."

She snapped her mouth shut before she could say the next thing on her mind.

I'm scared.

Alec's gaze darted over her. His eyes softened, like he understood her unspoken confession.

"I don't know ..." Piper swallowed again, forcing her throat to cooperate. "I don't know if we should open that door."

Alec hesitated. "You're sure the magic is stronger here?" he asked. "Stronger than at the house, with the mage trap?"

"Yeah," she whispered. "Yeah, I'm sure."

"All right." Alec ducked his head, rooting through his bag. When he straightened, he held something in his hands. He pressed them together for a moment, bowing his head. When he pulled his hands apart, something blue-black glowed between them.

"What's that?" Piper asked, edging closer.

"Spell," he grunted, like most of his attention was elsewhere. "Open the door, and don't get in the way if I throw this."

She put her hand on the doorknob, twisting it. It stuck under her palm.

"Fate damn you," she said, dropping to her knees.

"What?" Alec asked above her.

"It's locked." But it wasn't the first lock she'd picked that day, and if it kept going like this, it wouldn't be the last. Piper slid her picks out of the top of her boot, sliding her tension wrench inside and sticking her ball pick and rake pick between her teeth. She reached in with her diamond pick.

"Hurry up about it," Alec said above her head. "This is difficult to hold like this."

A few moments later, Piper felt the lock pop. She hissed around the pick still in her mouth, then tucked them all away and jumped up.

She glanced at Alec. He nodded, lines of tension around his eyes. His hands, on either side of that glowing blue, shook slightly. The magelight dimmed, until all Piper could see of him was his outline, and that glowing blue-black ball.

Piper eased the handle, then quickly pushed the door open. She stepped in and to the side, out of Alec's way. Nothing moved. Piper blinked as the dim glow of the magelight and the darker light of Alec's spell settled over the room, highlighting the edges of ... something. She wasn't sure what. Something large and blocky.

A movement darted across the room, towards her, and Piper sucked in a breath, her hand tightening on her dagger.

"DOWN!" Alec roared.

Piper dropped flat to the floor. She clipped her chin on the stone, blood filling her mouth as she bit her tongue. Alec's spell flew over her head, burning in the dark. There was a cry, then the spell went dark. Piper blinked frantically, willing her eyes to adjust. She heard footsteps, and Alec stopped beside her.

Piper pushed herself to her knees, squinting. Beside her, Alec held out his hand, and the magelight flared back to life. Piper threw up her hand, blinking at the sudden brightness.

"What do you think you're doing?" Alec growled. His boots tapped across the floor, and Piper dropped her arm, still trying to blink her eyes into cooperation.

Alec moved to stand next to a bubble-like structure wreathed in blue-black fire, glaring into its depths. He crossed his arms, his jaw tense. "Well?" he demanded.

Piper followed his gaze. She gasped.

"Stop!" She scrambled to her feet, half tripping towards Alec and catching herself on his shoulder. Alec twisted to her, raising one eyebrow, but Piper reached for the bubble.

"Don't do that!" Alec grabbed her hand, and Piper shook him off.

"I know him!"

A boy shivered within the bubble, his arms wrapped tight around himself. The fire and bubble turned his face a sick shade of blue, and his eyes were wide in a gaunt face. He was recognisable, barely, as the older of the two boys who had tried to pick her pocket, right before her meeting with Lore.

"Piper–" Alec began.

Piper spun to him. "Let him go, Alexander," she said. "He's just a boy!"

"He could be a skinwalker," Alec pointed out. "Or the Shiv'ek."

"He's a kid," Piper insisted. "I saw him barely more than a week ago!"

Alec caught one of her shoulders. Piper tried to twitch out of his grip, but he squeezed, holding her in place. "Piper," he said softly, "if I dismantle this trap, I can't redo it. I don't have a spare. This took me months to make. Are you sure?"

Piper looked over. The boy sank to his knees on the floor of the bubble. He looked so small, so thin. Piper's heart twisted. She rubbed at her arm. The magic pressed against her from all sides, writhing against her like an oily pet. But it didn't feel any stronger from the boy.

"Yes," she whispered. "I'm sure."

Alec made a hand gesture. The bubble disintegrated and the boy toppled out with a cry. Piper caught him, lowering him gently to the floor.

"Hey there," she soothed. "Shh. Shh. It's okay. We've got you."

The boy turned his face up to hers. "B-Bella?" he whispered.

"It's okay," she said softly, brushing his mop of brown hair back from his filthy face. His brown eyes looked huge, sunken in a face even more gaunt than the first time she had seen him – and then he had been living on the streets. "What happened?" she asked. Last she'd heard, he'd been safely settled with a family.

The boy shuddered. "They took me," he said, his voice still no more than a whisper.

Piper glanced at Alec. The mage stared at the boy, a frown on his brow. He dropped to his knees beside them.

"Who took you?" Alec asked.

The boy cringed back into Piper, and she wrapped an arm around his shoulders. "Three men," he said. He looked up at Piper, his long eyelashes spiked with tears that hadn't fallen. "One was tall, with eyes like yours."

Piper blinked. She glanced at Alec again, to find him staring at her now, the same frown between his black brows. Heat crawled up Piper's neck. She looked away, breaking the awkwardness, and back to the boy.

"Who else?" she pressed, speaking gently.

"Two other men. One was really tall, with black hair. The other one had brown hair and looked mean." He shivered again, and Piper rubbed his arms, trying to get circulation back into them. He felt cold and clammy.

A blanket, musty and crusted, wrapped around the boy's shoulders. Alec dropped back to one knee and leaned down. "When did this happen?" he asked.

The boy looked at him and hesitated.

"It's okay," Piper told him. "He'll help you." She brushed back his hair. "We both will."

The boy looked at her with eyes full of trust. "A few days ago."

She didn't know what to say. He was nothing but skin over a skeleton, as though he hadn't eaten in weeks. But it must be true – it had been only a week since she'd had news of him, and he hadn't been nearly so emaciated.

Alec rubbed his chin. "What happened, while you were here?" he asked.

The boy huddled, and Piper tucked the blanket closer around his shoulders. "The man ... the one with silver eyes," he said. "He put me in a cage." He jerked his chin across the room, and Piper looked up.

Her breath caught in her throat. She hadn't noticed before, but one wall of the room was full of child-sized cages. They looked empty, but the bars were smeared with filth.

"He ... he did things to me," the boy went on, his voice tiny. "Things that made my heart feel stretched and empty. It made me so, so tired."

Alec twisted, rummaging in his bag again, and pulled out a thin cylinder, barely as long as her thumb. He held it out. "Did he use something like this?" he asked, but the boy shook his head.

"The black-haired man did," he said. "At first. But the silver-eyed man never did."

"What's your name?" Alec asked.

The boy offered Alec a timid smile. "Raoul."

"Well, Raoul," he said, "have you ever been tested for magic?"

"Magic?" Raoul slowly shook his head. "No. No point. Mam and Da don't– didn't have any."

If Alec noticed his correction, he didn't say anything about it. Instead, he gave Raoul a small smile. "That doesn't necessarily mean you don't have any," he said. "My parents never did, but my brother, my sister and I all have magic." He held out the cylinder again. "If you don't mind, I'd like to check you for magic."

"Alexander, what are you doing?" Piper hissed out of the corner of her mouth.

"Trust me," he whispered back.

"Will it hurt?" Raoul asked, his voice trembling.

Alec shook his head. "No," he said. "I swear, I'm not doing the same thing that man did to you. I'm only looking in your eye. And I won't do it if you say no."

Raoul leaned into Piper for a moment, then he pushed himself up. "Okay," he said.

"Raoul, you don't have to," Piper said.

"I want to know," he replied.

Piper couldn't begrudge him that. She sighed, sitting back on her heels, as Raoul held his blanket closer and looked at Alec.

"What do I have to do?" he asked.

"Just sit still," Alec said, using the kind of soothing voice usually reserved for frightened animals. "I'm going to hold your chin. And I'm going to shine this into your eye – there will be a little light, but it shouldn't be bright enough to hurt your eye. Okay?"

Raoul nodded. Alec reached for him, then glanced at Piper.

"A little space?" he asked, and Piper realised she'd been leaning towards them both.

"Oh." Piper pushed herself up, feeling her face heat – thank fate that wouldn't be so obvious in the half-light of the magelight. "Sure."

Alec started to reply, but Piper turned her back to him. After a second, she heard him murmur to Raoul, asking him if he was ready.

Piper turned her attention to the room while they did what they needed to do. Now her eyes had adjusted, she could make out the space in stark grey-and-white relief. A workbench pressed against one wall, and she walked towards it for a closer look. The top was littered with a small distilling set – the only thing Piper recognised. The rest was decidedly more … mage-y. Herbs and crystals, cracked through the middle. A thick, leather-bound book with faded silver stamping across the front that she couldn't read. A blunt knife, something brown staining the blade.

Piper swallowed. She knew what was on that blade. She hadn't seen any marks on Raoul, but that didn't mean there weren't any.

She picked up the book, turning it over in her hands. The cover warmed, almost vibrating under her palms, and she dropped it quickly and turned away. Those empty cages loomed over her, bars like bared teeth. Piper shivered and kept moving.

The table in the middle of the room. That was innocent enough. Piper crossed to it, glancing at Raoul as she did. He sat like a statue, his thin, pointed chin in Alec's much larger palm, long fingers curving over his cheeks. Alec held the cylinder about a foot from Raoul's eye, shifting himself and the light alternately, frowning.

Piper's fingers traced over the stone, finding a divot in the tabletop. For cleaning, maybe, so the water ran off? Her fingers met something sticky. She jerked up her hand up into the magelight light, to see a brown-red substance covering her fingers.

She slapped her other hand over her mouth, just as Alec made a satisfied grunt at the back of his throat.

"I see it," he said, letting go of Raoul's chin. Then he looked at Piper. "What is it?" he asked, immediately seeing something was wrong.

"I need to get out of here." Without waiting for a response, Piper turned. She raced towards the door, only to be bought up short as a large hand wrapped around her arm. Alec pulled her back.

"What is it?" he repeated, but Piper shook her head.

"I need to get out." She tried to shove him off, but Alec pulled her closer.

"Piper," he said softly, and despite herself, Piper tilted her head back to meet his gaze. "If you run out, the two of us," he gestured to himself and Raoul, still sitting on the ground wrapped in his blanket, "can't get out. I haven't seen a single exit, except the one you can make by touching it. So please, stop for a second."

"Why does it only work for me?" Piper whispered, her gaze glued to her fingers and the congealed mess there.

"I don't know." Alec's fingers curled around her arm. "But just wait. Just a few minutes. And we can all leave together."

He was right. *But, fate, fate, fate …*

"I need to at least look at these cages before we go," Alec said.

"There's nothing in those cages." She held up her hand for him to see. Alec blanched at the substance on her fingers. "I just … We can come back in if you need to. But please. I need to get out." She was pretty sure she'd never begged for anything in her life. Alec's gaze flitted across her face. He must have realised, on an instinctual level, that she needed this from him.

"All right."

He turned, still holding her arm and extending his other hand to Raoul. "Can you walk, Raoul?" he asked. "Let's get into the fresh air."

If Alec hadn't kept hold of Piper's arm, she would have run. As it was, she forced them along at as fast a clip as Raoul could manage. Alec kept one hand on the boy's shoulder, drawing him along. Raoul shivered, arms and blanket wrapped tight around his thin body.

At the archway, Piper stopped. Hesitantly, she reached out, half expecting it to not work.

The stone turned to a shimmery gold.

"Come on." Alec squeezed Raoul's arm, before he turned to Piper. "Wait until we're through? If you come out first, we'll get stuck, and being stuck halfway … kind of hurts."

He held up his wrist. Piper blinked at the blackening bruise around his arm, exactly where it had got stuck in the stone the first time he came through. She opened her mouth, but Alec shook his head.

"I'm not looking for an apology," he told her. "And I know you want to get outside. But wait. Please?" His blue eyes fixed on hers. Piper swallowed.

"Okay," she said.

Alec offered her the ghost of a smile; just a tilt of one corner of his mouth. It highlighted the tense lines around his eyes, his mouth. Then he took Raoul's shoulder again and steered the boy through the wall.

Piper forced herself to wait. She counted to ten. Then counted again. Shimmery gold light flickered over the walls, over her hands and her clothes.

The ceiling, shrouded in darkness, pressed down on her.

Piper shuddered. Then she stepped through the arch. It turned to stone as she left it on the other side.

"Piper?" Alec called. Piper brushed past him, heading straight for the edge. "Piper!"

Piper dropped to her knees. Ignoring the scum and mud water, ignoring the patch of violet algae she could make out just a few feet away, Piper shoved her hand in the water and scrubbed. The already murky water turned a muddy red-brown, sticky, coagulated blood spreading into the liquid.

The algae drifted closer, drawn by the scent of flesh.

Alec grabbed her by the shoulder. "What are you doing?" he blistered.

"I–"

"You ..." Alec shook his head.

Piper held up her hand. The blood was gone. But she could still feel it. She tucked her hand into her armpit, twitching out from under Alec's hand.

"I'm fine." She didn't sound fine, even to herself.

Alec caught her shoulder again. He stooped, peering into her face. Piper tugged away from him, turning back to face Raoul where he stood, still shivering in a blanket Piper could now see was crusted in mildew, mud, and something that could only be dried blood.

Piper took a step towards him, but Alec wrapped a hand around her arm.

"His magic's been drained," he murmured near her ear.

"What?" Piper spun back to face him, her eyes wide. Alec wasn't looking at her. His attention fixed over her head, a frown between his brows. "How? What for?"

"I don't know," Alec replied. "If he hadn't been drained, the boy would have been quite powerful, once he had been trained."

"Would have been?" she asked softly.

Alec's eyes flickered to hers. "A few things can happen if you fully drain your *illis*," he said. "One of them is the irreparable damage, lessening, of your magic." He jerked his chin to the boy. He wrapped both arms, and the crusty blanket, around himself, shivering in the sunlight.

"Is that what happened to him?"

Alec shrugged. "Too early to tell," he admitted. He didn't sound optimistic.

His hand was still curled absently around Piper's elbow. She pulled it from his grip. "What else can happen?" She'd have to tell the family he was staying with, when she got him back to them.

"It's possible he might recover fully, with no damage to his *illis*," he said. "He's not dead, so that's something."

"You mean you can …"

"Die by draining your *illis*?" Alec glanced at her. "Yes. It almost happened to a friend of mine." A shadow passed over his face. He shook his head as though to clear it. "There were multiple cages in there."

"They were empty," Piper said softly. "I checked."

Alec rubbed his chin. "I don't understand. What would they have wanted those cages for, then?"

He didn't sound like he was asking her, but Piper replied anyway. Perhaps her search would yield some clue. "I found some things. There was … a distilling set. Crystals, and herbs I think." She frowned.

Alec caught the expression. "What else?"

"There was a book," Piper said slowly. "It looked … old. Faded." In her mind, Piper could see how it had moved under her fingers. "It … swirled."

Alec's hand gripped her arm, and Piper jumped.

"Swirled?" he asked her, urgency in his voice. "Are you sure?"

"I … I guess?"

"Piper." Alec's grip tightened. "Did it spiral?"

Piper opened her mouth to answer. Then she hesitated.

"I'm not sure," she whispered. "I think the cover vibrated. It felt … alive."

Alec rubbed his free hand over his face. "Fate," he breathed. "A grimoire."

"A what?"

"A grimoire," Alec repeated, his voice hard. "A book with a direct connection to the Winterland."

He didn't say it. But Piper's throat constricted at the implication behind that statement.

"And a direct connection to a Shiv'ek?" she whispered.

Alec's pursed lips were answer enough. "Maybe Raoul wasn't the first person they drained," he murmured softly. "But why? What are they trying to do?"

"The Shiv'ek could have drained more people?" Piper breathed.

Alec shrugged again. "Maybe."

Piper glanced back at Raoul. The boy sat now, blanket loose around his shoulders, his face turned to the sun. Then he shivered and tugged the crusty material close to his face. Piper pulled herself out from under Alec's hand, crossing the stone terrace towards Raoul. He jumped when she knelt down before him, dragging his attention back from wherever it had been.

"How are you doing?" Piper asked him. She tugged the filthy blanket off his shoulders, then, before he could protest, reached into her bag and pulled out a jumper. She held it out to him. Though Raoul hesitated – likely at the pale blue and decidedly feminine material – he reached out and took it.

"I'm okay," he said.

Alec settled down beside him, leaning forward to peer at the boy. "Do you mind telling us more about what happened?" he pressed gently.

Raoul flinched. But, clenching his fists in the fabric of Piper's jumper, he squared his shoulders. "I was" – he vanished for a moment under the wool – "in the Ilian, delivering a basket of fruit for Mary. Then someone grabbed me. I tried to shout, but they put something over my face, and everything went kind of fuzzy." He glanced at Piper, then at Alec. "When I woke up, I was in a cage and there were the three men there."

Alec pulled his bag into his lap. He rooted in it for a moment, then pulled out a small packet of beef jerky, and a larger packet of trail mix. He held both out to Raoul.

Piper saw Raoul swallow, his gaze fixed on the food. So, so slowly, like he expected Alec to take it away again, he reached out.

"How long were you in the cage for?" Alec asked as Raoul took the food.

Raoul shrugged. "Four … Maybe five days?" he guessed.

Piper frowned. That would mean he vanished almost as soon as she'd sent him off. She hadn't known his name to realise that it had been him on the list.

"Was there anyone else, beside those men, with you?" Alec asked, this time holding out his half-full water bottle.

Raoul nodded. "Two others," he said, his mouth full and his eyes on the bottle. "A lady, who looked tired and sad. And a boy." He looked at Piper. "Maybe your age?"

Piper's chest caught. She glanced at Alec, his own eyes wide.

"What did they look like?" Piper forced out.

Raoul frowned at her. "The lady, she looked kind, but she had a big bruise on her face like someone had hit her. She had brown hair. The boy also had brown hair. His clothes looked like they'd come from one of the nice shops, once, but they were all dirty and ragged."

"Did he have blue eyes?" Alec asked. "The boy? Blue eyes, and a piercing in his left ear? A scar on his neck?"

On his neck? Piper mouthed, but Alec didn't acknowledge her.

"I think so," Raoul said. "It was hard to really tell colour, in there, it was so dark. But I think so."

Alec sat back heavily, rubbing both hands over his face. "They were there," he whispered. Then he straightened, horror strangling his expression. "Fate, we just left them."

He started up, but Raoul caught his arm. "They're not there, anymore," he said. "The men, they took them away a few hours ago."

"Just a few hours ago?" Piper pressed, her heart beating in her throat.

Raoul nodded again. "They left me there," he said. "In a cage."

The air left Piper's lungs in a rush. "Fate," she breathed. She reached out, and Raoul let her brush his dirty hair back from his face.

"How did you get out?" Alec whispered.

Raoul looked down. "I can… pick locks," he admitted.

Both Piper and Alec stared at him: Piper in admiration and Alec in shock.

"What?" Alec asked. "Why?"

Raoul shrugged one baby-blue clad shoulder. "Ma always told us we couldn't get into the larder even if we were hungry after bedtime," he mumbled. "So I learned how to get in without the key. Marcel got hungry at night." Marcel was his younger brother, Piper assumed.

"So you picked the lock of the cage?" Alec asked. "After they'd gone?" Raoul nodded. "That was dangerous," Alec scolded after a moment. "If they'd caught you ..."

But Raoul just shrugged again. "I had to get back to Marcel," he said.

"Only clever boys can pick locks," she said, and Raoul looked up at her. "But only the cleverest boys know which locks *not* to pick."

Raoul offered her a small, shy smile.

"Raoul," Alec said. "Did you see where they went? The men, and the pri– the boy and the lady?"

Raoul shook his head. "It took me ages to get the lock open," he said. "I kept dropping my picks. And they kept bending. I had to bend them back into shape. I dunno how long I was out for before you came in."

Piper looked at Alec. "We missed them by hours," she hissed.

"Someone knew we were coming," Alec said, his expression dark. "Did you tell anyone?"

"Me?" Piper demanded. "Who, exactly, would I tell?"

"I don't know." Alec rubbed his forehead. "I'm sorry. I didn't really mean it like that. I just ..." He trailed off.

Piper rubbed her forehead. Then she stiffened. A smell reached her nose; one terrifyingly familiar. Piper scrunched her face and tried to breathe through her mouth.

"Piper, what–"

"Shh," Piper interrupted, holding out one hand. Alec snicked his mouth shut, his eyes narrowing.

"What?" Raoul said, but Alec shushed him and the boy fell silent.

The skin at the back of Piper's neck crawled. The mark on her arm felt like it twisted, tightening, and Piper clenched her fists. "That will not help me," she told it under her breath, and the mark loosened.

"What is it?" Alec breathed.

Piper pushed herself to her feet. Her gaze flickered over the terraces around them. Beside her, Alec rose too, his movements fluid. "Raoul," Piper said, her voice far too even, "stay down and stay between us. Understand?" She didn't hear the boy's assent, or see him nod, but Piper assumed she got it. She stooped, drawing her long dagger from her boot again. Her other hand found her leaf-shaped blade.

The scent of something rotting brushed over her again, so faint she was almost certain she imagined it.

"Argh!" Alec yelled.

Something huge and pale landed on Alec's arm, teeth gnashing, antlered head twisting to try and get at him. Piper spun on one heel, her dagger coming up. The weapon left her fingers before she could even remember throwing it. It landed in the fleshy part of its chest. The creature tumbled back, roaring in pain. Alec brought up both hands, glowing with dark blue fire.

The creature twisted to its feet, dislodging the dagger as it did. Fast as a scorpion, it ducked around the side of the building. Alec started after it.

"Wait!" Piper grabbed his arm with both hands, the hilt of her dagger digging into his shirt. Alec turned. Blue-black fire flared in his eyes, matching the magic around his hands.

"You can't run off after it," Piper said, fire or no. "It almost killed us the first time."

Alec growled. He blinked, and his eyes were their normal blue again.

"The first time, I was half dead from that stupid poison and you were carrying me," he growled. But he lowered his hands to his sides, the magic there fading too.

Behind Piper, there was a snarl.

Piper whirled in time to see the pale figure leap towards her. Its black eyes bored into her, its mouth stretched wide in an inhuman grin. Piper swore and threw up her dagger, bracing it with her free hand. The creature landed on the blade with a sickening crunch, throwing Piper to the ground. It flailed above her, one of its razor-sharp claws scratching a line across Piper's collarbone. She hissed in pain and brought up both feet to kick it in the stomach.

The creature was so thin she heaved it off her with ease, leaving a gaping would in its stomach as her dagger pulled free. Its body thudded into the ground, skidding over the stones, and Piper pushed herself to her feet.

There was a splash, and Piper wavered. Could it swim?

"Are you all right?" Alec was at her side in an instant, turning her to face him. He pulled the collar of her coat to the side to look at the scratch it had given her, but Piper smacked his hands away.

"I'm fine," she said, grabbing her first, thrown blade. Both knives dripped red-black blood to the stone.

There was a hissing behind her. Piper spun on her heel, her grip on her daggers tightening.

The creature sprung at her with a snarl. Before it made contact, a dark blue flash seared across her vision. It hit the creature square in the chest. The creature flew backwards.

Piper lunged, unwilling to take a chance. But there was no need. The thing lay at an unnatural angle, its antlered head twisting the wrong way, its white flesh covered in black burn marks. The smell of death and rot forced its way down Piper's throat, and her stomach rolled.

"It's dead," she said. Alec stepped past her, kneeling next to the creature, a frown etched deep between his brows.

"What was that?" Raoul whimpered. He crouched a few metres behind Piper, his hands over his head, his face bone-white.

Piper tore her gaze away from the broken, emaciated body.

"We're not sure," she told him, speaking as gently as she could. "But it's okay. It's dead now; it can't hurt you."

Raoul's eyes widened. His mouth dropped open and he raised a finger, pointing.

"Piper!" Alec roared.

Piper spun, eyes widening. On the ground, Alec's face contorted, and the glow around his hands got brighter.

She was hit in the back, unable to bring her hands up in time to break her fall. Her chin bashed into the stone. Something hissed in her ear, its weight digging into her shoulders. Raoul shrieked, scuttling backwards like a crab in front of her. Lines of fire scored down Piper's back. She felt it to her bones.

Piper screamed.

Her daggers lay pinned underneath her; their hilts dug into her stomach.

The weight on her back twisted, then shifted to beside her shoulders. Piper forced herself to roll over.

A second creature crouched over her, dripping with floodwater. Its black eyes bored into Piper's, and its emaciated lips pulled back from teeth as long as her forefinger. Instead of branching antlers, this one's horns twisted away from its face.

It spat, its putrid breath rolling over her. Hot saliva dribbled against Piper's neck.

Piper's fingers grasped at her coat. The creature lunged.

She buried her stiletto in the creature's chest before she realised she had drawn it. It collapsed on top of her, crushing Piper under its weight and radiating an immense cold down on her. She tried to gasp in a breath, but her lungs wouldn't expand. The hilt of her dagger dug into her chest, and the creature's teeth rested against her neck.

It rolled off her, and Piper gasped. She was too focused on drawing in air to even check if the thing was still alive. Her next breath turned into a cough. Someone grabbed her arm and pulled her onto her side.

"You're okay." That was Alec's voice. He kept a tight hold on her, stopping Piper from moving. Piper winced in annoyance. She really wanted to get off the dagger hilt that was sticking into her hip. She shifted.

"Don't move." His voice was tense. Instead of letting her flop backwards he pulled her towards him, and the hilt dug further into her side. It was nothing compared to the agony that flared across her back with the movement.

Piper bit her lip to stifle her cry. Placing her hand on the ground, she tried to push herself upright.

"Fate damn it, Piper!" Alec's fingers dug into her, holding her in place. Piper tensed, then hissed as pain flared in her back again.

She couldn't see, she realised.

"What were you thinking?" Alec demanded. "Fate, Piper!"

"I'm fine." Was that her voice? She sounded like a ninety-year-old smoker who'd never had a healer clear out her lungs.

"You are not fine," Alec ground out. She could see him again, and Piper realised she had just opened her eyes.

Alec hovered over her. Piper waved him away, though her arm felt rubbery.

He didn't move. "You insufferable woman, stop!" he ordered.

Piper ignored him, pushing herself up on one hand. She also ignored the spots dancing across her vision.

"I'm fine," Piper insisted a second time. "I–" She stopped, gasping, as pain lanced across her back. She felt it against her bones. The spots in her vision took over, twisting so fast that Piper lost all sense as her vision turned black.

THIRTY

S unslight flittered across Piper's left eye. She groaned, turning her
face into the pillow and throwing both arms over her head.

She was lying on her stomach. Her back felt tender. Almost like–

Piper threw herself upright with a gasp. It was a bad idea. Pain tore
through her, and Piper choked. She braced both arms against the bed,
forcing herself to remain still. Her shoulders heaved with each ragged
breath, her arms trembling.

Piper lifted one hand off the bed. It shook in the air, and as much as she
tried to clench it into a fist, it didn't want to. She reached behind her. She
tensed, expecting jagged flesh and hot blood.

Her fingers met something thick and cool. Ointment? No gashes.
Piper's fingers slid over her skin, until she reached a raised line, and she
understood. She'd been healed.

Piper looked up from the crisp white sheets underneath her. She knew
this room, she'd been in it before. It was Alec's room.

The one in the palace.

"Fate," she groaned, rubbing her forehead.

Cool air brushed her shoulders. Piper started, realising something.

"Fate!" she cursed, for an entirely different reason, yanking the sheet against her bare chest. She glanced around, her eyes wide.

The room was empty. No mage, no guards, no anyone. The gauze curtains in the window were mostly drawn, sunlight entering through a tiny gap between them.

Her eyes fell on the bedside table. A note lay there, written in the messiest handwriting Piper had ever seen; even worse than Caleb when he was learning to write. Glancing around one more time, Piper edged over, still holding the sheet to her in a death-grip.

Piper,

I'm going down to the library. If you wake up before
I get back, I brought you some clothes. They're on the
chair. You're free to use my shower.

Alec.

Piper looked up. Her bag sat on an armchair that had been pulled up to the side of the bed. Clothes were draped across the other arm. Piper frowned, rubbing her collarbone. Someone had been sitting on that chair. And, judging by the signature on the note ...

It was fine. The sheet had been drawn up when she woke. She shouldn't give it another thought. Piper shook herself and pushed to her feet.

It took a moment, grasping at the side of the mattress, for the room to stop spinning. Piper sucked in a breath, but that just made the light-headedness worse. Her stomach rumbled loudly. A headache pounded behind her eyes. Piper winced.

From the sun, she hadn't lost too much time. A few hours at most. A few hours to get back to the palace, get healed, and wake up.

Fate, what was that thing?

Piper winced again as she stood up, her tender muscles protesting. She ran her fingers through her hair. Someone had undone her braid, and it fell in wild curls to her waist.

Her skin prickled. Piper shivered, rubbing at her arms. But there was none of that sticky, oily feeling of magic clinging to her anymore. Instead, a faint, ticklish feeling brushed over her. The smell of citrus and mahogany permeated the room; she hadn't noticed that before.

Her daggers. Piper stumbled towards her bag, catching herself on the back of the chair. She breathed a sigh of relief as she opened the bag and found the blades. Her fingers wrapped around the hilt of her long dagger, then traced the flat of her leaf-shaped blade. There was a line of dark brown under the hilt; someone had wiped it, but it hadn't been properly cleaned. Her stiletto and both throwing knives lay underneath; all there, all accounted for.

Her belt lay on top of the nearby dresser, her boots underneath it.

Piper froze.

Her coat. The one Abby gave her for Yule, with the collar that stayed up against the cold winter air and a pocket for every knife she could desire. Torn to shreds when those claws sank through her flesh.

She shivered, wrapping her arms around herself. Despite the sunlight, the breeze in through the window was cold; off the water, possibly.

Piper grabbed her bag and the clothes, holding them against her chest as she crossed the room. The bathroom was barely more than a cupboard, not much larger than the one in her apartment. Piper locked the door behind her, glancing around. There were no windows, but a magelight brightened the space like day. Dark blue towels hung on a rail on one wall. The shower took up an entire end of the space, large enough for two people to stand in together. The lavatory sat behind its own half-height wall to give extra privacy.

Small, but far, far nicer than her own little bathroom.

Piper dropped her bag on top of the vanity and stepped into the glass shower cubicle. Half an hour and a continuous stream of hot water later, Piper carefully eased a shirt over her head. She'd only front-faced the spray, careful not to wash off any of the ointment if she could avoid it. She wasn't certain what it was for, but hoped it might prevent infection and scarring.

She finished dressing and, back in the main room, slid on her boots and belt. Piper sighed in relief as she slipped her daggers into place, the familiar weight even better than the hot water for easing the tension in her muscles.

She stretched. Then froze.

The fate mark no longer wrapped around her right wrist and arm. She extended her fingers experimentally. Then she ran her other fingertips over her wrist. No more feeling of scales. No green–purple–black lines over her tanned skin.

Nothing.

I am still here, a voice said.

Piper yelped. She tripped over the leg of the armchair, holding herself upright by grasping on to the back. "What by fate?" she gasped.

Piper, please, he – for the voice was definitely masculine – said. *Don't act like this is the first time I've spoken to you.*

"Oh no," she said. "No, no, no, we are not doing this."

Of course we … He grunted. Piper felt it down to her bones. Then he shook himself.

"What's going on?" Piper demanded, her heart pounding in her throat.

She felt the sigh travel through her body. *It's hard to … talk right now*, he said. *It will get easier.*

"Look, dragon–"

Kostin, he interrupted. *My name is Kostin.*

"Kostin," Piper acquiesced. "I don't think I'm the person you're looking for, here."

Yet you are the one I was able to reach, he said. *You are not the first one I tried, either.*

Piper forced her mind blank. Fate knew how much the dragon could get from her thoughts.

He sighed again. *I am struggling to hold us*, he said. *Find your mage. Stay with him. He will know what to do next.*

"Look, I really don't think …" Piper trailed off. She couldn't explain how she knew. But the dragon wasn't there anymore. It was like a part of her mind echoed, in his absence. Like he wasn't there to absorb the sound.

A flash of silver, lit by the afternoon sun, caught her attention. A mirror sat on top of the largest dresser. Piper marched up to it, gathering her hair in one hand. She turned.

Stark through her pale grey shirt, clear through the layer of ointment, black lines slashed and swirled over her back. Piper could make out the ridge of a wing, the curve of a tail. Kostin's head rested on the back of her left shoulder, as though he was watching the world go by. She dropped her hair, obscuring him. Fate knew how she was going to explain this to anyone. It had been bad enough when he took up her entire arm. Now, not only had he moved, he was also bigger.

Piper rubbed the back of her neck, then her temples. Fate, she needed coffee. And food.

Find your mage, he'd said. He wasn't her mage, for fate's sake.

But she did know where he was.

Piper edged through the palace, her heart beating an uncomfortable staccato in her chest. Her hands trembled, and she shoved them as far down in her pockets as she could to try and hide that fact.

Without her coat, she felt exposed. Which was stupid. But she couldn't push the feeling away, now that her blades were strapped on beneath the thin layer of her shirt. Piper shuddered. A guard glanced at her, and Piper felt her shoulders hunch. She sidled past him, heading west.

A maid, wiping down the tables in the little alcove near Alec's room, pointed her in the right direction. Piper crossed the mezzanine on the third floor, looking down into the entrance hall below. Elaborate, swirling white stone made up a railing that would be waist high on most people, but came up to Piper's chest. Below, the floor tiles flowed in a stunning pattern of waves crashing against a cliff, the colours muted like looking through snow.

It wouldn't be visible unless you were looking at it from this height, she realised. No one on the ground floor would ever know.

She crossed to the other side and into a hall. Thick green carpet covered the timber floor, muffling her footsteps. Doors lined both sides, each with a brass frame beside it displaying a typed slip of paper. Some were blank, but some, Piper recognised. *Chalink*, a family of extremely wealthy dwarfsmiths. *Airida*, the family name of the sea elf ambassador and her family. *Massey*, second cousins to the High Lady on her uncle's side.

No Riannivh, here. But several blank spaces. Maybe it had been here, once.

These living quarters were much larger than Alec's one room, judging by the spacing of the doors. The carpet here felt thicker under her boots, and watercolours lined the halls. The important families in residence here would be horrified to the point of aneurysm, knowing Piper walked down their hall. Knowing she took stock of their doors, made a mental note of where each family slept. She could sell that information for a small fortune to the right buyer.

Something ugly twisted in Piper's stomach at the thought. She turned away, wrinkling her nose.

She traversed a gentle corner, and stopped. A wide hallway cut across the floor, light flooding in through floor-to-ceiling windows on either side. A trio of soft, velvet-clad chairs sat in front of one of the windows, a small table between them. On the other side were double doors leading back the way Piper had come. Potted plants stood in front of the windows, though none so large someone could hide behind them.

In front of her, a set of carved redwood doors blushed red against the pale walls. Owls and ravens sat in carved branches; towards the floor, foxes and a family of mice sat together amongst the tree's roots. In the background, a ptereleon – a huge, winged lion native to the Khedoran Archipelago across the other side of the world – stood on an outcropping, its wings flared. Something that wasn't quite human or animal stood next to it, more parts of it animal than any puka Piper had ever seen. Its eyes glowed at her, even though they were just divots in the warm timber.

Piper pressed her hand against it and pushed. The door swung silently on well-oiled hinges. She took one step inside.

She was on the top floor of a three-storey space. A balcony, the railings wrought iron in the shapes of dayflower and nightflower blossoms and leaves, wrapped around the entire floor. Books filled floor-to-ceiling bookshelves on every wall, curving gently with the shape of the building. Above her, huge glass panes framed with dark metal showed the sky. Clouds flitted across the blue, wisps of white and long, trailing tendrils, not a rain cloud in sight. Strings of tiny little magelights wrapped around the edge of the skylight, then over the narrow ceiling curving over the balcony. They wrapped down the columns supporting the edge, and continued down to the lower levels.

Ahead of her, a wrought iron staircase patterned with the same leaves, vines and flowers as the railing spiralled downwards. It was wide enough for three people to walk comfortably abreast. Piper reached it and placed one hand hesitantly on the railing. She took a deep breath.

Warmed by the afternoon sun, the vines of the bannister pressed into her palm.

All the way down on the ground floor, an empty fireplace sat against one wall. A love seat, three armchairs, and a narrow coffee table sat in front of it. Behind that, a longer table, with six chairs around it, sat near a small cart piled with books. Piper could see a beverage nook against one wall, and freestanding stacks of books radiated out from under the balcony overhang.

Facing the front of the room, overlooking the palace drive and the groomed gardens on either side of it, and with a superb view of a rather ugly serpentine topiary, floor-to-ceiling windows broke up the upper-storey balconies. Sunlight flooded in, soaking into a smaller worktable and a familiar black-haired figure.

Piper tightened her grip on the railing and started downwards.

Her footsteps echoed on the iron in the huge space, and by the time she reached the floor, she was slightly dizzy from all the turns. Alec propped his chin on his hand, his gaze flicking over her.

"You're awake," he said.

"I'm awake." She pulled out a chair opposite him, sinking to the table. The sunlight fell across her back, and Piper bit back a sigh of pleasure.

Books lay open on the table in front of Alec, and a small tray holding a silver urn and a clean mug sat beside them. Another mug, half empty and filled with something black that smelled amazing, was by his elbow.

"You okay?" Alec asked.

Piper reached across the table. She checked the urn to find it was, indeed, coffee, and grabbed the spare mug. The first sip made her screw up her face – she much preferred her coffee with milk – but she needed the caffeine more than anything else right now.

Piper offered Alec a small smile. "I'm all right," she said. "Just a little tender, but that's normal after a healing."

Alec nodded. His gaze continued to flick over her, taking in everything from her unbound hair to her pale shirt, to the pull at the corner of her mouth where she was worrying at her lip.

She forced herself to take a deep breath. "How did we get here?" she asked tentatively.

"After you passed out," he said, frowning, "I carried you."

Piper blinked at him. "You carried me? All the way from the Lower Ilian to here?"

"Well, no," Alec admitted. "Maybe I panicked a little. When we got to the Ilian, I commandeered an autocart. It was a bastard to drive, but it got us here more quickly than anything else would have." He hesitated. "You nearly bled out on the drive here. I had Raoul trying to keep pressure on your wounds, but they were so big ... It was hard."

"Is he okay?" Piper asked. "Raoul?"

Alec nodded. "Yeah, he's fine," he said. "I want him to stay nearby so I can monitor him while he recovers, but I've sent a message to his family. They should be visiting him now."

Piper let out a long, relieved breath. He was okay.

Another sip of coffee, and the pounding in Piper's temples faded a little. Enough for another question to occur to her. "Why here?" she asked. "Why not a hospital?"

"You were bad, Piper," Alec said. "Literally bleeding out, while I'm trying to drive one-handed, and Raoul and I are trying to stop the bleeding. That bad. The most powerful healer I know is here." He hesitated. "The High Lady."

"What?" Piper's chair shrieked against the floor as she pushed herself back. She was on her feet in a heartbeat, staring at him. "The High Lady?"

"Healed you, yes," Alec said. "I'm not a healer. I could slow the bleeding with mundane methods, but I couldn't stop it. And I think you were in shock."

"Does she know who I am?" Piper asked, bile crawling up her throat.

Alec shook his head. "I didn't tell her," he said. "I ..." He rolled his coffee cup between his hands, but didn't drink. "Piper," he said after a long moment. "What happened to you?"

Piper frowned at him. "I think you're in a better position to tell than me," she said carefully. "I seem to remember being unconscious."

Alec didn't smile. He braced his elbows on the table, and took a breath.

"The High Lady told me to go get some water," he said. "So I did. And ... when I got back, she'd cut open the back of your shirt."

Piper's entire body went cold.

"How much did you see?" she asked through numb lips. Alec peered at her, but Piper couldn't tear her gaze away from the patch of sunlight on his blue shirt.

Alec rubbed both hands over his face. "Honestly?" he said finally. Piper flinched, uncertain if honesty was what she really wanted. "Your back was covered in blood, with claw marks so deep I could see your ribs in two places. But once she stopped the bleeding and started to heal you …" He sighed. "It was obvious."

Piper tore her gaze away from him.

"Piper–"

"I don't want to talk about it, Alexander."

"Piper, please–"

"I said I don't want to talk about it!" Piper snapped. "So leave it alone!"

"I don't think I can do that," Alec said, his gaze steady on hers and his voice too even.

"Let me rephrase it, then." Piper braced her hands on the tabletop. "It's none of your damn business."

"For fate's sake!" Alec exploded to his feet, reaching for her.

Except she was already gone. Piper fled to stand ten feet away, her back against the window, the table, chair and book a barrier between them. She balanced her weight on the balls of her feet.

Alec's eyes raked over her. He took in her hands, clenched so hard by her sides her knuckles turned white, and the set of her jaw. Her chest heaved as her breath sawed in her throat. Slowly, he raised his hands.

"Did you think I was going to hit you?" His voice returned to that too-even tone from before.

Piper's heart spasmed.

"I don't know," she admitted. It had been an instinctive reaction. What she did know was that a reaction like that had saved her life more than once.

Alec edged around the table, moving slowly, like he was afraid of spooking her. He couldn't hide how his blue eyes had darkened, or the tight line of his jaw.

Piper tensed as he took the last few steps, but she forced herself to remain in place.

They stood that way for a long moment.

"Is that why your back is the way it is?" he asked, his voice low and rough.

Piper dropped her gaze to the ground, feeling a flush race up her throat. She didn't want to answer that.

Alec reached out. Piper flinched, but she didn't pull away as Alec swept her hair over her shoulder. One hand caught her chin, tilting her head up and to the side. His other thumb brushed the skin behind her left ear.

Piper swallowed against his fingers. "I'd forgotten about that one." She surprised herself with how even her voice was.

Alec frowned. "I didn't notice it until you flushed just then," he murmured. "You're lucky you didn't lose your ear, or your hearing."

Piper offered him a tight smile. "That was the idea," she said. Alec pulled back to look at her, and Piper extracted herself from his hands. "I was eavesdropping."

"Fate, Piper," Alec breathed. His eyes darted over her neck and arms.

"You won't find anything."

He started, a guilty look crossing his face.

"Aside from the one on my neck and elbow, and a few on my arms and hands" – Piper held out her left arm, where the mark from a deep whip wheal sat around her wrist – "they're all on my back."

"So nobody can see them? Is that it?" Alec scowled.

"Basically." Piper hesitated. "Hardly anybody knows about them." She wouldn't beg him not to tell anyone.

Alec reached for her shoulder, then stopped himself. "How did you stop the hospital from working it out?" he asked. "This has clearly been happening for years. Child abuse–"

"Is overlooked, by certain people," Piper interrupted. "And I let some heal naturally. At least those– those didn't scar." She had to force the last words out.

Alec's eyes softened in sympathy. "Human healings always scar," he murmured, and Piper nodded. "Fate." Alec rubbed both hands over his face again.

Piper cleared her throat. "Anyway," she said, shaking out her hair and sidestepping the mage, "it's getting late. I should head back to Caleb and Madelyn. If I hurry, I can pick them up from school." She really, really wanted a few minutes away from Alec's penetrating stare.

"Piper ..." Alec hesitated. Then he took a deep breath. "Piper. It's not Pyros. It's Asdiel."

"What?" Piper stopped short. "Oh fate." She hadn't lost a few hours, she'd lost an entire day. "Caleb and Madelyn." Piper shoved past Alec, running for the exit.

"Wait!" Alec's hand wrapped around her arm, pulling her to a stop.

Piper spun to him. "Let go of me!" She lashed out, but Alec caught that wrist too.

"It's okay," he said. "Caleb and Madelyn are fine. They're here, actually."

Piper blinked at him. "They're ... here?" she asked.

"Yes." Alec's fingers on her wrist gentled. "They're here." A small smile curved the corner of his mouth. "They really took to the princess, actually. Acting like they've known her for years."

"Oh." The panic left her body in a rush, and Piper's knees turned to water. She pulled away from Alec's hands, then teetered the few steps to the table. She caught herself against it, pressing her palms to the timber as the flash of panic slowly left her body.

"Piper?" Alec edged around the table until he stood opposite her.

Piper held up one finger and dragged in a long breath. "How did they get here?" she asked when she thought her voice wouldn't shake. She misjudged, but Alec didn't comment.

"I went and got them," he said. "I didn't really know what else to do. The High Lady said you couldn't move, not until you woke up, or the healing would be incomplete."

Piper nodded woodenly. It sounded about right for other major healings she'd had. Slowly, she sank onto the tabletop. She didn't realise how cold her fingers were until she wrapped them back around her coffee mug, and shuddered at the heat there.

"Okay." Mechanically, she sipped from her mug, tucking her feet up onto the chair she'd vacated. A whole day. At least that explained the headache throbbing behind her eyes, and her growling stomach. She hadn't eaten or had any caffeine in over twenty-four hours.

She took a breath, then squared her shoulders. Part of her wanted nothing more than to find Caleb and Madelyn, then leave. The other part ... was curious.

"So what are you doing?" she asked, gesturing to the books Alec had spread across the table.

"Research." Alec dropped into the chair opposite her, refilling his coffee mug and adding sugar. "I think I've figured out what attacked us in the Lower Ilian."

Piper blinked at him. "Is that important?" It wouldn't help them find Abby or the prince, and the things were both dead.

"I started looking because I needed to recharge my *illis*," he admitted. "And then I got a bit carried away."

Piper frowned. "How does research help you recharge your *illis*?"

Alec sighed and clasped his hands before him. "Mages only have one way to recharge their *illis*," he began. "Well," he amended. "Ninety-five percent or so of mages only have one way to recharge their *illis*. I have a friend whose *illis* recharges through cooking, and another who recharges through landscape design. He can also recharge a little through gardening, but it's not as effective."

He glanced at Piper, clearly asking if she was following. She wasn't certain that she was, but she nodded anyway.

"It's why most children don't manifest any magic until they're twelve or thirteen. It takes that long for it to build up naturally, unless they happen to find their calling early." He ran his hands through his hair again. "Reading is how I recharge my *illis*."

"So you just ... read anything?" Piper asked.

Alec shrugged. "Fiction is better," he said, "but I can work with anything I've not read before. Fiction I *have* read before is kind of useful, and rereading anything nonfiction is absolutely useless." He spun a book around. "I also remember almost everything I've ever read. Which is how I found this."

The book had a rich, burgundy colour. Stamped in gold on it was the title *A Fool's Guide to the Ridiculous.*

Piper blinked at it. "Are you sure this is the kind of book you can actually use for research?" she asked. It certainly didn't look legitimate.

Alec waved one hand. "Just because it isn't a historically viable source doesn't mean it's not useful," he argued. "Winehart was a lunatic, yes. But he does have a certain amount of information in here, things that other zoologists overlooked as being too obscure and unlikely to really exist."

He thumbed the book open to a page near the end and pushed it across the table.

Piper didn't need to see the text. Ice drenched down her spine at the illustration. A gangly, humanoid creature, with long, branching antlers on top of its head.

"That's it," Piper breathed. Then her gaze flicked up to the title. "That can't be right."

Alec leaned forward, bracing both elbows on the table. "I think we've proved that it *is* right," he said. "I seem to remember getting your unconscious body out of the Lower Ilian after an attack by one."

Piper rubbed her cold cheeks. "There are wendigos in the Ilian," she breathed.

"Wendigoag," Alec said, and Piper stared at him. "The plural is wendigoag."

"*Why?*" Then, Piper held up one hand and shook her head. "Actually, I don't want to know." She tapped the page, skimming the test as fast as she could. "Thank fate they're dead." Alec made a noncommittal sound, and Piper looked up at him. "What?"

"Well…" Alec rubbed the back of his neck. "One of the theories Winehart had on how wendigoag reproduce or multiply is that they're infectious."

"But that's …" Piper blanched. "It scratched me!"

"It's okay." Alec's hand landed on hers, and Piper jumped. "Most people accept that it's the saliva that's infectious. And your wounds were cleaned by magic. It won't have infected you."

Piper yanked her hand from underneath his, trying to rub heat into her frozen cheeks. Then she realised something. "How did the drawing get inside?"

Alec rubbed his chin. "Inside the wall only you could open," he mused softly. "Inside that awful place."

Piper worried her lip. "Is it because of my *illis?*" she asked. "You said it was …" She searched for a word. "Loud."

Alec pursed his lips. "I'm not sure," he said. "I'm not even sure why you could open it. If we could go back there, and look at that arch some more …" He sighed loudly. "Could one of those things have even made the drawing?"

"The male," Piper said. "The drawing was definitely female."

"Drawing his mate?" Alec shook his head. "That makes no sense."

Piper hesitated. "If wendigoes – wendigoag," she corrected herself before Alec could, "are infectious, does that mean they were human once? Maybe that's how he could draw his mate?"

Alec shrugged. "I couldn't tell you," he said. "I don't have enough information."

Piper wrapped her arms around her knees. "But how did the arch open for them?" she murmured, not really expecting an answer.

Alec shrugged again. "Something about your *illis* activated it," he said. "But I have no idea what."

They lapsed into silence for a moment. Then Alec cleared his throat. "Something's been bothering me," he said. "How did they know we would be there? I didn't tell anyone. I mean, Liam knew, but he's an inspector, he's used to keeping secrets. Even Hazel wasn't listening for most of that conversation."

Piper clenched her fists. "You'd better not be accusing me."

Alec's blue gaze met her silver. "I've been wrong about people before."

Piper pressed her hands to the table, spreading out her digits to stop them from curling into fists again. "I didn't even tell Rose where we were going," she said. "Just that we might be late. My birdie might have guessed, but he's tighter than a steel trap."

Alec's eyebrows forked up. "Is he now?" he asked.

"No one is getting information from him he doesn't want them to," she said. "Trust me. That's been tried." Twice. She'd stitched him up both times. "If they knew, it wasn't from me."

"Raoul said we missed them by hours," Alec said. "They must have known." He frowned, flipping the pen through his fingers.

"Could they have …" A shiver tried to work its way down Piper's spine, but she pushed it back. "Could they have *seen* it, somehow?"

Alec shook his head. "The Shiv'ek couldn't," he said. "Aside from select Immortals, seeing magic only appears in humans and elves. A Shiv'ek can't have it." He rubbed his hands together. "Maybe one of the others with him."

Piper frowned. "Can your kraken see?" she asked. It would be useful to have a hint of what the future might offer them.

"Laithos," Alec corrected. Then he shook his head. "No, he can't." His gaze darted over her. "What about your dragon?"

"Kostin," Piper said without thinking.

A smirk crept across Alec's face. "So you did talk to him," he said smugly.

Piper glared. "Yes," she admitted. "Or more, he spoke to me. In the Lower Ilian. We spoke again when I woke up, but it was … brief." And confusing, but she didn't bother adding that.

"It's like that at first," he said, like he had read her mind. "It'll get better."

"I'm not sure I want it to get better," Piper muttered, mostly to herself.

It might have been her imagination, but she thought she felt a rumble of disapproval from the tattoo on her back.

Alec didn't reply. Piper placed her chin in her hands, watching him flip through the pages of the book, neither of them really seeing them.

"I need to talk to Norrix," Alec said finally. "As much as I don't relish that."

Piper stiffened. "What do you mean?"

Alec, his attention on a far away bookshelf, didn't notice. Instead, he shot her a half-hearted smile. "I'm about to go and convince one of the most practical men in existence that there were two near-mythical monsters in the Lower Ilian, and that we need to go check for more." He shrugged. "Not my idea of a fun night."

"Right." Piper rubbed her face. "Have fun with that."

Alec raised one eyebrow, and Piper crossed her arms.

"I really don't want to meet the Lord General. And I need to see Caleb and Madelyn. They can't stay here all night, they need to sleep in their own beds."

Alec hesitated. "All right," he said. "I'll come and find you." He pushed himself up from the table and marched out of the library, his long legs eating up the ground.

Piper wavered a moment, staring at the books spread out on the table. Then she turned to the iron staircase. Time to find her children.

THIRTY ONE

Through trial and error, and trying more than one door that led to a cranky staff member shooing her away, Piper found herself in front of the staff common room. She knew it was the common room, even without opening the door. A delighted squeal that could only come from a little girl reverberated down the hall.

That sound meant she was okay. And happy.

Piper pushed the door open.

"Piper!" She'd barely set foot inside when a mass of white-blonde curls crashed into her, wrapping her in a tight hug. Piper hugged her back, mindless of her tender back.

"It's good to see you, baby girl," she whispered.

Madelyn squeezed harder. Then she looked up. "Are you okay?"

"Alec said you were hurt." Piper looked up to see Caleb stop in front of her, twisting his hands together. Piper offered him an arm, and he only hesitated for a second before letting her draw him into a hug.

He moved away almost immediately. But Piper counted it as a win; any hug from him was a win, at his age.

"I was hurt," Piper said. "But the High Lady healed me, so I'm okay now."

Caleb gave a small smile, and Madelyn squeezed her again before she drew away.

Piper looked around. The staff common room was stunning. Timber floors were covered with thick rugs. Armchairs and couches were dotted around, creating cosy nooks for reading or talking. Bookshelves lined the walls, as well as windows looking over the gardens and towards the stables. There was a billiards table, balls set in a neat triangle in the centre.

Piper frowned. "Were you here alone?" she asked.

"No." Caleb shook his head.

"The princess is here!" Madelyn bounced on the balls of her feet. "She's *soooo* pretty, Piper!"

"Is she now?" Piper's gaze darted over the room again, but there was definitely no one there. "Where is she?"

"She's right …" Caleb trailed off, looking around. "She was right here."

"I see." If she had gone, that made things easier. "Come on, then. Grab your things. We should head back to The Lily."

Madelyn pouted. "But it's so nice here, Piper," she whined.

"The beds are softer here," Caleb agreed.

"Yes, but it's not home," Piper said.

The corners of Caleb's mouth turned down. He scowled, crossing his arms.

"Neither is The Lily," he said. "It's a pub, not a home."

Piper reached for him, but he jerked away.

"We can't go back to your home, Caleb," Piper said. "Let's go to The Lily."

"I don't want to!"

"You don't get a choice!" Piper snapped.

Caleb flinched. His arms came up, wrapping around his chest. Immediately, guilt coursed through Piper.

"Caleb," she tried, reaching out. But Caleb stepped back.

"Fine," he said. "Let's go."

"Caleb, please," Piper said.

Caleb ignored her. He grabbed Madelyn's hand. "Come on," he muttered.

"Caleb!"

But Caleb pulled Madelyn after him, dragging her from the room even as she looked back at Piper over her shoulder, her hazel eyes wide.

Piper closed the door to their suite behind her. Sighing, she pressed her forehead to the timber and closed her eyes.

Caleb hadn't spoken to Piper the entire way to The Lily. When they got there, he stormed into their suite, dragging Madelyn behind him, and slammed the door to their room. Piper had heard it lock. No matter what she'd said, no matter how hard she'd begged, he hadn't unlocked it.

That had been an hour ago.

Piper sighed again, fitting her key into the lock. When the door was locked behind her, she turned to the stairs. It took missing a step and nearly turning her ankle for Piper to shake herself out of her own mind.

Downstairs, the main room of the pub hummed with activity. Rose darted between tables, serving with a smile. It was busy enough that Patrik had ventured out from behind his bar, a notepad in hand. Judging by their trips to and from the kitchen, he spent so long talking to his usual customers that Rose took five or six orders for each one of his.

Lily poked her head out from the kitchen to observe the barely controlled chaos. When she met Piper's eyes, she offered a small smile, before withdrawing again.

Piper's usual booth by the window was taken; a couple, canoodling in the shadowy corner. Piper's lip curled, and she turned away. Some people had no tact, acting like that in public. All the tables were occupied, so Piper pushed past a group of men standing around the empty fireplace and made her way to the bar. She threw herself onto a stool with a huff, fighting back the desire to bury her face in her hands.

She'd just wanted a quiet night. Some space, some breathing room away from Caleb and his unspoken condemnation. She didn't want to come down here, not be able to sit in her favourite chair, and have to deal with all the ... sheer socialness happening.

Piper winced. It wasn't fair of her to wish a quiet night on Patrik and his family, not when they had bills to pay. It hadn't been fair of her to snap at Caleb, either. He just wanted his mum back.

Piper pushed her hair out of her eyes. She almost jumped off her stool to leave, when a voice stopped her.

"Piper?" Beks pushed past two women chatting loudly about hats, one hand going to the scarf wrapped around her head. Purple, today, it clashed awfully with her auburn eyebrows. Not that Piper would ever tell her that.

"What are you doing here?" Piper asked, and then grimaced. "Hi."

"Hi." Beks edged in between Piper's seat and the man next to her, earning a glare from him when she knocked his glass, almost tipping it. "I'm looking for you."

"What?" Piper blinked at her. "Why?"

Beks reached up and adjusted her scarf again. Her dark blue eyes flicked over the pub, her lips pursed. She leaned forward.

"I'm here because you need help," she said softly. "I had a vision."

"You had a vision?" Piper said, not entirely certain she'd heard correctly in the loud room. Beks nodded, and Piper grimaced. "That I'd need help, sitting in a pub on an Asdiel night ..." She trailed off, going cold. "Oh fate."

She'd forgotten their meeting. Completely and utterly. She'd been distracted by traipsing through the Lower Ilian, fighting off not one but three other assassins and getting ten knife-like claws in her back. They were all good reasons on their own, let alone combined, but guilt still crawled through Piper's stomach like a living thing.

"Oh fate," she repeated, jumping off her chair. "I have to go. I have somewhere to be."

Beks frowned. "Piper, wait," she said, catching her arm. Piper turned to the other woman, her gaze flicking over her.

"That's perfect," Piper said.

Beks blinked at her. "What?"

"It works perfectly," she said. "You're here. You can stay with Caleb and Madelyn for me tonight."

"What?" Beks shook her head. "No, Piper, that's not why I'm here. You need my help–"

"If you want to help," Piper said, "you can stay with Caleb and Madelyn. I can't leave them by themselves. And I need to go meet– I need to go somewhere."

A line appeared between Beks' brows. "Piper, wait," she said. "That's really not what I meant. I mean you need my help out there tonight!"

"I'll be fine," she said. "I can look after myself."

"I still think that–"

Piper didn't let her finish. "If you want to help," she repeated, "this is it. Thank you, Beks."

She pushed her spare key into Beks' hand. Then, before Beks could argue again, Piper hurried out the door. She forced herself to keep her gaze forward, and not glance towards the stairs. They'd be okay. They loved Beks. And Beks cared for them both as well.

She wasn't leaving them alone. She was probably leaving them with a person better suited to care for them than she was.

Now all she had to do was convince herself of that fact.

THIRTY TWO

Piper jogged through the Market District to the nearest tram stop. She glanced up at the sky as she did; it was the faded purple of an old bruise. Light came from streetlamps now, magelights on them high in place. The yellow banners for the Market District flapped in the breeze, making ropes rattle against the metal.

Piper jumped the garden at the station and joined the end of the line, waiting for the woman in front of her as she fumbled with her old-fashioned purse strings. Piper tapped her foot, shifting her weight. The woman's hand shook as she reached for the railing; the conductor handed her up with far more patience than he had for any other passenger.

Then he turned to Piper. "Where to?" he asked.

"Coral Square," Piper said absently, patting her pockets.

She froze.

Her wallet. The brown leather was soft from the beeswax her father had applied to it every weekend as they sat in front of the fire, and always smelled like the dried nightflower petals she had pressed under the fold. In the front, there was a photograph of her with Caleb and Madelyn, eating ice cream, mint-green liquid running down Madelyn's face and a smear of chocolate on Caleb's cheek.

A thin gold necklace, the only thing she had left of her mother's, was in the billfold.

And it had been in the pocket of her coat.

Piper's hands shook. "My wallet," she breathed.

The conductor's face creased in sympathy.

"There's a lot of pickpockets around on an Asdiel," he said. "Sorry to hear that." He hesitated. "I can't let you on if you can't pay."

Piper didn't bother to correct him; no pickpocket had ever stolen from her. It wasn't like someone had taken it, to steal what little money it held and drop it off at a police station as something "found" on the street.

Fate knew what had happened to her coat. It was probably at the bottom of the floodwater, on some street in the Lower Ilian. Maybe some lucky soul would find the wallet, when the waters receded. Maybe the violet algae would eat the leather. Leather was just skin, after all.

The tram whistle sounded, and Piper blinked. The conductor, leaning on the balcony railing, offered her one last grimace as it trundled away.

Piper's hands groped at her hip. But no familiar lump hung there amongst her coat folds.

No coat. No wallet. No necklace.

Piper took a shaking breath and ran her hands over her face.

No identification. She had no idea how she'd get into her bank accounts, let alone access the money she had in trust, without them. She'd never get a new card – not a clean one. And she couldn't pay for a dirty one, now.

Woodenly, Piper turned. The sound of boots slapping against cobblestones met her ears before she even realised she was walking. But walking was her only option, now.

Walking halfway across the city.

Piper forced her way through Illusion Square. On an Asdiel night, minor mages, the type with just enough magic to amuse, packed the square. Tricks and performances abounded, and to one side, Piper could see a line of parents standing with children about Caleb's age; getting them tested, to see if they had magic.

Piper pushed past them all. She avoided an elbow to the face as one particularly inebriated man spun around, guffawing at the mage juggling tiny balls of fire in front of him. She stepped around a father, his daughter clinging to his hand. Past a girl who had to be an older sister, her brother leaning against her side as they watched someone breathe a plume of smoke twelve feet long.

Tricks, all of them, and nothing more. But ones that entertained, nonetheless.

Forty-five minutes later, Piper jumped over a deep rut in the road, one that had collected enough rain to turn into a huge puddle. She wrinkled her nose at the smell of stagnant water, then again at the smell of unwashed bodies. Three women in patched and ragged clothes peeled themselves out of a doorway halfway down the side alley. One of them reached for Piper's shirt, but she twitched out of her grip. A second bared broken, red-stained teeth at her, and the third dropped to her knees.

"Please," she said, her voice hoarse. "I just need one more."

Her stomach twisting, Piper dodged around them and out of the alley. She didn't have the kind of thing those women were looking for.

She ducked around a tall man in a burgundy coat and wove between two women arguing over a bolt of sapphire blue cloth. As Piper passed, one of them grabbed it, while the other held it to her chest. A ripping sound tore through the murmurs and shouts around her, and Piper winced. That would be one unhappy shopkeeper.

A tram station loomed ahead. Behind Piper, the honking of a horn sounded, and Piper ducked off the tracks in time for the trolley to pass her.

As it trundled by, Piper looked up. The tram stopped and Piper kept walking, closing the distance between them. The conductor was frowning at something inside.

A few people got off. Quite a lot, actually, for a nowhere stop between the two large squares. One woman looked back over her shoulder, muttering something that Piper couldn't hear. The man walking beside her shook his head, a frown between his brows.

"... unseemly ..." Piper caught as they turned, heading on towards Coral Square. Piper frowned.

She turned her attention back towards the tram. The conductor vanished through the door, letting it snap behind him. Piper stared. The conductors never entered the tram carriages.

The first fist flew, and Piper frowned. A fight of some kind, the conductor stepping in to break it up she assumed. No wonder everyone else had got off.

Piper glanced at the street. The people from the tram had mostly moved on. No one else on the street paid any attention; fights on trams weren't that interesting.

The tram readied to move, the driver ignoring the fight happening behind him in favour of remaining on time. Piper picked up her pace, her gaze fixed on the railing. She reached the station as the tram began to move. It edged away, and Piper lengthened her stride, not quite running until–

A hand wrapped around her wrist.

Piper spun, lashing out. A wall of black met her eyes, then a familiar flash of bright blue eyes made her suck in a breath. She pulled back at the last moment, her punch going wide. Her back slammed into the plastic wall of the shelter. One hand pinned her wrist beside her head. The other pressed against her hip.

"It's me," Alec said unnecessarily.

"Well, obviously, Alexander." Piper scowled. Pressing her free hand against his chest, she pushed him away. "If I hadn't realised it was you, you'd have a broken nose again!"

Her breath caught in her throat, the flash of panic catching up with her.

Alec let go of her wrist, his fingers sliding over her skin. "Sorry," he said, reading her reaction. He glanced back over his shoulder at the tram, now well out of reach. "What were you doing? I thought you'd be with Caleb and Madelyn."

"I left them with someone I trust for the night." Piper rubbed her hands over her face. "I was trying to catch the tram. I lost my wallet when I lost my coat. I've had to walk across the city."

I, I, I, I. Piper gritted her teeth. She sounded like a whiney teenager. She hadn't even been a whiney teenager when she *was* a teenager.

In front of her, Alec cleared his throat. He rubbed the back of his neck. "Yeah, about that," he said.

"About what?" she asked.

Alec twisted, pulling the bag he had slung over one shoulder around to the front. There was a flare of blue-black light as he pulled open the flap. Then, from within, he drew a length of black.

Piper pressed her hand to her mouth. Her coat, long and black and somehow whole, hung in Alec's hand.

He held it out. "Here," he said.

Piper grabbed at it. Her hands shook as she hunted through the folds, looking for the inside pocket.

"You still had it on, when we left," he explained gruffly. "And I thought, well, I thought that ... Piper? What are you doing?"

Piper's fingers closed on smooth leather, and she bit back a sob of relief. Looping her coat over one arm, Piper cradled the leather in both hands, bringing it up to her face to breathe in the scent of beeswax and nightflowers.

Piper threw one arm around Alec's neck. "Thank you," she whispered, pulling him down to her and forcing him to bend almost in two. "Thank you, thank you."

Hesitantly, Alec's arm slid around her waist.

Then, Piper realised what she was doing. "Oh!" She jumped back like she'd been electrocuted. Alec's hand dropped to his side, and he cleared his throat again, the tips of his ears pink.

Casting around for a distraction, Piper held out her coat. "I can't believe it's not ... ruined," she said.

"It was, actually."

Piper's gaze flicked to him, and she frowned. "What are you talking about?" she asked.

Alec glanced down the street. The crowd from the tram had well and truly dispersed, and otherwise the street was quiet. He sank onto one of the benches for waiting passengers.

"It's what I'm good at," he said after a moment. "Items, I mean. I hadn't once seen you without that coat on, either. So I wanted to see if I could fix it."

Piper hovered next to him, not quite certain if she wanted to sit or not.

Then Alec looked up. The corner of his mouth curled, and his eyes crinkled in a small smile. "Well," he said, "that's not all. And please don't stab me for this."

"What did you do?" Piper asked, her eyes narrowing.

"Yours is the strongest *illis* I've ever felt," Alec said. "If I can feel it, can track it, it's only a matter of time until someone else realises they can, as well."

"What are you saying?" Piper interrupted. Then she frowned. "Someone like whom?"

Alec shrugged. "Someone like the Shiv'ek."

Piper froze. "What ..." She trailed off, licking dry lips.

Alec nudged her foot with his. "It should hide your *illis*, stop anyone from tracking you," he said. "Try it."

Piper's fingers tightened around the wallet in her hands. It was stupid to be nervous about putting a coat on. Wasn't it?

She shrugged it on, working the hand with the wallet through the sleeve carefully so it didn't get stuck. Her daggers settled into place; stiletto against her right hip, and throwing daggers near her left breast.

"Well?" she asked, feeling ridiculous.

Alec's gaze darted over her. "Put the hood on," he said.

Piper hesitated a moment more. Then she reached behind her, pulling the hood up over her curly hair.

Alec nodded. "I feel nothing," he said. "It's like stepping out of full sun into deep shadow. I can actually feel the *absence* of your *illis.*"

Piper tugged the hood back down off her head.

Alec let out a breath, closing his eyes for a second, and nodded again. "It's back," he said. "It works."

Cradling her wallet in both hands, Piper lowered herself to perch on the bench beside him. She hesitated. "Thanks," she murmured, hoping he understood. One word couldn't possibly sum up everything: the charm, repairing her coat, getting her out of the Lower Ilian. Saving her life.

Alec just nodded. "It's what I do," he said. "Item magic."

Piper fiddled with the edge of her wallet, worrying it between her fingers. She had it back. Had everything back. She opened the fold.

There was a bulge in the coin section not shaped like any coin. Piper flipped it open, her fingers finding the fine gold chain. She put it over her head. For a moment, she held the ruby shard attached to it in her palm. Then she tucked it into the neck of her shirt.

Alec glanced sideways at her.

"That's a man's wallet," he said after a moment. Piper stroked the photograph of Caleb and Madelyn, thinking of the one underneath it; the only photo she had of her parents. It was too painful to look at their faces every time she opened the wallet.

"Yep," she said. Piper closed the wallet and slid it into its pocket on the inside of her coat.

Alec braced his elbows on his knees. He said nothing. But Piper could almost hear the wheels in his head turning, see him mentally sorting through their conversations over the past few days.

"Why couldn't your parents do anything about you being put on a black ship?" he asked gently.

Piper touched the lump of her wallet through her coat. "They were already dead."

Alec nodded, like he had expected that. "I'm sorry," he said.

"I don't like it when people say that," Piper warned, looking at him sideways.

Alec shot her a small, sad smile. "Most people really don't know what they're saying when they say they're sorry."

Piper turned to face him, trying to read his expression. He held her gaze.

"But you do," she said.

Alec clasped his hands together, eyes turning towards the tram tracks in front of them.

"I lost my father a few years ago," he said.

Piper nodded. There wasn't really anything else she could say.

Like they sensed the gravity of their conversation, a bare handful of commuters approached slowly, glancing between the two of them. Piper ignored two men, who went to lean against the wall, but she did move closer to Alec so an old lady could sit on the end of their bench. The rumble of the approaching tram finally sounded, and the lady beside Piper stood.

"Come on, then," she said, jerking her head towards the tram as it pulled up beside them. "Let's go."

THIRTY THREE

They left the tram in Coral Square. Though it was less busy than Illusion Square, people still pressed in around them, browsing the Asdiel nightmarkets. Delicacies from all countries lined the stalls, and Piper stopped as they passed to purchase a *frede* from one of them. After a glance over her shoulder, she bought one for Alec too.

Alec raised his eyebrows as Piper handed him the pastry. She tucked hers in the top of her bag. She'd eat it later.

"Why are we here?" Alec asked, leaning down to her so he didn't have to shout. "We should be looking for Jai and your friend."

"I need to meet someone," she said. "It shouldn't take long."

If she brought Abby back, maybe Caleb would forgive her.

One street back from the square, a white building loomed a full storey over the buildings around it. Someone had recently cleaned the render on the walls; it reflected shards of moonslight to fragment against the ground. A sign on top showed a cocktail in a refined glass, its contents purple. A line of patrons snaked down the large set of stairs leading up to the club. At the top, two guards checked identification and for weapons. Piper's gaze trailed over the line, taking stock of the people there.

She stopped so suddenly that Alec bumped into her. "Beks?"

Beks stood at the base of a set of stairs, her hands clasped so hard before her that the knuckles had turned white.

Panic burned in Piper's chest. She darted forward.

"Piper!" Beks gasped in relief. "Thank fate–"

Piper gripped her wrist. "Where are Caleb and Madelyn?" she demanded.

"It's okay," Beks said, "they're still at The Lily. The girl who waits the tables promised she'd keep an eye on them. They'll be fine."

"Beks ..." Another favour from the Edlams. They'd already done so much, and they were so busy, running their pub. Piper clenched her fists. There wasn't anything she could do about it now. "What are you doing here?" she asked instead.

"I tried to tell you," Beks said, frowning. "You need me tonight. I had a vision. I have to be with you."

"But–"

"No buts!" Beks interrupted with uncharacteristic firmness. "This is important, Piper."

Piper wavered for a second. "What did you see?" she asked.

Beks pursed her lips.

"Seers have to be careful what they say," Alec said from beside her. His face was paler than usual, lines of tension around his eyes. "If they say the wrong thing, or too much, they can make it come true instead of avoiding it."

"How do you–"

"My brother is a seer," Alec said before Piper could finish. His gaze flicked over Beks, over her scarf and back to her face. Then he looked at the club behind them. "Why are we here?" he asked, frowning.

"I need to see someone," Piper said.

"Surely we should be–" he started.

"Piper, I think–" Beks said at the same time.

"No," she said firmly, cutting them both off. "You both inserted yourselves into my evening, and I need to do this. Understand? So come along and try to look like you know what you're doing, and for fate's sake, do as I say so you don't get yourselves killed."

Beks' mouth dropped open. Alec raised an eyebrow.

"By fate, who are you seeing?" he asked.

Piper ignored the question, waving her hand at them both. She turned her attention back to the building. Behind her, Beks' clothes rustled, and Alec hissed something. Piper tuned them out. She headed upstairs, taking the steps two at a time. She heard a soft curse behind her, then two sets of footsteps; one heavy, and one far lighter. At the top, Piper dodged around a man with a keg thrown over his shoulder, and pushed open one side of the double doors.

"Hey!" a guard snapped. "You have to wait your turn!"

Piper glanced at him, then stepped through the doors.

A hand wrapped around her arm. "I said," the guard growled, "you have to—"

Piper grabbed him by the hair, and he let out a high-pitched yelp. She wrapped an arm around his throat, using her much shorter height to drag him backwards and put pressure on the veins in his neck. A moment later, he slumped in her arms. Piper gripped his shirt and lowered him to the ground, careful not to hit his head.

He'd only be out for a minute; she hadn't really wanted to hurt him.

The man with the keg stared at her, his mouth hanging open. The second guard shrugged.

"You're expected," she said to Piper. Then, with a head tilt towards her unconscious colleague, "He's new." Piper dipped her chin in acknowledgement, then stepped through the doors.

A wave of heat slapped Piper in the face. The air smelled like beer and soap; someone must have spilled or vomited, and recently. The room looked like someone had gutted the entire bottom level of a mansion, leaving only columns to hold up the upper storey. Piper ducked around a pillar so she could see better.

People of all sorts crowded the space. Booths lined the walls, filled with couples and groups, each with a drink in front of them; beer, commonly, or a purple cocktail, the house specialty. A low, thrumming music filled the space. The lighting was cosy, but dim, creating plenty of shadows in the corners.

To Piper's left, two people conducted a conversation in low voices. Then, in full view of everyone in the club, the woman passed him a clear bag filled with violet dust in exchange for a single cream-coloured note. Silver winked in the lamplight, then she pocketed the stars, turning to the next person, who hovered nearby as they waited for their own dose.

In one booth, a sea elf with long, silver-white hair sat in a man's lap, leaning against his shoulder with the ease of long partners. Across from them, a wood elf with night-black hair trailed his fingers through a pretty human woman's hair. Both wore the purple shirt that marked them as part of the inner circle, truly trusted employees.

Interesting. She'd have to ask about the elves. They were new, and clearly very comfortable here.

Piper strode towards the back of the room, her shoulders squared and her chin high – walking tall despite her meagre height. She met no one's gaze, instead stepping past them as though they meant nothing to her. They didn't.

She reached a small crowd and pushed through it, ignoring the disgruntled exclamations as she elbowed someone out of the way. Complaints followed behind her; Alec and Beks, she presumed. She didn't look back to check. That would ruin the effect.

At the back of the room, the crowd thinned around a small, raised dais. Three steps led up, and on it were two very comfortable chairs, one significantly larger than the other. A little table sat between them, a bottle of violet gin and two glasses on it; one was untouched, the other almost empty.

As Piper watched, a dark-haired man lifted the almost empty glass. He sat in the smaller chair, seeming at ease despite the crowd, and despite the man who sat across from him.

Piper climbed the three steps. One guard put her hand on her pistol and stepped forward. Her partner caught her arm, shaking his head.

The man in the larger chair looked up from his conversation as Piper's boots tapped on the timber. Sea-green eyes took her in, flicking over where the daggers were concealed in her boots and coat. His hair was pulled back in a severe horsetail; the near-white colour of it almost glowed against his tanned skin.

Piper sank into a shallow movement somewhere between a bow and a curtsey, equal parts flamboyant and mocking. Her eyes never left his.

"Belladonna." His deep voice echoed across the dais, causing the man beside him to freeze. The silence was almost deafening, despite the music still playing in the background.

Out of the corner of her eye, Piper saw Beks stiffen, the colour leaving her face.

"Alchemist," Piper replied irreverently. She had to maintain a strong facade in this place, in front of one of the most powerful underground leaders in the city.

THIRTY FOUR

Piper rose from her less-than-respectful bow and rocked back on one heel, crossing her arms over her chest.

His piercing green eyes stayed in contact with hers. "How kind of you, to take time out of your busy schedule to visit me." Achard steepled his fingers and stared at Piper over the top of them. At only a few years older than Piper, Achard was the youngest crime leader in the city. That hadn't stopped him from becoming one of the most powerful.

Piper shrugged. "I was bored, and I wanted a word. *Alchemist.*" One of Achard's eyes twitched at the use of his title, but aside from that, he kept his face blank.

"Go on, then." He made a dismissive gesture, giving Piper permission to speak. Piper narrowed her eyes at him, ready to tell him exactly what she thought of his offer.

"Hey!" Both Achard and Piper tensed, attention darting towards the interruption. Piper's fingers brushed a hilt through her coat. Achard didn't move at all.

Below the dais, a man had his hand wrapped tight around Beks' slim arm. Alec was beside Beks, one hand on her shoulder, possessively, and the other clenched in a fist by his side.

"Let go of her," Alec growled.

Panic flared, hot in Piper's chest, but she shoved it back down. "What's this?" she drawled. She took the stairs down, inserting herself between Beks and the guard. The guard glared down at her with cold eyes. It was the man she'd knocked out, Piper realised. It looked like he wasn't too happy about his impromptu nap.

"They can't be here," he said. "They haven't been screened." His fingers tightened around Beks' arm, and Beks hissed in pain.

"They're with me." Piper reached up and pressed a single finger to the hollow of the guard's throat. She felt him swallow.

"You shouldn't be here, either."

Piper traced her finger over the pulse point of his throat. A warning.

"I heard she poisons her fingernails, and just one scratch can kill you," Alec rumbled, in a whisper designed to carry.

Piper bit the inside of her lip. That was just stupid. What if she accidentally scratched herself? But the guard edged back from her. Stupid enough to believe Alec's ridiculous lie, but smart enough to back down when he was clearly outclassed.

Achard sighed. "Don't antagonise the Belladonna, Eric," he said. Then, "Who are these two?"

Piper turned back to him and shrugged. "They're king and queen of my fan club," she said, her expression completely blank. Achard bit the inside of his cheek. It was such a tiny movement; she doubted anyone else noticed. "Now, about that word."

She retrieved one of her twin throwing knives. She slid the point under her nails, unnecessarily cleaning them. The threat was unmistakable.

"Leave them alone." Achard jerked his chin at Beks and Alec, then his gaze returned to Piper. "You have five minutes, Belladonna."

"Privately," Piper said. "And they come too."

For a long moment, Achard regarded her over the tops of his fingers. It was always a delicate performance between them. If either came across as weak, they risked an attempt being made on their life. There would be a certain cachet for being the one to kill the Belladonna, and whoever killed Achard would be a strong contender for his empire.

So Achard waited. He waited for so long that the people closest to the dais, those pretending not to listen in on them, began to shift and glance at each other. He was letting them, and Piper, know that he could refuse her. That this "word" was on his terms, not hers.

"Fine." With the fluid grace that came from spending countless hours with a sword in hand, Achard rose to his feet. Though shorter than Alec, he was still over six feet tall and muscled in the classic build of a swordsman. His green eyes were hard, and though his blonde hair would have softened the harsh angles of his face if worn out, he rarely let it fall from its horsetail.

He made a gesture to one of his guards, and she stepped forward to refill the gin glass of his companion. Achard then turned and moved towards the large staircase behind the dais. Not another family leader, then, Piper surmised. Achard would have taken a moment to excuse himself if he were. A business deal, or maybe a petition of some kind.

Achard led Piper's group upstairs. The balcony ran around the outside of the level, with several closed and, if he were smart, locked doors leading off it. Achard didn't live here; that would be asking for trouble, if everyone knew where he slept. But he made it look like he did, and that kept most potential issues at bay.

He unlocked one of the doors, opening to a short hallway. With a few steps down it, and a second locked door, they were at his study. Half-full bookshelves lined the walls, and not just with books. Weapons, rolled-up maps and figurines littered the shelves, as well as a wine decanter. A soft red rug covered the timber floor, and two armchairs and a couch flanked the fireplace, where coals glowed merrily in the grate.

Beks stopped in the centre of the room. Her eyes glanced from Alec, who stood at her side with one hand still protectively clasping her shoulder, to Piper, to Achard. Achard crossed the floor and dropped into his chair, the larger black one. Piper dropped into the green one opposite him, closest to the fire. She crossed her legs, sitting tailor-style in her seat.

"Fate, Piper." He rubbed his hand over his face. "You nearly made me laugh with that fan club comment. Then what would I have done?"

"Appointed me your court jester?" she suggested, and he laughed.

He looked over at their guests. When his gaze landed on Alec, he frowned. "Wasn't he the one you were supposed to kill?"

Alec swore. He stepped forward, his entire arm glowing with blue-black fire. Beks gasped.

"Alexander!" Piper leaped from her seat, putting herself between him and Achard. Despite the magic glowing around him, she grabbed his arm and shook her head.

Alec didn't move, but neither did he stop the magic engulfing his arm. Piper glanced down at her hand. It was more than a little disconcerting to see her wrist vanish into the dark blue flames. They licked at her skin, tickling and stinging mildly.

She looked at Achard over her shoulder. "He *was*," she said firmly.

"So the rumours of you going rogue are true," Achard mused. Then he smiled. "Good for you."

"Good for you?" Alec asked, his eyebrows rising towards his hairline. "Last I saw, being attacked by three other assassins isn't 'good for you' criteria."

Achard glanced at Piper. "I killed Iso and Ratt," she said, walking towards the sideboard. "But Saxe got away. Not before I stuck him, though."

Piper busied herself pouring two glasses of water. She could feel their eyes on her.

"Achard, there's Red Rot back in the city," she called over her shoulder, placing the glass decanter back down on the timber table.

Behind her, Achard swore. "Are you sure?" he asked.

Piper turned and walked back to them, glasses in hand. She handed one to Beks, who watched them all with an impassive expression Piper was certain hid absolute terror. The other she handed to Alec, who nodded his thanks. She dropped into her armchair again.

"Of course I'm sure." Piper shuddered at the memory of those poor women, so desperate, clutching at her and begging for *just one more*. "I saw the teeth."

Achard raised his eyebrows at Alec's glass of water, then looked pointedly at Beks. "What, none for me?" he asked.

Piper flicked her leaf-shaped blade through her fingers, then tossed it at him. Achard barely seemed to twitch, then the dagger was in his hand.

"You're old enough and ugly enough to get it yourself," Piper told him.

Achard glanced down at the dagger.

"What would you do if one day you did that, and I didn't catch it?" he asked.

Piper shrugged. "Not apologise, because that would mean you've gotten lazy," she replied.

Achard snorted and tossed the weapon back to her. Piper tucked it away, then gestured to the couch.

"You can both sit," she said to the others. "This shouldn't take long."

"As always, your ability to underestimate an issue astounds me," Achard muttered.

Piper sighed, wishing to fate for just one quiet night. "You have to get back to your darlings out there, and I'm assuming you need me to go beat someone up, or you wouldn't have called me here."

Achard grimaced. He steepled his fingers – his classic thinking position.

Piper swivelled her bag around, pulling her *frede* out and unwrapping it.

His eyes narrowed. "And you find time to eat?" he asked.

He was stalling. Piper could tell that. Whatever he wanted her to do, it wasn't going to be pleasant.

"Turns out I haven't eaten since dinner the day before yesterday," she said, tearing off a piece of bitter flaky pastry. "I'm not superhuman. Even I need to eat sometimes."

Achard's mouth popped open. "What–"

"Before we broach that subject," Beks interrupted, cutting off Achard's questioning. "I don't understand this." Beks gestured between Piper and Achard. "You two are ... what? Friends?"

Achard glanced at Piper, who shrugged. She trusted Alec, and Beks was no one. It didn't matter what she knew, no one would believe her.

"I'm not the only man of my ... profession in the city," Achard said after a moment. "The others, and the people under them, can be difficult."

"Difficult how?" Beks asked.

"Like importing Red Rot into my city," he said, and Beks winced. "But I have something they don't have."

"What is it you have?" Alec asked, his eyes narrowed.

"The Belladonna," Achard said.

Piper glared at him. "You don't 'have' me," she said. "We work together. *Alchemist.*"

Like she had known he would, Achard shuddered.

"Why Alchemist?" Beks asked.

"I didn't choose it," Achard said. "They could have called me anything, you know. They could have called me the Winter Sword!" He gestured to his hair. "But no. I got the Alchemist."

Piper laughed. "The Winter Sword?" she asked. Then she put a hand to her forehead. "Oh save me, Winter Sword! For I am a swooning damsel!"

It was Achard's turn to throw something at her. Piper ducked as a metal figurine sailed over her head, clattering to the floorboards behind her. "It's better than the Alchemist!" Achard insisted. Piper laughed again.

"But surely it came from somewhere," Beks pressed, frowning.

Achard sighed. "I oversee the entire Violetta and Purple Gin trades, amongst other things," he said. "I try to keep the rubbish like Red Rot out of the city, in favour of more harmless drugs like Violetta."

Alec's eyes narrowed. "No drug is harmless," he said.

"Compared to Red Rot? Yeah, they are," Piper said. "Red Rot literally rots out the inside of a person's mouth over time. Healers can't do anything to fix it." She shook her head. "You can use Violetta to wean the addicts off it."

"Is that the one made out of violet algae?" Beks asked, glancing between them with curiosity in her eyes.

Piper narrowed her eyes at her. "You're taking this rather well," she said. "Is there something you're not telling us?"

Beks blushed bright red. "No," she squeaked, her voice a little too high. "There's nothing I'm not telling you."

Alec twisted, staring at Beks like she'd grown an extra head.

Piper ignored them both and turned to Achard. "Why am I here, Achard?" She gestured to the others. "I'm kind of in the middle of something."

Achard made a face and looked away from her, into the fire. "I need your help," he said.

Piper tensed. The last time he had started a conversation like that …

"What happened?" A sick feeling of dread curled in her stomach.

Achard pursed his lips. "That rumour I told you about," he said slowly. "I've heard some things. Regarding a certain … young man, who is missing." Piper sucked in a breath. Her chest burned, and she rubbed at her breastbone. "I've only come by this information recently," he protested, and the burning in Piper's chest eased. "I'd originally asked you for something else, but it's less important."

The burning in Piper's chest flared, and she gritted her teeth. "Action or inaction, Achard," she said. "This is counting as inaction. Hurry it up."

Alec's blue gaze darted over Piper, frowning at her hand, still pressed against her breastbone where the burning pain centred.

Beks leaned forward, crossing one leg over the other in a very delicate and feminine way.

Achard sighed loudly. "I shouldn't be telling you this," he muttered. "Fate. I'm going to get her killed."

340

Piper bit back a gasp as her chest caught fire – or so it felt. "Achard," she said.

He directed his gaze from the fire back to her, and his eyes widened. "Fate!" He braced his elbows on his knees. "All right. I'm telling you." The pain in Piper's chest eased enough for her to suck in a full breath. She tried not to cough.

Achard rubbed his face.

"This young man who's missing–" Achard said.

Beks interrupted him, delicately clearing her throat. "I presume," she said, "that this young man is Prince Jairus. You can stop dancing around the point."

Achard stared at her. So did Piper. A heartbeat after, Alec turned to look at Beks as well.

"How do you know that?" Piper asked.

Beks huffed. "Why do you all look so surprised?" she demanded. "I'm a seer. I see things. Like, you know. The future." She crossed her arms over her chest, fixing all three of them in turn with a dark blue stare.

Piper ran her hand through her hair. Finding half of it out of the quick braid she'd thrown it into when she left the palace, she pulled the tie out of the end, shook it out, and started again. It felt like the kind of night she'd need her braid good and tight, with no loose curls for someone to pull on.

"So everyone in this room knows the prince is missing," she summarised. Her hands worked in her hair so she was unable to press them against the flare in her chest to try and ease it. "Achard, stop dancing around the point. Whatever you know, I need this information. Yesterday."

"I didn't have it yesterday," Achard said, his voice very even.

"For fate's sake man, just hand it over," Alec snapped. "She meant that figuratively."

"But I didn't." Achard's gaze fixed on Piper's again.

The truth in his words did help with the pain, and Achard knew that.

"It would seem," Achard said, "that a certain individual who runs in your circles is behind the prince's kidnapping."

Piper frowned. She shifted her hair over her shoulder to work on the end of her braid. Then she sucked in a breath. "Lore."

Achard nodded.

Piper leaped to her feet. Her boots wore the familiar track between her chair and the bookshelves and back again, where she gripped the top of her armchair. "I don't understand," she breathed. "He makes the rules."

"Rules can be broken," Achard pointed out. "Who would make him take any oaths?"

There was a clear answer to that: no one. Lore wasn't accountable to anyone but himself; even the families could barely keep him in check, and Piper was certain a lot of money traded hands to keep it that way.

She rubbed her face. "The Shiv'ek must be paying him," she muttered. Lore never did anything that wasn't for money or power.

Beks gasped. "A Shiv'ek?" she demanded, her eyes round as an owl's. She rounded on Alec. "You didn't tell me this involved a Shiv'ek!"

"Nor me," Achard thundered.

"Stop!" Piper held up both hands, wincing as that tugged her now sore chest. "Stop. Neither of you needed to know because neither of you have to deal with the Shiv'ek."

"Then who *will?*" Achard demanded.

"That would be me," Alec said, crossing his arms. "The Shiv'ek is my problem; the people working with him, Piper and I will deal with together."

Achard's lips pursed as he took Alec in. He glanced at Piper, and she shrugged in answer to his unasked question. She had to be okay with it.

The oath she'd taken didn't like this information gathering. Piper rubbed at her chest gingerly, then looked at Achard.

"Tell me what you know," she said.

Achard sighed. "You know our rules." He gestured to himself, meaning all family bosses. "Anyone who goes after the royal family dies."

"You need me to cull Lore," Piper said woodenly. A new burning started in her chest at that thought, and Piper grimaced.

"He's threatening the royal family," Achard said. "We can't have that." He hesitated for a moment. "This is no different to the black lace gang, really."

Piper begged to differ. "I can't kill him," she reminded him.

"That's okay," he said. "I can. But I can't go after him."

"Why not?" Beks asked, frowning. "You certainly look like you can handle yourself. Why make Piper do this?"

Achard sighed. "Because," he said, "if I interfere, he'll kill my daughter." He rubbed his face, his hand hiding his expression and muffling his next words. "He knows about Madelyn."

The room swayed. "Fate damn him," Piper hissed.

Achard dropped his hand, his face pinched. "You're the only one who even knows about her," he said. "She's just a kid."

Piper bristled. "You're not suggesting I told him."

"Of course not." Achard shook his head. "But I don't understand." He hesitated, glancing at the others. He wanted to say something, Piper could tell.

"What?"

"Do you remember that time, seven years ago?" Achard's gaze flitted down her arm.

Piper gripped her elbow, covering the star-shaped scar there with her palm.

Seven years ago. When Saxe had nearly succeeded in permanently disabling her. When she'd had no one she could go to, except Achard.

The strength left Piper's legs, and she sank back into her chair.

"I understand," she said softly. Achard nodded. "Fate."

Across from her, Achard leaned forward. When Piper looked up, it was to find his gaze fixed on her right hand. "What did he do?" he asked, and Piper glanced down.

She'd almost forgotten about the bandages there. Piper stretched her fingers, feeling a shadow of pain lance through her. It wasn't the worst sprain she'd ever had, but it was up there with them. Even clenching her fists still hurt, sometimes.

"He smashed my hand into the corner of a table when I didn't kill *him* the first time," she said, jerking her chin to Alec.

Alec's blue eyes widened, while Achard's eyes narrowed.

"Will you still be able to fight him?" Achard asked.

Piper stretched her fingers out again, ignoring the pain. "Of course I will," she said. She had to be.

"There's something else," he said. "He has magic."

Piper frowned at him. "No, he doesn't," she said.

"I assure you, he does," Achard said.

"Achard, I think I'd know if he has magic," she said. "I've been trying to figure out a way to get rid of him for fourteen years."

"I've no idea what to tell you, Piper," he said. "Maybe it's new. But he most definitely has magic, and strong magic at that."

Piper opened her mouth.

"Wait." Alec held out a hand, interrupting them. Piper frowned at him, but he wasn't looking at her. "Are you certain the magic is new?"

"I didn't think you could newly develop magic," Beks said softly.

Alec pursed his lips. "It's possible," he said. "If someone else gave him his magic."

Three pairs of eyes turned to him.

"What?" Piper said.

"It's too much of a coincidence, Piper," Alec went on, his voice soft. "Powerful magic, when we know there's a Shiv'ek working out of Silversdale ..."

"A Shiv'ek can give someone else their magic?" Piper breathed.

"Well," Alec admitted after a heartbeat, "everything I've read says they can. At least temporarily."

The room buzzed. After a moment, Piper realised it was the others, talking. But she couldn't hear them.

"All right," she said softly. The buzzing ceased, and all three turned to her. "I'll do it."

The corner of Achard's mouth tilted up in a small, relieved smile.

"I knew you would," he said, and Piper rubbed her eyes.

Of course he'd known she would. She always did.

"An act like this means payment," Achard said, and Piper's gaze snapped up to him. "Payment that's been overdue for fourteen years."

He didn't say it. He didn't need to. The magic that bound them together tugged at her *illis*.

"I accept," Piper breathed.

The tugging stopped. It was still there, but now dormant. Maybe would always be.

Alec looked between them. "What payment?" he asked, his eyes narrowing.

Piper shook her head and pushed to her feet.

"It's not important right now." She couldn't lie completely and say it wasn't important at all.

Achard leaned forward again. "Thank you," he breathed softly.

Piper offered him a small smile. "I'll drag him back here by his hair," she promised.

Achard's smile turned predatory. "I think I will enjoy that."

Piper got to her feet. "Stay here," she told Achard. "He'll have a spy; someone will know you've talked to me. But hopefully, I can catch him off guard all the same." She hesitated. "She's safe for tonight, I think."

Achard nodded, relief crossing his face. "Be careful, Piper," he said. "I don't want him to kill you."

Piper's smile was sharp. "I'm not easy to kill," she said.

Beside her, Alec snorted. "Nine lives, I swear," he muttered under his breath.

Beks kicked his ankle. "Don't say that," she hissed. "You'll tempt fate."

Piper beckoned to the two of them. She'd have to shake Beks, but having a blackcoat with her would be useful, if Lore had magic like Achard said.

Then she paused.

"What was the other thing?" Piper asked, almost at the door.

"Tanner's back," Achard said softly.

Piper froze. "I thought he was dead," she breathed.

Achard frowned. "I did too."

"I'll add him to my list," she promised.

Then, gesturing to Alec and Beks over her shoulder, she vanished through the door.

THIRTY FIVE

Avoiding eye contact with everyone else in the hall, Piper led the others back down the pale staircase and out the front door. The male guard glowered at them as they passed, but his female counterpart offered Piper a brisk nod.

Piper nodded back. She'd be back, at some point. It didn't hurt to be polite.

She clattered down the stairs, not bothering to be quiet. Then she turned, heading down towards the Oldtown. The cobbles slapped under her feet. Every so often, one wobbled underneath her. A few people crossed her path, mostly heading for the magical display happening in Coral Square. The fastest way to get back to Lore's headquarters would be heading right, avoiding the square.

"Let go of me!"

Piper spun.

Behind her, Alec's hand wrapped around Beks' elbow. He tugged her back, away from the street, towards one of the cab stops.

"I said let go!" Beks slapped ineffectually at Alec's hand.

"Absolutely not," he growled. "We are not—"

"What's going on?" Piper demanded. She didn't have time for whatever this was.

Alec glanced at her. "I'm sending her home," he said, and Piper blinked.

"Oh." That made sense. It made everything much easier, actually. Except that her chest set up an uncomfortable burn at the thought. Something about it felt wrong.

"I'm not going anywhere," Beks snapped, yanking her arm from Alec's grip. "I am coming with you, whether you like it or not."

Alec's jaw clenched. "Please," he said, his voice strained. "Your parents will kill me if you get hurt. They must be beside themselves already."

Piper frowned. *Her parents?*

Beks shook her head, brushing at her three-quarter sleeves. "I can't, Alec. I need to help. And you need me, tonight. I've seen it."

Alec's hands clenched by his sides. "Please, Beka."

Beka. Not Beks.

Piper tore her gaze from Alec's distraught expression to look at Beks. She was tall. Slim. Her clothes were well made, though not showy. She had auburn eyebrows. Piper cast her memory back. She was just the right height ... Piper pulled her bag around in front of her, rooting through it until her fingers landed on a slightly worn envelope. She pulled out the photograph that had been part of Alec's profile, and held it up, glancing at Beks and Alec. They were the right height, comparatively. When Piper traced her eyes down the woman in the photograph, she noted that she was wearing a pair of low-heeled, black-and-white spat boots.

Beks had her jeans tucked into the exact same shoes.

Piper sucked in a breath. "Take off your scarf," she said.

Beks started. Her face paled, and her hand darted to her head.

"Please don't," Alec begged.

Piper turned the photograph around. Beks gasped, and Alec grimaced.

"You're Jai's sister?" Piper said, her voice rising. It wasn't what she wanted to ask. But in a crowded street just metres away from Coral Square, she couldn't exactly throw around a word like *princess*. She stuffed the photograph away before anyone could get a look at them.

Beks took a deep breath. "Yes." Her face was pale, but her eyes were stubborn, determined.

"Fate." Piper scrubbed both hands over her face. "So much for finding some way to ditch you tonight."

"You were going to ditch me?" Beks – Beka? Rebeka? Her Highness? – snapped.

Piper groaned softly. "Yep," she said unashamedly. "You're a liability with us." She rubbed her forehead. "Unfortunately, you're now more of a liability by yourself."

"I am a seer," Beka said. "I get visions. Sometimes I can force them." She fixed Piper with her blue gaze. "I will find you again if I need to."

"And you're stubborn," Piper sighed. "I wish you'd get in a cab and go home." She glanced at Alec.

"That's what I'm trying to tell her." Alec rubbed his forehead. "Please, Beka."

Beka shook her head. "No." And Piper got the distinct impression she was just as stubborn as Piper herself. "I'm coming with you. You're my friends."

She couldn't really argue with that. Then she blinked. Fate. She'd been friends with the crown princess of Silvaein for two years without even realising it.

Alec's jaw clenched. He looked like all his worst nightmares were coming true at once. "You. Have. To. Leave," he said, punctuating each word with abrupt, jerky hand movements. Beka crossed her arms.

Piper rubbed at her chest, but … it wasn't burning.

"She comes with us," Piper said softly.

Alec whirled to her. "What–"

"See, I–" Beka started at the same time.

"Wait," she told them both, holding up one hand. She took a breath. "We find Lore," she said carefully. "We stop him."

Still, her chest didn't burn. Piper frowned, and tried something different. "We put her in a cab and–"

Flames tore through her chest, and Piper gasped. Blinking back tears of pain, she looked at Alec. "She's safer with us," she said.

Understanding lit his face. "You're under a fate oath," he said.

Piper nodded. "More than one." She cleared her throat. "Come on, both of you. We're too close to Achard; we need to move."

She turned without waiting for a response.

For a moment, Piper wondered if Alec would try and drag Beka to a cab anyway. Then footsteps sounded behind her. Smaller, lighter ones, jogging to catch up. Beka fell into step beside Piper. A moment later, Alec joined on her other side.

Piper touched the side of her neck, feeling the roughness of scales there, and sighed.

Fate, this was not how she'd planned for her night to go.

"How long have you known him?"

"Hm?" Piper blinked, drawing her attention away from Lore's hideout. They stood around the corner and down the street, where she could keep the exits in view. "What, sorry?"

"How long have you known him?" Alec asked. "Achard."

Piper sighed. But, she supposed, she did kind of owe him an explanation. Even if she didn't really want to get into it. "He was the first person I met in Silversdale," she replied. "So, fourteen years."

"What did he mean about the black lace gang?" Alec asked.

Piper flinched. In that quiet intersection, the darkness wrapped around the three of them. She heard the scuff of Beka's shoes as she moved closer.

"Achard took power from his uncle about six years ago," Piper said softly. "There were plenty of people who weren't happy with the changes he was making. About a month into his rule, a group of people decided the new ruler wasn't powerful enough to keep them leashed any longer."

Piper looked up. Beka's lips pressed together, her mouth nothing more than a thin line. Alec's blue eyes looked dark in the shadows.

"This group, they ..." Piper couldn't say it aloud. "They hurt and killed children, and left a black lace shroud over their faces, hence the name. Achard asked for my help to deal with them."

"Deal?" Alec asked.

Piper turned back to the corner, pretending not to hear.

"Every day for a week, the police found a man stabbed through the heart and slit from throat to groin in a public place." Beka's voice was so quiet it was almost inaudible as she took up Piper's thread. "Each had a black lace shroud on their face and belladonna berries in their chest cavity." Beka hugged her elbows.

"It was meant to be a warning." Piper felt like she had to defend herself. "No one's been dumb enough to try anything like that since."

"And that's what you call a cull?" Alec pressed.

Piper pursed her lips, but nodded. "Yes," she murmured, leaning against the side of the building. "We do it when we're trying to stop something even more horrific."

Alec glanced back at Beka, then shifted closer to Piper. "Let me guess," Alec said. "He's the one who stitched you up after your injuries. And he's also your little birdie."

"Two for two," Piper said, blinking up at him.

A small, reluctant smile curled the corner of his mouth. "Sometimes I can be smart," he said. "He mentioned payment. What's he offering you?"

Something in the mage's voice told Piper he wouldn't leave her alone until he knew. She sighed again, too tired to fight with him any longer.

"Repayment for a life debt," she said. "Achard saved my life when we first met. And his uncle, who was a greedy bastard, decided that meant I owed a life debt."

Alec let out a low whistle. Piper didn't blame him. A life debt was a particularly volatile type of magic. Much like a fate oath, once one was declared it was unbreakable unless released.

"He couldn't release you for the black lace gang?" Beka asked softly, like she'd read Piper's mind.

Piper shook her head. "Too impersonal," she said. "Believe me, we've tried a few times over the years. It never sticks. But this one ..." She rubbed her chest. "I think this will stick."

"Protecting his daughter is probably enough to satisfy the magic," Alec murmured. He glanced sideways at Piper. "Does Madelyn know?"

Piper shook her head. "Abby and Achard weren't together very long," she said. "Abby didn't want her to know."

"They fought?" Beka guessed.

"No," Piper said. "He became the Alchemist. Abby thought it was too dangerous for Caleb and Madelyn, and Achard stepped away." It had just about killed him to do so. She'd been the one picking up the pieces. Madelyn had only been two months old, but the pride, the love on his face whenever he looked at that little girl ...

They stood in silence for a moment until, beside Piper, Beka shifted. "What are you waiting for?" she whispered.

"I was hoping he'd come out," she muttered. "Or I'd see someone go in. Anything to give me an idea of what they're doing." She looked at the two of them and made her decision. "Stay behind me. Alexander, can you see through your shield?"

Alec shook his head. "Not well. That's why I had so much trouble with that other assassin. He was so quick, and I could barely see him."

Piper sighed. "All right." She looked back at the street. "Just be ready to throw one over the two of you."

Beka touched Piper's elbow. "What about you?" she asked.

Piper offered her a smile that she knew was pure predator. Beka drew a quick breath in, and Alec's eyes widened.

"I'll need to be able to stab people."

THIRTY SIX

Piper eased open the inner door, peering around it from relative safety before pushing it the whole way open. The room beyond was dark. Moonslight filtered in through the dirty skylight, lighting the stairs down. Behind her, she heard someone sniff.

"This place smells … unique," Beka said after a moment.

Piper laughed darkly. "It smells like sweat and blood and metal," she said. She kept her voice low. "Stay with me." Piper didn't wait for an acknowledgement before she took the steps down. She slipped across the room, her boots shushing softly against the stone.

Behind her, Alec's shoes tapped on the steps. Beka followed him, her tread far lighter.

Piper pressed her ear to the door. Then, slowly, she eased it open.

The golden-white light of Azah filled the training yard through the skylight. The overhang cast a shadow over the doorway. Piper stepped through cautiously.

No one stood there, waiting to decapitate her as she came through the door. Just in case, Piper checked the doorjamb at her throat height, then further up for Alec and Beka.

A flash of white on Lore's study door caught her eye, and Piper frowned.

"What is it?" Alec breathed.

"No idea," she whispered. "If he's not there, he just ... isn't there. He never gives an excuse. But ..." She trailed off as she stepped close enough to read the note.

Belladonna,

It's my immense pleasure to tell you you've lost.
Despite your traitorous actions, you weren't
good enough.

Abigail Brown dies tonight. Her slaughter will fuel
something much, much more important.

"No," Piper breathed.

"What?" Beka asked. Alec, reading over Piper's head, swore. Beka tore the letter from the door, gasping when she read the words.

Piper spun. "Can you track him?" she demanded, grabbing the front of Alec's shirt.

"Piper, calm down," Beka said.

Alec grabbed both of her hands, stopping her from ripping the material.

"You have no idea where they could be?" he asked. Piper shook her head, and Alec swore.

"Can you track him?" Piper repeated. "You're a spellbinder! A compass, anything?"

Piper knew she was begging. She also no longer cared.

"I can try," he said, sounding uncertain. "I need something personal to him to do it."

"What kind of thing?" Lore had a room here. There were spare weapons, clothes ...

Alec let go of her hands. "Something he's invested himself into," he said. "The whole 'blood, sweat and tears' cliché is a cliché because those things are important. Diaries are the best, or something handmade, like a ... a knitted jumper, or something he's carved or ..." He trailed off, shrugging.

"What about regular clothes?" Piper asked, and Alec shook his head. "Weapons?"

"Not unless he pours his soul into them," Alec said. "The kind of thing he'd be devastated, inconsolable if he lost." His gaze darted to her waist. "Like that blade you dived after, in the Lower Ilian."

"What about ..." Piper trailed off, an idea hitting her.

"What is it?" Alec asked.

Piper didn't answer. She threw herself over to Beka, landing on her knees with an audible crack. Ignoring the pain shooting up her legs, Piper yanked her picks out of the top of her boot.

"What are you doing?" Beka asked.

Every click, every fumble, every tremor of her hands was excruciating. It felt like fire ants crawled over her hands, biting at her exposed skin, making her fingers tremble with their venom.

The lock clicked. Piper shoved the door open with her shoulder.

Not a pen was out of place in the office beyond. Piper stumbled to the desk, her knees protesting as blood flowed back in them. She tore open the drawers.

"Come on, come on, come on," she muttered. Sure, surely, this once he could have been sloppy. Could have left it out. This important thing he was planning was surely enough to distract him.

But no. No ledger.

Alec stood in the door, frowning. Beka stared around the room, her mouth pressed into a thin line. Piper's gaze flicked from them to the black safe tucked into a corner. Her heart sank with certainty.

"It's in there," she said, pointing.

Alec looked at the safe, then back to her. "So open it."

Piper squeezed her eyes shut and shook her head, feeling tears sting. "I can't." The room swam for a moment when she opened her eyes. "I've tried. I can't."

Alec strode over. In three steps, he knelt before it, his hands tracing over its hard case.

"Can you break it?" Piper's voice cracked, and she cleared her throat.

Alec sat back on his heels. "What's inside ... is it flammable?"

"Very," Piper admitted.

Alec made a disgusted noise. But he reached out, placing his hands on the safe again.

"Wait." Beka's soft voice cut across the room.

Alec spun to face her. Piper looked up.

Beka traced a hand over the bookshelf, her eyes ... misty.

Alec swore. "Beka." He shoved himself off the floor, crossing to her and catching her arm. "Don't force it. Just let it come."

"I need to force it." Her voice ... wasn't hers anymore. It was deeper and higher at the same time. The hairs on the back of Piper's neck and arms stood up on end, and she shivered. "It won't happen soon enough, otherwise."

"If you force it, you could hurt your *illis*," Alec said. "Maybe irreparably."

Beka's pale gaze landed on Piper, and she smiled. "It's worth it," she said. She closed her eyes.

For one heartbeat, nothing happened. And another.

Beka gasped. Her back arched. Alec swore again, still holding one of her arms. He slung an arm around her waist as Piper jumped over the table to grab Beka's other arm. The muscles trembled under Piper's grip.

Just as suddenly, she went limp.

"This is why we don't force them!" Alec snarled.

"What's happening?" Piper asked.

Alec lowered Beka to one of the hard chairs in the corner of the room. His fingers found her wrist, and he glanced at his watch. "She forced a vision," he muttered. "Which she shouldn't be doing."

Piper frowned at him. "If she can force a vision," she said, "why didn't she force one for Jai?"

"She did," Alec said shortly. "Nearly put herself in a coma doing it. Bedridden for a week. That's how I knew he was still in the city."

"It was my choice," Beka said weakly. Piper rocked back, giving Beka more space. Alec leaned closer, grabbing Beka's chin to peer into her eyes.

"Stop it." Beka smacked at his arm. "I'm fine. Just have a headache." From the way she winced and covered her eyes against the dim light, it was a bad one.

Piper hesitated. She glanced at Alec, guilt eating at her stomach. Then she looked back at Beka. "What did you see?" she asked.

Alec glared at her. But Beka took a shaking breath.

"He's going to change the safe combination next week," she whispered. "But to do that he has to put in the original numbers."

Piper's heart skipped in her chest.

"Twelve," Beka whispered. "Thirty-eight. Nineteen. Sixty-two."

It took a moment for that to sink in. When it did, Piper threw herself across the room.

"Come on, come on, come on," she muttered, for the second time that night. "Please, please, please, please." The dial spun out of her fingers, and Piper swore.

A large hand landed on her shoulder.

"Breathe," Alec murmured, kneeling behind her. "Slow down. It feels slower, but it will be faster."

As much as she was loathe to, Piper did. She closed her eyes, taking a long breath in through her nose and holding it for a few seconds. Then, just as slowly, she let it out. When she opened her eyes again, her heartbeat had slowed. Her hands shook less, and Piper grabbed the dial again.

"Twelve," Alec murmured. "Thirty-eight. Nineteen. Sixty-two."

The lock clicked and Piper depressed the handle. It swung forward, and she almost sobbed in relief.

Inside, the leather-bound ledger sat amongst a small bundle of gold-threaded notes and a larger stack of copper- and silver-threaded ones. Her hands shaking, Piper reached in. Butter-soft leather met her fingers. Piper cradled the ledger in her arms like a newborn, then looked up at Alec.

Alec leaned around her and took the ledger from her hands.

"Yes," he murmured. "Yes, this will work nicely." He stroked his hand over the leather cover. "It's saturated with his *illis*."

"And that's what you need?" Piper pressed.

"That's what I need." Alec glanced up. "Give me some space."

Piper pushed herself up, using the safe for leverage. Alec shifted so he sat cross-legged, the book in his lap. Blue-black magic sparked at his fingertips. It rolled over the backs of his hands, winding through his fingers like a pet. He reached out and stroked his finger on the cover.

The ledger burst into blue-black flames.

Alec swore. Piper grabbed the ledger, heedless of the heat licking her fingertips, and threw it on the ground. She jumped on it, stomping on the flames as they licked at the sole of her boots.

Alec swore again, on his feet at Piper's side.

Beka pushed them both aside and knelt, something in her hand. Carefully, she poured a water bottle over the leather.

Piper watched, her heart in her mouth, as the ledger steamed and hissed. Beka flipped it open, pressing both covers into the small puddle of water underneath it. She dribbled the last few drops over the corner, where a few paper pages smoked, shaking her bottle to get the water out.

Piper blinked, steam stinging her eyes. The only sound in the room was the sizzle of hot leather, the smell thick and acrid. Alec coughed.

Beka sighed. Standing up, she gathered the dripping ledger in her hands and held it out.

"I don't think it's too damaged," she said.

Piper pressed a hand to her chest, feeling her heartbeat race under her fingers.

"Good thinking," Alec admitted grudgingly. When Piper glanced at him, the tips of his ears looked pinker than usual. He rubbed both hands over his face. "Fate damn this stupid magic," he muttered, so low Piper didn't think either of them were meant to hear it.

Beka turned to Piper, shoving her empty bottle back into her small bag. "Do you have any more water?" she asked.

"Um ... I ... guess?" Piper hedged. She pulled her own water bottle out of her bag and shook it. "It's maybe half–"

She didn't finish her sentence. Beka took the bottle out of her hands and unscrewed it. Then she tipped it over Alec's head.

"What the f-fudge?!" Piper snapped, jumping back as droplets splashed at her. Alec blinked, looking like some kind of sea monster with long, black hair plastered all over his face. He shoved it back with both hands, grimacing as large droplets of water splashed around him. Piper threw him a dirty look, shielding the ledger with her body. A drop slid down her neck, and Piper shuddered.

"What, by fate, are you doing?" she demanded, glaring at Beka.

"Reducing his magic," Beka said primly, screwing the top back on the water bottle.

Alec pushed his wet hair back from his face. "Give it here," he said, holding out one hand.

Piper glanced at the ledger. There was a burn mark almost clear through the leather cover. "Will that help?" she asked cautiously. She didn't think the book would survive another fire.

Alec nodded. "I can barely cast when I'm wet," he said. "Like at the Ilian. This will help."

Beka touched her arm. "It really does work like that," she said. "I've seen it."

Piper looked at the other woman. Beka's blue eyes softened, and she smiled uncertainly.

Piper unfurled her arms from around the ledger and held it out. "Please don't break it."

"Don't worry," he said. "I barely need any magic for this."

He glanced at the floor. Then, with a put-out sigh, he knelt in the puddle of water Beka had created. Piper scuttled back, tugging Beka with her. Alec laid the book down and put both hands on the cover again. He murmured something.

Magic sparked at his fingertip again. It flickered, almost going out. Then it strengthened, covering his index finger. Only his index finger. He traced it over the book.

The leather didn't catch fire.

Piper let out a sigh of relief. "Good idea," she murmured to Beka.

Beka nodded, a gracious – and royal – tilt of her head. "I've known him a while," she said. "Once he tried to close a window with magic. The window shattered."

Piper shook her head. "I can't imagine having that much magic."

Beka offered her a small smile. "I don't think I'd like it," she admitted. Then she winced, lifting a hand to her head.

"Are you okay Be– Reb ... ah ... Your ...?" Piper trailed off.

Beka chuckled, rubbing at her temple. "Rebeka is fine," she said. Then she hesitated. "Or Beka. I mean ... that's what my friends call me."

"Are we friends?" Piper asked. "Neither of us really knew anything about the other before tonight."

"I knew the important things," Beka said. She nudged Piper's arm.

Piper hesitated. "I don't think that you're a ... *you*," – she still couldn't make herself say the word *princess* out loud – "and I'm, well ..." She trailed off, gesturing loosely to her coat and the daggers it contained.

Beka hesitated for a moment, then she shrugged with one shoulder. "I don't think it's that important. And if this doesn't make us friends ..."

There was uncertainty in her voice. Vulnerability in her eyes.

Piper smiled. "I think this makes us friends," she agreed.

Beka laughed.

Piper dragged her gaze back to Alec and the ledger. Glowing, blue-black marks covered the leather. The mage brought his palm down to the cover. He hissed.

"I know where he is," he said.

THIRTY SEVEN

Alec led them out of the Oldtown, the book held between both hands. His long legs ate up the pavement, and both Piper and Beka had to jog to keep up with him.

"Where are we going?" Beka panted.

Alec grunted. "Not really sure," he said.

Alec turned. Piper caught Beka's arm, tugging her to a stop as she tripped over a raised cobblestone, almost tumbling into the street.

"Thanks," she panted, and Piper nodded.

"Don't mention it."

Piper kept hold of Beka's arm as they chased Alec across the bridge. Below them, water crashed against the pylons, churning like a living entity. The purple algae frothed with it, colouring the water with hues ranging from violet to lilac.

Alec stepped off the other side of the bridge.

"Alexander!" Piper hissed, catching his sleeve. "Wait for us!"

He checked his stride. When he turned and met Piper's gaze, lines framed his blue eyes and the corners of his mouth.

"Sorry," he said, breathing heavily. "The stronger the *illis*, the more this spell pulls me." He peeled one hand off the book and rubbed his eyes. "I can't even imagine the time spent on this."

"Years and years," Piper said. She laid a hand on the cover, and Alec flinched. "Everything every one of us owes him, or owes whoever he bought us off, is in there."

Beka made a noise beside her. "Everything we need to condemn him?" the princess whispered, her voice hopeful.

Piper hesitated. "Everything that condemns me too."

Beka fixed blue eyes on her, her mouth a hard line. "We'll see about that," she said.

"Come on," Alec said. "We need to keep going. The trace will only last another half an hour."

They wove through the Ilian, avoiding factory workers and sailors out after a day's work, foremen and managers and captains heading for a late drink. Those well-dressed men and women in the Ilian worked hard, staying well after the last of their employees had left for the day, balancing ledgers and ordering supplies and organising things for the next shift. Either that, or they were up to something shady. Piper frowned as they passed an alley where a man in a top hat handed a woman a small package.

His wide eyes landed on Piper, and he froze.

Piper ground her teeth, her short nails digging into her palm as she clenched her fist. *Abby*, she reminded herself. She looked away and kept moving.

They rounded another corner. Alec slowed. "He's nearby," he murmured.

Piper looked around. She didn't know this area. They stood in between three buildings, the two on the right three storeys high. On their left, a single-storey roof sloped up gently, before changing to a sharper pitch.

Beka frowned. "Why here?"

"This area was sealed off for dragonfever last year," Piper murmured. "It's been hard to get tenants into these factories again."

"Another deserted area," Alec murmured.

Piper nodded. "He seems to be good at finding those."

"There's a lot of them in this city," Beka said. "I've found many in the last few years, since I've been staying in the city more."

"And they're all in the poor areas, where new people aren't noticed as much," Piper agreed.

Alec ran his hand over the ledger, stroking it like a cat. "I think he's on the other side of that building." He pointed to the one with the lower roof.

Piper chewed her lip. "Stay here," she said softly. "I'm going to check it out."

"Are you mad?" Alec grabbed her arm, holding Piper in place. "You can't take him on by yourself if he's got Shivian magic!"

Piper yanked on her own elbow, hard. It barely moved in Alec's grip. She glared at him.

"I can look after myself!" she hissed.

"Could you look after yourself when the wendigo attacked you?" Alec growled.

"Both of you stop it!" Beka hissed. "You're both big, and you're both bad, so quit it with this macho crap!"

"Macho crap?" Piper laughed. "Is that the language they teach you at those fancy universities?"

Beka shot her a withering look. "You both know what I mean," she said. "Now." She crossed her arms. "What are you going to do?" Her eyes bored into Piper, like twisting daggers.

"I'm just going to look," Piper said. "I swear it."

For a moment, Beka held her gaze. Then she looked up at Alec. "You have to learn to trust us, too. We *both* know what we're doing."

Alec gritted his teeth, squeezing his eyes shut. He let go of Piper to rub his eyes with his thumb and forefinger.

"I am a dead man," he muttered. "Your mother is going to kill me for letting you get involved in this." There was a note of resignation and respect in his voice.

Beka smiled. "You already knew I'm not the type to back down from something," she said. Then she turned to Piper. "I know you think you can do this yourself. But you can't. Please let us help you."

Piper sighed. "You make far too much sense," she admitted. "I promise, I will just look. I need to see what's around there before we do anything else. Okay?"

"Okay." Beka squeezed Piper's hand. "Fate guide you."

"And you," Piper replied automatically.

"It had better," Alec muttered.

Piper turned, marching up the street. She slowed as she reached the corner. Her heart jumped to her throat, and she pushed it ruthlessly down. She leaned, barely poking her eyeball around.

The alley was empty.

Piper slipped down it, imagining smoke, water, shadow. Things that were slippery and easy to overlook. Her limbs felt like they were being controlled by a three-year-old. Piper swallowed to work moisture into her dry mouth. Her hands shook. Piper clenched them into fists.

She hesitated at the corner. The tattoo on her back rumbled, like it was encouraging her. She took a deep breath and leaned forward.

About six feet tall, and broad-shouldered. Light brown hair. A bastard sword strapped over his shoulders.

Piper slapped a hand over her mouth to stop her gasp, and jerked quickly back.

He hadn't seen her. She was certain. His back had been to her.

Her heart crawling up her throat towards her mouth again, Piper edged silently back up the street. She found Beka and Alec where she had left them. Beka had her arms wrapped around herself, her teeth sunk into her lip. Alec paced the entrance of the alley, three steps each way. Piper caught his arm, and he jumped.

"Fate, Piper," he breathed.

"Shh," Piper whispered. "We have a problem."

"What kind of problem?" Beka asked.

Piper glanced back over her shoulder. "A guard that knows me too well," she admitted. "Getting past him won't be easy."

"What do you need?" Beka asked.

Piper turned. Her gaze slid over the alley: the puddle under the drain, the bars over the window. The first-storey roof overhead.

Piper turned to Alec. "Give me a boost," she whispered.

Alec frowned, his gaze sliding to the roof. "How's that going to help?"

"Just trust me."

Alec pursed his lips, like he wanted to retort. "Fine," he said instead. He stooped, cupping his hands together. Piper placed one hand on his shoulder for balance. Then he lifted.

Piper scrabbled for the gutter as it approached far too fast. She caught it, then Alec lifted her higher. She scrambled onto the roof, almost as easily as stepping off a bridge, and glanced back down over the edge. "Stay here," she said.

Alec's frown deepened. "I really don't think …" he started in a whisper. But Piper ignored him, turning to cross the roof as silently as she could.

The metal, just like in the Lower Ilian, creaked under her feet. Piper shifted further in, seeking a beam that would help distribute her weight. A third of the way over, the roof steepled sharply. Piper stayed on the narrower, lower edge, crouched down to make herself less visible. Finally, she made it to the other side. The metal under Piper's foot groaned, and she froze.

There was no sound from underneath her. Leaning forward, moving like a tseoun on her knuckles and balls of her feet, Piper crawled to the edge. She didn't dare lean the whole way over for a look. Instead, she watched the shadow cast by the moonslight move across the ground before her. Saxe stood just under the roofline, almost entirely in the shadows. But the moon landed on his hair, his head making a circle cross the ground as she shifted positions.

The prince could be in there. Abby. Piper pressed a hand to her chest. Fate, she wanted her friend back. Wanted to go back to a time when they could sit by the fire late in the evening, sipping wine and laughing while the children slept in the other room.

Piper leaned back. She took a deep breath.

She jumped.

THIRTY EIGHT

S axe roared out a curse as she landed on top of him. Piper grabbed at him, but he ducked, throwing her off over his shoulder. She grunted as she landed hard on the ground, then spun around to face him again.

Saxe glared at her. "I knew you'd be here," he spat. His hand twitched towards his shoulder.

Piper lunged. She lashed out with an elbow, and he blocked it from landing in his throat. Piper seized his arm, twisting it hard, and Saxe spat a curse.

He'd made one mistake already. His bastard sword lay strapped across his back; while that was easier for carrying, it was much more difficult to draw than it would have been in a hip-sheath. Piper just had to make sure he never got a chance to get to it.

She grabbed Saxe by the hair, dragging his head down and bringing her knee up. His face crunched against her knee.

Saxe swore. His fist landed hard in Piper's side, and she gasped, stumbling and losing her grip.

He straightened. Blood dripped down his face, staining his teeth red as he bared them at her. "You're going to regret that," he said thickly, murder in his eyes.

Piper settled her weight back on one leg. "Make me," she said.

Saxe charged. Piper danced out of the way of the shoulder that would have landed in her stomach. As she dodged, he got a hand in the folds of her coat, pulling her up short.

She lashed out, catching Saxe's already broken nose with her elbow. He bellowed and let go of her to clasp both hands over his nose, his eyes streaming.

Piper didn't let him recover. She seized his shoulders, bringing up a knee to incapacitate him. Saxe twisted at the last moment, and instead of his groin, her knee hit his inner thigh. Piper jerked back, her eyes on his face.

Saxe swept out one foot. Piper slammed, back first, into the ground, the breath leaving her body in a rush. She scrabbled, willing her limbs to work properly, as Saxe reached for her, a vicious light in his eyes.

Piper rolled onto her hands and knees. But a hard yank on her braid forced her head back, and she twisted backwards, trying to lessen the pressure. Saxe wrapped an arm around her throat. She scratched at his arm, but her short nails had little effect against his long sleeves.

Saxe squeezed.

"I'm not allowed to kill you," he whispered, his breath hot and moist against her ear. "But know this. I am going to take her away from you. Like you took him from me."

Piper dug her fingers in, clawing ineffectually at Saxe. His arm tightened. Spots danced over her vision.

"Piper!"

Somewhere in the distance, hazy, a familiar tall figure appeared.

She'd told him to stay out of things. At least, she thought she had. Her head was heavy, fuzzy.

Piper clawed for her coat, her hip. She couldn't bend to reach the dagger in her boot. Saxe grabbed her right hand in his free one, pressing down hard on the bandage on her hand.

A strangled scream left her throat, and Piper's vision went white.

"Don't move!" Alec bellowed. What did he think was happening? She couldn't move even if she tried – and she was trying.

Something blue and black flashed past her right ear. Saxe howled. The pressure on Piper's throat and hand vanished, and she fell forward, catching herself on both hands. Breath sawed in and out of her abused throat.

Piper threw herself over.

Saxe staggered to his feet, one hand pressed over the side of his face. He fixed Piper with his good eye. "You'll be sorry for that," he hissed.

Another flash of magic rushed past him, and Saxe jerked out of the way. He turned tail and ran into the building.

Piper scrambled to her feet. Two very tall figures appeared. Alec caught Piper's arm. Beka reached for her throat, frowning. Piper pulled away from both.

"Stay with Beka," she croaked to Alec.

"Piper, wait!"

Piper didn't. Dodging around Alec's outstretched hand, she barrelled through the open door.

Darkness greeted her. Moonslight cast faint shadows over the furniture, highlighting them in grey against black.

Piper tripped on a chair, likely tipped over for that purpose. Above her, a door slammed. Piper staggered around the chair and through the room.

The wreckage of the interior came into focus as her eyes adjusted. Furniture toppled into the walkway; it had once been an office, she thought. The big desk must have been too heavy to move. It sat near the wall, the papers from on top of it strewn everywhere.

Piper shoved the door open, tripping over the step down, her boots echoing on the metal floor. The smell of well-oiled machinery coated the inside of her mouth, leaving a metallic taste behind.

Steps led upwards. Saxe had gone that way; the sound had come from there.

Piper leaped up the stairs two at a time, her boots ricocheting off the metal with a clamour.

I am going to take her away from you.

He knew where Abby was. He had to.

The metal was slick under Piper's feet. She slipped on a step, her heart leaping into her throat as she caught herself on the railing, her ankle sliding between the metal treads. She hauled herself up and kept going.

Piper jumped three steps and landed on the metal landing, staggering on impact. Her pulse thrummed in her throat, like a hummingbird.

The landing led to a narrow catwalk. At the end, a door stood ajar.

Piper clenched her fists.

It occurred to her, too late, how loud the metal was. Piper ran for the door on tiptoes, trying to put her weight on the edges where the metal wasn't so hollow, so loud.

Saxe could be in that room. But so could Lore.

So could the Shiv'ek.

Piper heard the door open below.

"Piper?" Alec's hiss carried through the building, loud as a shout.

Piper ignored him. She reached the door. Peering through it, Piper couldn't see anyone within. No Saxe. No Lore.

No Abby.

Pushing the door just enough that she could slip through it, Piper eased inside.

Nothing. The room was empty; in the wall, one door was firmly shut. Across from her, the window stood open, letting in the night air.

Piper swallowed and stepped forward.

Something cracked down on the back of her head, and Piper's vision went black.

THIRTY NINE

Piper's head throbbed. Something sticky ran down the back of her neck. Her arms and legs felt awkward and stiff.

She was sure she hadn't blacked out for more than a moment. But now she sat in a chair, her arms and legs bound to it. The dingy walls of the factory pressed in on her from all sides.

Light stabbed at her eyes, making the sick pounding at the back of her skull worse. Piper squeezed her eyes shut, drawing in a long breath through her teeth.

Something rustled behind her. "You try," Saxe breathed in her ear, "but no matter how hard, you never quite manage to beat me."

Piper smashed her head back. White hot pain flashed in front of her eyes as the back of her head connected with Saxe's nose. There was a bang as he fell against a wall.

Saxe swore. "You bitch," he snarled.

"Don't touch me," Piper snapped back, forcing down the bile rising in her throat.

Against the wall in front of her, someone *tutted*. "Really, Piper, is that how you treat your partner?" Lore peeled himself off the wall; she hadn't noticed him before, standing in the shadowy corner. She'd been distracted, trying not to throw up.

"He is no partner of mine," Piper said, lifting her chin.

Lore's eyes narrowed as he took her in.

"Piper," a voice whimpered. Piper twisted towards the sound.

Her eyes widened.

Abby sat, pushed against the wall. Tear tracks marked her face, a bruise on her cheek. Her hair was scraggly and tangled, like she hadn't brushed it in a week.

"Abby," Piper breathed. Abby choked back a sob, more tears spilling over her brown eyes; eyes just like Caleb's.

Beside her sat a young man, a boy really. He had brown hair, blue eyes, and a gag in his mouth, both hands tied behind his back.

The prince. He had to be. He looked just like Beka, aside from the hair colour.

Piper's breath shuddered in her chest. She'd found them.

Then her gaze tore back to Lore, keenly aware of Saxe behind her. She'd sort of found them.

Fate, where was Alec when she needed him? He'd been right behind her.

Something sticky, something oily and viscous, rolled over Piper's arms, and she shuddered.

Footsteps sounded behind her. They weren't alone. She could barely move, but she could turn her head. She twisted as far as she could, her heart palpitating in her throat.

Two men stood behind her. One was tall and thin. He had black hair and eyes like a bruise.

He wasn't the one who held Piper's attention.

The other man was also tall. Almost as tall as Alec. His hair was sandy blonde.

His eyes were the silver of new coins. The exact same as the ones Piper saw every time she looked in the mirror.

She tilted up her chin, a sick, queasy feeling in her stomach.

"What do you want?" she demanded.

The Shiv'ek smiled.

"You're smart," he said. "That's good."

Behind her, Piper heard Saxe growl.

The Shiv'ek shot him a look that could have flayed skin from bone. When he looked back at Piper, his smile softened. Turned cajoling. He crossed the room in two strides and knelt down in front of her.

"Now, Piperlyn," he said softly. "Let's say we have a little chat."

Piper narrowed her eyes. "Untie me, and sure," she said.

She could go for her stiletto. Chaos Demon or not, he'd die if she stabbed him in the heart.

He chuckled. "Nice try." He traced his fingers up from her throat, scowling as he touched the line of blood tricking from her hair.

Piper flinched away from him. Her coat shifted, and the final man, the one with the black hair, hissed.

"Fate," he said. "Her *illis* is the strongest I've ever felt."

Piper swallowed. A mage then, she assumed, if he could feel her *illis* like Alec could. She squeezed her hands into fists, feeling the bite of nails against her left palm – the one without the bandage. It helped keep her breathing steady.

The Shiv'ek didn't even look back at him. Instead, he smiled.

"Of course it is," he said. "How astounding. Except for your eyes, you look just like Keeva."

"Keeva?" Piper asked. Her gaze flicked past him, towards Abby and the prince. Tears still streamed down Abby's cheeks.

"Look at me," the Shiv'ek snapped, making Piper jump. Her heart leaped into her mouth, her stomach swirling with something ugly she didn't want to look at too closely.

The Shiv'ek's expression softened as she met his silver eyes again.

"That's better, isn't it?" he said. "We must look at the people who speak with us. Isn't that polite, Piperlyn?"

"Stop calling me that," Piper growled. She tugged at her wrists, but the ropes didn't budge. "What do you want?"

"Ah." The Shiv'ek smiled. "That's really quite a simple thing. I want you to come with me."

Piper blinked at him. "You what?"

The Shiv'ek sat back on his heels, his expression turning almost smug. "I want you to come with me," he repeated. "Away from here. Away from the city, the squalor. Away from the people who don't appreciate everything you do for them" – his eyes cut sideways to Abby for a moment – "to somewhere you will be looked after."

Piper swallowed. "I don't need looking after." She was proud, for a moment, at how strong her words were. "You need to let all three of us go. There are people looking for us."

"The mage and the princess, no?" He glanced back at the fourth man. "You stopped them, didn't you?"

The man smirked, his lips pulling away from teeth that were too straight, too white. "Of course," he said in a deep voice. "He won't be bothering us tonight."

"Good," the Shiv'ek said. His gaze darted sideways to Lore. "We all know how well 'taking care of him' went, last time."

Lore bristled. "You have *her* to blame for that failure," he spat. "Even with the promise of millions, she couldn't manage to kill him."

Cold rushed through Piper. "It was you?" she forced out. "Why?"

The Shiv'ek's gaze returned to Piper. "He was trying to stop me from getting what I want," he said simply. "He had to be removed."

For a moment, Piper sat there. She felt paralysed. Even breathing was hard. Then she looked up at Lore.

"There was never any money, was there?"

Lore snickered. "Catches on quickly, doesn't she?" he said.

Piper's heart thudded sickly in her chest, her breath sawing in her throat. Her chest burned uncertainly.

"If you've hurt them–" she started.

The mage – he had to be a mage – laughed.

"You'll do what, Belladonna?" he asked. Piper flinched. Across the room, she saw the prince's eyes widen. "You'll have a hard time coming after me tied to that chair." His bruise-blue eyes fixed on her mockingly.

"That's enough," the Shiv'ek said mildly, waving one hand at the mage. He turned back to Piper. "But it's true, my dear. Your friends aren't coming for you tonight."

Piper glanced around the room. There was the door in the wall behind her and to her right. On her left, a large window stood open, letting in the evening breeze.

Maybe, if she screamed, someone would hear her?

"Just take her with you," the mage said. "You can convince her when we're out of here." He glanced towards the door again, and Piper's heart leaped in her throat. Maybe he wasn't as certain that Alec wouldn't follow them as he sounded.

"I won't go with you," she said. She needed to stall for time. "Your game is done. I don't know what you're trying to pull here, but–"

"I assure you, Piperlyn, there is no game," the Shiv'ek said. "I want exactly what I've told you. You come away with me." He glanced around the room. "We can leave this horrid place, go somewhere warmer. Less dank. You'd prefer that, wouldn't you?"

His voice was soft. Cajoling. And he was right. She *hated* being cold. And wet.

Piper swallowed. "No." Her voice didn't sound as certain as before. From the way the Shiv'ek smiled, he could hear it too.

The only sound in the room was Abby's soft weeping.

"So ungrateful for our hospitality," the Shiv'ek murmured to Piper. "Whatever would your mother think?" His silver eyes sparkled with something Piper couldn't place.

"My mother is dead, you *ass*," Piper snapped.

He smiled. "Well," he said, "I am a Shiv'ek. You know I can do something about that one small fact."

Piper froze. "What are you talking about?" He couldn't mean what she thought he did. He *couldn't*.

"Your mother," the Shiv'ek said. "We could bring her back. There is a price, of course. But you'd pay it, wouldn't you? To see her again?"

Piper's breath stuck in her chest.

Fate. She'd heard, somewhere, that a Shiv'ek actually *could* bring back the dead. She hadn't thought it was real.

"It's real," he promised, like he could read her thoughts. "You want to see her again, don't you? It's been such a long time."

Fourteen years.

Piper heard Saxe growl behind her. "You said that—" he started.

"Enough." The Shiv'ek didn't shout. But Saxe stopped talking immediately. Maybe that was a skill he could teach her, if she went with him.

Piper shook her head. She wasn't really thinking of taking him up on it. Was she?

The Shiv'ek smiled. "Come with me, and we bring your mother back," he told her. "There'll be a trade, a small price to pay. But, once that's done, she'll be back. Like she never left."

She'd never understand.

She licked her lips. "What price?" Fate, she *was* thinking about this.

The Shiv'ek held out one hand. For a moment, Piper stared. Then she followed the direction he was indicating.

Towards the wall. Towards where Abby sat, curled against the prince's side, tears streaming down her face.

Like she'd always known.

Piper sucked in a breath. For a heartbeat, no one moved.

Then, "Fnt lilen 'o 'im!" the prince shouted.

Piper jumped. The Shiv'ek leaped to his feet. "You keep your opinions to yourself, boy!" he roared.

Abby flinched, cringing back against Jairus. The prince glared at the Shiv'ek, his face red from yelling through the gag.

The black-haired man flicked his fingers. Something almost colourless left them, wrapping around the prince's face. The prince screamed. He doubled over, his face almost against the floorboards.

"Leave him alone!" Piper strained against her ropes, the coarse material tearing the delicate skin around her wrists. Her chest burned, and she cried out.

"Stop that!" The Shiv'ek snapped.

The mage stopped. Piper could breathe again.

The Shiv'ek stalked to the mage, his footsteps making the ground shake.

"You," he growled, poking the mage in the chest, "made her hurt herself. Made her bleed." He stepped back, glaring at all three men. "I will kill the next person who makes her bleed."

"She deserves to bleed," Saxe muttered above her head.

The Shiv'ek spun around.

"What did you say?" he thundered. Power, more intense than anything Piper had ever felt before, pressed against her chest, and she choked. She heard Saxe stumble back a step.

Piper's breath caught in her chest. "I won't do it," she said.

The Shiv'ek turned his attention back to her, his lips twisting into a sneer.

"You stubborn, reckless, *ungrateful* little woman," he snarled. Spittle landed on her face, hot against her chilled skin. Piper shrank back in the chair, feeling the hard spines of the back press into her. "I'm going to—"

Behind him, the mage cleared his throat. "I hate to interrupt," he drawled, "but we do have a schedule to keep."

The Shiv'ek spun around so fast Piper felt sick from watching him. He grabbed the mage by the collar.

He didn't wear a coat, Piper realised. She had no clue what kind of mage he was, nor how strong.

"*You* have no schedule," he growled. "Take the boy and get out of my sight." The Shi'vek pushed the mage away. The mage stumbled back a step. Then, tugging his collar straight, he grabbed the prince by the arm.

"No!" Panic – or the fate oath – flared in Piper's chest. She gasped, doubling over in pain. Her vision doubled, and nausea ripped through her along with the fire of the oath.

At the edge of her vision, she saw the mage drag Jairus across the room. Saxe stepped out from behind Piper. He tossed her a curled-lipped look. Then he followed the mage towards the window.

"Interesting," the Shiv'ek murmured. He knelt before Piper, his fingers taking her chin and lifting her face. "You're under a fate oath." He tilted his head to the side, and for a moment Piper saw two of him as she struggled to draw in a breath. "Don't worry. I won't kill him yet."

The burning faded. Piper coughed, drawing in a breath that tasted like wine, despite the stale air of the factory.

She blinked, forcing her eyes to focus on the face just centimetres away from hers.

"Screw," she panted, "you."

His silver eyes flashed in ire.

"You are irritatingly wilful," he growled at her. "I'm offering you your mother back if you come with me quietly."

"See my previous statement," Piper gasped.

He stood suddenly, so fast he shoved Piper back in her chair. Her head smacked against the timber, and she yelped in pain.

"Just remember," the Shiv'ek murmured, "I gave you an option. It didn't have to happen like this. It could have been painless. At your own hand."

He stepped away.

Piper's eyes slid closed. She forced them open, her head aching like she'd held her breath for too long and passed out.

Abby looked at Piper, her brown eyes wide and frightened. The Shiv'ek leaned over her.

Panic spiked in Piper's chest.

"Wait." She jerked, the entire chair rattling. "Wait!"

The Shiv'ek ignored her. He grabbed Abby's arm, hauling her to her feet. She stumbled, her left leg buckling, blood seeping through the fabric of her jeans.

"Abby!" Piper screamed. She threw herself forward. The chair toppled and her head hit the ground with a resounding smack. For a moment, black filled Piper's vision. She groaned.

"Use this," she heard the Shiv'ek say, and Piper forced her eyes open.

Lore cradled a dagger longer than Piper's forearm between his hands. The Shiv'ek touched his forehead, between his eyes.

When he turned, a spot glowed there, blacker than night. He didn't look over at Piper again; his gaze was fixed on Abby.

"Ab-by." Piper couldn't force the word out.

Something glinted on Abby's cheek. Piper's vision went fuzzy, until she blinked, and something hot and wet slid over her face.

"Leave ... her ... alone!" Piper gasped out.

Lore placed a hand on Abby's shoulder. She shrank back, but the Shiv'ek grabbed her hands from behind, holding her in place.

"Abby!" Piper yelled. "Stop!"

Lore raised the dagger.

"Please stop!" Piper begged. "I'll do anything, I'll–"

The dagger fell. Abby's mouth opened as it sank into her stomach, but no sound left her. Lore lifted the dagger again. And again. Drops of crimson splatted the floorboards.

Someone was screaming. Distantly, Piper realised it was her.

Lore withdrew the dagger.

"Do it," the Shiv'ek said.

Abby stared at Lore, her mouth still open, blood sliding out over her lip.

Lore raised the dagger. Taking its tip carefully with his other hand, he raised it to his mouth. Piper stared as he licked its length, careful of the razor edges.

"Wh … Wh …" Piper stuttered insensibly.

Lore turned the dagger over and licked the other side.

He shuddered. Then he hung his head back.

"I feel it," he growled.

Blood spattered the floor.

The door behind Piper burst open with a crash. "Piper?!" Alec roared.

Lore twisted. He bared his teeth, the dagger clenched in one hand. His face was painted in blood.

The Shiv'ek let go of Abby's arms, and she collapsed to the floor.

"ABBY!" Piper screamed.

"Stop! You're under arrest!" A tall wood elf, a purple streak in his hair, stepped forward, followed by half a dozen other officers. A series of legs filled Piper's vision, blocking out the Shiv'ek and Lore. She heard Lore snarl.

"Come on," the Shiv'ek snapped, "we're leaving."

"Stop right there!" There was the sound of a scuffle. One man screamed, staggering backwards, smoke rising from the hand he clasped to his chest. A crunch came from the direction of the window.

Liam lunged out of Piper's vision.

"No," she gasped, panic flooding her chest and stealing her breath.

Someone swore. More legs in uniform pants crossed in front of her.

"Abby!" she screamed again.

"Piper." Alec was on his knees in front of her. He gripped her shoulders, and Piper wriggled, but the ropes didn't budge.

"My boot!" Piper gasped. Alec leaned over her, pulling her long dagger from its sheath on the inside of her boot. Despite his inexperienced grip, the dagger sliced through the ropes like they were made of cream.

Piper fell out of the chair. She rolled, her head throbbing, and scuttled between two pairs of legs, stopping when her knees bumped into Abby's arm. Beka was there, her hands pressed to two of the many wounds in Abby's abdomen.

"Abby," Piper whispered.

Abby's eyes flickered open.

"Just hold on," Beka said. "A healer will be here soon." She didn't sound like she believed that.

Piper caught Abby's hand in both of hers.

Abby blinked, too slowly. "I knew you'd come," she breathed, her voice barely audible.

"Of course I came."

Piper's eyes stung, but she didn't let go of Abby's hand to wipe at them.

Abby drew in a shaking breath. Blood beaded on her lips.

Her eyelids fluttered.

"Look after them for me," she whispered.

"No, Abby," Piper breathed. "You have to stay. You have to look after them yourself. You can't leave them alone."

"They're not alone," Abby said. "They have you." She coughed, then drew in a long, rattling breath.

"I'm so sorry." Piper pressed Abby's hand to her cheek. "I'm so sorry. I didn't mean it."

Abby squeezed her hand.

"I know." She offered Piper a tiny smile.

Her head sagged backwards, her eyes staring unseeingly upwards. Her fingers went limp in Piper's hands.

A shudder rocked Piper's body.

"Abby?"

Abby didn't reply.

A hand landed softly on her shoulder. "I'm sorry," Alec murmured.

Piper's shoulders were shaking. She couldn't breathe.

She couldn't … She didn't …

Beka reached up and gently closed Abby's eyes.

A sob tore through Piper's throat. Pain tore at her chest, worse than any fate oath.

She couldn't *breathe*.

A laugh like a hyena tore through the room.

Lore stood between two officers, one arm held by each of them. His eyes flicked over Abby's body with a feral light, his lips twisted in something that resembled a smile.

"Serves her right," he said.

Piper was on her feet before she even realised what she was doing. Lore choked as she landed on him, her hands closing around his throat. The police officers stumbled back, shouting.

"You bastard," Piper screamed. Her fingers closed on his dagger.

His hand lashed out, catching her in the side of the face. Piper flew backwards, landing hard enough to wind herself, and slid across the floor. She choked in a breath.

Lore laughed again.

"By the way" – Piper lifted her head to see him crouched on the windowsill – "that woman is the Belladonna." He pointed at her.

Piper leaped up, his dagger in her hand.

Lore jumped.

Piper lunged. A hand around her arm pulled her up short.

"Drop the weapon!" an officer barked. He twisted Piper's wrist, and she had no choice. She gasped, and the dagger fell through her fingers.

Another officer grabbed her other arm. "Let's not do anything hasty," she said, warning in her voice.

"Let her go!" Alec snapped, striding up to them. Liam intercepted him.

"Alec, calm down," Liam said. "We'll get this sorted out, but–"

"My left arse cheek we will!" Alec snapped, power burning in his eyes. "Let her go now!"

"Stand down!" Liam ordered him. He turned to the officers. "She hasn't tried to hurt anyone except that man, and we know he's a criminal."

"Inspector Riveralli, are you letting your personal alliances get in the way of your work?" a voice asked. An older man stepped forward.

Liam gritted his teeth. "No, deputy commissioner, but–"

"Good," the man said. "The woman goes to Silvaein Prison."

Piper's knees went weak. Only the grip of both officers kept her upright. "No," she breathed.

"No!" Alec echoed, appalled.

"Deputy commissioner, you have to let her go!" Beka stepped out from behind Alec, her fists clenching. "She just had her friend murdered in front of her!"

"That shouldn't bother the Belladonna, with all the people she's murdered herself," the older man said dismissively. "Silvaein Prison. The Pit. Now."

"No!" Alec darted to the doorway, bracing his hands on the frame.

"Alec, stand down," Liam warned. "Deputy commissioner, we have no proof–"

"You, girl." The deputy commissioner clicked at her. "Are you the Belladonna?"

Piper opened her mouth. Her gaze fell on Abby's body.

It was too much. She hadn't been able to save Abby. Jairus was fate knew where. Sitram, and all the others. Almost Alec. Even Iso.

Maybe she belonged in the Pit. And she was too tired to lie.

"Yes."

"Piper!" Alec snapped.

"They didn't know," Piper whispered.

The deputy commissioner scoffed.

"A likely story," he muttered. "Arrest them all."

"No!" Panic – or maybe the fate oath – flared in Piper's chest. Liam grabbed Alec's arm; to arrest him or to hold him back, Piper wasn't certain.

"That's enough!" Beka snapped.

There was a flutter of fabric. Bright copper waves tumbled down from the top of Beka's head, caressing her shoulders.

The deputy commissioner stared.

Beka took one step closer to him, and jabbed at him with her finger.

"You are going to move this poor woman's body to the hospital," she said. "That is an order. And then, deputy commissioner, you are going to escort us all to the palace to see my mother." Her eyes narrowed. "The High Lady."

FORTY

Piper let them cuff her. Then, one guard on either arm, they frogmarched her back towards Factory Lane.

A large autocart with a square back and two long bench seats awaited them there. The deputy commissioner bundled Piper in the back. He climbed into the front passenger seat – the slight given by not offering it to Beka was not lost on Piper. Then, more police officers in between Piper and her friends, they left the Ilian.

The wailing siren and flashing light on top of the autocart gave them quick passage through the city. They pulled through the palace gates in a spray of gravel that Piper heard against the side of the cart.

The police officer had to click in front of Piper's face to get her out of the autocart. Abby's slack face lingered in her vision. She blinked, rousing herself enough to step out of the cart, instead of being dragged.

"Stop there," someone called. Piper blinked, and then Beka stood before a guard in palace uniform, talking softly to him. His grip on his pistol loosened, and his gaze flickered over them. Recognition lit in his eyes when they landed on Piper, and she blinked again. That was the guard from the garden, from when she had broken in.

Fate. It felt like months ago.

The two palace guards escorting them, Beka led them inside, across the tiled foyer and towards the glass staircases. Piper tripped up the translucent stairs, barely able to stay on her feet. The back of her head throbbed sickly, and more than once, Piper swallowed down bile. It had to be a concussion.

Beka pushed open the door to a room. Inside, a large square table took up the centre of the room. Two long windows overlooked a garden.

That was all Piper saw before the police officer on her right arm pushed her into a chair.

"Stop that," Alec warned, only to have Liam silence him with a warning look.

The officer removed the cuff from Piper's wrist, but only to pass the chain around the table leg. "Stay here," he told her unnecessarily.

"What do you think she's going to do, teleport?" Alec snapped.

"Why?" the deputy commissioner asked. "Is she a mage?"

Liam started to speak. "Deputy commissioner, I don't think you realise this is—"

"I don't care who he is, boy!" the deputy commissioner snapped. He pointed to one of the palace guards. "You, there. Go and wake the Lord General."

The guard cleared his throat. "Excuse me, deputy commissioner, but I don't take orders from you," he said. The deputy commissioner went beet red.

Beka stepped forward. "Harry, would you please wake Norrix for me?" she asked. "I will wake my mother."

The guard clicked his heels together. "Yes, your highness," he said.

The deputy commissioner glowered. "You and you," he said, pointing to Liam and one other police officer. "Watch her."

"Deputy commissioner, I'm not under your command—"

The older policeman ignored Liam, turned on his heel, and marched from the room. The other officers trailed out after the deputy commissioner.

Liam sighed and leaned against the wall. They had different stripes on their sleeves, Piper realised. Liam's were purple. The deputy commissioner's were blue.

She sighed. She rested her head down on the table, closing her eyes.

Caleb and Madelyn needed to know. How was she going to tell them?

The chair beside her squeaked. Piper opened her eyes to see Alec lower himself down next to her. He hesitated, then he reached out.

"You okay?" he murmured. He brushed Piper's hair back, frowning at the blood down the back of her neck.

Piper shrugged. "I'm here," she murmured.

Alec nodded, his mouth twisting in sympathy. "I got the daggers," he told her. "Both of them. I thought you'd want them."

Piper nodded, her throat tight. She swallowed.

"He was there," Piper whispered.

Alec blinked at her. "What?"

"The prince. I saw him. He's alive." Her voice faltered. "I couldn't save him." She squeezed her eyes shut.

"I couldn't ..." She trailed off.

Alec squeezed her arm. "It wasn't your fault."

Piper shook her head. "They took her because of me. The Shiv'ek, he wanted me."

The door opened and Alec jumped to his feet. Three men entered. The first, Piper recognised from the parades through the city. Lord General Norrix, leader of the empire's military, strode in first. His eyes narrowed as he took in Piper, slouched over the table, and Alec, standing beside her.

The second man was shorter, thinner. He had ink stains on his fingers and longish brown hair, raked back from a prominent widow's peak.

The third man caught Piper's attention. He was tall – even taller than Alec, by half a head. His long brown hair was pulled away from his face, and grey touched his temples.

The High Lord glanced over Piper, his lips compressing. Then he stepped to the side.

Two redheads walked in.

Piper sat up straight. Beka met her gaze and offered a small, sad smile.

The High Lady's eyes flashed at Piper. Then she turned her attention to Alec.

"Blackcoat Rylan," she said. The deputy commissioner, who'd followed her, went white as a sheet. "Why, exactly, is this woman in my home? Near my daughter?"

Piper flinched.

"My Lady ..." Alec started.

"I told you, Mum, she's not like that!" Beka whispered furiously.

"Beka," her father admonished gently.

Beka shook her head. "You'd agree with me if you were there tonight, Dad," she said. "It was ..."

She trailed off, righteous fury fading from her face and leaving weary sorrow behind.

"It was awful," she admitted.

Norrix spoke to Piper. "You will let me restrain you, Belladonna," he said.

"Norrix!" Beka snapped.

"She's already handcuffed to the table!" Alec protested.

Piper sighed. "If I wanted to hurt any of you, I already would have." Her soft voice cut across the room. "I'm an assassin, Lord General. Handcuffs or not, you would not see me coming."

Norrix took a step towards her.

"You really don't want to do that," Alec warned.

"Blackcoat Rylan," the High Lady said again, and Piper saw Alec flinch. "Explain yourself."

Those four words froze the room. Alec glanced at Piper. Piper shrugged one shoulder.

He took a deep breath.

"You'll remember, Piper and I had a ... run in," he said. "A little over a week ago. I tracked her down, thinking she was the one behind the prince's disappearance, but ..." He glanced at Piper again. "But her friend also vanished under the same circumstances." He nodded towards Beka's bloodstained hands. "That friend was killed tonight, by the men who did take Jai."

The High Lady turned to her daughter, taking one of her filthy hands in her own pale ones. Beka shuddered.

"It was awful, Mum," she whispered again.

The High Lord wrapped an arm around his daughter's shoulders. "Tell me the whole story," he said. His tone broke no argument. "Both of you."

Alec sighed. "All right."

He did. In more detail than Piper would have ever remembered. It took him over an hour to summarise their week.

Finally, he got to the Ilian, and hesitated.

"There was ... a mage trap," he said. "Set by someone quite powerful. It took me a while to break it. Beka went for the constabulary."

"I was unconscious for a moment." Piper frowned. "There were four men. Lore and the Shiv'ek, Saxe, and a mage I've never seen before. And Abby and ..." She looked up and met the High Lady's gaze. "The prince was there too."

Beka pressed a hand to her mouth. The High Lady sank into the nearest chair, her hands shaking. The High Lord squeezed her shoulder.

"Was he okay?" Beka demanded. "Was he hurt?"

"He didn't look badly hurt," Piper said. "Gagged, and bound, but I didn't see any bruises or blood."

"Oh fate." Beka slid into a chair next to her mother, burying her face in her hands.

The High Lord sat next to his wife. "He's alive," he whispered.

"That's ... not all," Piper went on. She recounted what Lore and the Shiv'ek had done. Then she looked at Alec. "What was it?"

Alec rubbed his chin. "I don't know," he admitted softly. "But I will find out."

Beka looked up. "Deputy commissioner," she said. "I'd like you to remove her handcuffs."

For a heartbeat, there was silence.

"What?" the deputy commissioner gasped.

"Your Highness, that is a bad idea," Norrix said.

The last man, the one with the ink stains, looked up from the huge leather book he had been scribing in. "The young lady has a point," he said, his voice cutting through the others. "She did break into the palace, and she caused no harm." Alec scoffed softly enough that only Piper heard it. "Do you really think you could stop her if she decided to attack?"

"Piper is my friend," Beka insisted. "She won't hurt any of us."

Norrix ground his teeth.

"It's fine, Beka," Piper said softly. She lifted her hands. There was a faint click, and the lock on the handcuffs opened. They hit the table with a soft thud.

Piper leaned down and tucked her lock picks back into the top of her boot.

Norris started towards her.

"Norrix," Beka said, holding up one hand. "Please."

"You could have done that at any time," the ink-stained man said, fixing his gaze on Piper.

"I could have," Piper agreed.

"Don't think this means I trust you," Norrix growled.

Piper sighed again. "Of course not," she said.

The High Lady's lips pursed. "After this," she said, "you will be arrested."

Piper's stomach swooped. But … it felt half-hearted. Like her body couldn't be bothered to respond.

"Wait, my love," the High Lord murmured.

The room turned to look at him.

"What is it, Rhys?" the High Lady asked softly.

The High Lord propped his chin in his very large hand and looked Piper and Alec over.

"Alec," he said, "has she been helping you? Really helping, I mean?"

Alec nodded without hesitation. "Yes, sir," he said. He glanced sideways at Piper. "If not for her ... I'd still be chasing loose ends."

Piper nudged him. "Give yourself some credit," she murmured.

Alec frowned. "I am," he said. "And I think I can guarantee, without you this would not be happening."

"Too right this wouldn't be happening," the deputy commissioner snapped. "She freed a known criminal!"

"She was a bit beside herself at him killing her friend," Liam finally snapped. "And if you had handcuffed him, like you're supposed to do ..." He trailed off as the rest of the room looked at him. "My apologies, My Lady, sir," he added to the High Lady and her husband.

The High Lady waved a hand.

"No matter," the High Lord said. He shared a glance with his wife.

"This is a matter for another day, I feel," the High Lady said. "Preferably after our son is returned to us."

Alec's hand gripped Piper's wrist under the table, hard enough that she winced.

"I agree," the High Lord said. "Juan?"

"Yes, sir?" The man with the ink-stained fingers looked up.

"Let's ... table this discussion," the High Lord said. "We will revisit this woman's crimes after the prince is returned to us."

"Very good, sir," Juan said. Juan – the Lord Justiciar in charge of the judicial system – jotted something in his ledger.

"You can't possibly–" the deputy commissioner started.

"Don't presume to tell the High Lady what she can and can't do," Norrix said, glowering.

The High Lady nodded. "I am retiring," she announced. "Come, Beka." She gestured to her daughter.

Beka stood. She ducked around her mother to go to Piper and Alec. "I'm sorry," Beka whispered, squeezing Piper's hand.

Piper nodded, her throat tight.

"Beka," her father called. Beka offered Piper a wobbling smile, then turned.

Piper's chest ached. It was a painful, bone-deep ache, not the burning effect of a fate oath.

She turned to Alec. "I have to ..." Her voice broke, and Piper pressed a hand to her mouth.

Alec pursed his lips, his eyes soft. "I'll come with you," he offered.

Unable to speak, Piper just nodded her thanks.

Alec led the way out of the palace. Liam, the deputy commissioner and Lord Norrix all trailed behind them until they got to the gates – likely making sure she left. Then Norrix pulled both police officers aside. By the time they spoke, Piper was too far away to hear what they said.

Piper took a shaking breath. "I guess it doesn't really matter anymore," she said, "but ... what was the deal?"

Alec frowned at her. "What deal?"

"I didn't know what to think, after Li– Inspector Riveralli defended me in there." She sighed. "I'm so tired, Alexander. I can't keep running. I'd assumed the deal was for me to be arrested, but ..."

"Oh. That deal." Alec rubbed his chin. "Well, actually, that wasn't the deal. It was for me to take you to the High Lady, when everything was done." He glanced back towards the palace, now hidden by the buildings of Redwell. "Which I think I just managed. Without getting you arrested." He glanced sideways at her. "I didn't realise you even knew about it."

They quietly stepped onto a tram at the next station. Inside the car, Piper rested her head against the window, closing her eyes. Sometimes, late at night, the rocking of the trams lulled her into a doze.

Not that night. Instead, silver eyes and a flashing blade and Lore licking the blood off a dagger assaulted her vision. Piper's fingernails dug into the palms of her hands, and she felt a lump push its way up her throat.

Beside her, Alec said nothing. His arm pressed against hers on the seat that wasn't quite big enough for his shoulders.

He stood up without prompting at the station closest to The Lily. Piper glanced around, then followed him.

Her legs felt like lead weights as she stepped off the tram. The street stretched for eternity. The road was deserted. Whatever time it was, it was very late.

Piper led Alec around the back gate and up the inside stairs, avoiding the stragglers in the main room. In the hall, Piper hesitated before she put her key into the lock.

The room inside was empty. Piper glanced around for Rose, but she must be downstairs.

Piper crossed the room. Behind her, she heard the door shut softly. Piper placed her hand on the door handle.

Blood crusted under her fingernails. Dirt smeared her hands. Around her wrists, raw, red marks showed where Saxe had tied her to the chair.

Piper took a breath. Then she pressed the handle.

They lay curled in their beds. Caleb slept with both hands tucked up underneath his cheek. His eyelashes made a dark crescent against his skin. Next to him, Madelyn looked so small, so pale. Her white hair lay across her brow.

Piper bit her lip.

Soft footsteps. He didn't touch her, but Piper felt it when Alec stopped behind her.

Piper clenched her fists. "I think I'm going to wait until morning," she murmured.

"It seems … cruel to wake them for this," Alec murmured.

Piper nodded.

Caleb sighed. As they watched, he rolled over, tucking something under his arm.

Madelyn's rabbit. He held it like a lifeline.

Piper wiped at her face with the back of her wrist, the only clean part of her hand.

She sniffed. "Thank you for coming with me," she said, "but I need to be alone, now."

Alec hovered in her peripheral vision, and Piper turned her head to look at him.

He sighed. "All right," he murmured. "I'll be across the hall, if you need anything."

Piper frowned. "You're not going back to the palace?"

He offered her the ghost of a smile. "I'd rather stay here, just in case …" He shrugged. "The room here is bigger than my room at the palace, anyway."

"Thank you," she whispered.

Alec said nothing. He reached out, touching Piper's arm. Then he turned, his footsteps tapping across the floor as he headed out of the room.

Piper turned her attention back to her children. Her eyes stung, and she leaned her head against the doorframe. Caleb and Madelyn wavered, then cleared as she blinked.

Saxe was alive. He and the mage had taken Jairus with them. The Shiv'ek, whatever he wanted, was with them. And Lore. Fury and agony rolled together in Piper's chest. Lore was with them. He didn't deserve to live, after what he'd done.

And she had to tell these two children that their mother was dead. Dampness slid down Piper's cheek, sliding off her chin to pat against her hand. Tomorrow. She couldn't put it off any longer than that.

But for tonight, she could watch them blissfully, ignorantly, sleep.

ACKNOWLEDGEMENTS

There are so many people to thank, so many people who go into the writing, planning, designing and printing of a novel.

Firstly, thank you to Sam. You have been my rock, my biggest cheerleader. Thank you for talking me through the panic attacks and tears and celebrating with me through the milestones. I couldn't have done this without you.

Thank you Mum and Dad, for instilling a love of books in me from the time I could read. I remember thinking I was sneaking in extra pages reading by the hallway light in bed at night. Thank you for encouraging that girl, instead of telling her to get her head out of the clouds.

To Nick, my partner in crime. You're the world's best brother – see, I put it in writing – and the only person I'd want to have slow-motion Kung Fu fights in the hallway with.

To Ellie, even though you are a dog and you can't read this. You're the best writing companion, even if you do put your head on my keyboard sometimes, and try to steal my coffee or wine. You give the best cuddles (sorry, Sam) and spending time with you always makes me happy, no matter what plot hole I'm currently struggling with.

To Mark and Sonia, thank you both for being such fantastic cheerleaders! And thank you Mark for the thousands of photos you have and continue to take for me.

To the amazing Rebecca Sutherland, my editor. You helped me pull apart a novel that had something just not quite right in it and turn it into something amazing. I'm so grateful that I reached out to you and that you helped me find the right way to tell this story.

To Nadara Merrill with Nay's Notations, my proofreader, thank you so much for polishing this work so I could share it with the world.

To Im and Kate, thank you for being even more in love with this series than I am. Thank you for being the people I can bounce ideas off, no matter how kooky they sound.

To my beta readers, Imogen, Ivana, Maddy and Kate. Your input on so many early stages of this novel helped me shape it to what it is today.

To some of the best (and weirdest!) friends a girl could have – Lisa, Maddy, Selin and Kate. Our group chat and real-life antics always make me laugh. Thank you for not just accepting, but matching my weirdness.

To the amazing writing group of SydNaNo. Not only is it so much fun to hurtle towards 50,000 words with you each November, but you keep me grounded the rest of the year as well. I know whenever I want a writing buddy, there will almost always be someone online to chat with. Thank you for the amazing writing community we have built.

Thank you to every blogger, Bookstagrammer, Booktoker, reviewer or reader who's picked up my book and given it a chance. Thank you for sharing my story with the world.

And lastly, but certainly not least, thank you God for creativity and for books. And for so much more.

TF JOHNSON

TF Johnson has nurtured a love of books from a young age. She started creating stories before she started primary school and has never stopped.

She has 125 books on her to-read shelf, a number which is steadily growing. In her spare time, TF Johnson enjoys buying even more books to add to this stack.

When she's not reading or writing, TF Johnson spends time with her family, including a English bulldog who has an awful habit of putting her head on the keyboard and leaving it there.